Invasion
of the
Lesbian Zombies

A TALE OF DARK, EROTIC REVENGE

By **George S. Naas**

TO MALA

*I HOPE YOU ENJOY
MY BOOK. PLEASE tell
All of Your FACeBook
FRiends!*

Sincerely

*George
NAAS*

27/JAN/2019

Golden Publishing Company · Lakewood, CO
2018

Chapter 1: THE BETRAYAL OF BRENDA

As the rain beat down on a rusted blue Dodge van, inside, Brenda Ayler obediently performed oral sex on John Marshall. The floorboards were littered with fast-food trash, the ashtray was overflowing, and dust covered the dash and gauges. The whole place smelled like burnt oil, but this old beater was the best vehicle John could afford. Brenda took an oral break. "I don't think the rain is going to let up."

"Thanks for the weather report, now get it done." He pushed her head back down to his lap.

With his engorged cock in her mouth again, she felt all warm and fuzzy inside, so lucky that John actually loved her. The thought of him inside her dampened her panties, but she was determined to keep her virginity until her wedding night.

She came up for air, and after wiping saliva off her mouth she decided to press the subject. "John, we should get married right away."

"We can't right now, baby. I'd like nothing better but I'm low on funds. My ex-wife is hounding me for more money. That miserable bitch just can't accept the fact that I've found the girl of my dreams."

The compliment stirred Brenda to take his length deep into her throat.

"Oh, yeah, baby. It won't be long now." John groaned as he patted Brenda's head and played with her matted red hair. As promised, he exploded into her mouth. Sent shivers down his legs as she sucked him dry. When his orgasm eased, he lay back and rested his head on the seat. "That was great, baby."

Swallowing, Brenda sat up and took out her lipstick to fix the smears. She then leaned over and put her head on his shoulder. *Being in love is the best feeling.*

John pushed his dick back into his pants and struggled to zip up. She reached down to help him out, took hold of the zipper, and pulled it up. "All better now?"

John was thinking how to hit her up for money. She often helped him out on that front, too. Twenty bucks here, a hundred there, piddly stuff. Now he needed some big-time dough. He leaned over and kissed her forehead, but he had to hold his breath to do it.

What a fat, smelly, pimple-faced pig. She should be grateful I let her blow me. She does have pretty red hair, though, but I don't ever want to know if it matches her pubes. Shit. The only thing good about her is that she's loaded.

Brenda snuggled closer. *I know he loves me, and besides, all men want their women to give them blowjobs. I hope we can get married soon and have intercourse on our wedding night. Money's not really the problem. He's just being careful. Probably thinks I might turn out like that bitch he was married to, Jenny. He doesn't have to worry. I love him with all my heart, and I know he loves me. We're sure to live happily ever after.* "Let's set the date, John."

He lit up a cigarette. "We can't get married for at least another year because it'll take me that long to raise the money."

Brenda sighed. "We don't have to wait. I've been stashing cash all my life and have over fifty thousand dollars in savings."

He exhaled smoke. "I wouldn't feel right about taking money from the woman I love," he lied.

She kissed his ear. "Don't be a silly goose. It'll be our money...not just mine. Take it. Settle up with Jenny and use the rest for our wedding."

"You sure?"

"I know it sounds crazy, but I love you, John. If a little bit of money is all it'll take so we can be together, I don't mind giving it to you."

A little bit...fifty grand? She has more money than brains.

John could *not* believe his good fortune. He flicked the cigarette out the open window. "Brenda, I'll take you up on your offer. How about a check for the fifty-K? Is tomorrow all right? We can start planning our wedding and honeymoon right away."

Brenda squealed with joy and hugged his neck. "Let's meet at my bank at 11:30." She caught her breath. "John, I want you to know I'm ready to have any kind of wild sex you want on our wedding night. I'm so, so lucky."

Yeah, yeah. John was thinking about the fifty grand and his real relationship with his ex-wife. What a great time they'd have together in Las Vegas with Brenda's money. However, for now, he'd play the chivalrous fiancé. He got out of his cluttered van and strode around to open her door.

"Thank you, honey." She pulled her 248-pound frame out of his junk-mobile. As he walked with her hand in hand to her new Toyota Prius, two guys in their twenties walked by. They broke out laughing at the sight of the fatso and her slob of a boyfriend. He had tobacco-stained teeth, a scraggly goatee, and a snake tattoo on his left arm with the words: *Don't tread on me.* He was a real man's man.

Brenda scowled. "Nobody will be laughing at me tomorrow night at our high school reunion when they realize that you are all mine."

John scoffed. "Anybody laughs at you, baby, and I'll rearrange their face."

"Oh, John. You have made me the happiest woman on earth." She began to cry. "You really do love me, don't you, John?"

For just a fleeting moment he actually felt sorry for her. He gazed into her eyes. "Of course I love you. I love your voluptuous body and your sweet face and your kindness and your trusting eyes. Brenda, you said you were so lucky. You were wrong. I'm the lucky one. I can't wait until I can call you Mrs. Brenda Marshall. See you tomorrow, honey. I've got to get back to work, but soon we'll be together, man and wife, forever. Spend the night dreaming of our wedding. Love you."

One more kiss and she drove off in her Prius.

John waved goodbye, spit, then called Jenny. "Sugar, start packing your bags. The stupid bitch is coughing up...ready for this...fifty grand."

Jenny screamed with joy. "I love you, I love you, I love you."

"Easy, baby," John interrupted. "Tomorrow night you're going to be working off some of that fifty grand in a suite at the Bellagio in Vegas. I'll pick you up at noon tomorrow, cash in hand."

***

Brenda couldn't wait to get home to tell her mother the wonderful news. *Damn it. This traffic is a joke. I'll wait until our wedding night to tell him that I have a couple million in stocks and bonds. He doesn't like living in Denver with that bitch of an ex-wife only six blocks away. I think Florida would be great. I know he hates being an all-night janitor. I know he can do better and I want to have a baby right away. I won't be thirty-three forever. John is going to do his duty on our wonderful wedding night.*

Rushing into her house, she yelled, "Mom, where are you?"

"In the kitchen, dear."

"John proposed to me and I said yes."

Her mother, Ethyl, grumped. "I hope you're making the right decision. There's something about him that I just don't trust."

"Sure, he's not the best looking man in the world, and he's kind of a slob, but this is the first time in my life that I'm truly happy, so please don't dampen my spirits. He's a good man, an answer to all my prayers."

"In that case, I'm happy for you."

With that, Brenda rushed to her mother and hugged her.

"Do you want anything to eat? I have pork chops, your favorite."

"I'm too excited. I'll eat later."

Brenda sashayed into her bedroom and started making out a list of people to invite to the wedding. Propped up on her bed with a pen and notebook, she wrote down names of old school chums she'd be seeing the following night at the Lakewood High School reunion. She worked on the list, making revision after revision and then fell asleep at 2:30 a.m.

Ethyl got up to go to the bathroom. She saw the light on in Brenda's room and quietly opened the door to find her sleeping peacefully. She sat in a rocker by Brenda's bed and whispered, "I pray everything turns out the way you want it. You have suffered so much with people making fun of your weight in high school and even on your job. It was heartbreaking in art class when the kids were told to draw a picture of someone in the class, and some of the students drew pictures of you with pig's ears and elephant snouts. You came home in tears, saying how you hated yourself. I really hope this love affair is for real. You deserve it, honey."

***

Brenda got up at 7:00 and called in to work to say she was taking a flex day off. She didn't tell them why because she wanted to surprise her fellow employees the next day.

John was waiting at the Bank of the Rockies for Brenda when she drove up. He hurried over to her car and pulled her up to him and gave her a passionate kiss. *This kiss is going to cost her fifty thousand dollars. She'd better enjoy it.*

After getting the check, he walked Brenda to her car. "This money will go a long way to making our dreams come true."

She kissed his cheek. "Are you picking me up tonight?"

"Of course, sweetheart."

His cell phone rang. It was the *set up call* from Jenny.

"John Marshall," he answered.

Jenny sounded very official. "Your grandmother is in the

hospital in Cleveland."

"What happened?" He cast a puzzled look at Brenda.

"A car accident. You better come right away."

John hung up and held the phone to his chest. "Brenda, my grandmother is hurt. I have to go see her immediately."

"Yes, honey, I understand."

"But the reunion—?"

"Forget the reunion. There'll be others."

"I'm so sorry." Again, he lied.

Brenda touched his face. "I'm still the happiest woman on earth."

He gave Brenda a goodbye kiss then made a hasty retreat to his truck. He drove off and went just far enough to make sure she'd left the bank's parking lot then came back and cashed the check.

The wad in his pocket brought joy to his heart. *Poor Brenda. She's about to learn that happiness is fleeting.*

Chapter 2: A WOMAN SCORNED CAN BE A REAL BITCH

As Brenda got herself ready to go to the reunion, John and Jenny had gotten off their plane in Las Vegas. Walking out into the ninety-four degree heat, John answered his ringing cell phone. It was Brenda.

"How's your grandmother?"

He conjured up his solemn voice. "It looks pretty bad. Just a minute, honey." He put his hand tightly over the phone and whispered to Jenny while trying to stifle laughter. "She's as dumb as she is ugly." Getting back to Brenda, "I don't know when I can come home."

Sitting in a bathtub full of bubble-bath bubbles, Brenda caressed her ample breasts. "Guess what I'm doing right now."

"I don't know, sweetie."

"I'm taking a bubble bath. Wish you were here in the tub with me."

Looking at slim but big-breasted Jenny, John pointed his finger in his mouth as a *gag me* sign. "I would love that, baby."

An announcement came over the public address system. *"There is now long term parking adjacent to Terminal 1 on levels 1M, 3, 4, here at McCarran International Airport."*

John choked. His lie had been exposed.

"I thought you were in Cleveland? John. What's going on?"

Before he could say anything, Jenny grabbed the phone and yelled, "We're in Vegas to get married again."

A shot of hot adrenaline tore through Brenda's naked body. "Married?"

"And you're not invited."

Panic kicked John in the chest. He snatched the phone back from grinning Jenny. "Dear...I-I can explain."

"Was that your ex-wife?"

"Brenda, it's not what you think."

The bubbly bubble-bath felt like quicksand. "You stole my money and ran off with that bitch?"

"I never meant to hurt you," John lied once more. "But Jenny is pregnant." No lie. "I'll pay you back, honey. I just need a little time."

"Tomorrow, John, or the Las Vegas police will be paying you and your whore a visit."

"Well, if you're going to be like that, let me remind you...you said the money belonged to both of us."

"That's when I thought you loved me, you bastard."

Sweat ran down his forehead. "Well, just so you know, bitch, I never loved you. I never enjoyed one minute with you. While you were sucking me off, just so I wouldn't vomit on your bobbing head, I imagined you were Jenny."

Jenny shouted, "In an hour, you won't have to imagine it, baby. I'll be doing the real thing to you while we're lying on a pile of money."

"That's my money," Brenda snapped.

"John earned it by having to look at you. Your fat-ass body is disgusting."

"Gotta run now, sucker." John hung up.

Brenda dropped her cell phone into the morass of bubbles. Her heart felt like a dead stone in her chest. She struggled to stand but collapsed on the edge of the tub. Hot tears stung her eyes then flowed down her cheeks in rivers of shame.

Ethyl heard her daughter's sobs coming from beyond the bathroom door. "Are you all right, dear?"

"Leave me alone."

Invasion of the Lesbian Zombies

Brenda went to her bedroom at 3:37 a.m. but did not go to bed. She sat in her wooden rocking chair in the darkness, thinking how foolish she had been. Yeah, she was fat, but under the flab lived a vivacious and giving woman. John knew the real her and took advantage of her insecurities. If only she were attractive in the way men wanted women to look. She was angry and hurt enough to cut the fat off with a knife, just to show John what he was really missing. *Fat chance of that...*

She decided to turn on the TV. The Food Channel, of course. She quickly became engrossed in a commercial and quit sobbing.

Doctor Ernesto Gomez sat behind an impressive desk. He wore a white lab coat and the customary stethoscope, which gave him an official look as he explained his revolutionary weight reduction therapy. The usual pictures of patients who had undergone his procedure scrolled down the screen. These ex-fatsos were mere shadows of their former selves.

"Bah...photoshopped, for sure," Brenda muttered.

"I guarantee you'll lose a hundred pounds or you'll get your money back." Dr. Gomez leaned toward the camera. *"Gamble all you want in Vegas. I've never had to refund a single dime."*

"Vegas," she spat. Images of John and Jenny fucking each other's brains out in some glitzy hotel sparked another round of angry tears. She wanted to slaughter both of them, but not as *fat* Brenda, no. She'd get her revenge while wearing a slinky cocktail gown. They'd be so turned on by her beauty they'd never see the blade slashing toward their cheating throats.

Quickly putting the images of them screwing out of her mind, she went back to watching Doctor Gomez.

"My weight reduction therapy can only be administered at my health clinic in Port au Prince, Haiti, because the FDA has not approved it in the United States."

This was all Brenda needed to know. The government didn't like it, probably cut into Big Pharma corporate profits and their political contributions, so it had to be good.

"Give me a call and change your life forever."

What did she have to lose? *I won't look any worse than I do right now.*

Brimming with excitement, she left a note for her mom, telling her what she was going to do, and then hired an Uber to Denver International Airport where she got her boarding pass to Newark/Liberty. There she bought a ticket to Port au Prince.

Upon her arrival, she booked a room in the Habitation Hyatt. It was her lucky day. The hotel was only three blocks from the Haiti Health Clinic, Dr. Gomez, and her salvation.

Chapter 3: IT'S A BAD IDEA TO FUCK WITH MOTHER NATURE

T he next morning, Brenda walked the short distance to the clinic. It was not exactly what she'd expected. Instead of a sparkling clean medical center, the place looked in disrepair. The outside walls had been painted white decades ago, and the peeling flakes of paint revealed a dirty brown undercoat. There was a neon sign that flashed: *OPEN*; and a hand-scrawled note taped to the inside of the front window read: *Walk-ins Welcomed.*

She pulled on the dirty glass door, but it took both hands to get it to open due to the rusty hinges.

The reception office smelled like dirty socks. Ragged stuffed chairs stood about on a dusty wood floor. She walked to a small window to an anteroom that looked abandoned, but after peering over the counter she saw a thin Hispanic lady in a red dress, her head down on the desktop, sound asleep.

"Excuse me."

No response.

"Miss?"

Nothing.

A bad feeling wormed in her stomach. Maybe this wasn't such a good idea after all. She decided to leave, but the door wouldn't open on those rusty hinges. Finally, with a two-handed yank, she jerked the door ajar enough to squeeze her way out. Halfway through the process, she heard a voice say, "Wait, wait."

She saw Doctor Gomez ambling toward her. He looked exactly as he did on the commercial: maybe five-foot-nine, less than one hundred sixty pounds, jet black hair combed straight back, beautiful brown eyes, and a muscular build. He also sported the same stereotypical stethoscope. He certainly looked like a real doctor.

By the time he got to the stubborn door, she'd squeezed her way back inside. Doctor Gomez held out his right hand. "I am so pleased to see you here."

She accepted his hand, but to her surprise, he kissed it like a prince would kiss a princess's hand, made her feel a little special...even a little pretty.

"What brings a lovely lady like you to my clinic?"

"I saw your commercial."

"Oh, that. You want to lose some weight to become more attractive to a gentleman who scorned you."

"How did you know?"

"This is Haiti, miss. We know."

"Can you help me?"

"Maybe. Maybe not. You are already very attractive. I guess that you are an American. Am I right?"

His flattery stirred a tingling sensation between her legs. "I'm Brenda Ayler from Denver, Colorado. I want to lose one hundred pounds, get bigger breasts, and maybe have the pimples on my face removed. What will it cost me?"

Doctor Gomez smiled. "What does it matter the price? I sense your present condition has already cost you plenty."

She winced. "Try fifty grand for starters."

"I see." He offered her a threadbare chair and sat across from her. "Brenda, let me be blunt. I can do a complete makeover of your body and face but not your breasts. I am sure they are perfect already. As for the cost, I have the usual seven thousand USD plan, but for you I will do it for five thousand USD."

"Guaranteed or my money back? That's what you said—"

"Yes, of course. We can get started today if you wish."

A broken spring in the chair poked her ass. "I don't know..."

"And those nasty pimples will be gone too."

She touched her bumpy face and imagined a smooth, rich complexion. "All of them?"

"To perfection. What do you say, Brenda? Do you want a beautiful face and perfectly proportioned body to go with that very nice set of breasts you have there?"

"Do you take American Express?"

"The answer is yes, Brenda. Now let me show you to our operating room."

A jolt of dread hit her. "Operating room?"

"I call it that but the whole procedure will not take more than one and a half hours. You will be in a semi-state of consciousness the entire time."

"I thought you meant some kind of diet and exercise therapy."

"Nah. That takes too long. I am sure you want instant gratification, right, like all Americans?"

She thought about that. The quicker the procedure, the quicker she can fly to Vegas and kill John and Jenny. With any luck she could even get some of her fifty grand back. But still, an operation sounded risky. "Will it hurt?"

"I will make a small incision in your abdomen and then I will use a small suction tube to suck out the fat cells."

"Liposuction? That's nothing new or revolutionary."

"Ah, but mine is special. You will see. Come this way please."

Brenda followed him past the sleeping receptionist and down a dimly lit hall to his so-called operating room.

"Now disrobe and lie down on the table." He handed her a white sheet marred with yellow stains. "Cover yourself with this."

She took the sheet, looked at the rickety table and water-stained walls. The place made her stomach crawl, but such was the price of beauty and revenge.

Gomez left and shut the door behind him.

Brenda exhaled a big breath and stripped to the buff. Looking down at the folds on her stomach and the press of fat between her thighs, she realized this would be the last time she'd feel embarrassed by her body. No one would ever again look at her and laugh.

Meanwhile, Gomez retreated to the reception office to wake up Debbie Lopez, his receptionist and operating-room nurse. She was an import from Mexico who had gotten on the wrong plane in Mexico City and landed here just before the earthquake.

He had to shake Debbie several times to get her to wake up.

"What?" she cried out in surprise.

"We have a live one. Now get your white dress on and act like a professional medical assistant." He stood there and watched her take off her red dress and her bra and panties. At one hundred and eighteen pounds and flowing black hair like most young Mexican women, she didn't mind showing off her supple perky breasts and slender sexy thighs. She had the classic dark eyebrows, brown eyes, pouty lips, and perfect teeth of a Spanish maiden. What she lacked in talent for receptionist and medical assistant she more than made up for in bed.

Dressed now, she tucked in a stray titty and stood for him to admire.

"Very nice, my love. Now get in there and prep our patient."

After walking into the operating room, Debbie smiled at the now covered up Brenda. "I am going to start an anesthetic IV in your left arm."

She did just that but she made a slight mistake in the dosage, accidentally giving Brenda what would be a fatal dose of sodium thiopental.

Dr. Gomez came in wearing latex gloves. Thinking Brenda was just under sedation, he decided to give Debbie a free medical exam on the table next to his unconscious patient. He laid Debbie down on her back.

"Right here?" she protested.

"I know she's fat and ugly, but don't pay her any mind." He

pulled up Debbie's white dress, revealing a bush of black pubes and a wide-open pink valley. He promptly examined her with his penis.

"Oh, yeah, don't stop," Debbie cried.

His boner was about to pop when Brenda started choking beside them. Phlegm gurgled from her mouth, a clear sign of an overdose. He stopped pumping Debbie's pussy. "What dose did you give her?"

"450cc, just like you said." She thrust her hips upward in an effort to gain more of his length inside her.

"That's way too much."

"Don't stop, doctor. Give it to me."

"Oh, shit. My patient is dying."

"Forget her," Debbie shouted. "We are not done fucking. I am just getting started."

Brenda croaked.

"Are you nuts?" He pulled out of Debbie. "We have a dead body on our hands and I already ran her AmEx card. When someone comes looking for her, the police will know she was here. We have to do something fast or we're both fucked." Looking at Brenda's faraway gaze, he shook his head. "At least she died peacefully."

"Doctor, I am so sorry." She grabbed his dick. "Now come to mamma. Worry about her later."

"I'll have to tell the cops the truth. She died during surgery, complications, is all."

Debbie spread her legs and pulled his cock to her opening. "Finish me first."

He backed away. "How can you fuck next to a dead girl?"

"If we finish fucking or not, it won't bring her back. Let's screw in memory of her. What do you think?"

"Just get your ass out of here."

"But I am so horny for you, doctor."

"Now."

She rolled off the table and pulled down her dress. "I don't like it when you are mean to me."

"I should have put you on a plane back to Mexico City."

"If I were you, I would call your mother about this one." She pointed at dead Brenda and stormed out.

"Of course. That's it." Doctor Gomez picked up his phone and dialed his mother. It rang and rang. *Please pick up*, he prayed. His prayers were soon answered.

"Ernesto?"

"I'm in deep shit."

"You sound upset. What can I do to make you feel better?"

"Debbie gave my patient too much sodium thiopental by mistake, a dose that stopped her heart. So I may have the perfect candidate for you, just what you've been looking for."

"Bring the corpse to me at eleven tonight."

"Thanks, Mom. See you then." He poured himself a stiff drink and then another. He then laid his head down on his desk and went to sleep, woke up at 10:15 p.m. *I have to be there at 11:00.*

A now relieved Doctor Gomez bundled up poor Brenda in a green tarpaulin and sealed it with duct tape. He dragged her body down the hall to the loading dock. Leaving her on the dock, he made a quick trip to his 1978 black Toyota pickup truck and backed it up to the dock. After jumping out of the truck with the engine left running, he climbed up on the dock and pulled her body into the truck bed.

It dawned on him that, at this time of night, the local police might stop him to see if he had drugs in his truck. He came up with a brilliant idea. There was a large pile of cow manure in the lot next door for fertilizing the grounds around the park. He promptly took a shovel and administered the final insult on Brenda's body.

Driving through the rainforest on the outskirts of Port au Prince, he turned on the car radio, which was playing a most appropriate song. Gomez decided to sing along:

"Gonna drive down the road...

"Gotta deliver a heavy load...

"This whole shit business is a little creepy...

"The bitch in back is more than just sleepy."

He drove on what was a path rather than a road. With each bump, the truck bounced up and down, and Brenda's body did the same. The tailgate came crashing down and cow shit began to dump all over the road. All the while, Gomez just kept right on singing:

"Here we are and I bear witness...

"We wouldn't be here if she were more fitness...

"But in the land of the zombies...

"There is no forgiveness."

He slammed on the brakes and nearly missed hitting a tall, gaunt woman with a yellow marigold in her pitch black hair. She wore a red and black blouse and a brightly colored skirt of blue, red, yellow, and green, all in the shape of flowers with large leaves. Her face was covered with a Careta white mask that was worn to scare death away. She held a candelabrum that contained six candles burning brightly. Around here she was known as Cassandra, the Voodoo High Priestess.

"Hi, Mom."

"Hello, Ernesto."

"Where is your car?"

"Parked nearby." She walked over to the bed of his truck. In the dark night, she bent the candelabrum over to look at Brenda. The ride had exposed most of the tarpaulin. She pulled off the duct tape then proceeded to spread the green tarp so that she could see Brenda's face.

"She is a catrina," Gomez said sarcastically. "Pure and chaste, also a rich American."

"Rich? So what? With that cow shit all over her you have desecrated an honorable woman. Even in death there is kindness in those open and beautiful green eyes. If I can bring her back from the dead, the Lesbian Goddess Loa, in the afterlife, may allow her to come back with a vengeance in her heart after the one who killed her."

"I didn't do it. Debbie did."

"Since it would be woman to woman, your life may be spared, my son."

"Will she still be a fat slob, Mother?"

"It will all depend on what she wanted in this life and if Loa will grant what she asks for in the afterlife."

"When will we know, Mother?"

"When the moon reaches its apex. Now take her to the place where the blood of all saints has been spilled since the beginning of time. Strip her of all her coverings. Do it quickly."

He took Brenda by her ankles and slowly pulled her body from the truck bed until only her head and shoulders remained on the tailgate. Putting his arms under her arm pits, he groaned as he picked her up. Her head flopped over toward his right arm, but he managed to lay her gently on the ground.

Most of the tarpaulin had come out of the truck with the corpse. He dragged her and the tarp a hundred feet down the embankment, far from the road, and threaded her through a tangle of bushes. He laid her down by a six-foot by six-foot wide hole in the ground known as the Pit of the Ages. At six feet deep, the pit exposed the roots of the nearby Tree of Life. Then he sat beside her, out of breath, and waited for his mother.

Cassandra walked over to him. "Ernesto, I want her face up in the pit."

Exhausted, Gomez complained, "What's wrong with her lying on the side of the pit?"

"Because she has to be in the bottom of the pit, lying flat on her back for you to pour this blood into her mouth." She showed him an ancient glass vial. "The blood of the Lesbian Goddess Loa."

Doctor Gomez got down in the pit and pulled Brenda in after him. The heavy body came falling down and landed on top of him. Fighting to breathe, it was all he could do to push her up and over on her back. Her flab took up much of the space at the bottom, so he couldn't help but step on her as he moved around the pit and finally climbed out.

Up top, Cassandra had built a campfire that cast flickering light on the surrounding trees. After wiping the dirt off his clothes, he sat by the fire and watched Cassandra chant spell after spell over the open pit. From a leather pouch on her waist, she took out a doughnut glazed with pink-colored sugar and threw it to him. "Put it on her chest," she ordered.

"I just got comfortable."

Her pained expression sent him back into the pit. The doughnut looked so good he wanted to eat it himself but he did as he was told.

She then handed down to him a jar of *Mole*, a thick sauce made of chili, sesame seeds, chocolate and pineapple. "Rub it on the exposed Tree of Life roots."

As he did he asked his mother, "What's the *Mole* for?"

"An offering to Loa. It was her favorite food when the world was very young."

He pulled himself out of the pit. "Who is the doughnut for?"

"Brenda. If she is hungry when she returns to the living, it means Loa was not pleased and did not share her food with her in the afterlife. If she is not hungry, it is proof she dined with Loa and that Brenda has a good heart."

Doctor Gomez sat by the fire again and watched Cassandra place the lit candelabrum candles around the pit. She then lay next to him and waited in an eerie silence as the moon slowly moved directly overhead and shined down on the pit.

"Get back in there," she ordered.

Reluctantly and griping the entire time, Ernesto dropped in next to the corpse.

She handed him the vial of blood. "Now pour it in her mouth and then give me the vial."

Brenda's mouth was shut tight so he spread her lips and slowly poured the blood on her teeth. It took about ten minutes before the blood had seeped into her mouth. "I am done, Mom." After climbing out of the pit he handed the empty vial to

Cassandra. "What will the blood do?"

"It will make her loathe men and only love and desire women for sex."

"Why is that necessary?"

"It is the price the Lesbian Goddess demands in return for using her blood."

"What do we do now?"

"We wait."

It was like watching grass grow, so boring Gomez fell asleep. A crackling noise soon awoke him. The candles had all burned out, so he shined his flashlight into the pit. The roots of the Tree of Life were wrapping themselves around Brenda's body, probing her mouth and vagina, and smearing slime all over her like some kind of tree-cum.

Terror lit fires in his bloodstream. He shook his sleeping mother. "The tree is fucking Brenda."

Cassandra yawned. "Do not fear, my son. She is alive and now must escape the roots. Help her, Ernesto. She may forgive you, but be careful. She is no longer a woman who desires men."

Fear made him dizzy, but he scrambled down into the pit and, careful not to step on Brenda, began to pull the roots away from her body. He noticed she no longer took up as much room as when he put her in the pit, like the roots had shrink-wrapped her. Tugging and pulling, he uncovered her legs and thighs and could not believe how beautiful her body looked. Her skin was soft and a slightly pinkish color, like that of a newborn baby. As he removed the roots from around her breasts, he couldn't take his eyes off them. Perfectly round, perfectly plump, perfectly gorgeous. Her nipples stood erect and inviting. Brenda was definitely sexier than Debbie.

Now came the moment that he dreaded. He'd have to look into her eyes. With trembling hands he very slowly and gently removed the last of the roots from her face. Her complexion was as perfect as any makeup model's. She had a slender neck, pouty blood-red lips, perfect white teeth, and long bright red hair unfazed by the dirty pit and crusty roots. Curiosity led him to compare her hair with the curly bush between her thighs. It was the same color red, a perfect frame for the pink folds cupping her vagina.

His sudden erection gave him reason to be bold. He leaned over to kiss her mouth, but at that moment, she opened her eyes— those beautiful green eyes. A cold stare landed on him, no passion, no love, no humanity, just loathing. He recoiled in fear and scrabbled to the back of the pit. "Please. I am sorry. It was an accident. Debbie didn't mean to kill you."

Brenda sat up, slowly, like a vampire after a long sleep in her coffin, and smiled at him. "Don't be afraid." The doughnut rolled off her chest and into the dirt. "I'm a virgin, so I'm going to let you be the man to pop my cherry." She reached out and rubbed the hard-on in his pants. "I want to feel your cock inside me. Deep and painful. I want you to make me bleed." She spread her legs. "Take me. Take me now."

Gomez couldn't take his pants off quick enough. His great fear was that he would come before he could thrust into her. As he mounted her, she blurted out, "Wait. I want some saliva on that huge cock."

He spit on his hand and started to rub it on the head of his penis.

"No, silly. I want my saliva on your cock. So get up here, big boy, and shove it in my wet and waiting mouth."

Just the thought of sliding his cock between those blood-red lips made his pre-cum drip. He straddled her gorgeous breasts and tapped the slippery head of his dick on her lips. "Knock knock," he teased.

Grabbing his cock, she pulled his balls to her mouth and started licking them. "Remember what you said to Debbie about me being fat and ugly?"

"You heard that?"

"I wasn't dead yet." She popped one ball into her mouth, rolled her tongue around it and then let it go. "What do you think of me now?"

"You are the most beautiful and sexiest woman I have ever seen."

Looking up into his eyes, she told him a lie. "I'm just so, so hungry."

"When we are through fucking, I will take you to the best restaurant in Port au Prince."

"I can't wait that long." She sucked one ball into her mouth...and then the other.

His thigh muscles locked. "Oh, oh...that feels so good."

Before he could comprehend the danger, he felt the most intense pain he had ever felt as Brenda bit off both testicles with a single gnawing bite. He screamed and rose up on his knees, looked down on a face soaked in his blood and a mouth chewing his family jewels. "Oh, fuck no."

She swallowed.

He gained his footing and staggered to the back of the pit. His hands pressed the wound where his nuts had hung just a moment earlier. He looked up just in time to hear Cassandra say:

"I warned him but he didn't listen."

Brenda climbed out of the pit and gave a nod to Cassandra that all was well. Cassandra nodded back.

"For a doctor, he's not too bright." Brenda held out her right hand to Gomez and pulled him out of the pit as if he weighed nothing.

"I need a doctor," he insisted.

She threw him down by the fire and picked out a burning timber.

Gomez thought she was going to hit him, guarded his face with one arm, but he was wrong.

"The doctor is in." Brenda got down on her knees and pulled his hand away from his ball-less cock then thrust the hot timber between his legs.

He screamed and tried to wiggle away, but Brenda was too strong for him to escape. He dug his heels into the dirt and moved back and forth, trying to make the pain go away but to no avail. The night air filled with the stink of burning flesh. His flesh. And the sizzle of boiling blood. His blood. Strangely, his dick remained hard and bold.

Brenda jerked the hot log away and tossed it back on the fire. Sparks spiraled into the darkness. Disturbed flames threw shafts of light on Gomez's transformation. His hair grew long and flowing, his face paled, and though the hard features of his masculinity remained, the edges dissolved into smooth curves any woman would envy. Brenda admired her handiwork, figured he'd do well in female bodybuilding competitions. "Cassandra, he is no longer your son, but a lady-boy. She belongs to me now."

Cassandra bowed. "She will serve you well, my Queen."

Though this voodoo zombie phenomenon seemed perfectly natural, a question lingered in Brenda's mind. "How is all this possible?"

"The Tree of Life has blessed you with the zombie virus enhanced by the blood of the Lesbian Goddess Loa. The virus is transferred through your saliva. Every man you have sex with will be infected and transformed into a sex crazed zombie. Every woman you kiss and bring to orgasm will become a Lesbian Zombie. Bite off a man's balls, you get a subservient chick with a dick." She looked down at the lady-boy. "What will we call her, my Queen?"

"Aurora... after the goddess of the dawn, now a woman in a man's body, a new generation of fierce warriors for the lesbian cause."

Cassandra helped Aurora to her feet. "Ernesto, er, Aurora was never much of fighter, more of a ladies' man."

"Those days are over. Now take her with you and leave this place of my rebirth."

As they turned away, Brenda could see that Aurora already walked like a woman, that little sway to her hips... "Stay close to your mother and obey her like you would me. When the moon has made its return, I will find you."

Brenda watched as they drove off in Cassandra's white Nissan Xterra. She made a mental note about how she would put the car to good use in the near future. Right now, though, she would head back to Port au Prince in Aurora's truck. She didn't know what she'd find there, but she was sure Loa would soon reveal her reason for going there.

***

After dark and parked on a dirt road in the very poorest district of Port au Prince, stark-naked Brenda got out and walked on the rotting boards that passed for a sidewalk. A stray puppy greeted her, wagging its tail. "Well, hello there, little one." She stopped and picked up the dog, and being very friendly, it licked Aurora's blood off her face. She held it up to see its gender. "Oh, you're a little girl dog. In that case, you can come with me. Your name from now is Girlie Dog, yeah, Girlie Dog."

Standing in the doorway of a run-down shack and backlit by a dim light from inside, an 80-year-old infirm Haitian woman smoked a cigarette. Her black skin was heavily wrinkled from years of sun and stress. "Honey, you need some clothes. You can't walk around like that. I am surprised you have not been raped or arrested or both."

Before she could offer Brenda something to wear, a rusted out Jeep with no doors screeched to a stop next to naked Brenda. Headlights lit the dust rising from the road. The car's only occupant was a black man with a goatee, a bald head, and a small frame inside baggy army fatigues. He climbed out and marched to Brenda. "I don't know why you are naked, but your pretty white pussy is going to meet mister black cock. I'll put those tits and butt to good use too. He pulled out a pistol and stabbed the muzzle up under her chin. "You be comin' with me, bitch."

Brenda, cool as a summer salad, handed the dog to the old lady who began to beg the assailant on Brenda's behalf. "Please, sir. Do not harm her. I have a thousand dollars in my house. It is all yours if you leave her with me."

"I don't know." He ogled the patch of red hair between Brenda's legs. "Seems like mighty fine pussy here."

"A thousand dollars can buy you ten fine pussies, just like hers, only some maybe better."

"There's none better," Brenda insisted.

"Ten pussies beat one pussy any day. Okay, get the money. You can have her pussy then."

The woman put down the dog and, using a cane to support herself, lumbered into the wood-plank house.

While the old lady was gone, he began to caress Brenda's tits. "Nice and fine and white." He reached down and touched the fuzz between her thighs. "You ever have big black dick before?"

"I'm a virgin."

"Even better."

He was so engrossed with her body that the old woman returned without him noticing, now less than three feet behind him. "I don't have what you want but found what you are going to get."

The would-be rapist turned and looked into the barrel of a sawed-off shotgun. "Huh?"

The old lady pulled the trigger. His brains and eyeballs took off in opposite directions. The rest of his body dropped to twitch in the dirt. His legs and boots, which appeared to be new, were sticking up in the air.

Brenda smirked. "You really didn't need to do that. I was going to have some fun with the cocksucker."

"I didn't do it for you. I wanted his boots. I can get a really good price for them." With that, she hobbled over and pulled off the boots and then tried to lift the body back into the Jeep.

Brenda had to laugh at the old woman's tenacity. "Don't hurt yourself. I'll do it." She lifted him, easy as a rag doll, and tossed him into the passenger seat, but not without getting his blood smeared across her breasts. Then she removed the jerry can of gas from the back bumper rack and poured the fuel on Mister Army Fatigues. She sang a little tune that fit the occasion. "Come on, baby, light my fire."

The old woman dropped a lit match on the body. With a whoosh, the Jeep became an inferno.

Brenda pushed it down the road. In the night air and darkened street, the burning Jeep illuminated each house it passed by. It dawned on her that no one had come out of their houses to see where the gun blast had come from. "What is this place, New York City?"

"My people are afraid of the gunshot. They will be less afraid from now on."

"Why?"

"Because he was known as Blade, the leader of the FAd'H gang here in Cite Soleil. Now there will be peace, thanks to you, miss..."

"I'm Brenda Ayler. What's your name?"

"Monica Abelard. I have a pink dress with flowers on it. A little short above the knees, but it will be okay for you. You have beautiful knees, as did I many years ago. Come into my house and get cleaned up. Gotta wash Blade's blood off."

"Thanks."

"Come on now."

Brenda picked up the puppy, hugged her, and followed Monica into the house. Monica closed the door and moved slowly, as each step she took looked very painful. She ambled to a four-foot-high brown chest of drawers that had only two drawers left in it. Using a screwdriver, she pried one drawer open a crack, and then using both hands managed to pull the drawer out another eight inches. With her gnarled right hand she reached in and pulled out the dress. "But first we clean you up."

While Brenda admired her new body in the mirror on the wall, Monica shuffled over to a gray bucket where she wet a yellow washcloth then rung it out. After making her way back to Brenda, she began to wipe the blood off Brenda's breasts.

The sensation of the old-woman's caring touch stirred butterflies in Brenda's stomach. She couldn't help but wonder how beautiful Monica must've been in her youth.

Monica rinsed out the washcloth in the bucket and handed it to Brenda. "Wash your face."

"Thank you, Monica." Brenda washed her face and wondered how she could ever repay the old woman for her kindness. Then an idea struck her. "Do you believe in zombies?"

"Yes. Haiti has many zombie legends."

"I've been a Lesbian Zombie for a little over two hours now. Before that I was just a very ugly and a grossly overweight corpse."

"So you must have met Cassandra."

"And I dined in the afterlife with the Lesbian Goddess Loa. Then I was reborn a Lesbian Zombie. I have the power to take away all your pain and make you young and beautiful again, like you were in that picture on the wall."

In the photo, a young black woman's smile gleamed brightly.

"That is not me...but my sweet daughter who was raped and murdered forty-seven years ago by the Tomtons Machetes. They were soldiers for Papa Doc Duvalier, the dictator of Haiti back then. His great grandkids are visiting for a couple weeks from Paris where they live with their grandfather, Baby Doc, because their father was killed in Somalia. I am going to kill those kids so that Baby Doc can know what real sadness feels like."

Brenda wasn't too keen on that idea but played along. "I can help you with that. We'll hunt them down together and send Baby Doc a video of you ripping out their precious hearts and holding them in your hands and taking a bite out of each one. But first, you need to be converted to a Lesbian Zombie. Are you willing?"

"I have never been a lesbian before."

"Me neither. You'll be my first."

As she got down on her knees, Brenda let her hands slide over Monica's brown sagging breasts and down to the lumpy cellulite of her black thighs. She slowly pulled off Monica's dress and looked at her pussy like a vampire would admire a victim's neck. Juices began to flow down below. She licked Monica's clitoris, surprised at the softness and enticed by her fragrance. For an old woman, she was hot, hot, hot.

Monica spread her legs and pulled Brenda's face tightly to her snatch. "Oh, don't stop."

Brenda slipped her tongue into the woman's folds and savored the nectar therein. The sweetness made her potent saliva flow.

"Oh god." Monica moaned. "I'm going to come."

The transformation began. Old bones that ached stopped aching. Her fingers felt nimble as she combed them through Brenda's red hair. "They don't hurt anymore. This is wonderful."

Her pussy tingled like when she was a teenager cooing over her favorite movie star. The heat in her belly grew with every stroke of Brenda's magic tongue. Sagging breasts lifted to become round and firm with beautiful perky nipples. Doughy, wrinkled skin became ebony smooth and supple. Every muscle in her body tightened until her vagina let loose in surges of pleasure beyond any orgasm she'd ever experienced.

Her legs gave way and she dropped to her knees in front of Brenda, whose lips were shiny wet with saliva and Monica's cum. Gasping for air, she noticed her body was young, slender and sexy. She looked in the mirror on the wall and could not believe the black woman she saw. Her white hair was pitch-black, her eyes bright and dreamy, her mouth perfect for kissing again. She threw her arms around Brenda's neck and kissed her with a passion she'd never known.

Two hot naked women found love and satisfaction in a man's world that was about to change forever.

Chapter 4: BRENDA AND MONICA GO RECRUITING

A jubilant Monica strutted to a black cabinet that had no door, picked up a half empty bottle of Rhum Barbancourt, and waved it at Brenda. "I been saving this for a special occasion and, sweetie, they don't come any better than this one." After handing Brenda a chipped cup with no handle, she filled it to the brim. She poured a drink for herself in an equally beat up cup and made a toast that rhymes: "Here is to you and here is to me. Do Lesbian Zombies ever have to pee?"

"Yes we do, honey. We're just like any other woman except we are stronger than any man on earth. Oh yeah. We're also more intelligent, it's very hard to kill us, and we cannot reproduce. The male gender of the human race is *fucked*."

"You sound like you want to take over the world."

Brenda giggled. "Don't you?"

About that time they heard a dog barking.

Brenda laughed. "I wondered if Girlie Dog could become a Lesbian Zombie dog. Maybe that question will be answered one day." With that, the two of them had a good laugh and finished off the bottle.

Slightly drunk, Brenda said, "It just occurred to me that my cash and credit cards are still over at the clinic. So let's go get them and then go out on the town. I understand the New York Giants are here to help with a rebuilding project. If they're lucky, we'll fuck the entire team."

"Do Lesbian Zombies enjoy fucking men?"

"Well, Monica, there's no law against it, especially if it helps us get what we want from them."

"How about giving them a blowjob instead?"

"A blowjob will turn them into sex crazed zombies. But if you bite off their balls they become lady-boy slaves."

"I like the way you think, Brenda."

***

The next day, driving the truck with Monica giving directions to the clinic, Brenda got there in record time. The Nissan Xterra was parked out front, so she knew Aurora or Cassandra, or both were inside.

She left Monica in the truck and walked down the hall to the place of her previous death. Heavy breathing and giggles came from the so-called operating room. She leaned up against the doorframe and watched naked Aurora (aka the late Doctor Gomez) and an equally naked Debbie going at it head to toe on the operating table. "Ah-um."

Debbie lifted her head, and seeing Brenda, she let out a scream, rolled off Aurora, and fell off the table. "It was her...I mean his fault." She struggled to her feet. "Please don't kill me."

Brenda grinned. "Relax. I'm here for my credit cards and money. And I'll take the keys to the Xterra."

Debbie covered her tits with her hands. "You really aren't going to kill us?"

Brenda glanced at Aurora's impressive boner. "Go back to what you were doing."

Walking out of the operating room with keys, cash, and credit cards in hand, Brenda took one last look back and saw Debbie climb up on top of Aurora and start sucking her cock. This was followed by her deep-throated groans as her curvaceous muscles and sprouting breasts shuddered under Debbie's oral assault.

Aurora was one strange zombie.

Invasion of the Lesbian Zombies

Outside, the tropical heat of Haiti was stifling. Getting into the truck, Brenda looked at Monica. "Let's go for a swim. What do you say?"

"I think it would be fun. Lately, I would not have done it. People would have laughed at seeing an old woman, like I was, in a swimsuit."

Brenda dangled the keys in front of Monica. Let's take the luxury car. After they switched over to the Nissan Xterra, they stopped at a surf shop and bought matching bathing suits, and then drove a short distance to the beach. The white warm sand felt wonderful on their feet as they walked into the surf of the Caribbean Sea. As they frolicked in the warm water, hand in hand, Brenda realized that, in less than four days, she'd gone from being miserable to being happy. This all seemed surreal to her and yet it was really happening. She had always thought zombies were made up characters, gross, rotting corpses that lumbered about in search of living victims to tear to shreds, but now she was a zombie, and she wasn't anything like the Hollywood version.

And I must be the Queen of the Lesbian Zombies. Cassandra had called me her Queen. Well, if I'm the Queen, the world is going to see some colossal changes. Queen of the Lesbian Zombies. I like that title.

As they got out of the water, neither of them paid any mind to four guys in their twenties who appeared to be watching them. Men would watch them a lot from now on.

Monica had been doing some thinking too. She decided to broach the subject as to what the future was to hold for them. They certainly were in no position to take over the world, and she didn't know if she wanted to do that, even if it were possible.

Lying prone on the sand next to an also prone Brenda, she propped up on her elbow and just came out with it. "Okay, Brenda. What is next for us?"

"The first thing we're going to do is invite those horny guys to come over and join us and to bring their beer with them."

"Why don't we just go over to them?"

"Because I like this spot better."

"All looks the same to me."

"Look, two of them are walking this way and the other two are leaving."

Monica scoffed. "They must think they're hot stuff, all tanned and wearing those Speedos. Does nothing for me." She touched Brenda's firm and flat stomach. "But this, on the other hand, makes me wet."

"Save that thought and have some fun with these bozos."

"Why?"

"You'll see."

The two beachcombers arrived, beer cooler in hand and growing bulges in their Speedos. "Good evening, ladies."

"Well, look who's here." Brenda sat up in the sand. Before either of them could say anything, she came up with an obvious remark. "I suppose you guys want a blowjob."

The boys exchanged *BINGO* glances and shrugged. "Hell yes." The six-foot muscleman set down the cooler. "I'm Carlos, and this is Jason." He nodded to his Caucasian blonde and blue-eyed friend.

"Who cares?" Monica dragged Carlos to the sand. "Take off your shorts. I want to see the real thing, not just the bulge."

He scrambled out of his Speedos, a normally simple task now complicated by his enlarged cock.

"Oh my." Monica licked her lips. "Much better."

Carlos wasted no time shoving it in her mouth. She fought her gag reflex as she soaked him with her virus-laced saliva. Brenda's words of advice came to mind: *Bite off their balls.* She glanced around for Brenda and Jason but didn't see them.

Carlos was going at it hot and heavy, his hips thrusting up and down when Brenda appeared with a brown paper bag in hand, dripping blood. Monica glared at her with a *what-the-fuck* look.

Carlos was breathing ninety miles an hour. "Oh. Oh... I'm gonna come, bitch."

Before he could explode in Monica's mouth, she pulled away

and went for the balls. Those big bad-boys were a mouthful, but she managed to clamp down with her teeth and sheer them off.

Carlos screamed bloody murder, attracting the attention of other beachgoers, but his cries of pain were short-lived as he quickly passed out.

Brenda shoved the open bag toward Monica, who promptly spit the plucked delicacies into it to join Jason's pair. "Now let's get out of here before the cops come."

Monica took off running with Brenda down the beach. "Why did we clip those guys' balls?"

"Because men are so fuckin' easy."

"What are we going to do with their nuts?"

"I've developed a taste for gonads, thanks to Aurora, well, Doctor Gomez. We're going to eat them for breakfast."

On the drive back to her place, Monica stared out the window, the bloody bag seeping in her lap, the goo running down between her legs. During the blowjob she'd gotten sand in her pussy, made it itch.

Brenda broke the silence. "In a couple days we leave for New York City."

"Why? What's the plan? You just do shit without telling me what the fuck is going on. Like these balls." She lifted the drippy bag in evidence. "What's the point?"

"It had to be done. I need a couple more lady-boys to do the grunt work on the island for us while we're gone. They'll thank us later."

"No they won't do it."

"What do you care? Men are pigs that deserve to be neutered."

"Wow. Some guy must've really screwed you over."

"Yeah, something like that." *John and Jenny are in for a big surprise.*

"So we eat their balls?"

"We're zombies that prefer eating testicles over intestines and licking pussy over cock. Trick is to make it all mean something worthwhile."

"In New York City?"

Brenda glanced at her. "Don't you want to go?"

"Hell yeah. I hate this shit hole but first we kill that prick Papa Doc's grandkids like you promised."

"Tomorrow, honey, you can kill them."

A delighted Monica leaned over and kissed Brenda on her cheek. "When are we going to get some more followers? We can't take over the world by ourselves."

"I've already picked out our next candidate. Her name is Debbie Lopez. She's the doctor's assistant who killed me."

"Why would you want her on our team?"

"I'm not mad at her. I'm grateful."

Upon arriving back at Monica's place, they decided to go to bed. As they lay in each other's arms on a threadbare mattress, white and black, ying and yang, tied together as one, Brenda caressed Monica's backside. "Tell me about Papa Doc."

"When I was twenty-eight I was walking home from nursing school when an army truck pulled up and nine Tomtons Machetes soldiers jumped out and ran to me. I was not afraid because Papa Doc, our new leader, had told everyone over loud speakers that things were going to be wonderful in Haiti now. The soldiers forced me into the truck then drove into the jungle where they took turns raping me over and over for hours. When they had enough, they threw me out and drove off, laughing."

Tears burned in Brenda's eyes.

"My father went to the presidential palace to demand justice, arrests and convictions of the nine Tomtons Machetes. Papa Doc said he would look into it. He never did so my father went to the American Embassy, thinking the Americans would pressure Papa Doc. They did nothing because they were doing a lot of under-the-table deals with him."

Brenda sniffled. "I'm sorry my country failed you."

"It gets worse. A few nights later, a truck drove up to our house and those same soldiers jumped out. My father told me to escape through the bedroom window. I hid in the bushes and heard screaming and gunfire. When the truck drove away, I sneaked into the house and found my mother and father shot dead."

"I'm so sorry."

"I moved to the Dominican Republic where my rape-child daughter was born. When we came back, I thought things would be better with Papa Doc gone to France, but the Haitian people still suffered under Baby Doc's brutality. Five years later, my daughter was raped and murdered by the same Tomtons Machetes who raped me and killed my parents. Baby Doc did nothing about it either."

Brenda wiped her eyes with her arm then put it back around Monica. "We'll make them pay in blood and money."

"Let's start with Baby Doc's grandson, Francois, aka Baby Doc the Third, and his granddaughter Anya. When we kill them, Papa Doc's soul will be further tormented in hell."

"I think we shouldn't kill the grandkids. We'll convert Anya and make Francois a lady-boy."

"Killing them is better."

Brenda sighed. "The satisfaction would be fleeting. Better if Baby Doc should die."

"Then he won't be around to live with the heartbreaking loss of those kids."

"Kill him anyway. Leave the kids be."

Monica stretched her lithe body, so black, so smooth, so inviting. "All this talk of death when life is so beautiful for us now."

"It all comes with a price." Brenda slapped Monica's butt and it was game on.

After a peaceful night's sleep, they awoke to the sounds of Girlie Dog tearing up paper. Both now wide awake it dawned on them at the same time what Girlie Dog was eating.

In unison they said: "Damn that dog. There goes our breakfast."

"Monica, this city must have a McDonald's."

"About a mile from here but they don't serve balls."

"Their food isn't much better, but at least it's food. Let's go."

While both of them were stuffing down a big breakfast and drinking orange juice, the dining area television was broadcasting the news in Haitian Creole.

"Shit," Monica said while looking at the TV.

"What?" Brenda put down her orange juice. "I don't speak the language...what are they saying?"

"Baby Doc's grandkids are returning to Paris."

"Don't let it bother you. We'll get them another day."

Monica clenched a fist. "But I wanted to kill them today."

"Well, you're out of luck. We still need to get our tickets to New York, so let's get packed and ready to head to the airport."

"I want to take the pictures of my family and my precious daughter. By the way, what are we going to do with Girlie Dog?"

"We'll take her with us. First, I have something to do. I'll drop you off so you can get your stuff."

Monica glared at her curiously. "You know I don't like it when you don't tell me what is going on."

"It's a surprise."

Two hours later, Brenda was back with two additional people in the Xterra.

Monica threw a suitcase in the back. "Who are they?"

"The hottie is Debbie Lopez. She'll be going with us."

"Is she one of us?"

"Not yet. I'll convert her on the plane."

"Who is the other woman with all the muscles?"

"Aurora. She'll be staying with her mom, Cassandra."

"Eyee. Aurora? She is ugly as a mud fence."

"She used to be a he...Doctor Gomez. I bit off his balls. Now he's a woman with a dick."

"Like Carlos and Jason?"

"Aurora is their boss now, which makes her the queen of the lady-boys on Haiti. Right now he's dropping us off at the airport and taking his mom's car back."

"Then what?"

"Enough questions. We have to get our butts in gear."

"What do we use for money?"

"I have plenty of money and credit cards." Brenda kissed Monica on her pouty lips. "Don't worry."

**

Heading to their gate at Aeroport International Toussaint Louverture with Debbie in tow, Monica said to Brenda, "How do you propose to convert Debbie on the plane?"

"You'll be surprised."

Debbie was taking in the sights of the airport. "I have been here only once when I first came here. I was sixteen, from Mexico City, by accident. Since then, all I have done is screw Doctor Gomez, well, Aurora now."

Monica laughed. "You won't be doing that anymore."

Now waiting to board, Monica whispered to Brenda, "What section are we in?"

"Just wait 'til they call for all first class passengers."

"Good God, Brenda. First Class tickets must have cost a fortune."

Brenda grumped. "I've spent more money on bad men."

After a short wait on the boarding steps, Brenda sat in window seat 1A, Debbie in seat B, Monica across the aisle in C, and no one sat in D. Brenda looked at her traveling companions and saw how happy they were. Her past seemed meaningless, well, almost. She still had unfinished business with John and Jenny. *Let me see. What to do, what to do. I should thank them for how things turned out.*

On the other hand, John was really a lying slob, and Jenny who had an I.Q. of twelve, deserved to suffer. *She's definitely not Lesbian Zombie material.*

Brenda settled back in the plush first-class seat and thought about what to tell her mother. *I can't exactly call her up and say 'guess what, Mom. I'm the Queen of the Lesbian Zombies and I'm beautiful.'* No, that wouldn't go over very well.

With the cabin lights turned down and dinner and drinks long over with, Debby and Monica went to sleep to the drone of the plane's engines. Brenda fell asleep reading a Time magazine article about an oil tycoon named Alfons Duda. At about 3:30 a.m. she woke up. She looked at sound-asleep Debbie. Her long black Latino hair hung invitingly over a bare shoulder, and a bit of cleavage begged to be explored within the shadows of her low-cut blouse. Brenda's clitoris responded to the view with a tight throb. She nudged Debbie awake.

She sat up straight. "Are we landing?"

"Come with me."

"Where?"

"To the lavatory."

"There is not enough room for two people in there."

"Shhh. You'll wake up the whole plane."

After slinking down the aisle, they squeezed into the first-class lavatory and closed the door. Brenda immediately pulled up Debbie's pink skirt.

Debbie shoved it back down. "What do you think you are doing?"

"Shhh...I need to show you something."

"In here?"

"Didn't Aurora tell you?"

"Tell me what?"

"That I'm a lesbian."

"Well, I am not a lesbian."

"And therein lies the problem." Brenda pulled Debbie's mouth to hers and kissed her deep and passionately.

Debbie's first reaction was to push Brenda away, but as the virus-tinged saliva calmed her, protests turned to wanton need.

This time when Brenda pulled up Debbie's skirt, she got no resistance. She slipped her panties down around her ankles and opened her blouse, surprised to see no bra.

"Oh, Brenda...Brenda...I... I never felt this loved before."

"Get used to it, girl." Brenda started licking Debbie's nipples then made her way down to Debbie's clit and continued licking until Debbie's moans got loud enough for the pilots to hear. To Brenda's delight, her own juices were flowing and ready to ignite.

"Oh...oh... oh, yes..." Debbie came with a cry of delight.

"Ladies and gentlemen. We have begun our descent to JFK International. Please fasten your seatbelts. Flight attendants, prepare the cabin for landing."

"Shit," Brenda spat.

"Oh, no...don't stop, please don't stop." The hot Latina could never get enough, even if they were flying to Alaska.

"We'll finish this later."

"Damn." Debbie put herself together then followed Brenda back to their seats.

Monica leaned across the aisle to Debbie. "What was that all about?"

"I don't know." Debbie breathed. "But for some reason I want to kiss you."

"Me? Why me?"

"You are beautiful. I would love to explore every inch of your body."

Monica smiled. "You are one of us now."

Chapter 5: THE LESBIAN ZOMBIES TAKE MANHATTAN, THE BRONX, AND STATEN ISLAND TOO.

A s Brenda, Monica, and Debbie made their way out of Terminal 7, they were met by a cool night breeze that lifted up the skirts of all three women, much to the delight of every cab driver standing on the curb. The Lesbian Zombies opted for Sam's Limousine Service and Brenda decided to sit in the seat next to him. "Take us to the Waldorf Astoria in Manhattan."

"Of course, right away, ma'am." Sam was a guy in his mid thirties with a slender build and tattooed arms. He kept running his left hand through his light blond hair. *God I'd love to fuck these three.*

"Pardon me?" Brenda muttered though it sounded like a good idea.

He didn't answer her, as he was preoccupied with glancing in the rearview mirror to see Monica and Debbie getting it on in the back seat. *I would love to be in the middle of those two.*

Brenda purposely pulled up her skirt, exposing her creamy thighs. "How do you like this?"

He glanced at her, looked surprised. "Lady, I'm a married man." *But I'd fuck you in a heartbeat, given half a chance.*

She'd heard him speak but his lips weren't moving. It was then she discovered that she had developed a new ability: she could read his mind.

Sam began to make small talk. "Will you be in town long? How do you like the weather?" *How would you like to have a foursome in Central Park?*

She turned to hone in on the make-out session in the back seat, expecting some hot thoughts but got nothing from Debbie and Monica. *Hmmm. Doesn't work on Lesbian Zombies.* She didn't know why all of a sudden she could do this, but it was wonderful...and very naughty.

Returning her attention to Sam, "You're very attractive. I'll bet you fuck a lot of women who ride with you."

Sam didn't answer but she heard him think, *I'd fuck that hot Latina first, then her girlfriend, then last but not least, the redhead.*

Brenda scooted closer to Sam. "If you were to cut your fare in half, we would let you fuck whichever one of us you like. Isn't that right, girls?"

Debbie spoke up first. "I'm not interested in any cock."

Monica pulled her face out of Debbie's crotch. "Count me out." She returned to her muff dive.

Brenda scoffed. If they were going to get a lady-boy in New York, she'd have to do it herself. "That leaves me," she cooed.

Sam looked a little worried. "I don't know. I could get into a lot of trouble with the boss."

Debbie moaned with pleasure but stopped long enough to interject, "I thought the limo was yours. Your name is Sam."

"All the drivers are Sam. My real name is Roberto."

Monica looked up from her snatch snack. "Not Sam?"

Debbie pushed Monica's head back into position between her thighs. "Finish me." She gasped when Monica's tongue found its mark again.

Brenda decided to take the lead. "Roberto, pull off the road into that vacant lot and I'll fuck you like crazy."

"Okay, but no funny stuff. I have a wife and kid."

"Oh, I promise you won't be laughing."

He parked the car by a row of bushes. While Debbie and Monica waited outside under a streetlight, they could hear the two of them going at it. The heavy car rocked on its springs.

Inside, as Brenda straddled him in true lap-dance fashion, Roberto tried to kiss her but she turned her lips away. "No kissing."

"Who do you think you are...Pretty Woman?"

Now Brenda had to pee. She heard him think, *This pretty woman's going to kill me.* She'd been pressing him really hard for a blowjob, but he wouldn't take off his pants, so she hadn't gotten close enough to bite off his balls. He was a waste of time. "Let's take a break."

"But I haven't come yet."

"You don't know how lucky you are." As she opened the door his thoughts were very clear. *Thank God. Now's my chance to get the hell out of here.*

She got out and sashayed to her lesbian followers, giving Sam time to throw out their luggage and drive off.

"Just great," Monica yelled.

Debbie screamed, "Come back," and then glowered at Brenda. "Why did you let him go?"

"All three of us should have been in there." Monica was steamed. "It is your fault, Debbie. You said no first."

"You were eating me out, for godsake. That is no time to think about cock."

"It was Brenda's idea. It is her fault we are stuck in this slum."

Brenda threw up her hands. "Yes, it was my idea. I wanted to get his balls in my mouth, but no, he didn't want a blowjob. He wanted to go straight to the fucking, but I didn't want his cock in my virgin pussy. Win some, lose some, but lost balls aren't worth fighting each other over. Now let's pick up our bags and figure out which way to go to get to the Waldorf Astoria."

Grumbling, the girls followed her across the vacant lot to a lighted street. A drunk lying on the sidewalk asked, "What time is it?"

Brenda spoke up, "3:35 a.m. Is this Manhattan?"

"No, lady. This here is Navy Street...in Brooklyn."

"Do we have a long way to go?" Monica asked him.

"Can you spare a dime?"

Brenda gave him a twenty. "He's no help."

The three of them walked for several miles, carrying their high heel shoes, and then they sat on their suitcases on the sidewalk and watched the sun rise.

A Cadillac pulled up and a young woman in her late teens with auburn hair, gray eyes, and a small frame with small tits to match, got out the rear door and walked up to them. Her bloodshot eyes made it obvious she'd been crying and not trying to cover it up. "I'm Maggie Jensen. You look like you could use some help."

"We could use a ride," Brenda replied.

"My boyfriend..." she indicated the driver, "is known as Big Bad Brooklyn Daddy or BBBD for short. He'd be glad to give you a ride to a hotel, but you can stay at his house if you want."

"His house?"

"We can have a party."

They agreed.

Brenda couldn't wait to meet BBBD. She knew he was a pimp and Maggie was his prostitute. Monica and Debbie weren't experienced in the ways of a big city like New York, so they didn't have a clue.

Once more, Brenda took the front passenger seat and the girls took the back, with Maggie in the middle. It made a cozy threesome as BBBD drove the mile and a half to a two-story rundown house in an equally rundown neighborhood.

They sat in silence on the ride, but Brenda could hear what Maggie and BBBD were thinking. Maggie was thinking how BBBD was pleased that she was able to get the stranded women into his car, which meant she might not get beat for a while.

BBBD was thinking how he'd treat them as guests in his house, get them drunk and hooked on cocaine, and then start to slap them around. He would then invite some of his regular customers over for a free all-nighter to break the women into being his whores.

These nefarious plans made Brenda's blood boil, but she said or did nothing. She just sat there thinking how she'd kill BBBD and free Maggie from sexual slavery. There'd be no turning BBBD into a lady-boy. For him there'd only be a death sentence that would be carried out very soon.

Arriving at 121 Montford Lane, BBBD was the perfect gentleman. He marched around and opened the doors for all his women. All the time, Brenda was listening to what he was going to do. *Take them upstairs and lock them in.* He'd then get everyone a drink to knock them out. Problem was that his date-rape drug wouldn't work on Lesbian Zombies.

Soon the three of them were sitting on a worn-out couch, drinking BBBD's immobilizing concoction. They pretended to be getting woozy.

"I'll have another," Monica said.

Maggie brought her one but Brenda tripped her on purpose. The drink and Maggie hit the floor. "I'm so sorry."

BBBD took off his belt, grabbed Maggie by her left arm, and dragged her upstairs to the front bedroom.

The girls followed at a distance. "Leave her alone," Monica shouted.

As he drew back the belt to hit her, Brenda lunged at him and grabbed his right arm, stopping the belt.

"What the fuck, bitch?"

She threw him headfirst into the wall.

Maggie stood there in disbelief. Here was a woman half BBBD's size, kicking the shit out of him. He was a good two hundred-forty pounds and six-foot three inches tall with muscles the size of Michelin Man.

He staggered away from the wall with a very obvious broken nose. Muttering that he was going to kill her, he swung a fist and missed. As his fist went by her face, she took hold of it and bit off his thumb and index finger. He let out a bloodcurdling yell, pulled a gun from his waistband, and shot Brenda in the stomach. The bullet passed through her body. She fell to the floor.

BBBD turned and waved the pistol at frightened Monica and Debbie standing in the hall. "I'll kill all you bitches."

Maggie cried out, "Please don't kill them."

He cranked the gun to Maggie. "Don't fuckin' tell me shit."

"Don't kill me...I'll be good."

The women's eyes suddenly got big around.

He couldn't understand what the three of them were looking at until he turned around and saw Brenda standing right behind him. "Are you fuckin' kiddin' me?"

She slapped the gun from his hand. "You can't kill a zombie." With her razor-sharp fingernails she lashed out and slit his throat.

He stumbled backwards with more anger than surprise in his wide-open eyes, but as blood pumped from a cut artery, he instinctively cupped his hands over the gaping wound. He tried to say bitch, but all that came out was: "bpplttch."

Brenda ripped his shirt open, stabbed her fingers under his sternum, and yanked out his heart, still beating. "You won't be needing this anymore."

He dropped to the floor like the pile of shit he was.

Brenda held out her bloody hand and showed everyone her throbbing prize. "Anyone want a bite?"

Monica and Debbie rushed forward.

Poor little Maggie fainted.

Brenda tore a bite from the gushing organ and wiped the blood from her lips with the back of her hand. "It needs a little salt."

Monica and Debbie finished off the bloody mess.

BBBD's heart stopped beating just two days short of his 35th birthday.

Brenda headed for the bathroom and a quick shower. She noticed a prescription for Ziagen, an antiviral HIV medication with Maggie's name on it. *Maggie is sick and may be dying.*

George S. Naas

Brenda took the shower, and as the water beat down on her, she watched BBBD's blood flush down the drain. She felt overwhelming joy thinking how he looked as he knew he was about to die.

She walked out of the bathroom, naked, with water still dripping from her beautiful breasts. While drying herself with a white towel, she watched Debbie pat Maggie's face until she began to come around.

Drunkenly, she sat up. "What happened?"

Brenda tossed her the bottle containing the HIV pills. "You have two choices. Number one: Find a new pimp to slap you around and eventually murder you, or accept number two."

"What's number two?"

"Become a Lesbian Zombie like us."

She glanced at the bloody faces of Monica and Debbie. "I'm okay with the lesbian part, but I don't believe the zombies part."

"BBBD didn't either but I think he does now."

Monica added, "Us girls just wanna have fun, is all."

Maggie scowled. "Do I have to eat bloody hearts?"

"That was just a snack...but balls are our preference, mainly."

"Balls...like testicles?"

"We're Lesbian Zombies. What do you expect?"

"I don't know..."

"Get anything you want to take with you because you're coming with us."

All Maggie took was a picture of her drug-addicted mother and a teddy bear she'd had since she was five years old. "I'm ready."

Getting in the late BBBD's Cadillac with Brenda driving, they slowly made their way to the Waldorf Astoria hotel. The reservation check-in clerk, Chloe Dawson, was a very attractive young woman with long blond hair and eyes so blue the sky must've fallen.

Brenda couldn't take her gaze off her. "I just love your name."

"Thank you."

"So, Chloe, here's the deal. We'll be staying for at least a couple weeks. We want a suite with a large hot tub. One that can accommodate four and maybe five naked women. That is five in case you would like to join us. We have had one killer of a morning so we need to get some relaxation. You know what I mean?"

Chloe put her face just inches from Brenda's. "I know exactly what you mean and I'd love to join you when I get off at four. Will that work?"

"Four o'clock will be fine, and Chloe, I need you to do me a small favor. When we went through customs, we had to leave our little dog, Girlie Dog, at JFK International for a day to make sure she wasn't carrying some foreign dog disease. Could you send someone out there to pick her up?" Brenda handed Chloe the papers necessary to get Girlie Dog into the country.

Chloe looked at the stack of papers. "This has blood on it."

"Remember, I said we had a killer of a morning."

"See you in a few hours."

When they walked into their suite on the fifteenth floor, the ambiance blew them away. Everyone took off exploring.

A very excited Monica exclaimed, "This place is like a mansion...a very nice mansion."

Debbie came running out of the bathroom. "There is a separate shower and bathtub."

In the rec-room, tall sliding windows overlooked 49th Street across from the Intercontinental Barclay Building. The room was kind of like an indoor balcony that housed rocking chairs, exercise equipment, and a hot tub, in which lounged a very relaxed and naked Brenda gazing up at a blank 55-inch flat-screen. "This must be what heaven is like."

The girls stripped and jumped in.

Maggie appeared with a bottle of Dom Perignon, 1998. "This is the best booze I've ever seen in a rented room."

Brenda laughed. "You deserve a drink after what you've

been through."

"Oh, yeah. I forgot to thank you for killing that asshole. He's no longer BBBD. He's Big Bad Brooklyn Dead Daddy or BBBDD. You know, ladies, that has a nice ring to it. By the way, when do I become a Lesbian Zombie?"

Brenda curled a finger to her. "Get in and be patient."

She stripped down and climbed into the tub with the other naked women. They eventually finished off Maggie's bottle and ordered two more. To their surprise and delight, Chloe was the delivery girl...and a Lesbian Zombie to be. The girls' eyes followed Chloe through the steam and into the bubbling water, all ogling her already beautiful body and the fuzzy patch of blond hair between her legs.

As they relaxed with only their heads and necks above the froth, they began one by one to tell their life stories.

Brenda, being the leader, led off about how her journey started and how it led her up to this point.

Then came Monica ending her story with, "And that is why I am going to Paris to kill Baby Doc and his grandkids."

A dark mood settled over the girls. Brenda shook a pointed finger at Monica. "We don't kill women and children."

"We will see." Monica splashed water on Brenda to lighten the mood.

Next up was Debbie. "I did not mind working with Doctor Gomez and liked the fact that he loved to screw me. I quickly learned that I loved sex."

Next in line was Maggie. "I thought I was just supposed to be a whore. My mama sold me to BBBD when I was fifteen. I still remember the first time I had sex. He took me up to the bedroom and stripped me down, and then this big fat guy came in the room. He had paid BBBD five hundred dollars to be my first. Seems my virginity was sold to the highest bidder."

"Scum," Monica spat.

"So that's why I'm a whore."

Monica sat straight up. "Do not ever call yourself a whore

again. You are a beautiful young woman. You were too young to do anything but what you were forced to do. We will hunt down the assholes that defiled you, and when we catch them we will gut them as if they were fish."

Maggie scoffed. "That's a lot of fish."

Brenda chuckled. "Now what's your story, Chloe?"

She flashed her blue eyes. "I came to the Big Apple to get away from my husband, Tim. We met in college and were married for four years. He was never faithful to me. In fact, he screwed an old girlfriend on our wedding day and was late for the ceremony."

"What a pig," Debbie said.

"When he came home drunk and beat the fuck out of me for refusing to have sex with him, I finally decided to leave. I waited until he was naked and sleeping on the bed then squirted super glue in his dick hole. In the morning, when he couldn't pee, he went into a panic."

Monica laughed. "Now that's what I call getting even."

"He freaked out and ran down a street in Dayton, Ohio, naked and screaming for help. I divorced the asshole and flew here to start a new life." Chloe ended with a question. "What do I have to do to become a Lesbian Zombie?"

Brenda spoke up. "Kiss me."

"Really?"

"You'll feel the change inside, the heat, the passion, the want for female love. The thought of a cock in your pussy will be replaced by the hope for my tongue." She licked her upper lip. "Then you'll kiss me like you love me, and you'll mean it."

Smiling, Chloe scooted to Brenda, straddled her thigh, and wrapped her arms around her neck. "Like this?"

Luscious lips met, tenderly at first, then more wantonly, as tongues touched and mouths mashed together in the steamy mist. Chloe moaned with delight. Brenda's arms slipped around her and pulled her in tight, breasts to breasts, both now wriggling in each other's embrace.

Monica and Debbie joined them, touched them, and caressed them while Chloe rubbed her clit on Brenda's thigh, harder and harder, faster and faster, so much so that her breathing couldn't keep up, and the cry from her throat let them all know that the dam had burst and her libido was lit up with the color and intensity of fireworks. Every muscle in her body trembled as she clung to Brenda, nuzzling her neck. Slowly, Monica and Debbie backed off, leaving Brenda to sooth the newest Lesbian Zombie.

"Welcome to the sisterhood," she whispered.

Maggie didn't know what to think about what she'd just witnessed, though she'd have no problem admitting the girl on girl action turned her on something fierce. However, one thing was certain. She didn't feel like a zombie.

"Let's get Maggie," Debbie suggested.

"Game on," Monica cheered.

Both girls piled on Maggie, kissing her, caressing her, and fingering her in the churning hot water until she too came in a most wonderful way. When she drifted down from her heavenly high she still didn't feel like a zombie, but the lesbian part, now that was an experience of a lifetime.

Dreamy-eyed and on cloud nine, Chloe released Brenda and resumed her place in the hot tub.

Brenda got back to business. "Okay, ladies. It's time for us to get serious." Her ample breasts bobbed in the bubbling water. "After hearing your stories and knowing mine, it's obvious men are the problem with this world, more-so than I first suspected. So I say we put them out of business...for good."

"Here, here," Maggie said.

"How?" Debbie asked.

"Our immediate task is to find rich businessmen to fleece out of their money. Each one of you will be given the name of the man you are to seduce. You'll need to do a lot of research on your targets, but don't take too long. Our assets are a little over three million dollars. They won't last forever. Remember, the biggest asset you have is your good looks. Do whatever is necessary to get the man to fall so madly in love with you he'll do anything to keep you."

Chloe made an icky face. "Does that include fucking them?"

"Fucking, sucking, bondage, ménage à trios, and anything else the mark wants."

Maggie frowned. "What's a ménage à trios?"

"A threesome."

Chloe asked, "Does it have to be with men?"

"When you're counting his cash you'll forget all about the hairy bastards."

Monica spoke up. "I think we need a slogan and I have the perfect one. *Before we can* fuck them *over, we first have to fuck them.*"

Brenda smiled. "I like that. All in favor?"

A chorus of "Ayes" rose with the steamy mist.

One Nay came from Chloe. "Men are so icky."

"Sex is sex," Debbie chimed in. "Take what you can get."

"Now, ladies, let's go shopping and then out to dinner. I'm dying for a rare steak and several screwdrivers. Out of the tub now, and no drying each other off, otherwise we'll be here all night."

***

Three hours later, the five hotties walked out of an expensive and exclusive boutique locked arm in arm, sucking on complimentary lollipops. Maggie had grabbed a handful from a bowl on the counter. Three store clerks followed, carrying Sleeve Detail dresses, Slimming Strap dresses, Lace Midi dresses, Slimming Fringe dresses, and Sleeve Detail Floral dresses and, of course, Collar Detail Sweater dresses, all with several pairs of matching shoes. After the clerks piled all the clothing and shoes in BBBD's Cadillac, along with bras, panties, corsets, nightwear, socks, and hosiery, they thanked the girls and lit out back to the store to add up their commissions.

It was finally time for dinner.

Since it was only two blocks to the restaurant, they decided to walk. As they passed a Holiday Inn Express, they saw a little girl in a wheelchair, looking at an iPad. Monica took the lollipop from her mouth and stopped to talk to the mother. "What a cute little girl. I love the color of her hair."

The mother replied in a low voice. "We're praying that Caroline will be with us this time next year."

Monica's stomach dropped. "Oh, dear. That serious?"

The mother nodded and dabbed at a tear.

Monica bent down to Caroline. "What is that you are watching?"

"A zombie show. *The Walking Dead*." She spied the lollipop. "Do you like zombies?"

Monica patted the little girl's shoulder. "More than you know, sweetie. More than you know."

"Can I have a lollipop?"

Monica looked up at the girl's mother. "Can she?"

"Of course. She loves lollipops, especially cherry flavor."

"Stay right here. I will be right back." Monica took off running to catch up to her sisters. "Maggie. Can I have one of your lollipops? A cherry one?"

"It's the only one I have left. And I love cherry—"

"Give me that goddamn lollipop."

"Okay already." She surrendered the sucker. "Don't freak out."

With her back turned to Caroline and her mother, Monica carefully unwrapped it and switched it for the one she had been sucking on then wrapped it back up. She then ran back and handed the lollipop to a very grateful Caroline who promptly tore off the wrapper and put it in her mouth.

Monica smiled at Caroline's mother. "Caroline is going to be okay. Could I have your address so we can keep in touch?"

Caroline's mother gave her a Muscular Dystrophy card with her information on it. Monica hugged Caroline and then took off running back to her sisters. Out of breath, she caught up with them. Brenda stopped and, as a flood of pedestrians flowed around them, asked Monica, "What the hell do you think you're doing?"

"She needed my help."

"Help? Your saliva just turned her into a zombie. Her first orgasm will turn her into a lesbian. She'll have feelings she won't understand."

"Beats dying."

"Then what?"

"We'll bring her into the sisterhood with the rest of us." She wagged the card. "My first convert."

Brenda slapped her own forehead. "I need a drink."

Heading into Max's, a very swank and expensive restaurant, the five sexy zombies were promptly seated at a round table. The place was all decked out like an Aztec tomb.

Debbie commented on the décor. "This place gives me the willies."

"Spookeeee," Maggie teased while munching on complimentary strawberries in an old-looking pottery bowl.

Chloe laughed. "Let me get this straight, Debbie. We're zombies and you're scared of the dead. Don't you think the other patrons should be scared of us? Good thing they don't know they're sitting next to real live zombies in this dimly lit restaurant."

"Lesbian Zombies," Debbie corrected her. "Maggie, pass the strawberries around before you eat them all."

They all wanted a drink. Brenda ordered Bloody Marys for all of them. They didn't stop at one; they each killed off six. By the time their meal of rare steaks and Rocky Mountain Oysters arrived, they were three-sheets to the wind, loud, boisterous, and laughing at their own bad jokes.

At a table next to them sat two plump women in their mid sixties with their equally overweight husbands. One of the women with dyed brown hair whispered to the other three, "Those bimbos are drunk."

Unknown to the people next to them, zombies have the

hearing of a cat. Brenda had been amusing herself by tuning in on what the men were thinking. The one farthest from the sisterhood's table was pushing his chair up as close to the table as possible. He didn't want his wife to see that he was getting an erection, courtesy of the bimbos.

His wife noticed though. *I wish he could get an erection at home but I guess that is in the past.* She glanced at the sisterhood. *They're all loose women or maybe even lesbians.*

Maggie, the drunkest of all, yelled, "What are you looking at, you old bat? Do you know what your husbands are thinking? Well, let me tell you."

Monica reached over and covered Maggie's mouth. "I'm so sorry, ma'am. Our friend has had too much to drink. Please accept our apology. And Maggie, shut up. You want to get us thrown out?"

"They can't do anything to us. We're zombies. We can beat the hell out of everybody in this...hic...whatever this place is. I forget."

Brenda had heard enough. "Come on, girls. Let's get back to our hotel. I'll drive since I'm the only one who can still walk a straight line."

As they left, Maggie bent over and kissed the husband with the erection. "You wish you were going home with me, don't ya, honey?"

Brenda dragged her away. "Sorry, folks."

Back at the hotel with her sisterhood all tucked in and beginning to sleep off their drunken state, Brenda decided to call her mom. She knew that the two-hour time difference was such that her mom would still be up. Brenda strolled out to the rec-room by the hot tub, sat in one of the rocking chairs, and dialed the number. Her Uncle Fred answered the phone.

"Fred? This is Brenda. I'm sorry. I must've dialed your number by mistake."

"No you didn't, Brenda. I had no way to contact you. I'm so sorry to tell you this, but Ethyl passed away just hours after you left."

Brenda's stomach went into freefall. "Oh no. What happened?"

"The coroner thinks stress caused her heart to fail."

"A heart attack?" Tears blurred her vision.

"I didn't know of anything that was bothering her. Do you know if something had upset her recently?"

John, that fuckin' prick. Now tears ran down Brenda's face. "I think I know who upset her." *And his ex-wife Jenny.*

"I need help with her estate. She left everything to you. How soon can you be here?"

Be here? I can't show up looking this good. There's no way to explain what happened to the ugly, fat Brenda. Think fast, girl. Maybe I can go as someone else. That's it...

"I can't get away from business in Manhattan, so I'll send...er...Patty, a friend of mine, to help you. Mom knew her from when I was in high school. She'll get to the house by tomorrow afternoon. I'm sure she still has a key. She's absolutely trustworthy. I might get home by the end of next month."

"You'll miss the funeral, Brenda."

"Can't be helped. I'll see you when I can, Fred."

"I'll look for your friend to arrive. Bye now."

After hanging up the phone, Brenda put her head down on the window ledge and began to cry. *Mom's gone and it's John and Jenny's fault.* Her tears turned to rage. She dug her sharp fingernails into the wood as she thought about what she would do to them. *Disembowelment's too good for them. I should eat their livers...while they're alive to watch...* She suddenly felt Monica's hands on her shoulders.

"What's the matter, honey?"

Brenda straightened and turned around then cried on Monica's shoulder. "My mother's gone. Those two sons of bitches killed her because she thought John had broken my heart. The stress was too much for her so she died of a broken heart...instead of me."

"Everything's gonna be okay." Monica patted Brenda's back.

"Maybe I should have called her to let her know I was fine. Maybe she'd still be alive and happy right now."

"It's not your fault you were dead."

Streaming tears cut through Brenda's makeup. "They're going to pay. I promise you. Within a week there'll be three funerals. Tell the girls what happened. I'm going to JFK now. Uncle Fred needs me."

"How are you going to explain —?"

"I'm not. I'll tell them my name is Patty."

"But your red hair is a dead giveaway. You should die it. How about blond?"

"Just keep the girls in line. Any problems arise, call me."

"I love you, Brenda."

"I love you too. The only family I have now is in this suite." She kissed Monica and then went over and kissed each member of the sisterhood. She then hugged Monica, handed her the AmEx card, and headed for JFK with only the clothes on her back and her purse.

Taking the United Red Eye, Brenda landed in Denver where just a few days earlier she'd been downhearted. After getting her car out of long-term parking, she drove straight home, pulled into the driveway, and remembered how her mother would always leave the porch light on for her. She opened the front door and headed to her old bedroom where she looked at all her clothes that didn't fit anymore. Everything went in a pile that she threw into the garage. Then she methodically searched every room and trash-bagged anything that brought back the sorrows of her past, especially fat-girl pictures.

"Anybody home?"

She knew from the voice it was Fred. A chill skittered up her back. *Time to see if Patty can pull off the old switcheroo.* She rushed into the living room, and there stood fifty-five-year-old Fred, skinny and frail, with thick glasses and holding a cane in his right hand.

"Hi. I'm Patty," Brenda said. "You must be Fred."

He squinted at her. "You sure you're Patty? Your hair is exactly the same color as Brenda's."

Maybe I should have died it blond. "I'll take that as a compliment, Fred."

"I wish Brenda could be here."

"Me too."

"Ethyl didn't have any debts and the house is free and clear."

"Fred, Brenda wants you to have all her assets."

"Good lord. She really wants me to have everything? Doesn't she need some of the money?"

"Not really. She's overnighting the papers, and come tomorrow, everything will be yours."

"I don't know what to say."

"You're Brenda's favorite uncle and you never had a critical thing to say about her appearance. I've put all of Brenda's clothing in the garage. Please give it to Goodwill for me...I-I mean for Brenda."

"Why? Are you saying she's not coming home?"

"New York is her home now. Besides, she already bought new clothes. And as for the funeral, just scatter Ethyl's ashes in the mountains. Anywhere is fine."

"She said that?"

"Yes. Goodbye, Fred."

"Patty, thank Brenda for me, and please tell her she'll always be in my prayers."

"Will do." Brenda waved goodbye and got in her car and drove off. She had only one more problem to clean up.

Chapter 6: WELCOME TO SIN CITY

Stopping only long enough to sell her year-old Toyota 4 Runner for $21,000 cash she headed back out to Denver International. She knew John and Jenny would not leave Vegas until they were practically broke. After searching all the hotels on the strip, she got lucky at the Bellagio. They had signed in as John and Jenny Marshall. Knowing what a boozer the asshole was, she waited in the bar. Just when she was about to give up, in walked her ex man-of-her-dreams. When she thought about how she actually thought of the asshole that way, it made her ashamed of herself. *Never again would she be so foolish for love.* Trailing right behind him was Jenny. *Well, I'll be damned, she doesn't look pregnant.*

Waiting until they were seated, she took her drink and, acting like she was half schnockered, walked past them and spilled her Bloody Mary on their table. "I'm so sorry," she apologized profusely.

John, already thinking how he wanted to fuck this beautiful redhead, said, "Hey, things happen. Don't worry about it. Sit down and have a drink with us."

Brenda put on the coy act and the innocent voice to go with it. "Well, if I'm not intruding."

"Of course not. I'm John and this is Jenny."

Brenda squeezed in next to him.

He tipped his glass to her. "And what is the name of one of the most beautiful and sexy women I've ever seen."

"Brenda."

"Brenda, Brenda? I know a Brenda but she's nothing like you. She'd love to be you, though."

"What's the matter with her?"

"Everything."

It wasn't long before John had his right hand on Brenda's left leg and his left hand on Jenny's right leg. He was really more interested in what his right hand was doing than his left. He got it all the way up to Brenda's crotch until only her panties separated him from paradise. It was then that Jenny brought up the subject Brenda was waiting for.

"Brenda, have you ever had a threesome?" Jenny stirred her margarita with a swizzle stick.

"No. But I'm willing to try anything once, especially with you two. I'll let you in on a little secret, Jenny. John has his hand between my legs right now and it's getting me turned on."

John spoke up. "We should go up to our room and get the show on the road."

Brenda scoffed. "I don't want to get laid in this shitty hotel. My home in the desert is only five miles west of I-15. There's a swimming pool and wet bar. We could be there in less than twenty minutes."

John smiled. "Let's go."

They all stood and hurried to the parking garage. Brenda volunteered to drive John's rental car since she supposedly knew where she was going. Looking for a secluded spot to carry out the execution, Brenda passed many locations, trying to find the right place to turn. *Can't be too careful.* It was then that she noticed a Nevada State Highway Patrol cruiser right behind her and realized her driver's license had old Brenda's picture on it. Not to draw attention, she signaled and turned right onto what looked like the ideal road that headed farther into the desert. With her eyes glancing back and forth between the speedometer and the highway, she made sure her speed was only seventy-five. Finally, the patrol cruiser's lights came on and it passed her at a high rate of speed.

She exhaled. *I'm safe.*

Seeing what looked like a deserted road that had only ruts to drive over, Brenda turned.

Jenny said, "They should get the road paved or something. This bouncing about is shit."

After driving in ruts and sand and over rocks and not seeing a soul anywhere, Brenda set her plan in motion. "I have to pee...can't wait 'til we get to my place." She pulled over on a sandy flat. "Do you want to go with me, Jenny? Pregnant women always have to pee."

"Out here in the open?"

"There's some boulders over there."

"Okay."

As they were just about out of sight over a small hill, John yelled, "Hurry up. I'm tired of waiting."

After about twenty minutes, John went looking for them. He walked down the hill and saw Brenda sitting completely naked on a rock. He liked what he saw but was more concerned about Jenny's whereabouts. "Where is she?"

"Down by those cactus plants. I'm afraid she's had a life-changing epiphany."

"Are you fuckin' kidding me?" He took off running in the soft hot sand. For a brief moment he felt relieved when he saw her seated by a boulder. When he approached, he looked at naked Jenny and froze. She was breathing hard and staring at the horizon.

"What happened?"

"Something wonderful."

"What the hell is the matter with you?"

"I'm fine."

"Did Brenda give you something to drink?"

"Not exactly."

Now getting red-faced with bulging veins in his forehead he screamed, "What the fuck is that supposed to mean?"

A contented-looking Jenny replied, "We made love and that

is when it happened. I became a member of the sisterhood, and now I'm a Lesbian Zombie."

"You're fuckin' crazy. Did she give you some kind of drug?"

"No, only love for my sisters and hatred for assholes like you. You better run while you still can...before Brenda slaughters you."

"I'm gonna kill that bitch, but first I'm going to rape the hell out of her while you watch."

Brenda walked toward him. "You got it backwards, John. I'm going to kill you. Remember Brenda? Poor fat and ugly Brenda? Well, that's me."

"No way."

"I could tell you how this transformation came about but then I'd have to kill you. Oh. Come to think of it, that's what I'm going to do anyway. Jenny, go to the car."

Jenny grabbed her clothes and headed up the hill.

Brenda smiled. "Now where were we, John?"

"Fuck you, bitch." John bulled his way to Brenda only to be met with a hard right to his front teeth. They were shoved back into his mouth. His knees buckled and he hit the ground, gagging as he spit out his teeth. "Goddamn you." As he tried to get up, he was met with a right foot to his gut, which doubled him up in the sand.

Brenda walked around him in all her nakedness then sat on his stomach and bounced up and down, jarring the wind out of him.

"Let's play a little game, John. Tic-Tac-Toe."

Under other circumstances, he would have loved being this close to Brenda's pussy, lightly accented with a tuft of red hair he once thought he'd never want to see, but that was then and this was now.

"Get off me, you cunt."

Brenda ripped open his shirt and, using those wonderful fingernails, cut two vertical lines in his chest, followed by two horizontal lines, all of which began oozing blood. As he screamed and wriggled, trying to get away, Brenda started the game. "My turn." She cut an "X" in the upper left-hand square then pinched his cheeks together. "Your turn."

"I'm not telling you where to cut an O on my chest."

"Too bad. You took too much time so you forfeit a turn. She then cut another "X" in the middle square.

"You bitch," he screamed. "You can't be the same Brenda."

"Oh, I'm nothing like the old Brenda you fucked over."

"I loved her."

"Liar."

"Okay, I lied, but she loved the lies."

That made her stop and think. *Maybe I was partially to blame for getting fleeced.* It was then that she offered him a deal: "You can have all the other squares if you'll just tell me why you hurt me when I was always so kind to you, and loving."

He spit blood. "The Brenda you're talkin' about was ugly enough to make a freight train take a dirt road."

"You're no looker either, John."

"There's no such thing as an ugly man, just ugly women."

"Only a man would say that. I guarantee you're wrong."

"On top of fat and ugly, Brenda was also disgusting in every way."

She showed him a bloody fingernail. "Name one way or I'll cut the last X and rip out your heart."

"Okay." He panted. "When we went out to dinner, she used her fingers to take food off my plate. It wasn't sexy. It was disgusting. I couldn't eat another bite. She was all needy and ugly, and she stunk like dirty underwear. I liked to have gagged every time I had to kiss her. And she had an annoying way of trying to act cute. Her mother should have been shot for giving birth to the pig."

Hot anger spread through Brenda like wildfire. "I said *name one thing* and you recite a list. That's fine. You didn't like me. But then you went and disrespected my mother. You're not too smart, John. I might have let you live, like I did Jenny. I'm not really into killing women, just loving them. She'll serve me now, but you...sorry, John...got no use for you."

"Brenda deserved to lose her money. Tell her that for me."

"You already did."

"You're not the same Brenda. No way."

"Right again." She got off him, and as he tried to get up, she picked up a small boulder and brought it down on his head, crushing his skull. "That's for my mother."

After picking up the dress she'd discarded when converting Jenny to a Lesbian Zombie, she walked back to the rental car and used a bottle of water to wash off John's blood.

"He's not coming back, is he?" Jenny muttered.

"I left him for the buzzards."

"It's hard to believe you're the same Brenda."

"How much of my fifty Gs is left?"

"About thirty thousand...in the room safe at the Bellagio."

"Get in."

Brenda drove back to Vegas and took the turn to State Highway 171 heading straight to McCarran Airport. "Take the money, check out of the hotel, and fly to Denver. Buy a one-way ticket to Port au Prince. I'll call one of my lady-boys to pick you up at the airport. Her name is Aurora." She got out of the car and gave Jenny a hug. "It's hot as hell in Haiti. Buy some summer clothes."

"When will I see you again?"

"When I have everything settled in Manhattan. Here's my cell number."

A Las Vegas cop cut the conversations short. "Move this car."

Brenda waved as Jenny drove off toward the Strip.

Settling into her window seat as the plane climbed high into the Las Vegas sky, she looked out the window at the desert past Mandalay Bay where John lay dead. Happy about her decision to spare Jenny, she vowed then and there that the Johns and the Big Bad Brooklyn Daddies of the world would be shown no mercy, and that she and the sisterhood would never kill a woman. Men were the number one enemies of her envisioned Lesbian Zombie State. Soon the male gender would know what oppression felt like and endure the same discrimination women had suffered all this time.

At 7:25 p.m. she walked out into the Manhattan night and was quickly surrounded by a smiling sisterhood. Chloe said, "While you were gone, Maggie ran into a super rich guy that has a manufacturing company and a son who will be coming home from the army to work for his dad. She'll suck every dollar out of both of them, so to speak."

"I can't wait to hear about that. For now, I just want to get in the hot tub and relax."

"Sounds tantalizing," Chloe cooed.

"And no hanky-panky. I don't want a toe stuck in my pussy."

Back at their hotel, they all quickly disrobed and splashed into the tub. Maggie and Debbie got down to business, petting and kissing.

Brenda made eye contact with the others. "Remember what I said about no hanky-panky in the tub. I meant it, so Maggie, you and Debbie knock it off."

In unison both of them replied, "Yes, Mistress," and then started laughing.

"Maggie, you can tell me about your mark later. What have the rest of you been doing? I hope not trying to spend all our money."

Chloe took the lead. "I've been doing research. My husband Tim was a Jesus freak, well, when he wasn't out drinking and fucking around on me."

"Creep," Monica put in.

"On Sundays he'd watch the Christian Channel show *The Search for Jesus Gospel Hour*." The hot tub bubbles toyed with Chloe's breasts. "It's run by two ministers, Reverends Leroy and Janice Parker, out of their headquarters in Newark. *The Church of the Risen Jesus."*

"Hallelujah," Debbie mocked.

"One Sunday, the Reverends interviewed two lesbians who'd given up their husbands and families to live with each other. Good thing Leroy had a desk in front of him. He was probably getting a hard-on. As they told their stories of how they met and fell in love, Janice reached over and held Leroy's hand. The way she looked at her husband, I would bet she was thinking how great it would be to have a foursome with the lesbians or maybe a threesome and leave Leroy to play with his own pecker."

Monica jumped in, "What did the lesbians look like?"

"They favored you and Debbie a lot."

"What about the preacher couple?"

"Well, good news. I recorded the show so you all could see them, and it's obvious the preachers are rich assholes."

Brenda lay back in the tub with her buoyant breasts exposed. "Turn it on. Then I want a report from the rest of you."

As the 55-inch screen, which was situated ten feet away and six feet up from the hot tub, came on, everyone had a good view except Monica and Debbie. Their backs were to the screen so they turned around and leaned their elbows on the hot tub rim to watch the show. Bubbles danced around their shapely derrières.

Brenda climbed out of the tub and sat in the rocking chair, her towel draped around her shoulders to cover her boobs.

"Why did you get out?" Debbie asked.

"I got turned on looking at your behind, and I covered up with this towel so the guy on that balcony at the Barclay across the street won't be able to see my tits with his binoculars."

Maggie strained to look in the direction Brenda pointed. "I don't see anyone."

"Straight across, on the fifteenth floor. There's only one balcony."

"I see the balcony, but no binoculars."

"Oh, girls. In case you haven't noticed, you all have enhanced sight and hearing. It's another benefit of being a Lesbian

Zombie."

A silent Maggie couldn't see any better than she used to. *Maybe it just takes a while for the Lesbian Zombie virus to work on me. I'm not going to say anything though. I kinda like being a lesbian. Maybe I've always been one, just didn't know it. But what if I can't become a zombie? Maybe I'll always like men, too.* Quickly, she put that thought out of her mind, but one burning question remained:

What if I'm still HIV positive?

She decided to make an appointment with Doctor Jackson to get another blood test.

Meanwhile, Debbie got a great idea. "Sisters, let's give Binocular Man something really good to see. Let's all stand up and face his direction and wave at him. It'll probably be the highlight of his day."

Brenda said, "Girls, behave yourselves."

They stood and waved anyway, their hands and their tits.

"Wait a minute," Chloe said. "You see that woman standing beside him? Mexican, pretty, and with that obvious boob job, she'd make a perfect candidate for the sisterhood, don't you think, Brenda?"

Even from this distance, what Brenda could see of the Latino beauty made her insides tingle. "Sure, look her up. If she's interested, tell her the price of admission will be to throw Binocular Man's ass off the balcony. Now let's watch Chloe's show."

Reverend Leroy, at five-foot tall, five-foot around his waist, and pushing fifty, was the consummate television preacher. With his dark brown hair, which looked like it was glued to his head, and wearing a gray pinstriped suit set off with a red tie, he exuded unearned wealth. He held his hands up over his head. "Thank you, Jesus. Do I hear an amen?"

His 6,000-strong audience shouted, "Amen."

As if on cue, his wife, Janice, strutted onto the stage, waving at the crowd. She wore a St. John collection gray Belted Pant Suit and her brown hair style was stacked and layered with blond streaks. Talk about high maintenance, this woman was a Tammy Baker remake.

As the girls sized her up, they reached the same conclusion. The size-10, D-cup wearing wife was at least half Leroy's age.

Debbie said, "She has got to be in her mid-twenties. What's she doing with that fat slob?"

"Love is blind," Brenda said.

"God," Monica exclaimed. "He is such a fucking pig."

"A rich fucking pig," Brenda assured them.

"The only reason that gorgeous woman would have married him...for the money."

"Picture having a pig like that on top of you," Chloe said, practically gagging.

Debbie laughed. "Maybe all she has to do is suck him."

"I'll bet he has a puny dick," Maggie put in. "And I'll also bet he praises Jesus when he's fucking his wife."

Brenda clapped her hands. "Okay, girls, shut up already. She's introducing their lesbian guests."

The girls fell silent.

Reverend Janice said to Leroy, "Honey. Today we have with us Mary and Michelle. They are lesbians who want to change their sexual orientation in order to regain the love and respect of their families."

"I say fuck their families," Chloe spat.

"Please knock off the comments." Brenda was back to all business. "We're going to harvest information we can use to bring down Leroy's phony church, get his money, and convert his cute wife to the sisterhood."

Chloe countered, "I want first crack at her in the hot tub."

"If you do a good job seducing her and ruining her marriage to fat boy, you'll get your chance."

"Deal."

As Mary and Michelle sat on a black leather couch, someone in the congregation yelled, "Repent or go to hell."

This brought a response from Leroy. "Now, now, settle

down. We are here to help two of Jesus' children rise out of sin. Mary, let's start with you. When did you discover that you were attracted to women?"

Chloe yelled out, "When she discovered she had a pussy, you asshole."

In frustration, Brenda took the remote control, turned off the TV, and glared at Chloe. "Enough of that shit. We know what they look like now. Chloe, go to his service next Sunday and play up to him and the wife. Take your time. We're probably looking at several weeks just to gain their trust." Brenda turned to Debbie. "You go with her."

She winced. "I don't think they like lesbians."

"Say you're roommates. They'd have no reason not to believe you."

Debbie stood and crossed her arms. Water dripped from her lower lips, and bubbles lapped at her upper thighs. "But I hate going to church."

"Too bad. You and Chloe go together."

"She doesn't need my help to seduce Janice. Women are her specialty."

"Then you seduce Leroy. Can't be that hard."

"But he's gross."

Brenda turned to Maggie. "You're up."

Maggie pulled her heels up to her butt, giving her the room she needed to lay back and dunk her head under water.

"Sit up. We don't have time to play submarine."

This was met with a chorus of, "Boo, hiss."

Maggie resurfaced. Water cascaded from her auburn locks. She shook her head, flinging water droplets in all directions.

Brenda huffed. "This isn't a shampoo commercial. Tell us about your marks."

She leaned her back against the edge of the hot tub in front of a water jet and let the bubbly spray caress her butt crack. "I met the father several months ago at Sam's Donut Shop. I'd go there every Wednesday and Friday afternoon to get the Sam special, two rainbow-sprinkle donuts and a cup of black coffee with unlimited refills, all for $2.99. One day the place was packed and this real nice gentleman came over and asked if he could sit with me. I wondered if he was going to hit on me, but he didn't. We just talked. He owns a company that manufactures parts for the NASA space program plus equipment for the Department of Defense."

"Sounds lucrative."

"His office is in New London, Connecticut, and he commutes two and a half hours every day, but sometimes he spends nights there because he's a widower. His wife died a while back. I really felt sorry for him."

"That's your first mistake," Brenda said.

"He's such a good and kind person. We met a few times outside of Sam's, even went to Coney Island. He started buying me donuts and coffee then told me about his wife and son. He's very proud of his son, Robert Mark Johnson Junior. His eyes would light up when he talked about him."

"What's the name of the company?"

"Galaxy International. He has offices and plants in five states. One day BBBD saw me sitting with Mr. Johnson, laughing about something, and when I came out, BBBD dragged me into his Cadillac and beat me for not getting any money from him. My time is valuable even if I'm not putting out. I didn't go back for a month because I was worried that Mr. Johnson would ask about my black eye and the red strap marks on my arms. He might figure out I was a prostitute, but BBBD ordered me to go back and offer myself to him for a thousand dollars. If I came out empty handed he'd beat me again."

Monica reached over and rubbed Maggie's shoulder. "I would say Brenda solved the BBBD problem for you. So it sounds to me like it's free coffee and donuts time again."

Brenda was unconvinced the man would be a good mark. "You still didn't tell me about him. What does he look like? Is he cheap, a heavy drinker? Does he have any hobbies or vices that you know of? Could he be a womanizer?"

Maggie moved down on the water jet so it would massage her lower back. "He's about five-foot-nine and maybe one hundred and seventy pounds. Blue eyes. Mid fifties. His hair is almost white, and he always looks like he needs a shave. He has a pretty good tan, a soft voice, and he's always interested in what I have to say. He's in good shape, nice build, but he has a heart problem, AFib, but his doctor said it's not life-threatening. I doubt he's interested in another romance, but I get the feeling he's interested in me for his son."

I really don't want to hurt this man.

Brenda could've sworn she'd read Maggie's mind, but she knew she couldn't hear what a Lesbian Zombie was thinking. She leaned back in the chair and started to slowly rock while keeping her eyes on Maggie. "Go to the donut shop tomorrow then report back to me." Unease wormed around in Brenda's stomach.

Something wasn't right about Maggie.

"Okay, sisters, it's time to hit the sack. We've got a big mess to clean up in the morning, at Maggie's old place. Gotta get rid of a body."

In two king-size beds that they had pushed together, the sisterhood was soon fast asleep—except Brenda. She quietly got up, found a half full bottle of Veuve Clicquot La Grandeand, sat in the rocker, and slowly drank the wine straight from the bottle. She thought about all that had transpired in less than three weeks. Who would ever believe...

She spotted Binocular Man watching her again. *What a prick.* She wished the rec-room windows overlooking 49th Street had curtains she could close. Reasonable privacy was assumed this high off the ground. She chugged down the $190 bottle of wine, stood, and threw the bottle through the open window at the Peeping Tom's balcony some hundred yards away. The bottle missed his head by two inches but smashed through the glass sliding door behind him, shattering it to pieces.

His naked girlfriend, the Mexican beauty, ran out. He

pointed across the span at Brenda. With her super hearing, she was amused to hear the girlfriend tell the man he was crazy if he thought a woman, or any man for that matter, could throw a bottle a hundred yards. "You're drunk and broke the glass yourself. Now it's all over the bed. I'm going to sleep on the couch."

With that happy ending to the day, Brenda strode to the bedroom where her sisters snoozed, bodies entwined. She opened the bedroom drapes to let in the lights of New York City, and then slipped into bed. Propped up on her left elbow, she studied the faces of each member of the sisterhood. What a gorgeous group of women, so fun-loving but so deadly. She turned on her back and admired the pattern the lights made on the ceiling. Yawning, she clasped her hands together and said a prayer to Loa. "Please keep us all safe."

***

Brenda woke up at 9:45 and saw that the sisterhood was still asleep, minus Maggie. She checked the suite looking for her then it dawned on her where Maggie went: Sam's Donut Shop.

Back in the bedroom, she had to find a way to get her brood up and moving. She picked up a pillow and thumped Monica, who woke up, and seeing Brenda on her knees on the mattress, pillow in hand, she grabbed her own pillow and fought back. This started a pillow fight, and her sisters quickly joined in, all giggling and wrestling about in their nakedness. Soon there were feathers floating all over the room. After a few minutes of this ruckus, Brenda held up her hands. "Truce."

They all ordered room service.

Meanwhile, Maggie had gotten off the subway and hurried to Sam's Donut Shop. As she waited in line to place her usual order, she looked around for Mr. Johnson. He appeared to be a no-show. Berating herself for not getting an earlier start, she suddenly felt underdressed in the yellow miniskirt she'd chosen to wear for him. Now she just stood there picking at her fingernails while the plump woman in front of her attempted to buy out the entire donut supply.

Finally, Maggie got her order, and as she started to pay for it, a man standing behind her said, "The lady's order is on me and I'll take the same thing." Thinking someone was trying to hit on her, she turned and said, "No thank—" She never finished the sentence as she looked into the deepest blue eyes she'd ever seen. He was the spitting image of a younger version of Mr. Johnson.

She thought her knees would fail her.

He needed a shave too, just like his dad, and he looked rugged and strong in his khaki Army dress uniform, complete with super-shined paratrooper boots.

Her heart melted with desire, confirming she wasn't a lesbian. That revelation left her speechless.

"I'm Captain Robert Mark Johnson Junior of the United States Army Rangers. My dad told me to look for the prettiest girl in the place. So you must be Maggie."

"Y-yes, I'm M-Maggie."

As she struggled to find her voice, a kid with a bad case of acne complained, "Come on, get a room. I've gotta get to school."

Robert gave the kid twenty bucks. "For your trouble."

"Gee thanks, mister." The kid deserted the line and left with his newfound wealth. Ten people in line behind Captain Johnson gave him a round of applause.

Robert turned back to Maggie. "Now where were we?"

She gave him a wistful look then remembered what she was there for. "Your dad speaks very highly of you."

Robert handed another twenty to the clerk. "Keep the change," then looked around for a vacant table.

Patrons at three different tables offered their seats. "Thank you for your service, Captain."

"You're welcome, folks." He chose the nearest table and held out a chair for Maggie. "Ma'am."

Maggie sat and started the conversation. "So you're a Captain, huh? Is that like a General or something?"

He chuckled. "A General is a lot higher rank than mine." He

tested the heat of his coffee, careful not to burn his lips.

The last thing Maggie wanted was coffee and donuts right now. "Where did you serve in the Army?"

"Several places...but mainly Iraq."

"Did you ever shoot anybody?"

He stared into his coffee cup. "I don't like to talk about that."

Embarrassment heated Maggie's cheeks. *I should be a little more sensitive. He might have PTSD or something.* She plunged a straw into her coffee, stirred it around, then took a sip.

That seemed strange but cute to Robert.

One of her johns walked in, a businessman from uptown. She held her breath and dipped her head, and thankfully he didn't notice her sitting with the Captain. When he walked out she breathed a sigh of relief. "I thought about joining up, going to war. Women do it all the time these days, but my boyfriend..." *I dare not say my pimp BBBD,* "...wanted me to stay home to cook and clean." *I dare not say fuck for money.* "What's it like to be in a war?"

"Most of the time it's boredom followed by bursts of sheer terror when the bullets start flying."

As she sucked on her straw and looked at Robert, he was assessing her. *She's kind of ignorant on the ways of the world, so innocent and sweet. I owe my old man the courtesy of being nice to her.*

"What did you do for entertainment in Iraq?"

"Watched a lot of TV."

"Did you have any favorite shows?"

He chuckled. "The Walking Dead."

She gasped. "You're into zombies?"

"Seen every episode. What shows do you like?"

"I don't get a chance to watch much television." Maggie thought that sounded dumb and changed the subject. "I really like your father. He's a wonderful man. We run into each other here at Sam's. He told me you're getting out of the Army to help him run his business. Will you miss the Army?"

"I'll miss my friends." He tested his coffee and this time took a sip. "So, Maggie, my dad said you were in the health care business. What's that about?"

"I visit shut-ins in their homes," she lied through her teeth, "to make sure they're okay and take their prescriptions on schedule."

"That's honorable."

"I'm glad you agree, but it's actually hard work." Truth be told, in a sense Maggie was a caregiver...to 93-year-old Isabel Turner who lived three doors down from BBBD's place. When Maggie wasn't entertaining clients, she'd visit the old lady, do her dishes, and straighten up her house, which Isabel had left to her in a will. She was the closest thing to a real mother Maggie ever had.

Robert took a bite of his rainbow donut and studied Maggie. *God she's the sexiest woman I've ever met, and that yellow miniskirt, wow, she knows how to dress to impress. Maybe she's not as sweet and innocent as I thought. Too bad she has a boyfriend, though.* "So, Maggie, your boyfriend is lucky to have a girl as pretty and nice as you."

She dipped her head, tried to look glum. "Oh...he developed a heart problem and died suddenly a short time ago. We weren't much of a couple, anyway, and didn't have much in common."

"I'm sorry for your loss, but, to be honest, I'm also glad that you don't have a steady boyfriend...so maybe you'll go out with me."

She smiled. "I'd love to, Captain Robert Mark Johnson Junior." *Piece of cake.* She'd made her mark.

He leaned over the table until his face was only inches from hers. "Robert is good enough."

"Okay, Robert. Where're we going on our first date?" She chomped into her rainbow donut.

"Do you like seafood?"

"I love seafood," she mumbled with her mouth full.

"How about tomorrow night, say...6:00?"

She swallowed. "That would be perfect."

"Where do you live?"

"I'm staying with friends because my apartment is being renovated." *Namely body removal and blood cleanup.* Good thing she didn't tell him the truth.

"It must have been a real dump."

"It'll be like a new place soon, but until then, let's meet back here for our date tomorrow evening."

"That sounds fine." He downed the last of his coffee. "If you need someone to move furniture, or paint, or anything, I'll be glad to help."

She dusted donut crumbs from her hands. "That's kind of you to offer."

As they both stood up, he glanced down at that miniskirt and up to the low-cut blouse she was wearing.

Maggie didn't mind, in fact, she rather enjoyed his wandering eyes. She walked out ahead of him and felt his hot gaze on her ass and shapely legs. When she turned to say goodbye, her face nearly collided with his chest. "Oh, sorry."

"My fault. I didn't know you were going to stop."

Either way, they'd grabbed hold of each other in a near embrace. Butterflies took flight in her stomach. She'd been with many men, and men were men, nothing special, but Robert was a real man, and she was a real woman, free to love whomever she chose, and that made her feel special. Then her appointment with Doctor Jackson shattered her dreams of freedom to love. HIV could ruin her love life and even kill her in the end. She swallowed a hitch in her breath. "See you tomorrow."

They went their separate directions, Robert to the left and Maggie to the right. As if drawn by some magical force, they both turned to look at each other one more time. Smiling, they both waved. Maggie, bathed in her heterosexual feelings for Robert, continued on toward the sisterhood, suddenly feeling angst, knowing she would soon have to admit she wasn't a lesbian...to Brenda.

Getting on the BMT Nassau Street Line to take her back to Manhattan, she thought about Robert, her HIV problem, and the fact BBBD was still lying in a pool of coagulated blood on the second floor of his house. A little boy sitting across from her on the subway smiled at her. She smiled back. *I'm not going in that house to clean up the mess until BBBD's body is gone.*

Meanwhile, back at the hotel, Brenda was holding court in the rec-room. "Okay, all of you, listen up. There are two assignments that still need to be filled." She paced the redwood floor. "The first one goes to Monica."

Monica leaned against the wall with her arms folded. She wore only a white night gown with a flower pattern of Haitian design. "Who is the mark?"

"Your assignment is to seduce Alfons Duda. He immigrated to the U.S. from Warsaw, Poland, in 1985 and went to work in the oil business as a wildcatter in Montana. With money he borrowed from friends and relatives, he struck it rich in less than two years. He invested the profits in a new startup company drilling wells in the North Sea. He named the company KOMA LTD, using the first letters of his family members: Karol, his brother; Olga, his sister; Maria, his mother; and Alfons Senior, his father. He's worth somewhere around thirty-five billion. His office and home are in the Empire State building. He's forty-seven years old and he's a womanizer with a passion for gorgeous black women."

Monica grinned. "Wait 'til he gets a load of me."

Bikini-clad Debbie asked, "Where did you find all this information?"

"Someone had left a Time magazine in the seat pouch in front of me on the plane to JFK. They ran a story about the richest oil tycoon in the United States. I remembered everything in the article."

"So, Brenda," Chloe said. "Who is your mark going to be?"

She stepped to the doorway. "Jackie O'Neal."

"A woman? But—"

"We go where the money is, and she's one of the richest and most powerful women on earth. But she's going to take some work to fleece. She started out with a couple million bucks from a divorce settlement then turned that into billions with a line of skin care products."

Chloe gushed, "She's *that* Jackie? I love her products."

Debbie leaned on the windowsill above 49th Ave. "Brenda, are you going to make her a sister like us?"

"That's the plan."

Maggie walked into the rec-room. "What's going on?"

Brenda stared at her. "How did it go at the donut shop?"

Maggie sat on the edge of the hot tub cover. "I met the son, Robert. We're going out tomorrow night on a dinner date. I told him to pick me up at the donut shop. So that's what we agreed on. What did you do about BBBD's body?"

"We'll all go over there this afternoon."

"I don't want to go in there with his dead body."

Brenda sat in the rocker. "I'll take care of it. Once I get rid of the body we'll have the place cleaned up and painted, and then I want to meet your rich boyfriend."

"He's not my boyfriend."

Debbie giggled. "So, did you fuck him or suck him?"

"We just sat and talked. He's a very nice gentleman and good looking, to boot."

Laughing, Debbie replied, "We expect you to fuck him tomorrow night. You can be the dessert."

With that remark, Chloe gave a high-five to Debbie.

"Lay off of Maggie," Brenda snapped. "She's the only one to get any work done today."

"When we were talking, one of my johns walked in. Thank goodness he didn't see me, but I kept thinking, what if I run into another one when Robert is with me?"

"If the john says anything, just act indignant, as if you have no idea who he is and what he's talking about, that you've never met him. Your boyfriend will be glad to believe you, and if the guy persists, your boyfriend will handle the situation for you, be your knight in shining armor."

"He's not my boyfriend."

"He will be."

Maggie sighed. "Brenda, I hope you're right."

The girls started heckling Maggie. "He's not my boyfriend, he's not my boyfriend."

Brenda yelled, "Shut up and listen. We're going to BBBD's house to clean the place up. Before any of you start moaning about his body, I'll take care of it."

This brought out a reaction from the sisters. Maggie was the first. "I'm not going in there until you do."

Chloe, with a sullen look on her face, spoke next. "What are you going to do with the body? You can't just leave it for the trash man."

Monica interjected, "We are zombies. Maybe we should eat him."

Chloe frowned. "I'm not *that* hungry."

Brenda ended the debate. "I said I'd take care of the body. Take your showers and get dressed...and no messing around. It's already past two. I want to get to BBBD's by four o'clock. Chop, chop. Now move it."

As they walked past her, Debbie just glared at Brenda, but in unison, Chloe and Maggie gave Brenda the finger, but Monica looked at Brenda and held up her arms with her hands out and her palms up as if she were conveying to Brenda, *What did you expect? They're all just young girls.*

***

Once more Maggie was on the BMT, only this time she was with her sisters. As the train rattled toward Brooklyn, the interior lights blinked on and off as it skipped over the third-rail seams. All was normal until a gang of white supremacist thugs filed in, eight members of the Heinrich SS, who thought they could bring back the Nazi philosophy and create a new world order in the U.S. The other passengers scrambled out of the car, leaving only the sisters to face the SS gang.

The biggest Nazi, Hermann, clomped up to Brenda in his

combat boots. He was a typical banger: crew-cut, Nazi swastikas and Iron Cross tattoos all up his arms to his sleeveless shirt. "This is our car, bitch. You and your pussies get out."

Brenda looked up from her magazine. "Make us."

As they jumped the girls, the first to die was Hermann. He had drawn a knife on Brenda. The lights blinked off, and as they blinked back on, he was staggering toward the safety of his friends, grabbing hold of the seats as he tried to keep from falling. His tattoos were dripping blood.

At first, his punk friends thought it was Brenda's blood.

Hanging on to the last seat, he raised his head, revealing a six-inch cut across his throat that pumped out blood as he tried to catch his breath.

Wilhelm, his second in command, tried to hold him up. Hermann tried to speak but could only mumble and then he collapsed dead.

The sisterhood charged up the aisle a mile a minute, very pissed-off. Maggie brought up the rear.

Wilhelm was the second to die of a broken neck, compliments of Monica. Knives, brass knuckles, chains, and clubs did them no good. The beat-down was over in less than a minute. Heinrich SS bodies were stacked up like a log jam at the door leading to the next car. They were all dead except for Hans, a thirteen-year-old who was the brother of Wilhelm. He was too skinny to be in the Heinrich SS anyway. So what if he had a scraggly goatee and pop-bottle-bottom glasses? And so what if he was chickenshit? His baggie pants were wet in the crotch with his piss. Still, he was entirely under-qualified to be a Nazi.

Brenda grabbed him by the shirt and shoved him against the back wall. Nose to nose, she made sure he was scared enough to shit in his pants. "How many of you are there?"

"Fuck you."

With her free hand, she grabbed him by the gonads and squeezed. "How many?"

"Ahhggrh, lady, take it easy on the jewels."

"How many?" She squeezed harder.

The whites of his eyes were turning green. "Twenty."

She grabbed the kid's chin beard and made him look at the log jam. "Including them?"

"Thirteen, all right?"

"Where's the hideout?"

"You mean headquarters?" He said that in a girl's voice.

"Where do they meet?"

"Down by the old steel mill, a warehouse on the north side."

She threw him to the floor. "Go to school, get a life, before you end up like them."

They left him weeping under a seat and hurried to get off the train, leaving the bloody mess for the BMT to clean up.

As they ran up the stairs to street level, Brenda congratulated them all. "Job well done, girls."

Monica saw Maggie was upset and crying. "What's wrong?"

"Why did you have to kill them?"

"What do you think would have happened if you were alone on the train? They would have kidnapped you and taken you to some isolated place and raped you over and over and then killed you when they were done."

"You don't know that for sure."

"I know what happens to men when you give them guns and unchecked power. These Nazis are no better than the Tomtons Machetes who raped me, killed my parents, and raped and killed my five-year-old daughter. So don't feel sorry for that pile of dead shit that we left on the train."

"What about the kid?"

"No one will believe him," Brenda put in. "How can five women be so tough to kill seven Nazi wannabes?"

They walked pretty much in silence the remaining distance to BBBD's house on Montford Lane. Maggie unlocked and opened the door, and the sisterhood was immediately inundated with the worst odor they had ever smelled.

Maggie was the last sister to enter her previous home.

Invasion of the Lesbian Zombies

Horrible memories consumed her, the rapes, the beatings, the smelly men... She had all she could do to keep from vomiting.

And the stench didn't help.

BBBD's house had been around ten years before the Brooklyn Dodgers began playing a few blocks away at the old Ebbets Field, and the house looked like it had never been upgraded. Brenda led them into the living room, which was decorated like it was still 1920.

The girls sat on a dilapidated couch while Brenda walked around and examined everything in the room. She ran her hand up and down the wallpaper pattern, a yellowed background with flocks of black birds and ducks in flight. Built into the wallpapered wall was a fireplace that had seen plenty of use in the past. It had an ornamental mantelpiece made of oak and painted brown. Brenda saw that it was loose on the wall, took hold of one corner and ripped the whole thing off. She dusted off her hands. "Most houses built in this era had coal furnaces in the basement. I'll have to get the prick's body down there."

Monica decided to help.

Maggie spoke up. "There's beer in the refrigerator. I'm going to get one. Does anyone else want one?"

Since the place was giving Debbie and Chloe the willies, they each replied in the positive.

Monica and Brenda made their way up the stairs to the scene of BBBD's death. Looking at his bloated body, Monica nearly croaked. "Hell. He looks like he has gained a little weight in the past few days."

"Grab his left leg and I'll take his right. We'll pull him down the stairs and through the kitchen to the basement stairs."

In the old days, steps to the basement were usually built off the kitchen because, in the fashion of root cellars, the pantries were built in the basement.

As they started to pull the body down the stairs, Brenda was pulling mainly on BBBD's foot, which came off and sent her falling head over heels backwards down the stairs. "Fuck."

This brought an immediate response from Chloe, Debbie and Maggie as they came running out of the living room. "Are you okay?"

"Yes, Chloe." She tucked the foot under her arm. "Now go back into the living room and enjoy your beer. We'll be done in a little while."

Maggie took a quick glance at BBBD's body, which was partly on the top step. He looked blown up like a balloon, and his eyes were wide open. The hole in his chest where Brenda had ripped out his heart was clearly visible. She gagged, almost upchucked her beer.

Monica waved her hand at Maggie. "Go back with your sisters."

Fighting the reflex to puke, Maggie returned to the living room and sat with her sisters, no longer able to even look toward the stairs.

As Brenda and Monica pulled his body down the stairs, his head bounced off each step and made a clunking sound like a mallet striking a table. Once they got him in the kitchen, it was obvious the door to the basement wouldn't open wide enough to pull his bloated body through and down the steps. So leaving him by the refrigerator, Brenda found a hammer and screwdriver in a drawer and took the door off its hinges. Then they got him through and dragged him down ten more steps where they plopped him on the damp basement floor.

Looking around for a light switch and not finding one, Brenda used her superior night vision to find a pull-string that hung from a ceiling bulb. She reached up and pulled the string. Sixty watts lit up a partial basement. Most of the area under the house was a crawl space inhabited by dozens of rats all huddled together. The light also revealed a natural gas heater, not the coal furnace she'd expected. "Shit. This isn't going to work."

"We should have checked down here first." Monica wiped her brow with the back of her hand. "Now we gotta haul his body back up the steps."

Then what? Brenda pursed her lips. She needed a professional cleaner to get rid of the body. The Heinrich SS came to mind. *How many bodies have they made disappear?* "We can get the Heinrich SS gang to get rid of BBBD."

Monica put her hands on her hips. "I am pretty sure they would sooner kill us as look at us."

"Call Port au Prince. Get Aurora to fly here by morning. And bring her side-kicks, Carlos and Jason."

"What for?"

"She's going to be their new leader, and the lady-boys will supply the muscle to keep them all in line. I'll break the good news to them tomorrow...at their warehouse."

"You heard the kid. There are thirteen of them left."

"And that's a problem how?"

Monica stood there with a dumbfounded look on her face.

Brenda grinned. "Let's go home. The hot tub awaits."

The sisterhood, to a sister, was glad to get out of BBBD's stinky place. They kept asking Brenda the same question. "Now what are you going to do with BBBD's body?"

Brenda's answer was always the same. "Forget him. The next time you're in the house, his body will be gone and the painting, plumbing, and construction crews will be hard at work remodeling the place. It'll be squeaky clean."

Maggie shrugged, and the girls shared doubtful looks.

"Now I have some business to take care of tomorrow so I want all of you, except Maggie, to spend part of the day doing your research so you'll be prepared when you meet your marks. Maggie, the rest of the day you'll spend shopping for furniture and kitchen appliances. I want the house to look beautiful in a hurry."

Monica grumped. "A little overkill on the clean up, don't you think?"

"If everything works out, we're going to live there. You want it to look nice, right?"

After arriving back at their hotel, the sisterhood was glad to strip off their clothes and lounge in the hot tub while they waited for room service to deliver their supper and drinks. As they soaked in the tub, Debbie noticed the guy across the street (aka Binocular Man) was busy watching two servicemen replace the broken glass door.

The rest of the sisterhood was relaxing with their eyes closed, in heaven among the bubbles.

Chloe hoped to see the man's girlfriend, who soon came out on the balcony and looked interested in how they were fixing the door, but she'd occasionally glance across 49th Street. Chloe waved, but she didn't seem to notice. She went back into the apartment and returned with the binoculars. This time when Chloe waved, she lowered the spy glasses and rushed back inside.

Yeah, oh yeah. We can convert her easily.

She made a mental note to check out the Barclay Building in the morning and get the information on the little sweetie.

Brenda sat up and played with the bubbles that jiggled her breasts. "Sisters, it's time for a history lesson."

"Ahhh, not now."

"Boo."

"Do you know why the male gender thinks they're superior to us females?"

"They got cocks and we don't," Maggie guessed flippantly.

"It goes back to the time of Igor the cave man. Since he could slap a female around and have his way with her, he thought he must be more intelligent. All he really had going for him was more muscle mass. From then on and up to this very day, males still think they're more intelligent than women. We are going to change their way of thinking. It will take a while but we'll get it done. Now then, who's up for a game of submarine pussy licking while we wait for our dinner?"

They all shouted out in unison, "I am."

After steak, lobster, Caesar salad, and three bottles of wine, followed by a game of hot tub grab ass, where one blindfolded sister would touch another sister's tits and butt and pussy and try to guess which sister she was touching, it was time for bed.

The next morning, Brenda got up first, slipped into a summer dress, no bra, no panties, and high-heel shoes, and then rushed out of the hotel. Once she found the old steel mill, it was easy to find the headquarters of the Heinrich SS gang. Their warehouse was marred with anti-Jewish graffiti and swastika signs. After sizing the place up, she stopped by a flower shop and a tattoo parlor, and then headed straight for the warehouse.

With flowers in hand, she walked up to a steel door that led into the building. It was unguarded because only a fool, or a Lesbian Zombie, would venture into the lair of the Heinrich SS. Descending a flight of rusted steel stairs, she saw seven members of the gang sitting around a large conference table. The next step squeaked.

The gang looked up and saw her. Everybody went for their guns.

"Now, now, boys. Take it easy."

The skinhead at the end of the table spoke up. "What do you want, bitch?"

"Are you the new president?"

"Adolph. What's it to you?"

"I bring flowers in honor of your dead comrades on the train, and then I'd like to fuck your new president in honor of his new position, and then I want to join your club."

Adolph stood up, reached down to his crotch and took hold of his cock under his fatigues, and moving his hips back and forth, laughed. "In that case, make yourself at home, bitch."

Brenda slinked down the remaining steps and strode to the grinning men. She got up on the table and threw the flowers to Adolph. "Let me show you what I have to offer." She slowly took off her dress and danced around the table, showing off her beautiful body. Stopping in front of ogling Adolph, she slowly climbed down to his lap, and facing him with her legs spread, she began a lap dance he'd never forget.

He scowled. "You're asking to be gang raped, bitch."

"Really now," she breathed, gently put her hands on each side of his head, and kissed him on the nose. The sudden invasion of his finger into her pussy made her gasp. She felt the bulge on his left side and knew it was a gun. Kissing him on his neck, she whispered, "Goodbye."

"Huh?"

With both hands she twisted his head around with such force that the cracking of bones reverberated through the warehouse. But she didn't stop there. She cranked his head around and around until it popped off his neck.

His subordinates froze in a state of shock as blood squirted like a fountain from the stub of his throat.

She grabbed his pistol and swung it to the first thug that moved. "I'd think twice if I were you." But his gun came up anyway, so Brenda shot him in the forehead. He and the chair he was sitting on tumbled over backwards. She waved the gun at the rest of the Nazis. "You're looking at your new president, pro temp."

"Y-you," one bruiser stuttered. "You killed our people on the train."

"It was easy for me and my sisters to murder your gang of bozos. And fun. Just like it would be easy for me to kill all of you right now. And fun. We let the kid live. Maybe he won't grow up to be a dick like you motherfuckers."

The guy beside him gasped. "The kid was tellin' the truth."

One bold soul spoke up. "Sooner or later we're going to kill you, bitch."

"You can't kill me." She held up Adolph's head by the torn cords of his neck and swung it back and forth like a railroad lantern, splattering blood in all directions while she pranced around the table and taunted the disbelievers with the gun. "By the angry looks on your faces, I see you don't believe me."

"You're dead, cunt."

"Then watch this." She dropped Adolph's head on the floor where it hit with a thud then pressed the gun muzzle to her chest and pulled the trigger.

The blast made everyone jump in their seats. Surprise widened their now believing eyes as she rubbed the bloodless entry wound.

"I'm a zombie, a Lesbian Zombie, for obvious reasons. Get the picture, bozos." She threw down the gun and spoke softly. "Now I know you want to vote me in to be your new president. We're going to become one big happy family." Then her voice dripped hatred. "Otherwise I'll kill every one of you motherfuckers, so you cocksuckers had better get in line right now. Do you pricks have any questions?"

Mute, the scared-shitless thugs gaped at her.

She grinned. "I didn't think so." Her grin turned into a sweet smile. "Now I know you all want to do the right thing so we can all get along. You'll love and obey my sister Lesbian Zombies as you will obey me....if you want to live, that is."

The skinheads nodded to each other in agreement.

Brenda slipped the dress over her blood-spattered body and jumped off the table. She kicked Adolph's torso out of his chair and claimed the leader's place at the table. "Time to vote. Raise your right hand if you want me to be your new president pro temp." Brenda looked around and saw everyone's hand in the air. "Good. I thought the vote might be unanimous."

One guy had raised his left hand.

Brenda frowned. "What's your name, fool?"

"Reinhard, miss."

"Well, Reinhard. Next time there's a vote, use your other right hand."

Reinhard switched hands, and although he was shaking, he got bold. "Lesbian Zombie sisters? Does that mean we can't fuck any of them even if they want us to?"

Brenda chuckled. "I'd be careful about that. The sisterhood doesn't have sex with men unless we want something from them. The good news is that we won't hold it against you if you have a girlfriend or a wife or some guy you think has a cute ass you'd like to poke. We don't give a shit."

She read another punk's mind, Albert. "Tell your brothers what you're thinking but leave out the part about how you want to fuck me."

He looked at her like she'd grown another nose.

"Yes, Albert, I can hear your thoughts, so say what you're thinking."

He swallowed. "Brothers, we know she is what she says she is so we go along with her or we'll all die."

"Good boy, Albert. I have an address for you guys. 121 Montford Lane. Go there. The door will be unlocked. In the basement, you'll find the body of the late pimp known as BBBD."

The Nazis looked at each other frightfully.

"Yeah, you know how powerful he was, but he was stupid enough to strike one of my girls. When you see him, take a good look at the hole in his chest where his heart used to be. I plucked it out and we ate it, so remember, that's what we'll do to you if you don't get rid of the body for us."

"We get it, lady," Reinhard said. "You're a killer."

"Sorry, I got a little sidetracked. My name is Brenda, Queen of the Lesbian Zombies, and don't you forget it."

"Okay, queenie, how do you propose we get rid of BBBD?"

"I thought you guys would be experts at that by now."

"Lady, we bust some chops and break some bones, but we never killed nobody."

Brenda scoffed. "Take a garbage can and a chainsaw with you. Cut off the head and hands then cut up the rest of the body and stuff it in the trash can then dump it in the East River at 3:00 in the morning. Totally chop up the head and hands then flush the pieces into the sewer system."

"Why not do it yourself?"

She blew on her fingertips. "I don't want to risk breaking a nail."

"Oh, yeah?"

"Yeah."

"That makes sense."

All the guys agreed.

"Lastly, Albert, I'm leaving you in charge until Aurora shows up sometime tomorrow."

"Who's Aurora?" Reinhard asked.

"A chick with a dick. She's bringing two others with her, Carlos and Jason. I'm sure those ball-less wonders will let you fuck them and they'll give you all the blowjobs you want. In fact, they may insist, because Aurora will be your new president. I better never see any of your ugly faces again, because if I do—"

"Yeah, we know," Reinhard cut in. "You'll kill us. So how do we know when Aurora is here?"

"She has this cell number. I'm leaving you this phone." She handed it to Albert. "It belonged to the late BBBD. She'll call you when she arrives at JFK from Port au Prince. You'll pick her up and install her as your president until I can make other arrangements. She's not beautiful like me, however, she's very intelligent and used to be a man. Don't let that fool you. She's a killer at heart." Looking at two guys sitting at the other end of the table, Brenda frowned. "Who are you two bruisers?"

"I'm Karl and this here is Fenn."

"You're big guys. I want you to contact all the neighborhood gangs. Let them know they had better not mess with me or my sisterhood. Also, tell all the pimps to find a new line of work. They're ordered to set all their working girls free or die. The sisterhood will be checking to make sure this order is carried out."

No one said a word as Brenda examined the blood on her hands. She reached over and patted Albert's face, smearing it with blood. "Be a dear and hand me your bottle of water. I look a mess." She cleaned up, and as she turned to leave, she took one last look at each of the Heinrich SS. "One other thing. Reinhard has been thinking about my tattoo." Turning her left arm and peeking at her shoulder, she smiled. "Nice rose, huh? Do anyone of you dumb bastards know why the outer petals are black and the inner petals are blood red?"

They all looked at each other dumbly.

"I had it colored that way for a reason. Recognition. All of my Lesbian Zombies sisters will sport this rose tattoo on their left shoulders. If you meet a woman on the street, and she has this tattoo, you better leave her the fuck alone. Step off into the gutter and wait for her to pass. Don't make eye contact. Spread the word. Make sure everyone gets the message."

Reinhard nodded.

"You know, Reinhard, there's something kind of refreshing about the way your simple mind works. I know you're still thinking about how you'd love to fuck me, but it ain't never going to happen." She gave them the one-finger salute. "Don't any of you think about crossing me. That would be a one-way ticket to the cemetery." She turned her back to them and strutted to the door. "Goodbye, shitheads."

Brenda got back to the Waldorf, and since there was no sign of the sisterhood, she turned on her Mac and Googled *Jackie O'Neal.* Reading everything written about her, Brenda was most interested in the fact that Jackie fancied herself an artist. She was putting on an art exhibition of her own paintings. It had a pre-opening on Friday and official opening on Saturday, just days away at the Art for the Common Man and Woman Gallery in Manhattan.

Jackie must be a very good artist for such a gallery to show off her work.

She Googled information about the gallery and discovered it was owned by a foundation that Jackie chaired as the CEO. Maybe Jackie's work was being shown, not because it was good but because she was the boss and nobody was going to say no to her. *Then again, maybe her work is good.* Brenda exited Google. *I'll check her out on Friday instead of Saturday. All the kiss-ass people will be there on Saturday.*

The sisterhood bounded in all excited.

"So, girls, how did it go today?"

Chloe spoke up first. "To be perfectly honest, none of us

know a damn thing about appliances and stuff like that, so we went shopping for clothes."

Brenda furrowed her brow. "You didn't come in with any sacks and packages so you must not have spent any money."

"A little. Two hotel employees are bringing up the stuff we bought."

"Okay, Chloe. Since the others are too gutless to admit how much you all spent, how much is a little?"

"Fourteen thousand dollars."

Brenda's breath hitched. "Good grief. Monica, I can understand Chloe, Debbie, and Maggie going on a spending spree. They're young and naive, but you know better. I'm disappointed in you."

"We have to look pretty for our marks. Do you want us to take it all back?"

"You need to be more frugal, but it sounds like a good cause. You can keep the stuff."

Monica plopped down in a chair. "How did your day go?"

"Good for me, killer for the Nazis."

"What did you do?"

There was a knock on the door. The clothing had arrived.

Maggie ran to the door like a little kid expecting to see Santa Claus for the first time. Quickly going through the piles of clothing the girls had dumped on the floor, she found what she was looking for. With a big smile she showed it to Brenda. "Get a load of this."

"My, my." Brenda sighed. "A red dress."

"It's called the Home Before Daylight Red Dress. Only forty-six bucks. I found it at Lulu's." She held it up to her body. They say it's the perfect dress to make a stunning first impression. Knit tank straps, a sexy square neckline, lacy seams..." she turned it over, "...scoop back, no bra required. So, Brenda, what do you think?"

"It's a little short but that's okay. You'll look beautiful in it, honey. After dinner, Robert is sure to see how fast he can get you out of it."

"Do I have to let him do it to me tonight?"

"Yes," Debbie chimed in.

Monica spoke up. "Not so, sweetie. Wait 'til he falls madly in love with you first."

It was as if Maggie never heard a single word Monica said because she was bent over, busily looking through the pile of clothing for the single-strap red heels from Lulu's. "I know they're here somewhere. I saw the clerk put them in a sack."

About to panic because she was down to the last pile, she finally struck pay dirt. Now holding them in her right hand, her face was aglow. "I found them and here they are. The original *come fuck me* shoes."

Chloe displayed a questioning frown. "Now that we're Lesbian Zombies and prefer women over men when it comes to sex, what do we do when we're having intercourse with a man but thinking about women? Girls are soft and sexy and nice smelling. Compare that to some hairy slug who thinks he's being romantic by squeezing my tits and breathing his tobacco breath in my face while he's groaning and shoving his dick in me."

Monica answered the question. "Do what women have done since the beginning of time, honey. Fake it."

"That's going to take a lot of faking, Monica."

"Once you get his money, the reward will be worth it."

"A-hum." Brenda cleared her throat. "I can't believe that none of you noticed my tattoo."

The sisterhood gathered around Brenda. Debbie softly ran her fingers over the inflamed skin of Brenda's shoulder. "That is so cool. Can I get one?"

"Yes, dear. In fact, this design will identify us among all the other women walking down the streets of New York. At three o'clock today, the tattoo artist will be here to tattoo each of you. Maggie will be first since she has a hot date she'll have to get ready for."

"Brenda, what does the tattoo artist look like?"

"Margret is a redhead, covered in tattoos, has a ring in her nose, and likes to show off a nice, well-proportioned body in a tight tube dress."

Debbie giggled. "Are we going to convert her?"

"No."

"Why not?"

"Because she's as dumb as a post."

"So is Maggie."

Maggie burst into tears and ran into the bedroom.

Brenda shouted, "Debbie, you apologize to her right now."

After walking into the bedroom, Debbie sat down on the bed and rubbed Maggie's back.

"Go away. You might get contaminated touching some stupid person like me."

Turning Maggie over and holding her in her arms, she kissed her forehead and whispered, "I didn't mean it. You know how I am always shooting off my mouth. Us hot-blooded Latinos are like that sometimes. If there is anyone in the sisterhood that is stupid, it is me, Maggie, not you. Please forgive me."

Maggie looked up into Debbie's brown eyes. "It's true. I never had much of an education. I only went to the seventh grade, and then my mother sold me to BBBD. He told me that I didn't need an education because I was going to be his whore forever."

Debbie slowly rocked Maggie back and forth, her face pressed against Debbie's left breast. "Well, sweetie, you got the last laugh on him. Right now some rats are munching on his dick and balls."

"Debbie, what if I like Robert? Will Brenda kill him for his money?"

"Put that thought out of your mind."

Brenda announced, "Girls. Margret is here. "Maggie you're first."

After getting her tattoo, Maggie showered, fixed her hair, got dressed, and walked into the living room where Debbie was getting her tattoo. Maggie spun around in her new red dress.

To a sister, they all praised Maggie's beauty—including Margret.

Brenda came over and hugged her. "Do you have money and your cell?"

A smiling Maggie replied, "Yes, mother."

"I'm not your mother but I'm the closest to one you'll ever have. Now go. Have a great time with Robert, and remember, this date is just the first step."

"I will, and I will." With that, Maggie sashayed out the door and into a cab Monica had called for her.

All the way to the donut shop, Maggie kept going over the same thoughts: *Robert is so nice and smart and handsome.* She didn't like the thought of going out with him to steal his money. Just because Brenda hated men because she was treated badly by one...*doesn't mean I have to hate men.* Maggie only hated some men, like BBBD...and Dick, the used car salesman, who always bragged about how women all loved fucking him in the employee's lounge. *I should have said, 'Oh yeah? Then how come you're always paying me for sex?'*

She was happy that BBBD was dead. *No wonder I always thought I was stupid. He told me I was stupid every day.* She should have put poison in his coffee a long time ago.

What if Robert finds out that I was a whore? No. Monica was right. *I should never call myself a whore again.* Then the reoccurring question arose. *What if I'm not a zombie and still have HIV. I don't want to give it to Robert.* And if Maggie was a zombie, she didn't want to fall in love and be loved in return. Robert would grow old and she'd stay young and they could never have any kids.

Maybe Doctor Jackson will help her with the HIV. She couldn't exactly say to the doctor, *"Can you also check to see if I'm a zombie?"* He'd say *'just a minute,'* leave, and then come back into the room with a couple guys in white coats to take her to the mental ward at Bellevue. Maybe she'd be put in a room next to the Son of Sam. At least he didn't go around thinking like her. He just went around killing people.

The cab pulled up in front of the donut shop. Robert was standing at the door. *Oh. He's waiting for me. Gosh. He looks so handsome...and well built. If he wants sex tonight, I have to find a gentle way to turn him down. Well, here goes.*

Getting out of the cab, Maggie started to pay the driver, but he waved her off. "Your friend Monica paid the fare."

"Thank you."

The cab drove off as Robert, with a big grin on his face, walked up to her. *God! She's so beautiful and sweet looking. Man. Even the way she holds her purse with both hands on the strap and the purse hanging in front of her knees. This is going to be the best date of my life. I don't want to rush it. If I scare her off, I'll never forgive myself.*

"You are gorgeous." He breathed. *Way to go, genius. Shit! She's probably heard that line from a lot of guys. I must've sounded like a dumb ass.* "I hope you're hungry."

"Yes, I am." Maggie slung her purse strap over her shoulder. "You look pretty good yourself."

He blushed. "I parked my car right across the street."

Taking hold of her hand, he took charge of the situation and escorted her to his car.

As she got in, fine leather embraced her body, and luxury surrounded her senses at every turn. "This car must have cost you a fortune."

"It is one of my dad's cars."

"I've never sat in a Mercedes before."

"I can't afford a car like this, not on a captain's salary." He slid in behind the wheel. "You said you like seafood, so I made a reservation at the Sea Fire Grill in Midtown East. I've eaten there before with my dad a few times. The food is great. It'll take a little while to get there. The traffic in the city is a joke."

She put her hand on his shoulder. *My god I'm touching him and he didn't pull away.* "That's okay. I have plenty of time."

"New York traffic is the same as everything in the Army. Hurry up and wait."

"You'd said you're getting out soon. When will that be?"

"In two weeks I'll muster out at Fort Dix, New Jersey."

The car inched forward.

"Why not reenlist?"

"I've seen enough killing and grief to last a lifetime. Working in my dad's New London, Connecticut, plant will be a great change of pace."

Maggie broke a very short silence. "Tell me more about women in the Army."

"It's changed a lot over the four years I've served." He noticed how her red dress had pulled up high on her thighs by the way she was sitting in the seat. *God she has beautiful and sexy legs.* He immediately thought of how he wanted to fuck her but told himself again: *Don't rush it, Bobby Boy.* He wanted a relationship with her, not just a quick lay.

Maggie hadn't heard a word of his thoughts but did catch him looking at her legs and knew exactly what he was thinking. She pulled her dress back down, knowing it would make him want her all the more.

As Robert and Maggie walked into the restaurant and were seated, she almost fainted. At a table on the other side of the room sat the sisterhood. They were giggling and joking around as usual. She touched Robert's hand. "Please excuse me. I have to powder my nose."

"You've never powdered your nose in your life."

"You know what I mean."

He grinned. "Hurry back."

She got up from her chair and made a beeline for the ladies' room, passing right by her suddenly muted sisters. Out of sight of Robert and standing by the door to the ladies bathroom, she motioned to Brenda to come here.

Brenda joined her inside the unoccupied restroom.

Maggie blurted out, "What the hell are you all doing here?"

"Settle down. We didn't know the two of you would be here."

"I didn't even know I'd be here. Were you spying on us?"

"Of course not. Chloe suggested seafood for dinner, and the hotel concierge recommended this restaurant, that's all."

"Just don't look at Robert and me. I don't want him to see you because when you eventually meet him, he might remember where he'd seen you all before."

Brenda checked her lipstick in the mirror. "Distract him by getting real close to him and make small talk while we move quietly to the verandah. Okay, honey?"

Maggie sighed. "I guess that'll work." She too glanced into the mirror. "Does my lipstick look all right?"

"Yes. It's fine. Now go back to Robert before he thinks you ran out on him."

Returning to the table, Maggie sat down. "Now then...what do you recommend?"

He pointed out the Fire Grill special. "There's a different House Special every night. It's very good, but all their dishes are excellent."

Maggie had to distract Robert. She dropped her fork on purpose. "Oh, oh." As Robert bent over to retrieve it, that gave her time to see her sisters make their way out to the verandah, which made her breathe a little easier.

Robert straightened up and put the fork on the edge of the table. "They'll bring you a new one. What would you like to drink?"

"I'm not fussy. Pick a wine you think I'd like."

***

The sisterhood sat safely out of sight. "What are the odds?" Monica asked.

Debbie said, "She probably thinks we are spying on her."

"Yes she does," Brenda confirmed while tuned in to what Robert was thinking. *I hope she likes white wine.* Brenda's efforts to hear Robert's thinking were overwhelmed by the thoughts of the other one hundred-plus patrons.

Robert is such a gentleman. For a fleeting moment she thought she picked up on something Maggie was thinking but quickly dismissed it as a coincidence and reminded herself that a zombie cannot read the mind of another zombie.

After an hour of eating and drinking, the sisterhood got ready to leave. Debbie went to the ladies' room this time, and she quickly glanced to see how Robert and Maggie were getting along. To her surprise the table was now occupied by a different couple plus a small child in a highchair. She made a U-turn and went back to report her findings.

As they headed back to the hotel, there was only one topic of conversation: "Where did Maggie and Robert go?"

Debbie, the sister with sex on her mind most of the time said, "I'll bet he is fucking her right now."

"I don't think he's fucking her," Chloe put in.

"Then I bet dollars to donuts she has her pretty little mouth open and he has his cock in it, and she's sucking him like crazy."

Monica had to comment on that one. "We will know when she gets back. We should offer her dessert, and if she says she is not hungry for dessert, we will know she had him for dessert."

"I'll bet she loved it," Debbie added. "She's not a very enthusiastic lesbian."

They all laughed again.

The one person not engaged in the laughter was Brenda. Looking out the window at the passing cars she grumbled to herself. *What if she's not a Lesbian Zombie? What if she's not even a zombie? What will I do? I love Maggie. It wouldn't be her fault if she's immune to the virus. Could be those HIV pills she's taking. If she were to fall madly in love with her Army Captain, I'd not let any harm come to him. She has suffered enough in her short life and she deserves some happiness.*

***

Across town, very happy Robert and Maggie walked hand in hand and barefoot on the sandy shore of Coney Island and watched the moon rise over the Atlantic Ocean.

As they sat on a wooden step under a streetlamp, still holding hands, Robert pressed her. "Tell me about where you live and more about your roommates."

"The women that I live with I've known for several years." It broke her heart to lie to him, but some secrets must never be told. "We go to the same church and we're in the same line of work. It's very rewarding to help people, and since we bought the house together, it helps keep our cost of living down." The lies kept flying out of her mouth. Like a house of cards, one lie too many and it'd all come tumbling down.

Robert squeezed her hand. "I hope I get to meet them."

"I'm sure you will and maybe very soon."

"Maggie, it won't be for two weeks, that's for sure. I have to report back to the base and go through the mustering out process."

She squeezed his hand in return. "I'll miss you every day. Maybe I'll still see your dad at the donut shop."

His eyes darted around warily. He gently let go of her hand as if he didn't want to make any fast moves. "Oh, look." He'd found an empty beer bottle, which he quickly filled with sand.

"Why are you doing that?"

"It is just an old habit from my days in Afghanistan."

She squinted. "That's weird. I thought they couldn't drink beer in the Middle East."

"Any old bottle will do." He actually planned to use it as a weapon. Unbeknownst to Maggie, they'd been spotted by three thugs from the el Diablos gang.

"Maggie, we should head back. It's getting a little late, and I wouldn't want your friends to put out an Amber alert on you."

Maggie laughed at Robert. "I'm a little too old for that."

Within ten seconds of saying, "I'm only joking," they were confronted on the wooden steps by the gang-banger punks. There were two in front of them, blocking the stairs. When Robert turned Maggie around and ran down the steps, another thug appeared at the bottom, grinning. The one hundred forty pound, five-foot-seven cocksucker immediately met the beer bottle across his jaw. He fell into the rotted railing, which snapped and crashed down with a knocked-out-cold punk now lying on it.

Maggie screamed.

Robert turned to take on the other two rushing down the stairs. Both brandished knives and deadly scowls.

Maggie jumped in front of Robert and held out her arm. "Stop."

"Get behind me," Robert shouted.

Her black and red rose tattoo gleamed in the glow of the streetlight, stopping the punks in their tracks.

"Our mistake," the biggest thug said. "Please forgive us. We were just messing around." They turned tail and ran, leaving their buddy face-down in the sand.

Robert carried Maggie up the stairs. "I wonder why they turned chickenshit and fled."

"They probably knew better than to fight you."

"I don't think so. Maybe they thought we were someone else."

Now back in the Mercedes, Robert asked Maggie, "Where are you staying while the house is being refurbished?"

Her reply shocked him. "The Waldorf Astoria."

"Good lord." He started the car. "What is that costing you? Did you win the Lotto?" Tires squealed as he hit the road.

"My roommates and I split the cost, and our house will be ready in a couple weeks. Then you can meet my friends."

"Looks like I'll be home just in time."

"I'll feel a lot safer then."

"Maggie, I can't get over those dumb-ass punks. They acted like they were suddenly scared shitless. I've seen a lot of men in battle who acted like that, but they had something to fear, the US Army Rangers."

"Yup, you put the fear of God in them."

"Why would I put the fear of God in them? It was one against three. They could've easily robbed us, even beat us up, but something spooked them, something scarier than a guy and his girlfriend."

Remembering a line from Brenda, Maggie looked at Robert. "You're my knight in shining armor. Forget about those guys. We're safe because of you."

"Okay, but here I was trying to impress you by taking you to the Fire Grill, and you impressed me more when you suggested we just get a burger and some fries at Coney Island's Dream Burger."

"To tell you the truth, the seafood restaurant was a little crowded." *Too many sisters...*

Pulling up in front of the Waldorf, Robert was sorry to see their date end. Since it was pushing twenty minutes past one, there were plenty of empty parking spaces. They just sat there in silence for a minute with Robert holding her hand. Then Maggie broke the silence. "You can kiss me if you want to."

"Oh, I want to all right." He leaned over to her, and as they closed their eyes, their lips met in sweet surrender.

Maggie felt the strength in his arms as he pressed his chest against her breasts. Times like these, she was glad she wasn't a lesbian.

Robert was thinking about kissing her neck and down to her breasts.

They sat there necking and petting like teenagers after the prom. Future dates would definitely go to the next level. And Maggie knew that could be a problem, but for now she squirmed with delight, in love with the beautiful night. "Please open the moon roof and lean both seats back so we can get as close to each other as possible."

"I like the way you think, Maggie."

With the console between them, they looked up at the sliver of sky above the buildings, the dim stars, and listened to the constant buzz of traffic. Maggie thought she'd play down her first date with Robert, let her sisters bombard her with questions but not tell them how wonderful a time she's had with him. All they wanted to hear about was the sexual relations parts, which were none of their business.

Robert was thinking about the next date in two weeks and that he'd take her somewhere more comfortable to hold her in his arms, other than the front seat of a car.

Maggie cooed, "Robert, I hope we can do this again."

He kissed her and countered, "You can bet on it. I'll call you while I'm on the base. We can set up something then. I really won't have much to do there except wait out my last two weeks of active duty. Then I'll have two years inactive duty before I'm totally free." He powered the seats back up. "It's time to walk you to the door." With a look on his face that said he was sorry the date was over, he softly whispered, "I really had a great time."

"I did too. Just one thing, if you're going to call me, there's something you need."

"What?"

Standing on her tiptoes she said, "It's called a phone number."

Robert grinned. "I'll write it down but my price is a kiss for every digit. What is it?"

She whispered the number in his ear.

"Maggie, that adds up to 44."

"I think we should round it off to an even 50, Captain Robert Mark Johnson Junior."

"Affirmative, Miss Maggie Jensen." With that, he bent down and started giving her the most passionate kisses he had ever delivered.

After several minutes Maggie whispered, "How many is that?"

"I don't know. We'll have to start over."

They did.

***

Walking into the hotel suite and trying to be as quiet as possible, Maggie was relieved to see that all the lights were off.

She removed her shoes and tiptoed to the bedroom. *Thank God they're all asleep.* They probably finished off four bottles of wine and crashed in drunken stupors.

"Surprise!"

All the lights came on at once.

Maggie's heart flip-flopped in her chest. She was dizzy with a sudden fright.

The sisterhood quickly surrounded her and lambasted her with questions: "Did you fuck him?" "Did he strip you naked?" "Does he have a big cock?" "Tell us everything." "Don't keep us in suspense."

Maggie gathered her wits and caught her breath. "We didn't do anything but kiss...well...a lot."

Brenda asked, "What's the plan from here?"

"He has to report to his Army base so I can't see him for two weeks."

"Come on," Debbie prodded. "I know you gave him a goodbye blowjob, so you might as well admit it."

"No, Debbie. That's what you would have done, and Robert wouldn't have given you the time of day afterwards. In fact, he might not have let you touch his dick at all. I'm not going to scare him off."

"I guess some men like silly young girls."

"You better shut up."

"At least I was never a whore."

As a frustrated Brenda looked on, a cat fight broke out. Soon they were wrestling on the floor kicking and pulling hair and calling each other bitch and other names far worse.

When clothing started to rip: "Okay, enough is enough." Brenda grabbed Debbie, and Monica took hold of Maggie and dragged the two of them to the hot tub and threw them in head-first, splashing water in all directions. This quickly brought the fight to an end.

A still pissed-off Maggie yelled, "Now look. My nice red dress is soaking wet. All Debbie got wet was her stupid nightgown."

Chloe interrupted the yelling. "Oh, Maggie, your cell is ringing."

Running to get her cell and leaving wet footprints across the floor, Maggie made it in the nick of time. "Hello. I thought it might be you."

"I just wanted to make sure you got home safely."

Maggie giggled. "You walked me to the elevator and our last kiss as the elevator door opened was the best kiss of the night."

"It's going to have to last for a while but not the entire two weeks. If you can come down to Fort Dix this Friday about 1600 hours, there's an officers' party on the base."

"But that's in New Jersey. How far?"

"About seventy miles, just a couple hours at the most."

"I've never been out of New York. Can you come get me?"

"I can't leave because I have to go through a bunch of medical tests before I muster out. Can you take a cab? Oh... I know you're taking care of old lady Isabel. Can you work that out?"

"I'll think of something." Making a face at Debbie, Maggie added, "I can get my best friend, Debbie, to cover for me."

"Good. When you get to the gate just give them my name and rank and they'll give you a map that shows where the officers' quarters are located."

"Sounds easy enough."

"Now I have something really good to look forward to. See you then."

"Wait, what time is 1600 hours?"

Debbie stood next to her, showing her a note that read: *And we will fuck as soon as I get there.*

Robert said, "Four p.m."

"I'll wear something sexy."

"What you had on tonight looked sexy to me."

She pushed Debbie away. "I'll wear something even skimpier. Bye."

Now holding her cell close to her breast, Maggie chortled, "What do you think now, Debbie?"

"I still think you fucked him. When you wear that sexy outfit, don't wear a thong because taking it off will slow down the process of getting down to doing the dirty." This made Maggie and Debbie both laugh. They hugged as they both stood there with water dripping on the floor and agreed that the war was over.

Brenda had only one comment. "Thank God."

Monica threw an arm around Maggie. "Tomorrow morning, go to the coffee shop and see if Mr. Johnson shows up. Find out what his plans are for Robert. Maybe he will be more than just an employee helping out. Maybe some position closer to the money."

"I just want to go to bed and sleep."

"Goodnight then."

Maggie lay in bed, sandwiched between Brenda and Monica, thinking about Robert, of which Brenda was well aware. Though she hadn't tried to read Maggie's mind, her thoughts came to her without restraint. Psychoanalyzing herself, Brenda decided she was never going to be like a thief in the night, stealing the thoughts of one of her sisters, zombie or not. Maggie snuggled up to Monica on one side and Brenda spooned her on the other side with one arm draped on each of her sisters.

In the rec-room, with the double sliding glass window wide open over 49th Street, Debbie and Chloe decided to take another dip in the hot tub. They sat there in the bubbly steam, sharing memories of men in their lives.

Chloe went first. "I was sweet sixteen when I went out on a date with Tom Davis, the star halfback on our high school football team. He was really good looking, six-two, hair as red as Brenda's and blue eyes that seemed as deep as the sea. He drove me to a secluded spot on the banks of the Great Miami River."

Debbie questioned, "Isn't that in Florida?"

"It's not the same one. He had his dad's 1957 restored Ford 2-door Fairlane 500 hardtop. I remember that he parked and turned off the headlights. The full moon was shining directly into the car. So romantic. He kissed me and slid his hand up my dress to my pussy and started rubbing my clit."

"You weren't wearing panties?"

"No. I was so thrilled to be going out with the number-one heartthrob of Belmont High School that I forgot."

"Nobody forgets their panties, girlfriend. Maybe you forgot them on purpose."

"Could be I really wanted to get laid that night, I guess."

"I'd believe that."

"Tom was no stranger down there. I started getting his car seat wet. He must've noticed I was ready, quit rubbing me and unzipped his pants. I had to help him pull them down. He got his dick out through the opening in his shorts."

"Was it big?"

"I thought so. I'd never seen a dick before. He moved the seat back as far as it would go and told me to suck on him. I wasn't so sure I wanted to, gross, you know, but I got up on the seat on all fours and leaned over his lap. My god, being that close to him made my pussy gush, and I forgot about how gross it would be to have it in my mouth."

"Did you like it?" Debbie breathed.

Chloe smiled. "I took hold of his shaft with my left hand, opened my mouth, and closed my lips around the head. I kinda sucked on it, but I must've been doing it wrong because he put his hand on the back of my head and pushed it down. His cock hit the back of my throat."

"You must've choked on it."

"A little, but I kinda liked how it felt in my mouth, you know, hard but soft around the edges."

Debbie licked her upper lip. "I loved sucking Dr. Gomez's cock, well, Aurora now, but she still has a delicious dick... Just no balls."

Chloe grimaced. "Tom put his right hand between my legs and started first with one finger in me and then kept adding fingers until his hand was practically in my vagina. The feeling was so intense I really went all out on his dick. Didn't take long for him to start groaning and squirt a huge load of cum in my mouth. I wanted to spit it out but my vagina started throbbing around his fingers. My god that orgasm was intense. I swallowed so I could cry out and breathe."

"You go, girl."

"When we were through, I looked at myself in the rearview mirror and saw a streak of cum on my chin. I couldn't wipe it off fast enough, felt a little sick in my stomach. Guess I never developed a taste for it."

"What happened to you two?"

"We went out several times after that, pretty much fucked the normal way, and I found out what it was like to have my pussy eaten. I may have lost my virginity to his fingers, but I discovered I wanted to experience sex with a woman. Might say I developed a taste for eating pussy. What do you think?"

"I think I love you."

"Debbie, what about Aurora? Don't you two have a thing?"

"A threesome with her and you would be to die for."

"I believe you think so, but dicks are not my thing anymore." She flicked water at Debbie. "Your turn."

"I was raised in Mexico City. My family still lives there. My mother, Rosita, and my father, Francisco, they have a decent home. I have two brothers, Miguel, who is nine, and my other brother is Juan. He is eleven. On Saturday nights we would sing with a mariachi band at Polo's Taco Bar."

Chloe yawned.

"My dad is a leather belt maker. His best customers are people who have lost family members to the murderous drug cartels. He would engrave the dead loved ones' names on the belts the families will buy. He is never hurting for business."

Chloe rubbed her pussy, hoping to get some stimulation from Debbie's story. "Get to the sexy parts."

"One day a guy drove up and saw me with my dad and said

he wanted to take me out for a nice dinner. My dad knew the guy, a cartel drug lord known as El Paco, really wanted to fuck me, so he took me in the night to his friend's house. Pedro was to drive me to the airport and put me on a plane to the U.S. under the family migration plan."

"So you already had family in the states?"

"My cousins in San Diego. They were to pick me up at LAX."

Chloe pinched one of her nipples, which was erect from all the dancing bubbles. "But you never got there?"

"Pedro tells me to wait in a shack in the backyard. I saw a bunch of chickens in the yard, penned up to keep a pit bull from killing them. When I say a shack, I mean a shack. I walk in through a garage door, set down my suitcase and look around a tiny room, see a toilet that had a broken seat in a corner and an old pickup truck. The floor was dirt and the place stunk of oil and vomit."

"Were you afraid?" Both her hands were busy under the water.

"Not 'til he came in and closed the garage door. He had a bottle of Tequila and offered me to drink it with him."

"Was he cute?"

"If that's what you call forty and bald. He was short and muscular. I remember he was wearing a pair of worn out jeans and a dirty white t-shirt that had on the front, *Eltri Fifa*."

Chloe slipped a finger into her vagina, wishing Debbie's story would make her hot. "What does that mean?"

"It is Mexico's national soccer team."

"Can your story get any more boring?"

"We sat on the tailgate of the truck and drank Tequila until the bottle was almost empty. I never drank Tequila before, got woozy and had to pee. He told me I could use the toilet if he could watch. Guess I was just drunk enough to not give a shit. I pulled down my panties, took the bottle from him, and squatted over the broken toilet while he watched. What a pervert. Took a couple hits of Tequila before I could go. After that he told me to sit on the broken seat then he put both his hands on my thighs."

"Now you're talking." Chloe moaned.

"I wasn't that drunk, told him not to touch me. He said if I was a good girl then he would get me to the airport in time for my flight to the U.S. If not, he would give me to the cartel boss El Paco and he would teach me some manners, maybe kill me."

With that, Chloe lost all interest in finger-fucking herself. "Shit."

"I beg him not to rape me. 'I am only sixteen.' 'You are going to love it,' he says. Then his cell phone rings. He took his hands off me to answer the call. It was my dad. I heard him ask about me. When I started to scream, Pedro covered my mouth with his hand. 'Si, I get her to the airport right on schedule.' He hung up, all smiles. 'Now we fuck.'

Chloe felt a chill. "He raped you?"

"When he bends over to take off his boot, I smashed the Tequila bottle over his head. He goes headfirst into the truck fender, out like a broken bulb. My heart is racing, but I have to think fast. I throw my suitcase in the back of the truck and jump in the cab. The keys are on the visor, of course. I see him start to move on the dirt floor. My fingers are shaking. I'm trying to fit the right key into the ignition slot. Pedro is on his knees and getting to his feet when I turn the key. The battery sounds dead. *Ruugh, ruugh, ruugh—*"

"Debbie?"

"He's staggering toward the truck door, only two steps when the engine fires up. I slam the gear in reverse. The truck smashes through the closed garage door, and I am outside in the night. Dogs are barking. Pedro is yelling. I careen the truck down the dirt road. Tears in my eyes make it hard to see where I go. Good thing I am drunk. I would not have made it."

Chloe breathed a sigh of relief. "But you got to the airport."

"Somehow, I am drunk, I guess, I get on the wrong plane and end up in Haiti. No money. No way to call home. Doctor Gomez is at the airport, back from a trip, and feels sorry for me.

He gives me a job, lots of sex that I want, and I decide to stay. Now this. I am a Lesbian Zombie. My life is much better."

"Sounds like you've made the best of a bad situation."

She shrugged. "Maybe one day I will go home."

Chloe scooted close to her in the warm bubbling water and immediately embraced her in a passionate kiss.

"Oh, Chloe," Debbie breathed.

"What could be better than this?" Chloe let her hands follow Debbie's curves, down past her shoulders, over her breasts, and down her perfect tummy to the baby-smooth mound of skin between her legs.

Debbie responded with a deep moan. She arched her back, and as her nipples surfaced in the dancing bubbles, Chloe's lips found purchase on the nearest nub. Her tongue circled and circled and her teeth nibbled and nibbled. Debbie shuddered in her loving embrace. "Oh, oh...yes. I want you to eat me." She stood to sit on the hot tub ledge, legs spread so Chloe could maneuver her face between them. Her lips kissed sensitive skin, her tongue probed hot wet places, up and down the pink valley between her folds, sometimes flicking her clit and sometimes licking her opening before diving in to where Debbie's sweet nectar pooled.

"Don't stop." She gasped. "Don't stop. Oh, Chloeeee..."

Her thighs clamped around Chloe's head as wave after wave of orgasmic release swept through her. Every muscle in her body contracted. Again and again. She couldn't breathe and didn't care.

Chloe was rewarded with a gush of Debbie's honeydew. Her beauty, her passion, even the sound of her desperate breathing made the night of storytelling seem so long ago.

"A-hum."

Both girls looked up. Brenda stood only a few feet away with her arms folded under her bare tits. Her little red bush beckoned to both of them.

"Want to join us?" Chloe cooed.

"Maybe another time. Right now I want you two to join us and get some sleep."

"Yes, Mother dear. We'll be in right away."

Brenda was beginning to relish being the mother hen over her clutch of chicks. "And, Chloe, don't forget to brush your teeth."

Chapter 7: FATE CAN BE A CRUEL TASKMASTER

With the morning sun came the first real day of the fight to pay back the male gender for their sins. At 9:45, the sisterhood was up and ready to begin their secret war. As they enjoyed their breakfast, across town in a five-million-dollar Empire State Building suite, Alfons Duda was still in bed but hard at work. He lay on his back with a beautiful black woman bouncing up and down on his erection. Because he was a good forty pounds overweight, he could feel the sexual pleasure but could not see the action between his legs.

Adrienne, the object of his dick's affection, considered the whole episode something she had to endure to keep her job as his private secretary. He looked like a typical oilman: dark, weathered skin from years in the oil fields, a sharply trimmed beard, and a little nest of hair in the center of his man-boobs. For the fourth time in two days, the sex was finally over. It was a good thing because his mother had just entered his suite. "Alfons, honey. Where are you?"

Fighting panic, Alfons whispered to Adrienne, "Go into the bathroom, take your clothes, and hide in the closet. Don't come out until I tell you to."

"She's your mother, not your wife."

He was already in his slacks and throwing on his shirt. "Do you want her to fire you?"

Adrienne huffed then fled to the bathroom while Alfons

buttoned up and watched her naked body retreat. *Why do the good looking ones have to be such bimbos?*

***

On Long Island, in her multimillion-dollar home known as the Ranch, that also doubled as her corporate offices and art studio, Jackie O'Neal, dressed in her purple nightgown, admired her latest painting, a truly great work of art. While drinking a cup of black coffee and rocking in John Kennedy's original rocking chair that she bought at auction for the low price of 1.5 million, she tried to decide whether to display this piece at her upcoming art show. Putting her cup down on the coffee table, she screamed for Melinda, her live-in housemaid. "Has the fucking Times come yet?" In private, Jackie was nothing like the sophisticated woman she portrayed herself to be in public.

Fifty-two-year-old Melinda, with one leg shorter than the other from childhood polio, came limping in with the New York Times. "I have it here, Miss Jackie."

She snatched the paper from Melinda's shaking hand and quickly opened it to the arts and entertainment section where she found the art critic's column.

Melinda quietly tried to beat a hasty retreat.

"Wait. This so-called critic, Peter Duvoy, better have written something nice about my paintings or I'll buy that fucking paper and fire his sorry ass."

"Yes, Miss Jackie." Melinda cowered by the coffee table.

Jackie's face went from a scowl to a smile. "Melinda, he likes it. Sit down and listen."

Melinda obediently sat down on the coffee table.

"Jackie O'Neal has a unique style that would rival some of the artists from the early twentieth century. I can't wait to see her entire collection."

Melinda stood and clapped. "I never doubted you, Miss Jackie." Her forced smile revealed a mouthful of crooked teeth.

"Get back to work...and see a doctor about that limp. It

seems to be getting worse and I can't have an invalid parading around the Ranch when I have guests."

"Yes, Miss Jackie."

"And get me another cup of coffee. This one is cold. Next time make it hotter."

***

Driving down Interstate 280, Reverends Leroy and Janice Parker fought all the way toward their church. Looking at her husband and sitting with her hands in her lap, she decided to confront him for the hundredth time in their eight-year marriage. "Leroy, tell me the truth. Have you been sleeping with that young intern?"

"No, I haven't. Why would you ask such a thing?" He squirmed in the driver's seat of his $200,000 Mercedes and tried to think fast to cover his indiscretions. "You are the only woman in my life. In Luke it says—"

"Fuck what Luke says. I don't care who you sleep with as long as you include me."

"Sometimes I want to get laid by myself. You know how you are, always taking charge, licking her pussy when I want to do it myself. How many times have I told you to share the pussy, not hog it?"

"You know I have lesbian tendencies. You promised you'd help me with my problem. You get the women into your office. I join in so I can do my thing. That's the deal we made."

"Well, sometimes I want to do my thing too."

Looking at her face for signs of just how pissed off she was, and at the same time almost running off the road, he managed a smile. "I'm sorry you're feeling left out, honey."

"I want you to get us some new pussy. No more sneakin' it behind my back."

His heart skipped with joy. "Okay, honey. I'll take care of it. Let's pray on the matter." He pulled off at a rest stop and reached over and put his fat hand up her dress. Even though he was a disgusting slob, she was in the mood for love, and besides, she could always fantasize about the music director, Miss Flores. "Fuck me right here, Leroy."

He struggled to remove her panties, and just as he got his cock out of his pants, a cop pulled up in the rest area, and that put an end to their session of makeup sex. Leroy got himself put back together, and as he drove off, Janice came up with a great idea. She spread her legs. "While you drive, I want you to finger-fuck me 'til I come."

"Praise the Lord."

***

After finishing breakfast, the sisterhood was about to go their separate ways for the day when Brenda's cell phone rang. She quickly answered it as the sisterhood looked on. "Aurora, darling. When did you get in? 6:35 this morning? You must have taken the Red Eye to JFK. Carlos and Jason with you? Great."

Monica elbowed Chloe. "Shit is gonna hit the fan."

"And Albert picked you up all right? Yeah, I know he's a fucking Nazi. Give the phone to Albert."

"What's next, Brenda?"

"Albert, how did the meeting go after I left?"

"It didn't last very long. Karl and Fenn told Reinhard how they're gonna assassinate you when they go to the house to get rid of BBBD's body. They're gonna ambush you in the basement. They think Reinhard is in on the plot, but he's not. Me neither."

Brenda took over the conversation. "Let's see...it's only 10:15. Albert, I want you to tell the traitors that Reinhard told you about the plan. You think it's a good idea and want in. Get them over to BBBD's house at 1:45. Tell them we'll be there at 2:30. When you hear me and the sisterhood come in, back away and sneak out through the crawl space."

"You want to walk into an ambush?"

"I'll bring the ambush to them. I don't want anybody getting shot so tell the traitors to leave their guns at home, they'll make too much noise, and have them ambush me with knives."

"As you wish."

"Albert, you and Reinhard are going to be rewarded for your loyalty with a sex party, lesbian style, after we destroy Karl and Fenn. You ain't seen nothing until you see a naked Lesbian Zombie on a bed with her legs spread, tits sticking up, and pussy waiting for you with that vertical smile. I'm going to let Reinhard fuck me. As for you, you're going to the dark side with Monica. After the killing, I'll promote you to reign as president. Aurora will be going back to Haiti when the killing is done. See you this afternoon."

Pushing the end button on the cell, Brenda just kept looking at it. Then: "Debbie, you and Chloe go check out the church. Maggie, just hang loose. Maybe Robert will get hot thinking about you and call you up. I want you ready to go at a moment's notice."

A happy Maggie saluted Brenda and then Monica, Debbie and Chloe. "Aye, Aye, captains."

Brenda motioned for Monica to walk to the rec-room window with her. Debbie and Chloe watched as the two leaders stood there looking at each other with their arms folded. Both seemed to be talking at once, until Brenda put a finger on Monica's lips, shushing her. After a couple minutes, whatever they argued about was resolved. They embraced and kissed each other, and then walking back to the sisterhood, they were greeted with a chorus of, "What's that all about?"

Monica said, "It is top secret. We could tell you but then we would have to kill you."

A shocked Maggie spoke up in disbelief. "You wouldn't kill us...would you?"

Monica laughed. "It is a very old joke. Now go carry out Brenda's orders and wait for your boyfriend to call."

"Can I wait in the hot tub?"

Monica scoffed. "You can wait in the toilet for all I care."

Invasion of the Lesbian Zombies

***

The Heinrich gang, now supported by three apprentice gang members: Werner, Dieter, and Ernst, got to the house on Montford Lane earlier than instructed, just to be sure they weren't late for any reason. They brought with them a chainsaw and two trash cans. When this was over, there'd be two bodies to dump in the East River: BBBD's and Brenda's. May they both rest in peace.

Hiding in the basement next to BBBD's bloated body, Ernst threw up. Albert, Karl, Fenn, Reinhard, and the two other apprentices waited in silence with their knives drawn. The apprentices were all excited because they were told that, if they would help kill the zombie chick, they would instantly become full-fledged members of the Heinrich SS gang due to some recent openings.

Unfortunately for them, the zombies arrived; they heard footsteps upstairs.

It was then that Dieter noticed their ranks had thinned. "Where's Reinhard?" They all looked around, and in the dim light, Karl counted heads. He came up with five. "And where's Albert?"

He shined a small flashlight into the dark corners, illuminating a dirt bank that sloped up to the crawl space...and Albert who quickly disappeared into the twilight of the one-light-bulb basement.

"What the fuck?"

The door to the basement slammed shut. Rats stormed out of the crawl space en masse and scampered up the stairs, but their flow got dammed up at the closed door.

The gang of would-be assassins panicked and, clambering over the rats and fellow gang members, fought their way to the door, only to find it locked.

"You fuckers," Fenn yelled.

Brenda and Monica slinked out of the crawl space and pulled the gang members, one at a time, back down into the basement and cut their throats with their own knives. The butchery left the place and everything in it awash in blood.

The deed done, Brenda and Monica squirmed back through the crawl space to the storm door and out into daylight where Albert and Reinhard waited. "They're all dead—all dead."

Monica left to take a shower.

Brenda took Reinhard by the hand. "This is your lucky day." She led him into the bedroom where little Maggie had sacrificed her body and pride for BBBD's pocketbook. "Get your clothes off. I'm giving you five minutes, so you better not waste any time because when the five minutes are up, we're done whether you're done or not."

Reinhard had everything off in less than fifteen seconds.

Brenda was already on the bed, naked and ready to go.

The Nazi thug climbed on top of her. He stunk of tobacco and beer and treason. A typical hairy man, he was somewhat clumsy, feeling for her hole, then he jammed his erect penis into her. The way he grunted and pumped, she felt nauseous, but he'd earned his jollies. She already longed for a good woman.

"Tell me if I'm hurting you and I'll stop."

Brenda almost laughed at his attempt to give a shit about her feelings. "Just get it over with."

He held himself up on his strong arms so as not to crush her under his weight. The more he pumped, the more he dripped sweat on her chest, but she had to admit, his physical prowess felt rather pleasing. "You're more of a stud than I imagined. Better enjoy your one and only reward for your loyalty."

Without missing a stroke: "I've heard that some species' females kill the male after mating."

"I'm not a black widow spider. You'll be fine."

"God knows I've never fucked a woman so beautiful."

"And dangerous...don't forget dangerous."

"But you just said—"

"Not you. Not now. Just shut up and fuck me."

He was like a machine hammering away until his whole

body stiffened. His back arched and he let out a guttural moan as she felt a mighty throbbing in her vagina. He leaned in to kiss her, and for a fleeting moment, she thought to let him have the virus, but she turned her mouth away, though his performance deserved the intimacy she couldn't give him.

He collapsed and rolled off her. As he fought for breath, she rubbed his hairy chest. "Feel better now?"

Breathing heavy, he muttered, "I fucked up...didn't use a condom."

"F-Y-I, it was just fucking, nothing else. There'll never be a little Reinhard running around, not from my pussy anyway."

As his breathing slowed, she examined his body with a little less of a man-hater's perspective. Nice muscles, hard abs, blond hair and blue eyes of the Aryan race. She felt pleased she'd given up her virginity to him. He really was a fine specimen of the dumber sex.

Must be hard for the brain to compete with the little head down there.

She slapped him in the balls.

"Hey, what'd you do that for?"

"Time's up. You and Albert have a mountain of work to get done."

"Work? I want to take a nap."

"Save it, buster. You have six bodies in the basement and only two trash cans to put the pieces in. I hope there's plenty of gas in the chainsaw."

"Fuck." He sat up. "Being a skinhead just ain't what it used to be."

"Have fun." Brenda didn't bother getting dressed, just got up and, on her way to the shower, passed a now clean Monica. "Do I really have to fuck Albert?"

"I promised him a lesbian sex party. Who better than you?"

"He better not get cum in my hair."

Brenda stepped into the shower and, for more than five minutes, luxuriated in the hot water beating down on her. In the distance, sirens wailed. As she rinsed shampoo from her hair, she realized the sirens shut off somewhere close by. This unnerved her so she hurriedly dried off, and with just a towel wrapped around her, she hustled to the living room where naked Monica stood at the front window, looking out.

"What's going on?"

Monica spoke sadly. "It is the old lady that Maggie was taking care of, Isabel. The firemen brought her out on a gurney in a body bag. She must have pushed an emergency button on her wrist or called 911 but it was too late by the time they got here. A heart attack, maybe, or just old age. Who will tell Maggie? She really liked the old lady."

"I'll tell her. This can be a big break for us."

"How?"

"Remember, Maggie said the old lady had left her the house in her will."

"What are you getting at?"

"We don't have to clean up this dump or get rid of the bodies downstairs. Just burn the house down. Pour gasoline on the bodies and cook 'em good. By the time the fire reaches the top floor there won't be any proof we were ever here."

Monica agreed. "We will be doing Brooklyn a favor by razing this shithole. Let's think of it as a Lesbian Zombie reclamation project." She laughed at her own joke.

"We'll make the old lady's house our live-in headquarters, save a ton of dough on hotel bills."

"Brenda, that is a brilliant idea."

Albert and Reinhard showed up. They were dressed in protective garbage bags, and Albert toted the chainsaw. "What's all the ruckus out there?"

Brenda pulled them both into her and squeezed them tight. "Change of plans, boys." She felt giddy and giggled. "You're going to burn the house down. I want you two to handle this project in complete secrecy. No other members of the Nazi brotherhood are to be involved in this or know anything about what happened here or what will happen tonight at about two a.m. Capisce?"

"Capisce."

"Go get the gasoline and call me when it's done. Now beat it."

As the boys left, Reinhard turned and yelled at Brenda. "You were great."

"You too, Monica," Albert added.

Brenda asked her, "Well? How was Albert?"

"The fucker got cum in my hair."

***

Back at the hotel, they found Maggie lying on the floor with her legs up on the couch and her cell phone to her ear. Giggling, she didn't even notice Brenda and Monica were back from another killer day.

Brenda walked over and looked down on a very happy Maggie. "We need to talk."

Maggie went on gabbing with Robert as if Brenda were invisible. "So what did you have for lunch?"

Brenda just stood there listening to one half of the conversation.

"Two BLTs and a Coke? You should be starving by now."

Brenda's patience ran out. "Get off the fucking phone."

"Yeah, I have to go. See you soon. I love you too." She hung up and rolled to her knees. "Well, sisters, how are things going? I talked to Robert for almost two hours. This Friday at the base, they're having an officers' dinner and dance, so I have to find something pretty and sexy to wear."

"Maggie, I have something unpleasant to tell you."

"What is it?"

"Your friend Isabel has died."

"Oh, no." Maggie felt kicked in the stomach.

"I'm sorry for your loss."

Tears welled in her eyes. "She was such a sweet old lady.

What happened?"

"We don't know what killed her but her house is now your house."

"Yes." She sniffled. "Four bedrooms. Completely remodeled a couple years ago. She left it to me in her will."

"We know." Brenda embraced Maggie. "I want us to move into it as soon as possible. Is that okay with you?"

"Of course. Can I go to Isabel's funeral?"

"We'll all go with you, honey."

Chloe and Debbie rushed in like the wind, just in time to hear Brenda's comment. "Where are we all going?" Debbie asked.

Maggie spoke through her tears. "Isabel died today."

"So?"

"She was my friend when I really needed one." With that last comment Maggie started to bawl in Brenda's arms.

Chloe harrumphed. "Well, that sucks. Sorry to hear it." She inhaled and didn't miss a beat. "Can we go eat somewhere? I'm hungry as hell. Brenda, The Church of the Risen Jesus is fucking shit. We were in the building looking around when—"

"Shut up, Chloe. Just because you're a Lesbian Zombie doesn't mean you can't have a heart and compassion for a sister in mourning. What's the matter with you?"

Debbie jumped in. "That was a cold thing to say, Chloe."

"I said I was sorry and I said I was hungry. What's wrong with that?"

"It's the way you said it, just thinking about yourself."

"Good lord," Brenda cut in. "Both of you button your mouths. Now come here. We're going to have a sisterhood hug." Locked arm in arm, Brenda started by kissing Chloe on her right, who then kissed Maggie who kissed Monica who kissed Debbie who kissed Brenda. The circle of the sisterhood was restored, and the girls took a moment of silence to appreciate each other. Then Brenda released the group. "Now we can go to dinner where Chloe can tell us what they found out at the church."

Chloe embraced Maggie. "I'm sorry."

"I know." She sniffled.

"I get cranky when I'm hungry."

Brenda clapped twice. "It's my turn to choose, and being from Denver, I love Mexican food. So we're going to Vista Verde."

As they rode in a hotel limo to the restaurant, Chloe and Debbie took turns telling everyone about what happened at the church. Chloe went first. "We hadn't been inside for more than a minute, looking around the foyer at all the paintings and statues, when Reverend Leroy walked up behind us."

"The asshole was even fatter than he looked on TV," Debbie added.

"He asked us who we were. We told him we'd seen his television show and that we're looking for a church to join. His shifty eyes made it obvious he was interested in both of us, but he ogled Debbie more. Because she had a better chance to hook him, I excused myself to the ladies' room."

"Thanks a lot." Debbie took it from there. "As Chloe walked away, I noticed his eyes follow her until she was out of sight. The Reverend definitely wants to fuck us both."

"Pig," Monica spat.

The limo took a hard left.

"We walked down the aisle in the sanctuary where I asked him if he could forgive me of my sins. He went on and on about how his church was a strict Bible church then offered to help me *privately off the record*. I told him that was exactly the kind of church we were looking for."

"Good call," Brenda said.

"The pig kept wiping his forehead with a handkerchief. It was cool in the place so I knew his sinful thoughts were making him sweat. When we got to the pulpit, he asked about Chloe. I told him we had been friends since high school. No. He meant if Chloe needed *private forgiveness off the record* too. When I answered yes, he showed me directly to his office.

Monica laughed. "Hook, line, and sinker."

"He closed the door and I looked around. What kind of

preacher has a polar bear rug in his office? The thing was creepy with its open mouth, those sharp teeth and marble eyes. He offered me a plush chair in front of his desk. The bear was behind me so I forgot about it. I made sure my skirt hiked up high when I sat down. Oh, yeah, I had his attention all right. He leered at me as he sat behind his desk, and then he just kept smiling as he leaned back in his chair and laced his fingers behind his head. The asshole was trying to impress me, what a powerful man he was in my presence. Gag me. I adjusted my skirt a couple times to keep him thinking he was going to get lucky."

"I got lucky too," Chloe jumped in. "While she was seducing the fat bastard, I ran into his wife in the restroom. Janice looked at me, said *oh my*, and then pretended to fix her hair in front of the mirror. I walked up close behind her, close enough to smell her nice perfume, and introduced myself to her reflection. 'I'm Chloe.' I practically breathed it in her ear. I must've made her nervous, but she managed to stutter out her name. 'I'm Janice.' 'Oh, you're the reverend's wife.' She looked surprised. 'You know him?' I told her that my friend was talking to her husband in his office right now. That's when she looked me up and down. 'If your friend looks anything like you, I guarantee they're doing more than just talking.' Oh, there's trouble in Eden, all right. She was definitely annoyed at lover boy. 'Follow me,' she said, and we headed straight for his office. She didn't knock just opened the door and barged in."

Debbie picked up the story from there. "Scared the hell out of me. We both jumped up. She was on me like the wind in windmill. 'What the hell are you doing with my husband, young lady?' She was so pissed, her words came out with a spray of spit. I stepped back 'We were just talking about Jesus.'"

"I laughed at that one," Chloe put in.

"I licked my lips, and in my own defense I told her, 'Reverend Leroy said my sins would be forgiven. All I had to do was confess and make a big donation.' The missus wasn't convinced. She grabbed Leroy by the ear and dragged him out of the office. 'I told you not to fornicate with women without me,' she said from somewhere down the hall. That left Chloe and me standing in his office, laughing our asses off."

Pride ballooned inside Brenda for her girls. "Sounds like you have him right where you want him."

"Leroy told me about a Bible study group this coming Friday," Debbie said as the limo pulled into the restaurant parking lot. "At 7:00. We'll be there. Leroy has the hots for me. I know, icky, but sex is sex. Let's see if he takes the bait and gets burned."

Everyone was laughing as they piled out of the limo.

Walking in to the Vista Verde, the sisterhood was struck by the size of the bar. Chloe said, "That's the longest bar I've ever seen. There must be twenty-five barstools."

Monica's gaze locked downwind. "See those two women on the end by the staircase?"

"So?"

"They're lesbians," Chloe slipped in. "No doubt about it."

"Wait a minute." Debbie gasped. "The one in the yellow skirt, white blouse, tan...we've seen her before."

Monica made her point. "Looks like the hot Mexican drink of agave nectar on the balcony across from our hotel."

"Yeah, Monica, she's the same woman. I got dibs."

"Chloe, you can't call dibs."

"Yes, I can. I just did."

Brenda pushed the sisters toward their table. "Will you two knock it off?"

"I get to convert her to a Lesbian Zombie," Chloe cheered.

"Good luck with that. She's got a girlfriend."

So what if some butch-bitch was hanging on her shoulder? Chloe wouldn't let that stop her.

The sisterhood ordered Margaritas while waiting for their food.

Chloe kept an eye on the chick that got her all flustered. Hispanic like Debbie, and Chloe loved Debbie's Spanish maiden doll face and all, she was young enough, and she either got a very expensive boob job or was blessed with a hefty set of double Ds. In this light, her hair looked dark brown and soft enough to drown in.

I'd love to get her naked in the hot tub. Oh, oh. They caught me staring. Her girlfriend is looking at me. Miss Butch doesn't look too happy.

Chloe took a slug of Margarita straight from the glass, got brain-freeze. Fuck. Miss Yellow-Skirt got up off her barstool and started walking toward Chloe. Butch stayed behind. *She better not be looking for trouble. She has no idea who she'd be fucking with.* It looked like she was coming right to the sisterhood's table, but probably not; the restrooms were right behind them.

As the young woman in yellow strode past the table, she looked at Chloe and smiled. "Isn't this a great restaurant?"

As the sisterhood looked on, Chloe replied, "Yes, I love the place." This was the opening Chloe could use, even though the pleasantries were weak one-liners. Her eyes followed that gorgeous figure toward the restroom. She stood up and put her Margarita down. "I gotta go pee."

The sisters shrugged and watched her walk away.

Chloe, strutting toward the restroom, turned her head back and smiled at the sisters, but they weren't the only ones to catch the meaning of her sly smile.

Butch immediately got off her barstool and headed for the ladies' room, following Chloe.

This threat brought an instant response from Brenda and Monica. They joined the parade to the ladies' room. Brenda hoped there wouldn't be a fight but sized up the short stout butch anyway: in her forties, ring in her nose, black wife-beater shirt, arms solid muscle, baggy black pants with a forty-four inch waist. With her short-cropped hair and the stream of purple down the middle of her blond head, she looked menacing to the average woman. Her problem was that she wasn't dealing with an average woman, or an average lesbian, for that matter.

Chloe knew she was being followed but decided to converse with Miss Yellow-Skirt while she was busy rubbing a tissue on her front teeth to clean off some Mexican food. Chloe strolled up to the sink next to her. "Do you mind if I ask you a question?"

Her measured response was, "Go ahead."

"How does it feel to be the most beautiful woman in this restaurant?"

"After you, I suppose."

"Thanks, but—"

Butch busted in, followed by Brenda and Monica. Suddenly the restroom was very crowded.

Chloe stayed on course. "I would love to take you out."

"She's not interested in you, bitch," Butch blurted out. "She's my woman. Leave her alone or I'll kick the shit out of you."

Brenda stepped in and shoved Butch backwards. "Don't threaten my girl."

Miss Yellow-Skirt got out of the way and stood next to Monica to watch what she was sure would be Brenda getting a beating.

Brenda grabbed Butch's nose ring, pulled her into one of the stalls, and closed the door. It was a tight squeeze, but the fight was on.

Butch grabbed Brenda's hair. "I hate redheads, fuckin' bossy bitches."

Brenda leaned back on the stall door and without letting go of the nose ring put her foot in Butch's chest and shoved her down on the toilet, ripping the ring from her nose in the process. That took the fight out of her.

She screamed. "My nose."

Brenda saw a fleshy device sticking out of Butch's pocket and grabbed it. A phallic dildo?

"Give it back."

"You won't be using this on her anymore."

A dildo flew over the top of the stall door and bounced on the floor. Monica bent over to pick it up. "Well, well, what do we have here?" She grinned and showed it to Chloe. "A new hot tub toy."

There was silence in the stall. Monica and Chloe thought Brenda had killed the dyke.

The stall door flew open and promptly fell off its hinges. Out walked Brenda followed by Butch. She was holding toilet paper up to her bloody nose as she skulked to Miss Yellow-Skirt. "Donna."

"Oh my God, Joanne. You're hurt."

"Will you still go home with me?"

"Of course."

Brenda, Monica and Chloe just stood and watched as the two embraced. Donna had her arm around a totally beaten Joanne. "It'll be all right."

"I love you, you know."

"I know." Donna set her business card on the counter in plain sight of Chloe then escorted Joanne out.

Chloe picked up the card. "I could have taken her in a fight by myself."

Monica waved a finger at her. "Maybe, and then again maybe not. I just hope no one in the restaurant sees Joanne's battle wound."

Brenda took the dildo from Monica. "It might be a good idea for us to haul our butts out of here, now."

Stopping only long enough to gather up Debbie and Maggie and hand the waiter three hundred bucks, the sisterhood beat a hasty retreat to the exit.

Now in the limo heading back to the hotel, Maggie and Debbie wanted to hear all the details of the bathroom brawl. Chloe ignored their pleas, just kept looking at Donna's card and thinking about what she wanted to do to her in the hot tub.

Monica made the big announcement. "Donna is the woman from the balcony across the street from us."

"The address on her card proves it," Chloe affirmed. "I guess she's bi-sexual, though I personally would prefer Joanne over that asshole Binocular Man. Maybe we ought to tell Joanne about him. She would kick his ass. Brenda, I want to call Donna and see what comes of it."

A somber Brenda examined the dildo closely. "Hold off for a few days 'til things cool off." She had other things on her mind. *How do I turn this fucking thing on?*

***

At 121 Montford Lane, Reinhard and Albert were busy at work with several cans of gasoline. They first poured a gallon on the bodies in the basement and worked their way to the first and second floor with another gallon on each.

Meanwhile, in an abandoned warehouse north of the old steel mill, Aurora was busy presiding over a meeting with what was left of the Heinrich SS. Carlos and Jason flanked him on either side. The meeting didn't last long. There were only six members left, not counting Reinhard and Albert. Aurora, on orders from Brenda, gave Carlos and Jason the signal, the V for victory sign. The lady-boys promptly shot all six to death.

Now in a hurry to join Albert and Reinhard at the house, Aurora stole a bicycle and peddled as fast as she could. Once outside BBBD's place, she called Brenda before joining the Nazis inside.

The sisterhood was surprised when Brenda's cell rang in the limo as it sped toward Montford Lane.

Brenda answered, "Did you take care of our problem?"

"Going inside to do it right now," Aurora assured her.

"Call me when it's over."

Debbie asked, "What problem is that?"

"I'll tell you later. Now hand me that bottle of Tequila in the limo bar."

A very depressed Brenda, drinking straight from the bottle, stared out the window and then looked at her watch. She whispered a prayer over and over in her mind: *Take Reinhard and Albert to their eternal fate, Loa. Tell them I'm sorry.*

Having polished off the bottle, she rolled down the window and let the bottle slip from her hand to crash on the pavement. She laid her head on the car door and, fighting back tears, covered her face with her hands. *Some shit just can't be avoided.*

Her cell rang again.

Monica answered. She'd been laughing with the sisterhood just minutes before, but now had a serious look on her face. "I will tell her." She put her hand on Brenda's shoulder. "It is all over and done. Finished."

Brenda remembered Reinhard's face when he was fucking her. He truly enjoyed his reward for being loyal to her. Waves of remorse bent her over. The man who had so enjoyed the gift of her virginity was dead because she had sentenced him to death. Now he and Albert were burning along with the corpses of their brothers in crime.

Monica was still holding the phone. "What do you want me to tell Aurora?"

Brenda breathed, then: "Tell her it's time she goes back to Port au Prince."

"Go home," she said in the phone, hung up, and then tried to comfort Brenda. "I know you feel bad, but they would eventually turn against us. Everything we want to achieve could go down the drain."

Debbie spoke up, "Monica, Brenda, what is going on? We have a right to know."

"The Heinrich SS is no more. Aurora just killed Reinhard and Albert."

Debbie huffed. "Brenda, you said they would be working for us. What changed that plan?"

"I'll just cut to the chase. They were Nazis. Nazis want to rule, not be ruled, especially by a gaggle of lesbians. Sooner or later they would attempt to kill us, or rat us out to the police. It would come down to us or them, girls. I'll never, never put the sisterhood in danger by trusting Nazi gangsters."

The girls responded with silence.

"Tomorrow we'll go look at Maggie's new house." Brenda ran the window down that separated the driver's compartment from the back and told the driver, "Pick us up at ten a.m." With that said, she closed the window and her eyes then listened to the chatter of the sisterhood. *They took it pretty good about the Heinrich SS. Maybe they're starting to develop a hard side to their moral code, especially where men are concerned.*

Back at the hotel, they settled down in the hot tub. Chloe looked to the balcony across the street to see if Donna would appear. She didn't.

After more drinking and frolicking, one by one they turned in for the night—all except Chloe. She sat in the tub all by her lonesome for another hour, and then only minutes after she'd gotten out of the tub, Donna walked out on her balcony and surveyed the empty hot tub with binoculars.

For Chloe and Donna the evening ended on a lonely note.

***

The next morning, Monica left a note for a hung-over Brenda. *I am going to the Empire State Building. I understand that Duda is a stickler about starting every day the same way. He is superstitious about making even the slightest change in his routine. After he meets me, everything is going to change. Have fun at the new house.*

At 10:25 in the morning, Brenda was up and ready to head over to Maggie's new house, so she walked into the bedroom and got everybody up. "I ordered breakfast so get up and take a joint shower. I know you'll all enjoy that."

While the sisterhood was washing each other and giggling up a storm, Brenda turned on the local news channel. Leaning back in a black leather rocker and munching on a piece of toast with butter and cherry jam on it, she blurted out, "What the fuck?" She took the remote control and ran the newscast in reverse. The problem was that no matter how many times she reran the news story, the headline remained the same: *Six Gang*

Members Die in House Fire. Brenda added up the total dead. "There's the three apprentices, Werner, Dieter, and Ernst, plus the traitors Karl and Fenn," and she finished with "BBBD...that's six. There should be eight." Maybe the firemen hadn't yet found the bodies of Reinhard and Albert. *Yeah, that's probably what happened.*

She sat there watching intently as the camera panned the completely burned down building. As the camera started to look down into the now wide open basement, the network ran the usual warning: *The scenes you are about to see can be disturbing to some viewers.*

What aired could have been a burned out campfire, blackened timber collapsed into a hole in the ground. Talk about over-hyped news. "You fuckers."

The sisterhood came running out of the bathroom stark naked. Maggie shouted, "What happened?"

Maggie's eyes focused on the television. "Oh my god. Is that BBBD's old house?"

"Shut up." Brenda turned up the volume. "I want to hear what the fire chief has to say."

The news reporter asked, "Chief Miller, are you certain there are no more bodies in the house?"

Looking at the camera, he nodded. "Six deceased. Probably gang violence. Autopsies will tell us more."

Brenda stormed around the room. "God damn it, God damn it, God damn it." *What the hell is Aurora up to?*

Using her cell, she called American Express, and after trudging through the usual recordings and security questions, she finally got a live person. "Brenda Ayler, how can I be of assistance?"

"Check the charges on my card. Any American Airlines tickets purchased last night?"

"Yes. Five."

Aurora, Carlos, Jason, Reinhard and Albert.

"Fuck."

Looking at a very confused sisterhood, Brenda asked into the phone, "Let me guess, to Port au Prince, right?"

"Was the use unauthorized?"

"No, that's fine."

"Would you like to remain on the line for a quick survey?"

"Goodbye." She hung up and turned to the girls. "We've been betrayed. Aurora didn't kill Reinhard and Albert."

Debbie chucked the last of Brenda's toast. "Are you gonna kill 'em?"

"I never imagined my day would start this way."

***

At the café on the first floor of the Empire State Building, Monica was waiting like a cat when Alfons Duda came down for his morning constitutional. Each day he would sit and read the Wall Street Journal while waiting for a glass of fresh squeezed orange juice. Now, as he read the paper and sipped the juice, he didn't notice Monica walking by his table.

Pretending to slip, she poured her coffee on Alfons' newspaper and into his lap.

He jumped out of his seat and began to brush off the coffee from his light blue suit. "Fool."

Monica dabbed at his coat and pants with a napkin. "I am so sorry." Looking right at his ruddy face and gray beard, she continued to wipe the area around his zipper. "I...I will gladly pay the cleaning bill."

Alfons was immediately smitten by the black woman's beauty. "Don't worry about it. Sit with me and tell me about yourself."

She patted her hand over her heart. "Me? Really?"

He returned to his seat. "Breakfast is on me...ah...what's your name?"

Bashfully, Monica sat down next to him. "Please tell me you won't sue me."

He smiled wickedly. "It's no big deal. I have a lot of suits in my office." He pointed at the ceiling. "It's up there, twenty-five floors. And it has an attached suite where I live."

"Nice. I would love to see it."

"You still haven't told me your name?"

"I am Monica Abelard."

"Beautiful name for a beautiful woman." He took her hand, but not to shake it. "What brings you to the Empire State Building today, Monica?"

"I am here to see if I can get a job with KOMA LTD."

"Interesting." He continued to hold her hand. "How is it you know of such a job?"

"A friend of mine told me they were hiring."

"Interesting." He released her hand to sip orange juice then beckoned the waiter to double up for his new guest.

Trying to appear confident, she broke the awkward silence. "What do you do up there twenty-five stories?"

"I own a company. What kind of work are you looking for?"

"My last job was in Port au Prince where I ran an office of sixteen women. It was a medical supply company, Caribbean Pharma. We supplied medical products for hospitals all over the islands."

"Why would you leave such a good job?"

"Hurricane Matthew put us out of business so I came to the U.S. hoping to find suitable employment. What type of work does your company do?"

He leaned into her and whispered, "I own KOMA."

She feigned surprise and added a little gasp for effect.

"I have no job openings, so apparently you've been lied to...or maybe you are lying to me."

Monica plastered a pretend look of shock on her face. "Oh, no. I must look like an idiot to you." She stood, dug a card from her purse, and set it on the table. "Please send me a bill for your suit and I will pay you for it right away by return mail." Pretending to cry, she turned to the door...

"What about breakfast?"

...and ran out to the street.

Alfons sat there looking at her card, which had no address, only her name and phone number. He shrugged.

The waiter brought another orange juice and two plates of breakfast.

After eating his fill, he rode the elevator up to his office and strode into the attached suite. Naked Adrienne, his secretary and personal assistant, gasped at the wet stain all down his front. "You smell like coffee." She started to undress him.

"A woman spilled coffee on me."

As she continued to undress him, "Was she pretty?"

Adrienne was the jealous type so he chose his answer carefully. "Not particularly."

Now naked and heading for the shower with Adrienne hugging him and rubbing his white butt he said, "I have a lot of things to get done today. Put your clothes on and at least make it look like you're working."

A dejected Adrienne put on her clothes and left.

Alfons could not get Monica off of his mind as he poured liquid soap on his oversized belly and under his arms. He disregarded any further thoughts of Adrienne except how to dump her and put Monica in her place. With his eyes closed, Alfons kept visualizing what Monica would look like standing in front of him naked as he washed his erect penis more than was necessary.

He got out of the shower and dried off. *I'm going to call her up right now. Where did I put that card?* He took all the cash out of his wallet; he was certain he had put Monica's card in with his cash, but it wasn't there. He searched frantically through his clothes and then felt relieved when he discovered he'd put her card in his shirt pocket. He must've been in a state of shock at the time.

"Thank you, God."

He picked up his cell to dial the number but found it had been redacted with a black magic marker. Obviously a statement from Adrienne. Whatever it took, he was now hell-bent on finding Monica.

***

Monica walked into the sisterhood's suite. Everyone was sitting around with sullen expressions. She knew something was really wrong by the angry look on Brenda's face.

Debbie told Monica, "They are not dead."

A perplexed Monica uttered, "Who is not dead?"

"Reinhard and Albert." Brenda related the story of Aurora's betrayal.

"Are we going back to Haiti to kill them?"

"She doesn't know yet."

"Debbie," Brenda snapped. "Will you please shut up?"

Monica relayed the details of her encounter with Alfons Duda. "I am certain he will be contacting me shortly."

This relieved Brenda on one front, but she was still fuming about Aurora.

After dining in and taking another dip in the hot tub, the sisterhood celebrated with more booze and tub sex.

Brenda didn't join in. She sulked into the bedroom and sat in another rocker to contemplate what to do about Aurora.

I can only blame her. I can't say to Albert and Reinhard, I'm really disappointed with you two. You're supposed to be dead and burned up even though the last time I saw you, Monica and I were fucking you guys as a reward. What the hell am I going to do now? In some ways she was glad they weren't dead, but now they'd never trust her again. Her number one lady-boy had a lot of explaining to do.

***

Brenda was grateful when the sun rose on Friday. Looking around she found the sisterhood in all manner of poses. Chloe was lying with her head on Monica's thighs. Monica was propped up next to the hot tub. Maggie was in one of the other bedrooms, lying on the bed under a sheet like some kind of road-killed ghost. Two empty wine bottles lay on the bed with her.

It suddenly occurred to Brenda that Debbie was nowhere to

be found. Panic set in as she checked all the rooms, until back in her own bedroom she found Debbie sleeping on the floor on the opposite side of the bed where Brenda had awakened.

No wonder I didn't see her when I got up.

With all her chicks accounted for, Brenda got ready to check out Jackie O'Neal's artwork. She left orders for the girls to take pictures of Maggie's new abode and come up with some interior decorating ideas. And an additional order of the day: "Make sure you're back here by 2:00. Maggie has got to make herself beautiful and on time for Robert. Chloe and Debbie, do a good job acting like repentant Christians at Bible study, and Monica, be ready to go when Duda calls. See you later."

Brenda arrived at Jackie's Gallery in time to see workers hang the sign outside: *Art for the Common Man and Woman.*

Her art might be for the common man and woman but the gallery and the building are not. This place must be running her a hundred grand a month.

Since the door was open for the carpenters and painters to come and go, Brenda just walked in. All the lights were turned on in the suspended ceiling, and all the walls glistened a bright white, some displaying only one painting on a ten-foot-wide space. Others had four to five paintings of different sizes on a wall of the same size.

Brenda walked over to a woman who was bent over and touching up a few spots that had been missed with the white paint. At first, Brenda thought the woman was Jackie, but oddly she stood crooked because one leg was shorter than the other. Reading the woman's mind quickly revealed her name was Melinda, Jackie's maid, who was afraid that Jackie might find a spot that she had missed.

A black limo pulled up and the driver opened his door and ran to open the rear door for an aging Jackie O'Neal. Wearing a totally black three-thousand-dollar pantsuit, black pumps, and enough makeup to raise the Bismarck, she got out with as much glamour as a movie star, Santos De Cartier sunglasses and all.

Everyone stepped out of her way as she entered the gallery. Strutting over to a terrified Melinda, Jackie peeled off her glasses and examined Melinda's work. "It looks good. You can go now. Tell Jorge to take you home."

"Thank you, Miss Jackie." Melinda limped for the limo.

Jackie walked around, oblivious to Brenda's presence. She pretended to straighten pictures, this way and that way, and then put them back to their original positions. One of her paintings was her favorite: the two-foot by three-foot canvas of a yellow house. The painting owned the entire ten-foot wall. She stepped back eight steps and admired her work.

Brenda heard her think: *No one had better have a negative point of view about this one or I'll make them wish they were never born.*

"Vincent Van Gogh would be proud of you."

Jackie turned to the voice that came from across the room and saw a smiling redhead, about the same height as her with the most beautiful hair in the world. "Who are you?"

"Brenda Ayler. I know who you are, Jackie O'Neal, by the way you're looking at the artwork through loving eyes."

"Are you an art critic?"

"Not officially, but I'm better than a lot of them. You're work is pretty good."

Jackie flushed. "Brenda, do you have time for a glass of champagne?"

"Would you have offered that if I had been critical of your work?"

"Of course. I welcome all forms of criticism...as long as I agree with it." Jackie laughed at her truism and led her to a table-spread of wines, cheeses, crackers, and fruit she'd had laid out for the pre-opening that afternoon. "Dom Perignon Champagne," she said to a tuxedo-clad sommelier. As he poured, Brenda glanced around at Jackie's other paintings. They were all renditions of Vincent Van Gogh's work.

Just then Jackie, holding the entire bottle, delivered a flute of champagne. "Look what that nice young man gave me." She waved the bottle as evidence of her love of booze.

Brenda sensed that Jackie was doing her best to hide something of her true nature. "The whole bottle? Isn't it a little early for that? Maybe you should save it for tomorrow's grand opening."

Jackie led her to a waist-high table decorated with ribbons and flowers. "Tomorrow this place will be overrun with people who don't know shit about art, all telling me how great my work is and only because they want something from me."

Brenda sipped from her glass, a bubbly assault on her nose. "What makes you think I don't want something?"

"Because I didn't get where I am by not being a good judge of people. You are genuine. You say what you think because you're not trying to impress anyone."

Brenda, while concentrating on Jackie's thoughts, went to set her glass on the table but caught the edge and spilled the bubbly all down the front of her dress. "God damnit." She tried to brush it off but to no avail. The dress was ruined, but feeling the heat of embarrassment, she made light of the situation. "Excuse my French. The dress will be all right...it's not all that important."

Jackie reached over with the bottle. "Then here is a refill."

"Thanks." Brenda took a sip from her refilled flute. "I feel you and I, and poor Vincent, have one thing in common. We're all loners. Me because I don't make friends very easily and was betrayed by a lover, and Vincent because he was fucked up enough to cut off his own ear, and you, Jackie, I don't yet know what sets you apart from the crowd."

"Booze, my friend. I like being alone...nobody to interfere with my drinking that way."

"Since this is probably the only time we'll be drinking together, guess I'll never know the real you."

"I'm rich enough to not give a shit." She drank straight from the champagne bottle.

Brenda finished her flute. "I better get going."

Jackie reached over and took hold of Brenda's wrist. "If you can, please come to my opening tomorrow."

Brenda patted Jackie's bony hand. "Sure, I'll be here and spend more time looking over your entire collection. I'll also bring a bottle of the good stuff...the five-dollar variety."

With a sparkle in her eyes and a smile on her face, Jackie raised her bottle. "See you tomorrow."

Brenda walked out.

Jackie watched Brenda, admiring her backside. *I may have just made a real true friend.*

She was unaware that Brenda read her thoughts and was thinking that Jackie could be a real ally.

***

On the twenty-fifth floor of the Empire State Building, Alfons had a couple things on his mind as he walked into his office. He didn't even stop for his morning orange juice. He closed the door and sat behind his desk. Turning his chair around, he just sat there thinking and looking out the window at the Manhattan skyline. *What am I going to do about Adrienne and how am I going to find Monica?*

Within forty-five minutes, Adrienne Porter came into his office. Alfons turned his chair around and confronted her. "Why did you do it?"

Adrienne stood at his desk. "What's the matter, honey?"

He slid Monica's business card across the desktop to her. "This is what's the matter."

She picked up the card, looked at it, and then put on an innocent act. "So?"

"The phone number has been crossed out."

"Yeah. I saw this card when you were taking your shower. It was lying on the floor. I figured it must've fallen out of your pocket when you undressed. Right away I noticed the number had been blotted out, thought it odd, then put it in your shirt pocket."

Alfons' face reddened, and veins bulged in his neck. "Liar.

You're fired. Get out of here before I have security remove you."

Adrienne staggered around the desk, put her face in his lap, and began to cry real tears. "I need this job. Please give me another chance."

Her plea was met with a two-word response: "Get out."

Knowing it was now hopeless, she got mad. "You can't get rid of me so easy. I know everything. I know where the bodies are buried...well...not that you killed anyone, but I know your dirty tricks. I know you cooked your books to dodge taxes. I could put you away for a long time, Mister—"

"How much?" Alfons shouted.

"You can't buy me with chump change. A hundred grand will keep me silent...for a while anyway."

"Fine." He got the checkbook out of his drawer and wrote her a hundred-thousand-dollar check. "If I ever see you again, I *will* be burying a body. Yours. Now get the fuck out."

"I hope you never find this Monica woman...for her sake. I wouldn't want her to have to endure the filth you put me through to satisfy your sexual perversions...just so I could keep this job. Well, here you go, fucker. You can take this job and shove it."

Alfons picked up his desk phone. "Get me security."

Adrienne put the check in her purse and flipped him the finger.

"Not anymore, bitch."

She stormed out of his office.

Now feeling a little more freedom, Alfons called a friend at U.S. Customs and Immigration. "Check your intake logs, see if you can find a Monica Abelard from Haiti. Maybe there's a record of where she's staying."

Then he called his head of security. "Track down Monica Abelard. I'll pay a ten thousand dollar finder's fee...if you find her."

"I'm on it, boss."

***

Over at Fort Dix, New Jersey, Captain Robert Johnson Junior was lying on his bed, counting the minutes until he held sweet little Maggie in his arms once more. At that very moment, Maggie was waiting for the cab to take her to him. She wore a light green miniskirt with a tight cream-colored blouse that enhanced her breasts and matched her green pumps. She topped off her come-hither-looks with a green ribbon in her hair. She was now ready, not to meet Robert to fleece him for Brenda, but to be with a man she had genuine affection for.

That left Debbie and Chloe to inspect Maggie's new house.

Monica, having the suite to herself, got on her laptop and researched Papa Doc's son, Baby Doc, and his son, Baby Doc the Second, who died in 2001, and Baby Doc's grandson, Francois, aka Baby Doc the Third (in her mind), the great grandson of Papa Doc. The family had an extensive criminal career.

Too bad kids cannot pick their parents.

Brenda might think I will forget them, but I will not. I will kill them. I have a passport. I can go anywhere I want. I will wait, though. Brenda has plenty on her mind now. I don't need to cause her more problems.

Monica heard a click on the door and saw Brenda dance in. She picked up a bottle of wine from the bar then sashayed over and sat on the couch next to her. "I had great success with Jackie. I believe I can make her one of us."

Monica closed her laptop. "That is great news. Now let me open the wine."

Looking at her watch as Monica opened the bottle and poured two glasses of Merlot, Brenda thought Maggie should be just about to Fort Dix. She was correct.

At the main gate, an Army MP stopped the cab. Maggie handed Robert's information to him out the back window. As he looked it over, for a split second, Maggie heard his thoughts. *"That fuckin' Johnson has all the luck. I should fuck her first, get her warmed up for him."*

She swallowed a sudden gush of panic. *I must be a Lesbian*

Zombie...wait...I must not be because I want to have sex with Robert, but I just read his mind, so I must be.

Confusion wracked her brain.

The MP broke into her worry. "Miss, the officers' quarters are on Patton Road where it crosses General Sherman Lane." He bent to the back window. His face was close to hers, tantalizingly close as he showed her a small map and pointed out the building. "It's right here."

His nearness caused a reaction in her panties she hadn't expected, that little pull down there. She didn't have a lesbian bone in her body and couldn't wait to ravage Robert. "Thank you, sir...and for warming me up, too."

"Huh?"

"Go, driver."

The cab sped off.

She giggled.

Moments later, the cab pulled up in front of the officers' quarters. The meter read: $143. She pulled two Franklins from her purse. "Keep the change."

"Thank you, mum."

She got out and quickly found Robert's room. Even as she knocked on the door, she was still thinking that maybe she was a Lesbian Zombie, after all, but then she posed another possiblity: *Maybe I'm a Bi-Sexual Zombie. Is there such a thing?*

She forgot about it when Robert opened the door. He stood there wearing only olive-drab boxer shorts and drying his hair with a towel. "Oh. My god. I must've lost track of time. Come on in, Maggie."

"Actually, I'm a little early." She smiled at him as she walked into his living room and dining room combination. Everything was green or brown or gray. The place smelled of floor wax and mothballs. "Nice," she lied.

"Give me five minutes and I'll be ready to go."

As Robert was getting into his uniform, Maggie explored his quarters, especially the smallest kitchenette she'd ever seen. Army issue flatware, Army issue utensils, Army issue soap: all so boring compared to Isabel's house...*well, my house.*

In the bedroom stood one green locker and a twin bed with a green wool blanket. She discovered a small porch off the bedroom walkout so she stepped outside to have a look. Activity on the nearby airfield caught her attention. She leaned on a wooden railing that looked as though paint was the only thing holding it up and watched a long line of soldiers boarding an Air Force transport. They wore huge backpacks and carried huge rifles.

Seeing these men going off to war brought a sting of tears to her eyes. The wives and families left behind. The flag-draped caskets that would return to so many of them. She prayed that Robert would never have to go with those men again.

Robert stepped up behind her. She felt his arms slide around her waist. He began to kiss her neck.

She leaned back into his strength and kindness. "I wonder where they're going."

"Afghanistan, where I just came from. They're in Charlie 2-5, my unit, well, until I muster out." He turned Maggie around and brushed aside a lock of her auburn hair so he could look into her beautiful gray eyes. "Maggie, if you believe in God, you might want to say a prayer to keep them out of harm's way."

"I just prayed that for you."

"They're the ones who need His help now."

Maggie closed her eyes and made the sign of the cross. Opening her eyes, she saw the solemn look on his face. "I think I love you."

Robert pulled her in close. "I've had that same thought even though we've only been together for a short time."

She took a deep breath and let it out hard. "Brenda better not mess this up."

"Brenda?"

"My friend...it's complicated."

He gently broke away and straightened his collar. "I guess we can head on over to the hanger and join the party."

As they walked hand in hand toward the airfield, an officer marched toward them. Robert immediately let go of her hand and saluted him. "Good evening, sir."

The officer returned the salute and nodded to Maggie. "Ma'am." Then as he passed by, "You two enjoy your evening, and that's an order, Captain."

Maggie had a question. "Why did you salute him first?"

"I'm a captain, he's a major. He outranks me. The officer with the lower rank always salutes first. Enlisted men always salute first."

"I hope somebody comes by who has to salute you first." Maggie hugged his arm, proud to be at his side.

After walking into the huge hanger, they sat at a long row of tables put together for the party. Out of the blue, a sudden cramp threatened to buckle her over. She fought for a breath. "Oh, no."

"Are you all right?" Robert asked with a roadmap of concern on his face.

"This isn't supposed to happen." She looked around. "Ladies' room? Where's the ladies' room?"

Robert pointed to the far end of the hanger. "Let me go with you."

Another cramp and a wave of panic about killed her. "I'll manage. You stay here." She made a beeline for the ladies' room and burst in, holding her stomach. Four women turned to look at her. "Does anyone have a tampon?"

One lady dug in her purse. "Here you are, honey."

A very relieved Maggie said, "Thank you...this wasn't supposed to happen." The tampon wouldn't end the cramps, but at least now she wouldn't bleed all over everything. She ducked into a stall.

Minutes later, as she walked back to the table, hiding her pain, she had an epiphany. *I'm not a zombie. I can't be a zombie. Zombies don't have periods. So I still must be HIV positive.*

She was hoping to get laid tonight but now she didn't dare. *I'll just have to wait.* That would be okay. Robert would have to wait, too. *He'll be horny as hell when we finally do it. Come to think of it, so will I.*

As they sat there drinking wine and listening to an orchestra, a voice came over the loudspeaker: *"Attention all ranks, Commanding General is in the building."*

Robert stood. Maggie started to stand but he told her, "Stay seated."

"As you were." Major General Lawrence Taylor made his way past several tables, heading toward Robert and Maggie.

Maggie's throat went dry. She recognized the stout, potbellied man, even with his clothes on. Quickly, she fished through her purse, found her sunglasses, and put them on just as he arrived.

"I understand you're leaving the Army, Captain."

"Yes, sir."

"I'm sorry to be losing one of my finest officers."

"Thank you, sir."

"You two have a wonderful evening."

"We plan on it, sir."

General Taylor laughed and walked off, shaking his head.

Maggie breathed a sigh of relief, thankful she had brought the sunglasses.

Robert, on the other hand, questioned her motivation. "What's with the sunglasses?"

Maggie touched her temple for effect. "I have a slight headache is all."

General Taylor's aide-de-camp came over and handed Robert a note. "From the General."

Maggie's heart sank in a bog. Had the General recognized her and sent Robert a warning. *You're dating a whore, fool.* "What does it say?" She held her breath.

"I don't have to stay on the base. When we're done, I can take you back to your hotel."

"That's great." She exhaled. *Thank you, God.*

After the festivities, as they made their way back to Robert's quarters, Maggie held his hand, and swinging it back and forth, she had no idea they both had different expectations as to what was coming next.

***

At the Church of the Risen Jesus, Debbie and Chloe were not having the time of their lives. They hated sitting in a circle of chairs and listening to a plump, middle-aged woman reciting from the book of Proverbs. *Bible study, what a waste of time.* They were both going to raise hell with Brenda when they got back.

Just when it seemed the night couldn't get any worse, the bulbous Reverend Leroy came in with a video camera and began to record the proceedings...but with a special interest on shooting close-ups of Debbie and Chloe.

What the hell is he up to?

While all the other women had their hands clasped, their heads bowed, and eyes closed in prayer, Debbie and Chloe spread their legs for the camera and licked their lips for Leroy.

"Keep praying," he told the others as he backed up to get a better viewing angle under Debbie's skirt. In his haste for the perfect shot, he knocked a small crucifix and a picture of Jesus off the front table. This brought the prayer session to an abrupt end.

Debbie and Chloe quickly closed their legs, stood, and headed for the exit. Waddling, Leroy lit out after them but his loyal parishioners quickly surrounded him. "When can we see the video?"

"Ladies, please..."

Debbie led the way outside. "I hate this fucking place."

"Brenda should have sent Maggie. She's used to dealing with asshole men."

"She can't do double duty. Let's just go after Janice. If we can turn her, then it will be a lot easier to get his money."

"You're forgetting the Lesbian Zombie motto."

"Oh, right. One of us has to fuck him so we can fuck him over." Chloe grasped her throat with her hand and, tongue sticking out, made gagging noises.

"I'll tell you what, Chloe. Let's flip a coin. The loser fucks Leroy. The winner gets the wife. Deal?"

"Okay." Chloe pulled a quarter from her purse. "Ready?" She flipped the coin. "You call it."

"Heads," Debbie commanded the coin.

Chloe revealed the result on the back of her hand. "Damn. It's heads."

"You lose," Debbie chortled. "Enjoy giving short fat and ugly a blowjob. I won't be thinking of you while I'm kissing the wife and blowing her mind."

"Give me another chance."

"Okay. I'll call it this time." Chloe flipped the coin and called, "Tails."

The coin turned up heads.

Debbie squealed. "I win again. You lose again. He's all yours, Chloe."

She whined. "Let's go the best three out of five."

"No."

"I don't want to fuck the fat guy."

"Tough shit. I won fair and square. Janice is mine."

"I hope she has F.B.O."

As Debbie drove BBBD's Cadillac back to the hotel, a disgusted Chloe sat in silence, brooding over Reverend Leroy. It was bad enough she'd have to fuck a man, but this man was a lecher. He'd enjoy fucking her too much. The thought of his blubber bouncing on top of her made her stomach turn over, but she had to stiffen her resolve. Her sacrifice would be for a good cause.

I'll suck him all right...and bite off his balls.

***

Seventy miles away from Debbie and Chloe, a happy Robert and an even happier Maggie sat in a porch swing. She tried to stretch out her legs and reach the railing but couldn't, so Robert did it for her, which gave the swing an extra push.

"This is fun. I've always enjoyed swinging."

"Maggie, we really don't know very much about each other. Tell me where you grew up and a little about your family."

Oh dear. I'm not prepared for this. I'll have to lie again and hope he never learns the truth. "I'm an only child...*true*... Never knew my dad...*true*... He left us when I was eleven years old...*lie*... I never got to finish high school...*true*... because I had to help my mother make money...*lie*... for us to live in our Bayonne, New Jersey, one-bedroom apartment...*lie*..."

"I'm so sorry." Robert gave the swing another shove.

"When I was fifteen, she died of an accidental overdose...*lie*... I went to live with my aunt and uncle in Brooklyn...*lie*... They both died in a car accident when I was eighteen...*lie*... I've been on my own since then, working at various jobs to get by...*lie*." Keeping a straight face, she added, "Does this make a difference to you? I'll understand if it does."

Robert put both feet on the railing and stopped the swing. "Maggie, I'm falling in love with you...wait. Let me change what I just said. I am in love with you. It's heart-wrenching to listen to what a tough life you've had. In spite of that, you are perfect. You're sweet, kind, caring and smart, and did I mention you're beautiful? I love you the way you are and I want you to be my wife. You'll never be lonely or feel unloved or worry about money. The only job you'll have is being my wife, my helpmate, and the mother of our kids. What do you say?"

She couldn't breathe. Her heart was jumping around like a happy hamster in a cage and her eyes were all blurry from a rush of happy tears. *This is happening so fast, my mind can't connect the dots. Lesbian Zombie...loving housewife...mother of his children... HIV positive. Lesbian Zombie...*

"My god, I can't believe it."

"Breathe, breathe, Maggie. I wouldn't ask just any girl to trust me with the rest of her life."

Wiping tears away with the palm of her hand, she hugged

him, and with her head under his chin, she whispered, "I'll take the job."

He kissed her ear. "You've just made me the happiest man alive."

"I'm just getting started."

"I better take you back to your friends at the hotel so you can get some sleep. Tomorrow, I'll pick you up at nine to meet my dad at the donut shop. He'll be very happy with our news."

Maggie shuddered inside. *I hope my lies are never discovered.*

***

At the Waldorf, Brenda and Monica were each killing off a bottle of Merlot and looking down from the rec-room window at the people walking on the 49th Street sidewalk below. The entire face of the Intercontinental Barclay was aglow with lighted windows.

Monica took a swig from her bottle then brought up the subject that was always present in her thinking. "Remember, Brenda, how you said we would go to Paris and execute Baby Doc?"

"Of course."

"When I have things going really well with Duda, I want to take just enough time off to get the killing done."

"But not right now. Things are starting to go our way. Hey, look. There's Chloe and Debbie down there...on the sidewalk."

Chloe was waving her arms at Debbie, and Debbie stopped to poke her finger in Chloe's chest.

Brenda creased a brow. "I don't think they're very happy."

Monica yelled down fifteen stories, "Welcome back."

Chloe and Debbie looked up and promptly gave her the finger.

Brenda took another drink from her bottle and shrugged. "Ah, shit. More trouble."

Monica dropped her now empty bottle of Merlot in the trash and patted a depressed Brenda on the shoulder. "It might not be all that bad. Maybe they are mad about something other than their church marks."

Brenda and Monica didn't have to wait long to find out what had them steamed. Both girls came in fuming and immediately went into a rant. "We hate him."

"And his church."

"I am not too crazy over his wife either."

"Fuck you, Debbie. She'd be a better lay than the fat man." Chloe stripped off her clothes. "I'm not going back." She got in the hot tub and sank out of sight under the water.

Brenda looked at Debbie. "What's that all about?"

"She lost the coin toss. Gotta fuck Leroy. Sore loser."

Brenda scoffed. "It's not the end of the world."

All of a sudden Chloe surfaced, slinging water with her hair. "I got it...an epiphany...to solve the Leroy problem. Let's just kill him."

"No." Brenda nixed that idea but added, "Look up Donna across the street. That'll give you something else to think about."

Just then, the door lock clicked and in walked a very jubilant Maggie. "Robert asked me to marry him," she sang.

Brenda looked at her crosswise. "Really?"

"And I said yes."

Debbie jumped in. "Now that you two are engaged, did you finally fuck?"

"For the tenth time we did *not* have sex. When we do, I'll make sure you're the first to know. I'll take a selfie of us screwing and e-mail it to you."

"I will hold you to that."

"Robert's picking me up at nine in the morning to meet up with his dad."

Brenda, with some misgivings nevertheless, hugged Maggie. "I'm proud of you, sister, but always keep the goals of the sisterhood paramount. We're after his father's money. You don't have to marry the son to get it."

"I want to be Mrs. Robert Mark Johnson Junior, but I swear

the sisterhood comes first."

Brenda didn't believe her. Once she got married, she'd be gone, living the dream. Ha!

While the girls rehashed their goings-on, across town, Alfons Duda was on the phone with his head of security. He had some good news. "Monica is staying at the Waldorf Astoria, sir."

"Hmmm. Pretty expensive for being unemployed."

"Mr. Duda, what do you want me to do now?"

"Keep an eye on her."

Chapter 8: DECEIT CAN BE A TWO-EDGED SWORD

As the sisterhood lay around on a Saturday morning, Maggie was out the door without so much as a goodbye. On her way out to meet Robert, she stopped at the check-in counter to drop off a check that Brenda had made out to the kennel that was taking care of Girlie Dog.

She happened to see a somewhat chubby, bearded man step up to the counter and ask the clerk, "What room is Monica Abelard staying in?"

"Oh my god." She ran outside to Robert's car. "Wait a few minutes," and without further explanation headed back to the hotel door only to turn around and run back and kiss him then make a U-turn for the hotel again. Once inside, she grabbed the lobby house phone and couldn't dial her room quickly enough. *Pick up. Pick up, damn it.*

Brenda answered, heard Maggie shouting, "Duda is on his way up."

"Thanks for the heads-up," Brenda said calmly. "We'll take care of it. Now go meet Robert. Okay?"

"Yes, goodbye."

Brenda called out, "Monica, Duda is on his way up."

"What? How?"

"Go in the bedroom. I'll tell him you'll be back in an hour. Chloe. Debbie. Go with her."

The bedroom door closed not a minute too soon. Brenda

headed for the front door just in time to hear Duda knocking.

She opened the door, surprised to see a sharply dressed chubby man with a short gray beard, ogling her white bikini and red sheer. Exhaling, she acted perturbed. "I gather you're not room service."

Alfons leaned left and right to look around her. "I'm looking for Miss Monica Abelard."

Brenda played dumb. "Who are you?"

He extended his hand. "Alfons Duda. I met her yesterday and would've called, but I misplaced her number."

Brenda heard him curse Adrianne in his head and knew exactly what had happened. "So you're the KOMA CEO."

"She was going to apply for a job—"

"Monica was so upset about your suit, the coffee stain and all, she came back crying, said she messed up her chance to work at your company."

"She overreacted, I assure you, miss..."

"Can I guess that since you're here the job opening is still available?"

"A brand new position has just opened up. May I speak with her?"

"She'll be back in an hour. Should I have her call you?"

"Ask her to drop by my office at one o'clock. We can discuss the job over lunch."

"What kind of job?"

"It's complicated."

Brenda read his mind. Adrienne, his personal secretary and fuck buddy, was pissed when he fired her to make room for Monica. "I know Monica will be thrilled to meet with you for lunch today."

"Thank you, miss..."

"Brenda. Brenda Ayler."

"It's nice to make your acquaintance."

As he walked off down the hall, Brenda heard him think: *I wouldn't mind a threesome with Brenda and Monica. But first, I'll have my head of security check into them and their friends to find out what they do. They can't be living in a place like this unless one of them is rich.*

Brenda took warning in his thoughts. This security character found Monica. What would he find out about the sisterhood? Could mean trouble. *Fleecing Duda may be harder than I thought.*

The sisters in the bedroom, with their super hearing, heard all that had transpired. After coming out, they gave each other high-fives. Monica was in. "But I'm not going to fuck or suck him for a few weeks...to make him so horny that he'd pay anything to get it."

"That's not exactly how it works, girls."

Monica's expression turned serious. "So how does fucking and sucking turn into money?"

Brenda took out a business card from her purse and handed it to Monica. "Look at this and pass it around."

"The LZ Foundation?"

Brenda nodded "The trick is in my logline: *Saving the Lives of Women Worldwide.*"

Debbie jumped in. "I have a question. How do we save the lives of women worldwide?"

"With a lot of new Lesbian Zombie recruits. We'll start out in countries where women are put to death for merely looking at a man walking the opposite direction down the street. These women are slaves in those countries now, but an army of Lesbian Zombies will change all that."

"How?"

"First, our army will kill off the religious assholes in ways that'll terrorize the male population. Then we'll castrate a large number of them, but not all. And not all women will be converted to Lesbian Zombies. We need a core section of the population to be fertile to replace the people dying from old age, disease, accident, etc."

"What about the other countries?" Chloe asked. "There are a lot of religious pricks in every country, and even here in the

United States, like those two pricks that Debbie and I are going after."

"It will be even easier here, Chloe. Our ranks will take over the government, one congressional district at a time. It'll take a lot of money and fucking the right people, but remember our motto. *Before we can fuck them over, we first have to fuck them.* It'll sustain your motivation if the going gets tough."

"And this LZ Foundation? Is it up and running?"

"We'll set it up and get our marks to bankroll what will be their own destruction, eventually. It's kinda like sentencing them to death but they have to bring their own rope."

Monica said, "I like the concept, but how will I get Alfons Duda to donate big time from his oil drilling company, KOMA LTD? It's worth thirty-five billion. He's not dumb about his money."

"Yeah," Debby put in. "Why would he ever donate on a scale that would ruin him?"

"Because, girls," Brenda said. "If she doesn't get what she wants, then he's not going to get what he wants, and believe me, he wants Monica something fierce. Not having her, and not having her happy will drive him crazy. Why else would he fire his private secretary and sex toy?"

"So he could hire me," Monica said.

"All the powerful men we have in our sights don't care about money as much as they care about their cocks."

Monica was catching on fast. "We will supply them with what they really want, dominance over beautiful and independent women, make them think they own us so they can show us off to their equally rich asshole friends, who will also fall into our clutches. They will donate their wealth to get their rocks off in true Lesbian Zombie fashion. In the long run, the cocksuckers will be digging their own graves."

"Exactly." Brenda bounced another question off her girls. "Once the money starts rolling in, we'll have to funnel it through a third party outside the U.S. What country would that be?"

"Switzerland," Chloe said.

"Take another guess."

Debbie saw the light. "Port au Prince, Haiti."

"Correct."

"What if we get audited by the IRS?"

"No problem. The agents will become instant members of the clan...either as Lesbian Zombies or lady-boys, depending on their sexual orientation."

Monica wondered about something else. "Who's going to run the foundation in Haiti? Jenny?"

"She's too stupid for anything except screwing and stealing money, but I'll find work for her far from our bank account."

Debbie decided there was only one other. "Aurora?"

"She's a dilemma within herself." Brenda sighed. "The ball-less wonder turned out to have more stones than Stonehenge. She outsmarted me when it came to Reinhard and Albert. Showed cunning and compassion where I was quick to judge based on my own distrust of the Nazi wannabes."

"Aurora can't be trusted with our money." Debbie shook her head. "One-track mind...she'd fuck a woodpile if she thought there was a snake in it."

Brenda agreed. "That leaves Cassandra."

"The voodoo witch bitch?"

"She brought me back to life. Our money will be well protected under her watch."

"I still think we should kill all three traitors," Monica added, just to be on the record.

***

At Sam's Donut Shop, Robert and Maggie were seated, waiting for Robert's dad, with donuts and drinks on the table. Robert, not wanting to wait very long to get married, rubbed Maggie's ring finger, now sporting a diamond as heavy as a brick. "What do you think of getting married in Vegas the day after I'm mustered out of the Army?"

Maggie beamed. "That's fine with me. It seems sudden. I don't suppose that has anything to do with me holding off having sex until our wedding night."

"You never said that."

"What if I did?"

A little red-faced, Robert lied. "I'd respect your wishes."

She bent over and kissed his cheek. "You're lying, dear. You wouldn't let that stop you."

"I'm a man of honor. My word is my bond."

"I think about having sex with you all the time."

Robert confessed, "I've never wanted anyone as much as I want you."

An old man sitting at a table next to them said, "Take it from an old guy. Get a room right now. Before you know it, the old pecker is a noodle, and the lady's stockin' up on Double-A batteries to keep warm." He winked at Maggie.

Robert wondered what was keeping his father, got his answer as he flipped open his ringing phone. "Hi, Mike." It was his dad's CFO. "What's up?"

Robert's expression turned grim. Maggie knew the call was bad news.

He hung up. "My dad's had a massive heart attack. I gotta go. Please come with me."

"Of course I will."

Getting in his dad's Mercedes, they headed straight to New London, Connecticut.

Monica was getting ready to have lunch with Alfons Duda.

Chloe had decided to join Debbie in trying to track down Donna across the street.

***

Brenda was ready to go to the grand opening of Jackie's art gallery. Everyone was off on their assigned missions. *I miss my sisters already. It'll be interesting to hear about their day when they come home tonight.*

As Brenda and Monica walked out of the hotel together, Monica said, "Wait a minute. I need one thousand dollars from the safe."

"What for?"

"I will bring it back tonight. I'll tell you what I needed it for then."

"Okay." Brenda laughed. "I just hope you don't pull a Maggie and come walking in with a grand's worth of clothes."

"I promise...Girl Scout's honor."

"I'll wait for you here. Better hurry. You don't want to keep Alfons waiting."

"Oh, yes I do."

Brenda spotted a guy across the street. He looked at her as he answered his cell. Brenda listened to both sides of the conversation and knew he was talking to Alfons Duda. *So that asshole works for Duda and is keeping an eye on Monica for his boss. Well, fuck him.*

Just then Monica walked up. "What are you looking at?"

"The prick over there."

"I saw that guy the moment we walked out. He is trying to act as if he is not paying any attention to either of us. Look at that dumbass talking on his cell and reporting everything to Duda."

Brenda scoffed. "Let's see if he follows us to the subway."

They started walking.

He started walking, kept talking to Duda but kept a safe distance behind the girls. He reported, "They're going down to the subway." Duda said, "Let her go. She probably has a logical answer as to why she was hiding in the bedroom when I was at their suite."

Brenda hugged Monica and whispered in her ear. "Duda knows you were hiding in the bedroom."

"Good to know."

They went their separate ways. Monica headed for the line to take her to the Empire State Building, and Brenda took the train to meet up with Miss Jackie O'Neal.

***

Heading north on I-95 toward New London, Robert was already visibly shaken when his cell rang again. He and Maggie looked at each other and had the same thought: *Don't answer it.* They didn't. It rang again. Robert started to hand his cell to Maggie but pulled his hand back before she could take it. "I'll do it." He looked at the clock in the car right as he answered. "Hello?" He just listened for a moment, then: "Mike, as of now, you're running my company. We'll be there in about forty-five minutes."

Maggie looked at Robert. "I'm so sorry."

Robert took an off ramp, pulled into an abandoned gas station, and turned off the engine. He took off his sunglasses and covered his eyes with the palm of his right hand. "I-I can't be-believe he's gone," he said in a grief-stricken voice. Bending over on his right side, he laid his head on Maggie's chest and cried.

She put her hand on his head and sobbed softly into a tissue that she held in her other hand. Trying to ease his pain she said, "We'll have a baby as soon as possible, and if it's a boy, we'll name him Robert Mark Johnson the Third. If not a boy, we'll keep having babies until we have a boy. Then your dad will rejoice in heaven because his name will live on."

"I love you, Maggie."

"We better get going." She handed him a tissue.

They drove on. After covering the remaining distance, Robert pulled up next to his dad's rebuilt 1947 Studebaker pickup truck. They sat there for a few minutes, gathering themselves, and then Robert got out and walked around to open Maggie's door. Helping her out of the car, a now stoic Robert said, "This was going to be a happy occasion, but now it's anything but. At least he's with mom now and it should be a happy time for both of them. But not for us."

"We can still be happy."

"The last thing he said to me was that he hoped you would

soon be a member of our family and that you had overcome many terrible bad times in your life. I told him that you had told me everything about your past, but he said he didn't think you told me everything. What did he mean?"

A cold blade of fear stabbed her chest. What had she told dad that she hadn't told his son? What was the truth? What was a lie? Had dad seen her with BBBD? Would he even know who BBBD was? What she was...a whore? A prostitute? A caregiver? A Lesbian Zombie? Or not?

"Maggie? What did he mean by that?"

"I don't know."

She said nothing else as they entered Galaxy International, now the company of gloom, but her mind was a whirl of worry. *I want to get married before Robert discovers the truth about my past and kicks me out. I have to get pregnant right away. But if I'm a Lesbian Zombie, I can't get pregnant, but I had my period, so I can get pregnant. But with my HIV, I don't dare have unprotected sex, so I'll never get pregnant. If only I hadn't lied to him...if only I'd let the chips fall where they may. Oh god I'm going to get sick.*

Robert was a good man and he wouldn't go against his father's wishes to make her part of the family, especially if she were pregnant with his child. And even if she didn't get pregnant, or couldn't, she loved him, and she'd fight to keep him, even if it meant going against Brenda's wishes and the goals of the sisterhood. *If I have to, I'll have it out with Brenda. I'm never going to be a man-hater like the others.*

Maggie stood side by side with Robert and shook hands with a million employees, each offering both their condolences for Robert's dad and congratulations on their upcoming marriage.

She'd never been so frightened in her life.

***

One hundred twenty-six miles to the south, Monica was on an elevator to Alfons Duda's office. She thought it was interesting that she was ushered into a private elevator while at least fifty

George S. Naas

people waited for four elevators to open up. When the door opened on the 25th floor, Alfons was there to meet her. Taking one look at her black business suit, but with a Haitian style white blouse emblazoned with native flowers, he had to force himself to look away from her cleavage and into her eyes.

She knew what he was thinking. *Oh, yeah, I just fell in love.*

"I'm so glad I was able to find you. I was sick to death over losing the card."

Before he could say anything else, Monica reached into her purse and took out an envelope containing the thousand dollars and handed it over to him. "I hope this will cover your suit that I ruined. I was so upset over it that when you came over today I hid in the bedroom because I was so embarrassed."

"Monica, I like your honesty. I knew you were there when I overheard one of your friends in the lobby warn you I was coming."

"Please forgive me."

"I want you to be my private secretary, and I would start you off with a yearly salary of $125,000 plus a starting bonus of one thousand dollars." He handed her back the envelope. "This is for you. What do you say?"

She tucked the money in her blouse. "I say, let's talk about it over lunch. It will be my treat."

"Monica, you drive a hard bargain but, hey, we have to eat. Why don't we go down to lunch now?"

As they got on the elevator, Monica noticed twelve employees waiting for a public elevator, so she held the door open on the private elevator. "Get in with us."

They rushed to get in. "Thanks."

Alfons grumped and pushed the 'down' button.

"Okay, it's a little crowded."

The employees chatted away. "Now we'll have more time for lunch." "I have to go shopping." "Anyone seen the new movie Blade?"

Alfons reached over and pushed the *stop* button and the

elevator lurched to a halt. "Listen up. This young lady is Monica Abelard. She is my new secretary."

Everyone in the elevator spoke up. "Welcome to the firm, Monica." "We hope to see a lot of you." "Lucky girl." "We have a football pool."

She held up the palm of her hand. "I was really undecided but all of you just convinced me. How could I turn down Alfons' job offer when I would be working with wonderful people like you?"

Alfons made the elevator jerk back into motion. He wanted to spend as much time with Monica as possible so he bought himself another hour. "Take an extra hour for lunch and thank Monica for it."

They all applauded.

Walking down 5th Avenue with his hand around her waist to guide her, he stole glances at Monica's beautiful breasts while making small talk about New York. "Have you been to Times Square?"

"No."

"I should take you there."

"Where are we going for lunch? I need to know if one grand will cover the check."

He steered her to the left. "Here's where we're going. Albeties, best Italian restaurant in Manhattan, bar none, and I'm covering the tab. End of debate on the subject."

They were seated at a table where they had a great view of the Empire State Building. She and Alfons clicked their glasses, which were full of expensive red wine. "Where's your personal spy? Maybe he got lost trying to keep tabs on both Brenda and me."

Duda put his glass down and laughed so hard everyone in the restaurant looked at him. "You're very observant. Why would you have even noticed him? By the way, he has been with me since we left Poland."

"When I lived in Haiti, I had to be on the lookout whenever I went anywhere. Papa Doc's soldiers were everywhere. I hated them. They raped me, killed my parents, raped and killed my daughter."

"Oh, how terrible...how sad...wait a minute. Papa Doc died in 1974. You're not old enough to have known him."

Monica swallowed hard. Too much information had gotten her in trouble. "In Haiti, we call all the Duvaliers Papa Doc. It was his son, actually, Baby Doc."

The waiter came to take their order.

Alfons told him, "We'll have Strangozzi with black Truffle and serve our food before you serve anyone else."

The waiter took off to get their order started.

Monica looked puzzled. "Why would the whole kitchen staff give us priority over everyone else?"

"I own the restaurant."

She shrugged. "Of course. Let's talk about my job."

"Monica, your job will require some spur of the moment travel. Will that be a problem?"

"Sounds exciting."

"There's one glitch. My mother likes to think she runs the office. Don't let this bother you. If you want to make points with her, when she asks you what is special about September first, what will you tell her?"

"It was the day in 1939 that the Germans attacked Poland."

"Damn, I *am* impressed." He rubbed his trimmed beard. "My previous secretary never heard of World War Two and couldn't find Poland on a map using both hands."

"What was she good for then?"

"She was a good secretary...and I kinda liked her." *I fucked her every day but Monica doesn't need to know that.*

Wow, you are quite the man.

With lunch behind them and the wine dwindling down, small talk was in order until a bear of a man walked up. "Boss, you have an appointment in half an hour."

"Joseph, my word, I was so captivated by Monica that I had

forgotten the time. Monica, this is Joseph, my driver."

The goliath nodded. "Miss."

"My brother, Karol, I must meet with him this afternoon. Seems he always needs some damn voucher approved for one project or another." Alfons wiped his mouth and tossed the napkin on the table. "Monica, I'll see you on Monday at nine sharp. Joseph, take Monica to her hotel." He stood and patted his rotund belly. "A walk back to the office will do me good."

Monica smiled. "See you then."

***

At the grand opening of Jackie O'Neal's art collection, Brenda watched with interest as the rich and the wish-they-were-rich milled around, gazing at Jackie's renditions of Vincent Van Gogh's paintings. Drinking white wine and listening in to what people were thinking about Jackie's work made her chuckle.

A plump woman in her mid-fifties, wearing a dark gray dress and dripping with very expensive jewelry, was looking at the painting of a yellow house. *My god this picture is so poorly painted that Jackie should have called it the Piss Yellow House.* The woman in gray raised her glass to the painting, then realizing what she'd just thought, broke out in a smile and had to stifle a laugh.

Brenda felt a tap on her shoulder, turned, and came face to face with a very drunk Jackie.

"I'm so happy you came back." *Hic.* "This whole thing would be a flop if you were here...er...not here."

Brenda frowned. "Who is that old biddy in gray? She just made a very nasty comment about the yellow house painting."

Jackie bobbed on woozy legs. "She's Barbara Lowe...married to Harold Lowe, one of my invest...ment bankers. What did she say?"

Brenda put her hand up to Jackie's ear and whispered the comment about piss yellow.

"No, she didn't."

"Yes, she did. Ask her. Look right in her eyes and ask if your painting would be better named the Piss Yellow House."

"I'll do just that, the bitch."

Brenda folded her arms and watched Jackie, looking like a woman scorned, confront Barbara and obviously relay the words *piss yellow*.

Barbara dropped her glass and made a quick exit.

Now a victorious Jackie returned to Brenda. "You were right. How did you know she said that?"

"What are you going to do about her disloyalty?"

"First thing Monday...ah...I'm pulling eight hundred million out of an investment fund I have with her husband's firm and put it somewhere else. Maybe Barbara will piss yellow in her panties after that, huh." She laughed.

"You sure?" Brenda questioned her. "You could lose a lot of money over one snide comment."

"I'll do it even if I lose money on the trade."

Brenda saw the opening and took it. "I may have an alternative investment you might be interested in."

"I need a drink." She turned away then abruptly turned back. "Hell, I don't have to stick around here any longer. How about coming with me to my place where we can look at the sea and get drunk together?"

"You have a commanding head start."

"Brenda, you...*hic*... are amazing. How'd you like the way I plucked that old hen?"

"We can talk about that at your place."

"And you can see my place. My place is amazing...like you."

Brenda rolled her eyes. "Yeah, you said that already."

"Jorge," she shouted across the room. "Get the limo."

***

As the limo sped north on I-95 toward Jackie's house, traffic started to jam up. "Oh, crap. Jorge, what's the hold up?"

The driver glanced at her via the rearview mirror. "They're

working on the road, ma'am. For the next six miles it's one lane only in each direction. Looks like we're going to limp along at ten miles an hour for a while."

Both north and south lanes came to a complete stop.

"Shit. Now what?"

Construction crews were moving two large steel I-beams across the roadway.

Jackie poured herself a scotch from the car-bar. "I wonder what they're paying that guy holding the stop sign. I'll bet he's lucky to make nine dollars an hour."

It was at that exact moment Brenda picked up Maggie's thoughts. What the hell? Looking around, she figured Maggie and Robert were also stuck somewhere in this traffic jam. Maggie was thinking of their marriage plans and how she would spend the night with Robert in his quarters on base.

As Jackie continued on her rant about the traffic, Brenda listened intently as Maggie said, *"I'll go with you, Robert." "There's so much to do before the funeral."* Robert talked about the funeral plans for his dad. *"After that I don't know where we'll go." "I have a house we can live in on Montford Lane."* She mentioned Isabel's passing and the will.

As the traffic began to move, their voices faded away. Brenda huffed. *That's settled. Maggie is not a Lesbian Zombie. Somehow, she's definitely immune to the virus. However, this could be a blessing in disguise. Robert Junior was now the owner of a very rich corporation and Maggie has him wrapped around her little pinky. Sweet.*

She decided to tell Maggie that she knew her little secret, and she'd have the blessing of the sisterhood as long as Robert's company made a huge donation to the LZ Foundation, oh, and she and Robert would have to find another place to live.

I've already got dibs on the house.

***

Back at the Waldorf, Monica opened the door to find Debbie and Chloe naked in the hot tub and watching a Texas Hold'em poker tournament. Chloe waved at Monica. "Get a load of these poker players. They just had a pot worth three and a half million dollars."

Debbie had a mouthful of potato chips. "Monica," she mumbled. "Would you get room service to bring us another bag of chips and another sixer of Bud Light? Then come in and join us."

"Yeah," Chloe added. "And get a jar of those spicy dill pickles."

"Anything else?" She saw soggy Ruffles floating among the bubbles. "Ah...for the love of Loa. I want every one of those goddamn chips out of the tub."

Debbie was busy dumping the last of the chips out of the bag and into her open mouth.

"What's the big deal?" Chloe asked. "Hello? That's what the filter is for."

"I can't believe you two. Hello, yourself, Valley Girl. The filter will get plugged up, the water won't be fit to fart in, and the hotel will charge us to have it cleaned out. You two should be glad that Brenda didn't give you an I.Q. test before she turned you into Lesbian Zombies. You two wouldn't have made it past twenty."

Debbie laughed at that one. "We don't need to be brilliant to eat pussy."

"Speaking of which, Chloe, did you hook up with Donna?"

"Yeah. But she made it clear that she was staying with Joanne. Slammed the door in my face."

"Some girls like brawn over beauty I guess."

"I think Joanne was there with her, probably still nursing the ring-nose-job Brenda gave her."

Monica scooped up a floating chip. "Where does Binocular Man fit in?"

"The apartment is his." Debbie crumpled the chip bag and tossed it to the floor. "Donna gives him pussy service so he'll pay her bills—"

"And Joanne's too," Chloe put in.

"He is a U.S. Senator from New York who is only in Manhattan every other weekend. Otherwise he lives in Washington."

Chloe had to ask, "So, Monica, how did things go with Alfons?"

"He is a cross between a hardnosed businessman and a mama's boy. I know this much, though. He loves chocolate pussy. I start to work on Monday, and I will spend the rest of today and all day Sunday reading up on the history of Poland. The way to his bankroll isn't through my pussy. It is ultimately through his mom."

A phone rang causing all three of them to check their cells. Monica's cell was flashing. She answered. "Hello, Brenda."

"How are things with Alfons?"

"I got the job."

"Good for you. I'm at Jackie's place. In her bedroom to be exact. I'll be here until seven or eight then her limo driver will take me back to the hotel. Have you heard from our sisters?"

"Everyone except Maggie."

"She'll be spending the night with Robert. So don't expect her. Bye now."

"Wait. Don't hang up. Tell Debbie and Chloe there better not be any potato chips in the hot tub or there will be hell to pay when you get back."

"Sounds like you just said it all. Tell the girls to play nice."

***

Pulling up to the main gate at Fort Dix, Robert flashed his Military ID to the MP, and then drove to his quarters where he parked but just sat there. Maggie looked at him and cringed at the look of devastation in his tired eyes. "We don't have to sleep together tonight...I'll take the couch."

"I want you with me tonight. Close to me. Holding me. Naked or otherwise, it's up to you."

"I'm so sorry about your dad."

"I worried this would happen. He had several heart problems in the past. A stint. A bypass. AFib."

"He told me the doctors weren't worried...ah...not life threatening."

"Dad didn't want you to worry. He was a tough old goat. I know he really wanted me to meet you and fall in love."

"And you did."

Robert tapped the steering wheel.

Leaning into him, Maggie kissed his cheek. "If it wasn't for your dad, we never would have met. I'll always treasure the wonderful gift he's given me, and I'll always be grateful to have known him. I feel honored."

"We better get inside."

Robert opened the front door for Maggie. She walked to the window and looked out at the runway again. It was quiet, not a soul around. He took her hand and led her to the bedroom.

She sat on the sagging mattress and ran her hand over the rough wool blanket. "It smells like mothballs."

Robert agreed. "The Army has an affinity for wool, as do moths. Problem is, everything in the Army either smells like mothballs or is eaten full of holes. You get used to it after a while."

"It sure is warm in here."

"Let me take care of that." As he began to unbutton her blouse he kissed her.

She kissed him back and smiled as if to say *everything will be okay because I'm yours.*

Slipping out of her blouse exposed her shoulders. "You have a tattoo," Robert commented. "What's special about a rose?"

"I like roses," she lied.

"I have two tattoos."

"Show me." She was happy to have switched his focus away from her Lesbian Zombie tattoo.

Robert peeled off his shirt.

His dog tags caught Maggie's eye. She reached out and took

hold of them. "What are these for?"

"If I had been killed in action, one of the tags would have stayed with my body and the other would have been sent to Battalion."

"Thank God you don't have to worry about that anymore."

"I wasn't worried." Robert turned and showed her the tattoo on his left shoulder: *101 Airborne.*

Maggie ran her hand across the ink. His skin felt warm and firm. "What does it mean?"

"One Hundred and First Airborne Division. We're called the Screaming Eagles because we jump out of perfectly good airplanes."

She shuddered. "I'd scream too."

"The tattoo on my right shoulder... I'm just as proud of it...for my dad."

"The number five and a capital A?"

"The Fifth Army. My dad served with courage and honor."

"I don't know, father and son, so macho. What's a girl to think?"

He gathered her in his arms and kissed her again.

"Oh, Robert," she breathed.

Emboldened, he laid her on her back, slid his hands up her bare stomach to her bra, and worked his fingers up under the cups. *My god.* Her breasts were soft to the touch, by fingers that had pulled the triggers on M-16s and yanked the pins from grenades. Hands that had scaled rock walls and pulled ripcords now cupped the softest of human flesh. Lovingly. Wantonly. But carefully. His heart raced with more trepidation than that first step off the ramp of a C-130 Transport flying high over Kandahar.

When his fingertips found her nipples, she sighed. "I want you, Robert, but..."

"I know. Our wedding night." He kissed her neck and one-handedly unhooked her bra at the same time. The lacy garment fell to the floor. He had to take a moment to look at her, to savor her shape, the pallor of her skin, and the contrasting rounds at the tips of her breasts. His mouth watered and he had to kiss them. When he came up for air: "You're so damn beautiful...I'm such a lucky old soldier."

He pulled her naked breasts into his chest and felt the fire grow between his skin and hers. A small hand found its way to his erection, and to his surprise, she knew exactly how to handle it.

"Well, dear, you feel pretty damn good for an old soldier."

The old Army bed creaked as he got up on his knees and pulled off her skirt. Her panties weren't much bigger than a Band-Aid, a silky soft —

Maggie stopped him. She dared not tell him about her HIV problem. "I just finished my period. It's not a good time for this...unless you want me to get pregnant."

"Pregnant? No. Of course not. Not yet."

"Then use a condom or just hold me until dawn."

"Hell, Maggie. I'll do both."

The panties were history. She unbuckled his belt and unzipped his pants, which landed on the floor with the bra and Band-Aid.

Looking at a now totally naked Maggie, Robert couldn't believe the rapid pace of his heart. "You *are* by *far* the sexiest woman in the world."

"Remember those words when we're married and my belly's as big as a beer barrel."

"Got it."

Condom in place, there came a moment, as the two connected in the most intimate of ways, when time stopped. He didn't move. She didn't move. Their eyes met in a peaceful place, each one knowing, that before this night was over, their lives would never be the same. And when that moment ended, the lovemaking began. Slowly at first, gently, but with each ensuing stroke, each kiss became more frantic, each breath harder to inhale, and before long, every muscle in their bodies was called into action until the final explosion brought them down, down,

down slowly back to earth.

Gasping, Maggie looked at him and smiled. Oh, he was a little sweaty and a little weak, but he was beautiful, nonetheless. She put her hand on his biceps and thought they were made of steel. He was all man, and she was glad she wasn't a lesbian, or a zombie for that matter. Their first sexual encounter didn't last as long as she had hoped, but at least he'd worn protection, and besides there'd be many more opportunities to express their love for each other. For now, they relaxed in each other's arms and made small talk until dawn.

***

Up on Long Island, Brenda and Jackie made small talk too, but often threw in information that each one wanted to know about the other.

Jackie led off, "I was married for three years when I was young and stupid. It didn't work out. Men like to be king stud in the bedroom but don't want to be responsible for anything else." Pointing her glass of white wine at Brenda she asked, "What about you?"

"I was with a total loser who cheated on me, and I was so dumb that I never figured it out until he had taken me for fifty grand and ran off with his ex-wife."

"What did you do about it?"

"I killed him."

Pouring another drink for both of them, Jackie looked amused. "No really. What did you do?"

"I killed him."

"You really killed him?"

"Yep."

"This is fascinating. I have wanted to kill several men and you actually did it. I'm proud of you. I knew that there was something special about you the moment we met. Now I know what it is. If you had a dollar for every woman that, at some point in her life, wanted to kill a man, you could pay off the national debt. How did you kill him?"

"With a big rock. Gave him a headache to die for."

"What happened to his ex-wife?"

"Oh, Jenny? We're friends now. She works in my southern office in Port au Prince. She doesn't miss the asshole either."

"Here, Brenda, hold out your glass. We'll finish off this bottle and bury the dog. What exactly is it that you do?"

"I run a charitable group, the LZ Foundation. Our goal is to help save women's lives around the world."

"How do you propose to save these women?"

"By whatever means necessary. This could be as simple as making sure a restraining order is enforced and letting the perpetrator realize the consequences of violating it by acquainting him with a baseball bat to his face."

"Oh, my."

"Another approach is doing whatever is required to change the laws to protect women on the job, from sexual harassment and abuse, to getting less pay than their male counterparts, to not having the same opportunities at advancement, day care, and maternity leave."

"I was sexually harassed...once. *Hic.* I married him."

"Also we help women and their children escape from shithole countries to safety, by making sure they don't have to have ten kids because that's what their prick husbands demand. Something like the latter is simply accomplished with a pair of scissors and two people to hold the bastard down. We also want to help women make better decisions when it comes to abortion and birth control, decisions that are right for them and not the politically correct assholes who try to run everyone's lives. So that's how I spend my time."

With a serious look on her face, Jackie said, "I'll be right back." A few minutes later she returned with a check for Brenda. "Here's five million for starters. Count me in."

"Well, thank you. I certainly wasn't expecting a donation."

"I'm happy to help. Now I have a lot of business to take care of tomorrow, and I'm sure you do too, so I guess we better call it a night. Jorge will take you back to your hotel."

***

It was nearly midnight by the time Jorge pulled the limo into the loading zone at the Waldorf Astoria. He opened the door for Brenda. "Delightful ride this evening, Miss Brenda."

"You're quite the conversationalist, Jorge. I might have fallen asleep."

"Me too."

"Thanks for getting me here safely." She started off for the hotel entrance when Jorge shouted to her.

"Wait. Miss Jackie has a present for you. It's in the trunk."

"Really?"

"I almost forgot." He popped the lid and handed Brenda a large box containing samples of all of Jackie's skin products. There were a lot. The box must've weighed a ton.

"Tell her I said thanks." She pretended to muscle the box through the lobby and into the elevator where she set it on the floor and sat on it for the ride up fifteen stories.

At the suite, she unlocked the door and Debbie was there to meet her. "Maggie is spending the night with Robert."

Brenda set the box on the floor. "I know."

"She cannot possibly deny fucking him now."

"I don't think she's a lesbian," Chloe said.

"Where's Monica?"

"She went to bed."

"You and Debbie better get some sleep because tomorrow morning you've got to get up early. You don't want to miss the church service."

"Do we really have to go?"

"We were hoping you would forget."

"Well, I didn't."

As the sisters stormed into the bedroom, they made sure to slam the door to show their disapproval.

Brenda disrobed and took a well deserved dip in the hot tub. She turned on the water jets and was suddenly surrounded by soggy potato chips whirling around on the surface. "Girls, girls, girls..." She cupped her hands and collected then threw them out the rec-room window.

Two well-to-do couples looked up to see the cascading debris. One man brushed them off his suit as if they were spiders. "What the fuck?" echoed up from the street.

This brought a laugh from Brenda. Picking up a half full bottle of Dom Perigean Rose, she took a drink and turned on the TV. It went back to the previous station that Debbie and Chloe had been watching. Texas Hold'em Poker. She got caught up in the ritzy play just like Chloe had. It was then that an idea struck her. *We could play in these cash games, and with our ability to read minds, we could almost never lose.*

***

With the dawn, Chloe and Debbie were up and ready to go to church. They wore matching dresses, except Debbie's was pink and Chloe's was purple. Their shoes were the same style, except Chloe's were pink and Debbie's were purple.

Brenda was in the rec-room, sitting in the rocker and enjoying a cup of coffee when Debbie and Chloe came over for her approval. "You're wearing the exact same dresses, just different colors."

Chloe said, "What? We never noticed."

"Yes, you did. You two did that on purpose...so everyone will think you're lesbians."

"We are lesbians. So what?"

"Change your clothes."

"No. We are leaving like this. Goodbye."

Brenda sat there in silence with a big frown on her face.

Monica came in wearing her Haitian nightgown with flowers all over it, just like most of her clothes. Stretching and yawning she looked at Brenda. "What's the matter with you?"

"Chloe and Debbie just left wearing the same outfits. They're trying to sabotage their assignment. Pisses me off."

"Can you blame them? You pushed them into this church thing. What did you expect? You know they hate Reverend Leroy, and Chloe doesn't want to fuck him. Let them complain. They'll come through in the end."

"Monica, do me a favor. I need a drink...and make it a strong one."

***

At Fort Dix, Robert was up early too. He was on the physical training field working out with his company. When his men started making cat calls and whistling, he had no idea why until he turned around and saw Maggie up on the reviewing stand with her sunglasses on, watching them go through their workout routine. He turned back to his men dressed in green t-shirts, green shorts, green socks, and black combat boots. "At ease, you guys. That beautiful young lady up there is my very-soon-to-be wife, so show some respect. No cat calls. Now I want four laps up and down the field doing the bear crawl. Maybe next time you'll refrain from acting like idiots when a lady comes around."

"Yes, sir," the troops shouted in unison.

"Now I want to see some assholes and elbows. Move it."

They got down on all fours and scrambled across the field.

Robert waved at Maggie. She joined him and they walked off the field, holding hands, as usual.

"That was mean, Robert."

"It won't kill 'em."

"What are we going to do now?"

"We're going to that little PX over there and have breakfast then back to my quarters. You'll wait there while I see the doc for my discharge physical, then I'll take you back to your hotel."

"I had fun."

"Then I'm going back to New London to get things squared away with my dad's company, I mean my company. Hell, I doubt

I'll ever think of it as my company. Maybe our children will think of it as theirs someday."

***

At the Church of the Risen Jesus, Debbie and Chloe sat in the very back row in the upper deck of the massive auditorium to watch the televangelists' show. Debbie skimmed the program brochure she'd been handed at the door. "Two fuckin' hours. Somebody kill me."

At first, only a woman and her three kids occupied the other end of their pew. She was breastfeeding her two-month-old baby and paying no attention to the other parishioners who arrived and scooted past the girls' naked knees.

"Where do all these people come from?" They must've been six thousand strong.

The lights dimmed and the service started with several praise-Jesus songs, then Reverend Leroy came out on stage. He read from the book of Isaiah: "But he was pierced for our transgressions, crushed for our iniquities."

The congregation cheered, "Amen."

"The punishment that brought us peace was on him."

Debbie elbowed Chloe. "I wonder what that shit is supposed to mean?"

"Amen."

"I don't know, but this mob seems to get it."

Reverend Leroy then went on a rant about how the lord hates adultery. This went on for an hour and a half.

Debbie wondered just how observant these people would be of the goings-on around them. Her guess was they'd be so focused on the spew from the stage, a lesbian invasion would go unnoticed. She leaned into Chloe and put a large hymnal on her lap, thus blocking the view of anyone's wandering eyes.

"What are you gonna do to me?" Chloe breathed.

Debbie slid her left hand up Chloe's right leg, up under her dress, beneath the book, and began to rub her clitoris through her panties.

She gasped. "Oh god that feels good."

Debby whispered in Chloe's ear. "Forget about what we are here to do and enjoy this special time we have together." She rubbed a little faster...with a little more pressure. The softness of her folds warmed Debbie's heart, as well as every nerve down below. "Like it?"

Chloe inhaled shallow quick breaths. "Oh, yes, Debbie, oh yes."

As Leroy and Janice finished their joint sermon, Leroy bellowed, "Do I hear an amen?"

"Amen," the congregation shouted.

Chloe clenched her fists and arched her back. "Yes, yes, yes," she cried out from the crest of her climax. "A fuckin' men."

"Shhhh." Debbie slowed the pace, her finger now soaked in Chloe's sweet nectar. "You are going to get us busted."

Chloe's heart was beating a hundred miles an hour, then ninety and eighty and seventy, all the way down to normal again. Gasping air, "Debbie...that was the best orgasm I've ever had."

"Remember this one when fatso is humping you."

She glanced down at the stage. "How much more of this creep-show is left?"

"According to the program brochure, we are now on page two at the bottom. One more song, then they'll pass the collection plate while they sing another song, and then we can get the hell out of here."

"But we're supposed to make nice with Leroy and Janice."

Debbie licked her finger. "Who can fuck after a show this boring?"

"I missed a whole bunch of it." Chloe fanned her face with her hand.

As the offering plate was being passed from one person in the row to the next one, Chloe managed a sleight-of-hand maneuver, put a dollar bill in and took a hundred dollar bill out. The only one who saw it was Debbie. She worked very hard not to laugh.

As people left the church, the row Debbie and Chloe were in emptied out last. It was then that the person running the video equipment for the television broadcast just happened to zoom in on the girls.

In Dayton, Ohio, Chloe's ex-husband was watching the live broadcast. Still in bed, Tim sat straight up. "Chloe?" *Thank God she found the Lord. Perhaps she'll be glad to know the emergency room doc was able to fix my penis hole. Unleaded gasoline dissolves superglue. Burned like a motherfucker, but I pee really good now.*

Seeing her on TV couldn't have been a freak coincidence. The good Lord wanted them to get back together and procreate. However, that Latino bombshell Chloe was with could present a problem. They were holding hands on their way out of church. *What to do...*

***

Debbie and Chloe got back to the hotel at 11:00 and were met by an apologetic Brenda. "I'm sorry about the church assignment. I know you hate it. But you've gotta tough it out."

"We had fun anyway. Chloe, tell her."

"Debbie finger-fucked me under a hymnal. I had the best orgasm ever."

"In church?" Brenda huffed. "Have you no shame?"

"It gets better." Chloe held up the pilfered Franklin. "I made us a nice one hundred bucks from the collection plate."

"Good grief."

Debbie spotted the box Brenda had brought in. "What's in there?"

"Samples of Jackie's skin care products."

Chloe and Debbie tore into it just as Maggie rushed in, the taste of Robert's last kiss still sweet on her lips. "Yes, Debbie." Maggie beat her to the punch. "Counting last night and this morning we had sex three times."

Debbie looked up from the open box. "Finally. What kind of

sex?"

"Heterosexual intercourse...the good kind."

"Call it what it is, girl. It's plain ol' fucking."

"Not for Robert and me." She got up on the coffee table. "I have to be honest with you all. We love each other."

"Come on—"

"No. It's real."

Chloe asked Brenda, "Is falling in love with a man permissible for Lesbian Zombies?"

"Let her finish."

"I know why I had my period and why I love Robert's cock in me."

"Why?"

"You can't have your period."

"Yeah, what are you talking about?"

Maggie held up her hands to command silence. "I'm not a Lesbian Zombie."

Now Debbie jumped in. "Maggie, don't be silly. Of course you are a Lesbian Zombie. Monica and I did a number on you."

"It didn't work. Does that mean I'm out of the sisterhood?"

Chloe shrugged. "Now Brenda will have to throw you out the window."

"All because I'm not a Lesbian Zombie?"

"You are."

"I'm not."

"Girls." Brenda ended the debate. "I've known for some time Maggie is not a Lesbian Zombie, but she's still a sister and I'm sure she'll help us with our goals. Now, no more bickering or I'll be tempted to throw myself out the window."

"Won't life be grand," Chloe muttered.

"I want to check out of here tomorrow morning, so today we're all going to start moving into Maggie's house." Brenda flung her long red hair over one shoulder and focused on Maggie. "We still get the house, right?"

"What's mine is yours, Brenda...except Robert."

Brenda smiled. "That's my girl."

Taking a limo to 127 Montford Lane, Maggie was the first one out of the car. She dashed up on the porch of their new house and smiled broadly. "Brenda, we want you to open the front door for the first time." She handed her the spare key Isabel had given her long ago.

Brenda waved the key and put it in the lock and then opened the door. Girlie Dog jumped up into her arms and instantly started licking her face.

Brenda couldn't stop laughing. "Girlie Dog. I missed you too."

Monica said, "We got her out of the kennel for you as a surprise."

Brenda hugged both Girlie Dog and Monica. "Our family is complete again."

Monica's cell rang. It was Alfons. She rushed outside to answer the call away from all the chatter. "Alfons, what a pleasant surprise."

"Do you have a valid passport?"

"Yes, of course."

"I need you to fly with me to Paris."

"Paris? Oh, my. I have never been to France."

"We leave this Friday...and don't wear any of those flowery getups you got. Not very European."

"Wonderful."

On this warm Sunday afternoon, the sisterhood enjoyed a cookout on the back deck of Maggie's new home. A new hot tub had been installed, but it was vacant of naked Lesbian Zombies. Monica got up and told the sisterhood about what had happened to her and her precious daughter at the hands of Papa Doc's minions. She explained that Baby Doc was living in Paris with his grandkids and how badly Monica had wanted revenge for years...and now she finally had her chance.

"Fate has put me in a position to exact my pound of flesh. I will be there next Sunday. I won't be able to do anything that day, but the following Monday I expect I will. Alfons will be in a meeting all day long with oil executives. I know we all have free will, but I want a vote of the sisterhood to sign off on Baby Doc's execution."

"Kill the son for the sins of the father?" Chloe questioned.

"Like father like son," Monica spat. "When Father hightailed it to France, Son stayed behind to continue Father's legacy of tyranny, oppression, robbery, and murder. His death will make amends for both bastards."

They all voted in favor with Maggie abstaining. She didn't think she should vote—not being a Lesbian Zombie and all, even though the sisterhood told her she was as much a part of them as anyone.

Brenda clarified the plan. "This vote was for Baby Doc, and if it's impossible to kill him, then you're shit out of luck, Monica. The grandson, Francois, will not be harmed. The granddaughter Anya won't be harmed. Yes, Monica lost her daughter, an unthinkable death, but we're not animals like Papa Doc and Baby Doc. The grandson and granddaughter are off limits. We don't kill women and children, not ever."

They all agreed to the plan.

Debbie stood. "Since we are taking votes. I have something to vote on. I want to fly down to my hometown in Mexico and visit my family. While I am there I want to kill someone too. I told you all the story of how I escaped my would-be rapist and got on a wrong plane to Haiti. I'd love to kill the prick and bring his balls back as a souvenir, but still, I long to see my family. We all have a slack week coming up, except Monica, so it is not interfering with any other plans. Chloe and I don't have anything scheduled until next Sunday. If I leave tomorrow I can be back by Saturday. All in favor?"

Chloe waved her hands like she was trying to stop a bus. "Attempted rape isn't a capital crime punishable by death. Why kill him?"

"He betrayed my father's trust. Who knows how many

women he successfully raped...and maybe even murdered? Women don't need men like him on this earth."

"I'm good with it," Chloe voted.

All hands shot up in agreement.

"Good then, it is settled."

Chloe asked Maggie, "What will you be doing?"

"Robert is busy with work and his father's funeral arrangements. I won't see him until the end of the week."

Debbie had to laugh. "Don't kid yourself, Maggie. Your Robert got a good taste for your pussy. He ain't gonna wait a whole week to get some more."

Girlie Dog barked in agreement.

As the sisterhood watched her run in circles trying to catch her tail, Brenda got an email from Jackie. *I really need to see you tomorrow. Something terrible has happened. I will send my limo for you. Please be ready by 10:00.*

Brenda let all her sisters read the email and then texted Jackie back with their new Montford Lane address and: *I'll be ready.*

Monica touched Brenda's hair, lovingly. "What do you think she wants?"

"I have no idea but she obviously trusts me, and if I can help her, maybe she'll cough up another five million."

High-fives went all around.

A rainstorm ended the cookout for the sisterhood but even though they went into the house, Girlie Dog continued to play in the yard.

Maggie did get a call from Robert. As she ran up the stairs to one of the bedrooms for privacy, Debbie yelled, "I told you so. Yum yum pussy."

***

Waking up at 5:00 a.m., Brenda made a trip down to a small grocery store for some staples since the refrigerator was empty of just about everything except beer and wine. Waiting fourth in line to checkout, she reached over to get a package of dog biscuits for

Girlie Dog. For a brief moment her sweater slipped off her shoulder, exposing the rose tattoo. The two people directly in front of her saw the tattoo and told the clerk who immediately had another checkout lane opened up just for Brenda. She started to say she'd wait her turn but decided that might look like a sign of weakness so she went to the proffered checkout.

While the rest of the sisterhood slept in, Brenda and Monica sat on the back porch, each with a cup of black coffee in hand and huddled under the table umbrella against a relentless drizzle.

Monica turned on a small TV to watch the local news. Brenda wasn't paying any attention until she heard the announcer say, "The stock market is opening on a sad note this morning. Harold Lowe, of Lowe, Wright, and Morgan Investments was found dead by his wife at 6:00 p.m. last night. The Long Island coroner's office said *It appears he was killed by a self-inflicted gunshot wound to the head.*"

Brenda's stomach clutched with guilt. "Shit. He's dead because of me, you know."

Monica tisked. "Brenda, you didn't do anything wrong, so don't crucify yourself. Besides, you didn't close Jackie's account with him. She did."

Brenda wasn't comforted by Monica's words of assurance. To make things worse, the rain that started the night before was still coming down. Girlie Dog, who loved the rain, ran back up on the porch and started shaking the water off her body, splattering it all over Brenda and Monica. The difference being Brenda was dressed and ready to go meet Jackie whereas Monica was still just wearing her flowery nightgown.

Squealing against the cold, muddy spray, Brenda booted Girlie Dog in the rear end. "Do that somewhere else."

Girlie Dog let out a yelp, took off into the rain, and ran for shelter under the bushes at the back of the yard.

All the commotion woke up the rest of the sisterhood. Debbie came out first. "What the hell is going on?"

"Where's Girlie Dog?" Chloe asked.

Then came Maggie with her cell up to her ear, talking to Robert and obviously not all that interested in what happened.

Dripping wet, "Okay, ladies," Brenda said. "Since my clothes have dog water dirt all over them, I got a little upset with Girlie Dog. She's hiding in the bushes somewhere. Now excuse me. I have to go take a shower and change clothes."

***

As Brenda rode in Jackie's limo with Jorge at the wheel, she had one thing on her mind: *Is Jackie going to accuse me of Harold Lowe's death?*

While Monica rode in Alfons' limo with Joseph behind the wheel, she too had one thing on her mind: *Is Alfons going to start groping me the minute I walk into his office?*

Back at the homestead, Chloe and Debbie were busy drying off a wet Girlie Dog. The door bell rang. The girls exchanged puzzled looks. "A solicitor?"

"Salesman?"

"Maybe it's Avon calling." Chloe opened the door to find a soaking wet and crying Donna, a pleasant surprise at first, until she looked a little closer. "My god, Donna, you're a sight. How did you get two black eyes? And look at the bruises on your arms. Let me guess, Joanne did this to you."

A shaking and hyperventilating Donna managed to say, "Joanne thought I was going to leave her...to be with you. She got drunk and beat me and raped me with a broom handle."

Chloe ushered her in, hugged her, and then sat her down on the couch. "She won't bother you here. How did you find me?"

"The clerk at the Waldorf had your forwarding address."

Chloe gave her a glass of water. "Why didn't you call the police? They would have locked her up."

"What good would that do? They'd have let her out within hours. Then she'd hunt me down and kill us all."

"We're not afraid of Joanne."

"She has a gun."

"Not afraid of guns either."

"Huh?" she muttered.

"Since you found our new address, she can get it too. When did you see her last?"

"An hour ago...outside the Waldorf—"

"She's got our address." Chloe frowned then: "She could be on her way over here right now."

"What are we going to do?"

"Wait. And if she shows her mug anywhere near here, we'll call the cops."

"What if they don't get here in time?"

"Then I'll have to kill her myself."

Debbie chimed in, "Brenda said we are not supposed to kill a woman, ever."

"This is an unusual circumstance. If Joanne shows up, she dies."

Donna burst into tears. "I don't want her to die."

"It's her or us, Donna. When are you going to take a stand and stop coddling your abuser?"

"She has battered woman syndrome," Debbie said.

Chloe huffed. "Donna, would you rather sit on the porch, and when she shows up, beg for forgiveness? Maybe she'll calm down, or maybe she'll just start shooting. And if she comes through the door, the only way she leaves is on a stretcher in a body bag. So do you want to grovel or do you want to fight?"

"I'll stay here with you and fight."

Chloe smiled "All rightie then. You got some balls after all."

***

Unaware of what was going on back at 127 Montford Lane, Monica stepped out of the limo and met a smiling Alfons Duda waiting for her in the lobby of the Empire State Building.

"You're right on time. I'm impressed."

"I am efficient and dependable. Did you expect anything else?"

"No. Sorry. I guess not."

Monica read his thoughts: *This woman doesn't worship me like the others. I'll have a hard time imposing my will on her.* She came to the conclusion that she could make him a submissive and she would become his dominant. As he showed her around his office she decided: *I am going to turn the tables on him. He is going to worship me. Let me guess...this woman coming toward me has to be his mom.*

A woman in her seventies approached: short and plump and wearing a cheap black pantsuit. She had that commanding look on her face, furrowed brows and stony eyes.

"Monica," Alfons said. "I'd like you to meet my mother Maria."

Well, at least she has a nice name.

As Maria shook Monica's hand and smiled, Monica read her thoughts. *At least she is prettier than the last one, and she does seem to have a lot more class. I wonder if she knows anything about Poland.* "Monica, do you like to travel?"

"Yes. In fact, Alfons tells me that we are going to Paris."

"It's very nice meeting you, Monica. I'm sure we'll get to talk more in the near future." Maria turned and walked away.

Monica asked Alfons, "How did I do?"

"Very well. Your first day on the job is going to be a long one." *I may even get a blowjob after work.* "But that will be okay. You can come in late tomorrow."

Monica cringed. *The fucker thinks I am going to suck him off. He is sadly mistaken. The Lesbian Zombie virus in my saliva combined with his orgasm might not be healthy for this macho man.*

Alfons handed her a company AmEx card. "Use this to get a couple new outfits for Paris."

She snatched the card from his fingers, "Don't mind if I do," and headed to the office door. Most of his staff watched her gloat. They had seen the same expression on several other women over the past few years. "I'll be back in time for lunch, Alfons. Take me somewhere expensive."

***

Up on Long Island, Brenda had just gotten out of the limo when Jackie ran up to her. "I'm so g-glad you're here, Brenda." Her voice cracked with distress.

"Jackie, I'm so sorry about Mister Lowe."

"I don't give a shit about Lowe." Jackie hustled her toward the house. "He was an asshole anyway."

"Then why are you so upset?"

"My maid. Melinda. She had a massive coronary."

"Oh no." Brenda didn't fake her concern. "How is she?"

"If she dies, I don't know what I would do."

"How can I help?"

"Console me. Come on into the house. She's upstairs in her room."

In Melinda's bedroom, Brenda saw her hooked up to several machines. Some beeping. Some hissing. All keeping her alive. *So fragile is life. Not a day should be taken for granted. Not an hour. Not a minute...*

Jackie rushed over to the dying woman, sat at her bedside, and held her hand. "The doctors say there's no hope." Tears slipped down her cheeks.

Brenda could no longer watch the old woman weep. She strode to the window and looked out at the waves breaking on the shore. Endless waves, millions and billions and trillions of them over the millenniums past and the millenniums yet to come, while life is finite and minuscule in comparison. *But not like me, a zombie, perpetual in every way, immune to the frailties of the human condition.* She grappled with an epiphany. *I have the power...* Then without turning around, she asked, "What if there's a way to save Melinda?"

"It's hopeless," Jackie cried.

"What if she wouldn't be the same Melinda you now know, but she'd be alive and well. What would you say?"

Jackie looked at Brenda's back through a teary glaze. "What do you mean?"

Brenda turned to face Jackie. "There are forces at work in this world that only a few people know about. Me for one. I have the power of life over death."

"Brenda, you're talking crazy shit. I need you to be serious at a time like this."

"What would you give to see her live?"

"Anything, but that would take a miracle."

"Give me twenty minutes alone with her. You'll believe in miracles when I'm through."

"I don't know...I—"

"She's dying, Jackie. What do you have to lose?"

"Okay." She stood. "I'll go out, but I still don't understand."

"You will, very soon."

Brenda locked the door and pulled the covers off Melinda. She didn't look too good. Her saggy breasts were divided by a ragged wound stapled together after emergency bypass surgery, same with her inner thighs where the doctors had harvested her arteries. Blue veins webbed her pale skin, a sure sign of oxygen deprivation from faulty blood flow. Brenda could only hope Melinda had enough brain function left to detect what comes next.

Using the same technique she'd used on Monica, Brenda bent to the woman's dry lips and kissed her. Kinda felt like kissing a shoe, but with a little saliva and a probing tongue, her lips became suddenly supple and sweet. When Melinda's tongue greeted Brenda's, she pulled back, waited a few moments, and then unhooked all the tubes and wires that were keeping her alive. While the alarms sounded, Brenda kissed her again and let her fingers play between Melinda's labia, stimulating her clitoris into a massive orgasm.

Melinda's body tensed, shuddered, and she gasped. The surgery wounds closed, the staples dissolved, and her skin radiated with new vitality. She was now, indeed, a beautiful Lesbian Zombie.

Several people started banging on the locked door. "Let us in."

Melinda opened her eyes, all dreamy from sexual bliss. "I know you... You are my queen."

"And you are my sister." Brenda pulled the covers up over her rejuvenated body.

"Open this door." *Bang. Bang. Bang.*

Under the cacophony of annoying alarms and persistent pounding, Brenda strode to the door. "Say nothing except that you feel much better." She unlocked the door and stepped aside.

Jackie, a nurse, and a cardiologist rushed into the room only to stand at the foot of the bed in speechless amazement.

Melinda said, "I'm feeling much better, Miss Jackie."

Jackie leaned over and kissed Melinda's forehead. "Doc, is she going to be okay?"

The Cardiologist took her pulse. "Yes. Strong as a cheerleader at homecoming. I don't know how this is possible."

Jackie smiled at Brenda. "I do." Then she directed her next words to the medical staff. "You all can leave...and take this noisy junk with you." She pointed to the machines then hugged Brenda. "She looks so young. How did you do that?"

"First, we have to let her rest. She'll come downstairs when she's ready. Meanwhile, let's drink wine on the beach and watch the breaking waves. I'll tell you of amazing things."

***

Back on Montford Lane, the sisters spotted Joanne, called the police, and explained the situation. The cops were taking their sweet time getting there, but as luck would have it, from the sisters' perspective, a plainclothes detective was looking over the charred remains of BBBD's house when he saw Joanne stalking up the sidewalk. That in itself wasn't alarming, nor was the white bandage that covered her nose, but the revolver in her hand, that was a different matter. He immediately pulled the snub-nose .38 from his shoulder holster. "Drop the gun."

"Fuck you." Joanne fired, hitting the officer in his right thigh. As he went down, he fired three times. Joanne took two rounds in the chest and one in her side. She dropped the gun and fell face-down in a mud puddle. A few bubbles came up, and then stillness.

Donna rushed over to her. "Oh my god."

Chloe ran to the officer's side as he writhed in pain. "You're going to be all right." She applied pressure to the bleeding wound.

Debbie called 9-1-1. "Officer down," she screamed to the dispatcher. "Maybe now you will come quickly."

Weeping, Donna pulled Joanne out of the mud puddle and into her chest, and then showered her mud-covered face with kisses. "I love you...*sob*... I'm so sorry. This was my fault...not yours."

The wail of sirens tore up the morning calm. Patrol cars careened to a stop. Cops jumped out, guns drawn. "Show us your hands." A fire truck and ambulance joined the fracas.

"Show us your hands."

The wounded detective shouted, "NYPD. It's all right, officers. The suspect is down."

Chloe stepped out of the way so the paramedics could help the detective. When no one was looking at her, she licked the detective's blood off her hand.

Debbie rushed over to console a grief-stricken Donna.

"Don't touch me." She rocked Joanne in her arms. "I hate all of you. I wish you were all dead and my precious Joanne was alive."

"She beat the crap out of you," Debbie reminded her.

"But she loved me."

"Domestic violence isn't love. It poisoned your relationship, heterosexual or gay, and led to this kind of tragedy. You shouldn't have let it go on this long."

"Don't you get it? I loved her." Crying even harder she managed, "I wish I were dead. I wish I were dead."

Firemen had to pry Joanne from her grasp. "This one's DOA," a medic declared.

The police pulled Debbie and Chloe aside. "We need your statements."

They left Donna sprawled on the sidewalk, shuddering in despair.

***

As day turned to night, Monica discovered that Alfons did not have sexual thoughts about her, at least not at the present time. He needed her help setting up his conference room for a Texas Hold'em cash poker game. His rich friends would come over every other Monday night for a high-stakes game of luck and bluffing.

Monica made sure there was plenty of booze, food, and porn films on a giant screen for when someone wanted to take a break. She was ready to watch the game and to make sure everyone's glasses were full. However, there were seven players, plus Alfons, a chair for the dealer, and one empty seat because of a no-show. This gave her an idea. She whispered to Alfons, "If you will bankroll me, I will take that empty chair."

"What's in it for me?"

She batted her lashes at him. "If I lose, I'll do anything you want, and I mean *anything*."

All right, a blowjob is in the bag. "And if you win?"

"I get to keep my winnings and that *anything* I mentioned before is out the window."

He laughed. "There's no way you can win against us guys. We're pros."

"Then I guess you're right. That blowjob you thought about earlier is in the bag."

"Huh?"

"Let her play," someone shouted.

"Fresh blood," someone else put in.

"Okay." Alfons grinned. "Boys, I'll bankroll her for three hundred grand if you all have no objections."

"It's your money to lose," another said.

Alfons lit a cigar. "Monica, it looks like you get to play with the big boys."

When the dealer showed up, Monica got everyone a drink then announced, "Get your own drinks for the rest of the night." She pressed PLAY on the video. The screen lit up to an orgy scene that left nothing to the imagination. "And get a load of the porn video."

Monica sized everyone up as the dealer explained how the game was played and the rules. In seat #1 was John, an investment banker; seat #2 was Ralph, owner of CarNet, an internet company; seat #3 sat Alfons, no introduction needed; seat #4 Ted, Congressman from District 12 New York; seat #5 Charles, container shipping magnet; seat #6 Bill, VP United Petroleum; seat #7 Dale, President Western Capital; seat #8 Jackson, a lobbyist from D.C.; and seat #9 Monica. Larry, the dealer, sat opposite them.

As the first hand of two cards was dealt facedown to each player, Monica read their thoughts: #1 had a 5 and a jack, he folded. #2 had a pair of 10s, he checked. Alfons smiled at Monica because he had two kings. He raised. #4 had a 7 and a 2, he folded. #5 had 2 and 2, another folder. #6 held a 10 and a 4, he folded, # 7 had 5 and 6 of spades but folded, #8 had 2 fours and folded. Monica looked at her cards: Ace-Ace.

"Hmmmm... I raise ten thousand dollars."

Everyone folded except Alfons with his kings. *I can break her right now but I'll just call her ten grand.* He sweetened the pot.

The dealer laid the three community cards in the middle, face up: a king and two aces.

Alfons was beside himself but only checked to Monica who raised another ten Gs.

The forth up card was an eight of hearts. No help to either one.

Monica knew that even if the next and final up card was a king, Alfons would still lose. His big problem was that he didn't know that.

Invasion of the Lesbian Zombies

The last card was a fourth king for Alfons. He checked, hoping to lure Monica into making a big bet. Now all he had on his mind was how great it was going to be when he got her in the bedroom. He kept remembering her *anything* promise.

Monica fiddled with her stack of chips. "If I want, I can bet all my money. Is that right?"

Alfons chuckled. "Sure. You must have a good hand or a bad bluff."

"I think so. I bet all in." She shoved all her chips forward.

Alfons matched her bet. "I call. What do you have?"

Monica said, "What do you have?"

Despite the reversal of the call, Alfons was so eager to beat her, he laid down his cards. "Four kings," and with that said, he reached out to rake in the pot.

"Not so fast." Monica grinned. "I have four bullets." She laid down her hand. "Read 'em and weep, boys."

A shocked Alfons couldn't believe it.

Congressman Ted in seat #4 leaned forward. "She called her aces four bullets. I thought she didn't know how to play poker."

Monica giggled. "I never said I didn't know how to play."

"We just assumed it," CarNet Ralph stated stupidly.

Monica pulled in the pot. "I think I'll call it a night. Alfons, here is your $300,000 back." She slid him half the pile. "Cash me out."

Speechless, Alfons pulled stacks of cash from his safe, missing the blowjob more than the dough.

"Could you have Joseph take me home? I don't want to get on the subway with this much cash in my purse." Her rub-it-in-his-face comment brought a laugh from everyone at the table, except Alfons. "See you in the morning."

***

On Long Island, Jackie and Brenda finished off one and a half bottles of white wine while waiting for Melinda.

"There's something you have to understand, Jackie. You'll

never see the old Melinda ever again."

She scoffed. "I don't believe in the black arts and Voodoo religion. Zombies? Give me a break." She swallowed more wine.

"Then how do you explain that?" Brenda pointed down the beach.

A young woman in her early thirties strode toward them. The strong sea breeze tossed her long white gown to and fro, like something out of a beautiful dream. The sight of her stirred butterflies in Brenda's tummy.

As she got closer Jackie asked, "Who the hell is she?"

"That's Melinda."

"No fuckin' way. I'm not that drunk. She's not even limping."

Melinda sauntered up to Jackie. "See, no more limp, Miss Jackie. On second thought, I'll simply call you Jackie from now on."

A spellbound Jackie didn't know what to say, just sat there, mouth agape like a fish on a Long Island pier.

Again, Brenda tried to explain the unexplainable. "You see...Melinda is one of us now, the sisterhood of Lesbian Zombies. She has no more pain and she's young and beautiful."

"I-I..." Jackie stammered. "I want that for me. How much will it cost?"

"Even with all of your wealth you can't make yourself young again. Only I can do that for you, and if I do, you'll have to do something for me."

"Anything," Jackie cried.

Melinda just stood there all smiles, looking beautiful in the breeze.

Brenda sighed. "I have to go now."

"Go?"

"You and Melinda should finish off the last bottle and talk things over. I'll call you in the morning."

"Promise?"

"Jorge," Brenda called to the house. "Would you be a dear

and bring the limo around?"

She rode home, excited with the knowledge that one of the pieces she needed to take the world away from men was now in place. Jackie certainly wanted to be young and beautiful, but would she pay the asking price?

Later, while Chloe and Debbie were telling Brenda about Joanne's shooting, in walked Monica doing a happy dance. "Girls?" She turned her purse bottom-side-up and dumped three hundred grand on the floor. "Get a load of this."

Chloe's blue eyes got big around. "Man. I don't even want to know what sexual act you had to perform to get that kind of cash."

"Just one hand of Texas Hold'em, but now I have to hope Alfons doesn't fire me tomorrow morning."

Brenda shot her a stern look. "Why would he do that?"

"Because I won and he's out the best blowjob of his life."

"Nah," Brenda scoffed. "He's not going to fire you. Now he wants that blowjob more than ever."

***

There was another member of the sisterhood who was also very happy. Maggie. She was lying on her back in Robert's loving embrace, their connection made in heaven with only a thin prophylactic between them. Her thoughts were only of her true love and their future together. She relished the day they'd be man and wife and couldn't wait to be pregnant with their first child. Her life would be complete and her terrible past just a fading memory, *as long as Doctor Jackson pulls off a miracle.*

Robert not only fulfilled her sexually, he filled her heart and soul with hopes of better days to come. Now basking in the afterglow of their lovemaking, she snuggled into him. Jet engines roared outside the window, the flight-line abuzz with a flurry of new activity, more Charlie 2-5 soldiers off to Afghanistan. "I wish we could get married right now."

He put his finger on Maggie's lips. "Soon." He propped his

head up on his right elbow. "After the funeral."

"Have you made all the plans?"

"Dad wouldn't want some big affair. He just wants to be buried next to mom. So, that in mind and the fact that he'd said his goodbyes to all his employees in a video he'd made, there's nothing to do except carry out his last wishes. This Friday we'll go to a private service. Just you and me."

"Then we can get married?"

"Get some sleep so we can make love again in the morning."

"But I'm wide awake."

"Then why wait until tomorrow?"

Maggie giggled. "I don't mind."

Game on.

***

Back at Maggie's house, well, the sisterhood's haunt, Debbie was on her cell with United Airlines, booking her round trip ticket to Mexico City. "That's right. Arriving Mexico City at three p.m. Tuesday afternoon and returning Friday at nine p.m."

As Debbie got off her cell, Brenda spoke up. "Don't do anything rash. Just see your family and enjoy the time off."

"I should call them."

"Nah, keep it a surprise."

"I am going to bed now." She dashed up the stairs toward her new bedroom but stopped to pick up Girlie Dog and hug her. To bug Brenda she whispered to the dog, "Don't worry, Girlie. If Brenda kicks you in the butt again, I'll report her to the Humane Society."

When Tuesday morning rolled around, Debbie was out the door in a flash. She caught a shuttle to JFK International. Monica was sitting on the front porch steps as Joseph drove up. He got out of the limo and tipped his hat at her. "Ready, ma'am?" He opened the rear passenger door.

Monica stood and dusted herself off. "I will ride up front with you."

Driving off, Joseph commented, "You made a big splash last night. The boss ain't never going to get over losing to you. The guys make cracks like, *"Look out, Alfons. Monica just may come back to see if she can win the whole company from you."*

"I hope he is not a sore loser."

"He's going to be out to get even with you."

"Silly man." Monica laughed. "Tell me about his family?"

"His dad is a big boozer. Karol, his brother, he's kind of a shifty guy but doesn't mind spending Alfons' money. You already met his mother. She's all right, but for god's sake, don't repeat anything I tell you or I'll be back in Poland, working with the Nazi hunters."

"Joseph, World War Two has been over for seven-plus decades. There can't be anyone left to hunt. They have to be all dead by now."

"You are right, but for some Polish families like the Dudas, they want to keep looking. So if you want to make points with Alfons' mom, kiss up to her about the Polish sympathizers. The Nazis should all be killed."

I guess she wouldn't like the Heinrich SS gang. On second thought, she might like to hear how Brenda and I trapped them and killed them.

The limo pulled into a loading zone at the Empire State Building. Joseph ran around and opened her door. As she got out, she patted his smooth cheek. "Thanks, Joseph, for the ride and the information."

In the lobby café, she saw Alfons sitting in his customary place, obviously waiting for her. She sat across from him, his face obscured by the Wall Street Journal. Reaching over the table, she pulled the paper down and looked right at him. "Do I still have a job or am I fired?"

With a sly look on his face, and thoughts of how he wanted to fuck her, he said, "Of course you still have a job. You're just not invited to any more of my poker games. I'd hate to see you send all my rich friends to the poor house."

She smiled. "In Paris, I am going to give you a chance to win what you really want, and it surely isn't money. You don't give a damn about the cash. You just didn't like losing when you had thoughts of taking me to bed after the game. The same way you did many times with that bimbo that you finally fired. Am I right?"

Alfons picked up his orange juice glass and leaned back as far as he could in the chair. "Monica, are you a physic? I have never met a woman like you in my life."

"No. I'm not clairvoyant either. Careful though, I don't want to see you spill orange juice on yourself."

"The way you spilled coffee on me? The more I think about it, you did that on purpose."

"You will always wonder." Playing on his ego, she added, "I do like you, though. Powerful men turn me on, and you are about as powerful as a man can get."

He downed his juice. "I like the way you see me."

As they got on the private elevator and the door closed, Alfons pushed her up against the wall and tried to kiss her on the mouth, but she turned her head to the side. "No kissing on the lips." So he groped her breasts instead. This she didn't complain about, a little tease, as she wanted him to count the days until they left for Paris. When his hand dropped to her crotch, she pushed it away. "Not so fast, Romeo. We will see how things are between us when we go to France. What do you want me to do for the rest of the week?"

Alfons didn't hesitate a beat. "I want you to make our itinerary, set up everything, hotels, limo, and restaurants, everything except the flight. We have our own company jet at LaGuardia."

"Nice."

"One thing we need get straight right now." He squared his shoulders to her. "We'll only need one hotel room with one king-size bed. Saves cash that way. Is that going to be a problem?"

She stepped off the elevator on the twenty-fifth floor.

"Maybe for you." She winked.

A moment of speculation passed...then a smile gleamed in his eyes. "Good." He harrumphed. "Now I want you to get familiar with the office. Your desk will be in my office foyer. You'll be given an AmEx card with your name on it, so you can give me my card back any time now. Use your card for all costs on business trips plus incidentals plus use it to make yourself look like a million dollars. One last thing, Joseph will take you wherever you need to go. Do you like the way your new job is starting out?"

"When do I get my AmEx card?"

***

At 35,000 feet, Debbie was watching a movie in Spanish and counting the time until she would be back in her homeland and far away from the kid sitting behind her; he kept kicking the back of her seat. For a fleeting moment she thought what a pleasure it would be to throw the little bastard off the plane, but there was no way to open the door in flight.

Leaving Chloe all alone in the house with Girlie Dog, Brenda was once more on her way to Long Island. At the same time, a tired Tim Dawson had just arrived at JFK with one goal in mind: to find Chloe, though he had no idea where to look for his ex-wife, except for the Church of the Risen Jesus. He rented a car, checked in to a motel, and planned to go to the church tomorrow, hoping someone would remember seeing her there.

After the usual one hour and thirty-five minute trip, Brenda found herself being ushered into Jackie's house, only this time it was a beautiful Melinda who did the honors. She led Brenda all the way through the house to the swimming pool out back. She scanned an area of tall potted ferns intermingled with padded deck chairs, various umbrella-shaded tables, and other chairs set out helter-skelter in the sunshine. The kidney shaped pool had steps to get in at each shallow end, and it was nine feet deep in the center. Several individual air mattresses floated about. A single wrought-iron gate in the three-foot redstone perimeter wall opened to a path that led down to the beach. Jackie was nowhere to be seen.

Brenda sat on a folding pool-side recliner. Melinda brought her a glass of white wine. A splash behind her prompted a quick glance to the pool where Jackie's head soon popped up out of the water. She swam to the edge and smiled at Brenda. "Before you even ask, I'm still thinking about your offer."

"How do you like the way Melinda turned out?"

"I like it a lot, and Melinda is girl-crazy over the outcome. She can't keep her hands to herself."

"Then what's your holdup?"

"I don't know what you'll have me do in return."

"What does it matter?"

Getting out of the pool revealed that she was stark naked and butt ugly. She picked up a towel and began to dry off her hair and bump water out of her ears. "What if I don't like being a Lesbian Zombie? Do I get a refund and my old self back?"

"No."

"How about if I keep the zombie part, live forever, and not the lesbian part, and still get laid? Do I get a partial refund?"

"Afraid not."

Jackie plopped her bulk on the recliner next to Brenda. "Melinda is beautiful, I have to agree, but to be honest, it's not natural. She's a rendition of Melinda, not the original Van Gogh."

"You should have seen my original Brenda Van Gogh. Look at your tits. They're already sagging below your ribcage. One day you're going to trip over them. The only way they can go back to perky and cute is my way. Besides, you're more interested in women than men anyway."

"How do you know that?"

"I neglected to tell you that Lesbian Zombies can read the minds of normal people. That's how I knew that Barbara Lowe made that crack about your painting. At the time, you thought she had announced it to the world, but in fact, she only thought *piss yellow house*. Because of that, you pulled your investments, and her husband is now six feet under. Technically, his suicide was both our faults. Still, I'd say you got your pound of flesh."

"She'll get over it. He was running around on her anyway. He even tried to fuck me. I never liked the prick. Barbara should thank me."

"So what do you say?"

"How much is it going to cost me?"

Brenda grinned. "Is everything too much?"

***

At last, for Debbie, the long arduous flight came to an end in Mexico City. Taking a rental to the Mexico City suburb of Colonia Condesa, she got out of the car and made her way to her parents' front door. She was so excited to see her family that her heart was beating double-time. Then the excitement turned to confusion. The house had been painted a light brown over the white stucco. Why would her father do that? Why would her mother allow it?

She stepped up on the wooden porch. Trembling fingers retrieved an old key from her purse. Another setback struck when she discovered that her house key no longer worked the lock. Made no sense. Her confusion led her to knock on the door, ready to surprise her family.

The door opened to reveal Pedro wearing a wife-beater shirt, stained with only God knew what. Panic prickled down the back of her neck. The guy who had tried to rape her years before grinned at Debbie's shocked expression. Pedro laughed. "Debbie, Debbie, you are back. You must want to fuck me after all."

She fought the instinct to flee. "What are you doing in my parents' house?"

"This is my home now, compliments of El Paco for my loyalty." Pedro laughed even harder. "I abandoned my old place with the shack in the backyard. Ate the chickens. Shot the dog."

Terror drove icicles of fear into her throat. "Where is my family?"

"Would you like to come in for me to explain? Perhaps some tea, or do you still like Tequila?"

"Don't be a dick. What happened to my family?"

"Oh, such language you have learned since you left."

"You have no idea, so start talking."

"Your dad crossed the wrong people. All he had to do was let you pleasure the kingpin, El Paco, go out to dinner with him, to start, and maybe fuck him later, but your father said no and tried to smuggle you out of the country."

"Why would he let that snake touch me?"

"Your family paid a very big price for his disloyalty."

"But you were my father's friend. You betrayed him."

"The fool overestimated my loyalty to him. When you escaped, El Paco executed your father and brothers, your mother last, after he raped her. Their deaths are on you, little girl."

Her heart almost stopped. "I do not believe you."

"They are all buried in the old cemetery. Go see for yourself, but I assure you, I watched while El Paco raped your mother. She looked like she was enjoying it, well, before he cut her throat."

Debbie's zombie nature began to boil over, but she had to steel herself against the disgusting comments and quell the urge to rip out Pedro's heart and eat it for a snack.

"I thought he might let her go, or at least lock her up in one of the cartel's sex-trafficking whore houses, maybe to fuck her again later, but she was so stupid to say she was going to El Paco's rival cartel, Bendoso, so he had to kill her to prevent a gang war, at least that was his excuse."

Debbie slumped to the porch wood. "Now what am I to do?"

"If you have no place to go, you can stay here with me. However, you know the price for the room."

"Never." Debbie ran out to the street, crying. *I must tell someone but who? The Policia? Hell no. This is Mexico. There is no justice here. Just corruption at every level.*

Hoping Pedro was lying, she drove to the cemetery where she found the graves of her family. Crushed and overwhelmed with grief, she leaned on her mother's tombstone and hugged the rock as if she were hugging her warm mother. Debbie stayed this way for several hours, until the sun began to set. She then went back to her parents' house to kill Pedro and eat his liver. To her dismay, another setback. The place was surrounded by the *Policia*. More corruption at work, she knew, cops protecting bad guys for a share of the drug money.

She couldn't kill him now, so she drove back to the airport. On the way, she tried to contain her emotions and dry her tears. Sunglasses went on.

While changing her return ticket to a flight out that night, the woman agent couldn't take her eyes off Debbie. "Do you have any luggage?"

"I travel light." She sniffled.

"Your gate is A3." She handed Debbie her boarding pass. "Are you all right, Miss?"

Debbie adjusted her sunglasses, realizing they weren't hiding her despair. "I will be back with my friends, maybe on the Day of the Dead. Then I will be better."

"You will have a wonderful time."

"I am counting on that." She looked at what appeared to be a very sympathetic ticket agent. "Would you do me a favor?"

"I don't know. Does it involve any nudity?"

Debbie appreciated a little lesbian tease. "I have the names of four people buried in the old town cemetery." She helped herself to the agent's pen. "I want some flowers put on their graves." She wrote the names and slid the note and pen to her. "My family."

"Ouu, how did they die?"

El Paco, the snake. "A snake killed them."

"Huh?"

With her chest hurting from the unbearable pain, she took five hundred dollars from her purse. "For the flowers and your trouble."

"This is way too much money."

"I am sorry...what gate did you say?"

"A-3. You have an hour before boarding starts."

She tipped her sunglasses up to show the sincerity in her bleary eyes. "Thank you."

With compassion in her voice, the agent said, "I'm sorry about your family."

Debbie walked away without a reply.

All the way back to Manhattan, all she could think of was how each family member looked the last time she saw them. She remembered how her father had said, "We will see you soon in San Diego, and then he put two hundred dollars in her purse for emergencies. She recalled hugging him goodbye, the warmth and love. "I love you, Daddy."

Then her thoughts turned to Pedro and his sickening smile. Vengeance boiled in her heart. Pedro and El Paco would pay for the death of her family with deaths of their own. She would make them suffer terribly, perhaps during the Day of the Dead celebrations when their screams would blend in with the festivities. Each would beg for mercy, but she would kill them anyway.

***

Back on Long Island, Jackie and Brenda had just finished their dinner when Jackie suggested a late-night swim in her lavish pool. Brenda set her cell on the poolside table. "I don't have a swimsuit."

Jackie's response was to strip to the buff. "Neither do I." She giggled and watched Brenda disrobe. The stunning redhead had all the right stuff in all the right places. Comparing Brenda's perfect breasts to her own sagging jugs, she again thought about being a Lesbian Zombie.

Brenda had heard her thoughts and assessed the situation. *If she converts, then we'll have two powerful allies onboard: Jackie and Alfons. The jury is still out on Maggie and Robert. Maybe she can get a few million out of him for the foundation. But how can I break through Jackie's reluctance?*

After a swim and more drinking, Jackie dried off and asked Brenda to rub some of her, *Jackie's Soft Skin Restoration Cream* on her entire body. "A massage with a happy ending would be nice."

Brenda agreed and went in the house to Jackie's bathroom to get the skin cream. She picked up a jar of the greasy concoction and imagined the rubdown to come. A dilemma tripped her up. Jackie had no idea that the outcome of her *happy ending* could change her life forever. All it would take is one juicy kiss... Brenda thought to warn her but realized Jackie's doubts about joining the sisterhood could easily be overcome. She just needed a little push to get her onboard.

Then I can conquer the world and no one will see it coming until it's too late.

She found Jackie lying, not by the pool, but on a massage table she'd set up in her room. The lights were low, and candles flickered around the perimeter. Ribbons of delightful incense smoke rose from burners strategically placed on the dresser and nightstands. She was lying naked on her stomach with a bath towel covering her backside. Brenda had to chuckle. *To bring out the lesbian in Jackie, just add alcohol.*

She started on Jackie's doughy back, rubbing in the cream, softly and methodically, kneading the tense muscles until they relaxed.

Jackie moaned with pleasure. "You missed your calling, girl."

"You haven't felt anything yet." Brenda went to work on the backs of Jackie's thighs with the same precision, but she added intermittent forays under the towel to teasingly touch her woman-flesh, only to quickly retreat and run her slippery hands down her legs. An occasional shudder told her Jackie was enjoying herself tremendously.

She bent to Jackie's ear. "Turn over," she whispered.

As Jackie obeyed, the towel slipped to the floor.

Brenda started applying the cream on Jackie's neck and slowly rubbed down to her breasts. That garnered another moan of approval. Brenda cupped more cream in her hand, and as she massaged Jackie's breasts, she squeezed them a little, sometimes with one hand, sometimes with two, and then worked circles around her nipples, often pausing to pinch the hardening nubs between her thumbs and index fingers.

Jackie whimpered with delight, then: "If you don't kiss me, I'll go totally insane."

The invitation was made. The die was cast.

Brenda leaned to Jackie's mouth and kissed her, tenderly at first, but as Jackie raised up her knees and spread them, her mouth became more wanton and her breathing more rapid. Brenda responded with her tongue to create a juicy and passionate kiss Jackie would never forget.

Knowing the time was right, Brenda slipped well-lubed fingers between Jackie's folds and into her pink valley, causing her to gasp and arch her back. Her nub swelled in response to Brenda's gentle caresses, her legs straightened, and her hips thrust upward to increase the pressure on the hand that so lavishly loved her.

"I love you, Brenda," she whispered.

"I know."

She cried out, "Oh, how magical you are." Waves of orgasmic pleasure rippled up her spine. She clamped her thighs tight around Brenda's hand so as not to let the ecstasy end until a final surge of quivers released her from carnal bliss.

Breathing hard, her mind a-blur in colorful explosions, she failed to notice the changes taking place: the smoothing of her skin, the uplifting of her breasts, the slimming and trimming of a body once besieged by gravity, general wear and tear, and alcohol abuse.

Brenda backed away to admire her handiwork. *How fitting the artist has become a work of art herself.*

Jackie's heavy breathing subsided. She closed her dreamy eyes, and even as she slept, she didn't stop smiling.

Melinda joined them, but not with good news. "Your cell

was ringing down by the pool. I answered it for you. Monica wants you to call her back, some kind of emergency with Debbie."

Brenda felt a jolt of trepidation. "Stay with Jackie for me."

"Of course." Melinda retrieved the towel from the floor and covered Jackie's gorgeous body.

Down at the pool, Brenda dialed Monica. "What's wrong now?"

"Debbie is flying back from Mexico."

"Why? She's not due back until this weekend."

"Her family has all been murdered."

Brenda's stomach lurched. "That's terrible. When will her plane get in?"

"One a.m."

"Okay, I'll leave here right away." She hung up and ran into the house. "Jorge, ready the limo."

"Yes, 'm."

She ran upstairs to Jackie's room. "Melinda, I have to go. Family emergency. Keep an eye on her. When she awakens, she'll be confused."

"I know. Been there, done that."

"I just hope she's not angry at me."

"I'll tell her it was her skin restoration cream."

"Ha. Good one."

Downstairs, the limo idled in the drive. Brenda jumped in. "The house on Montford Lane."

She rode the entire way in silence, stewing over yet another complication in her plan.

At the house, and with the sisterhood intact, minus Maggie, they piled into Jackie's limo. "The airport, Jorge."

They got there in time to see Debbie at passenger pickup, flagging down a cab. "There she is."

Jorge blocked the cab and opened the door for a very sad-looking sister. He'd been listening to the sisterhood discuss the tragedy in Mexico City. Even though he didn't know Debbie personally, he thought he could help. "Ladies..." he peeled away from the curb. "I have friends in Mexico City. Dangerous friends. All I have to do is snap my fingers and the murderers of your family will all be dead before the sun comes up."

Debbie looked at her shaking hands. "Thank you...but my sisters and I will handle it ourselves, I hope on the Day of the Dead. It would be so fitting a time for revenge."

The first to hug her was Brenda followed by Chloe and Monica. Debbie put her face on Brenda's shoulder and cried while Chloe and Monica rubbed her back and cried with her.

Brenda's motherly instinct flared up in a rage. How dare anyone upset her sister in this way? She would count the days left until the Day of the Dead, *and then it'll be killing time in Mexico City...Lesbian Zombie style.*

The days counted up to seventeen.

***

Wednesday morning brought little relief for the sisterhood. They all took the day off except Monica who went to work dressed in black. She met Alfons in the first floor café of the Empire State Building.

"Jesus Christ, Monica. You look dressed for a funeral."

The waitress brought her a cup of coffee.

Monica conveyed the whole sordid mess with Debbie's murdered family.

"That still doesn't explain your black clothing today."

"In Haiti, black is practically the color of the day, every day, due to all the murders."

He sipped his orange juice. "I have friends in the Mexican government. Let me get them to investigate these cartel crimes for your friend Debbie."

"No. It will be handled in the same manner as the Polish Nazis."

"I don't know exactly what you mean and something tells me I don't want to know."

"Consider an old Polish quote. Blood demands payment in

blood."

"I wonder who said that."

"Henry Slawik. He fought for the Polish underground in World War Two and killed many Germans. Your mother would know about him, and she would agree with us. The killers of Debbie's family must die by her accord."

"Okay. As long as it doesn't involve you."

"I cannot imagine that you thought I would get blood on my hands."

"Good. I feel better."

She tasted her coffee. "I wish I did. I do not feel like working in the office with a bunch of nosey coworkers. I can hear them now: *Why the black clothes? Who died? Are you dressed for a funeral?* Sound familiar?"

"Then take the day off. You can access the company's computer network remotely and set up everything for the trip from your home. I'll have one of my people call you with the passwords."

"That is so compassionate of you."

Alfons dialed Joseph on his cell. "Take Monica back home."

She bent over and kissed his cheek. "I will reward you in Paris in ways you have never imagined."

"I should warn you, I have a very vivid imagination." He grinned.

Joseph pushed through the door. "I'm double parked, sir."

Alfons said to Monica, "You better go before I get such a hard-on that I'll have to sit here for another hour."

Leaning over, she put her hand between his legs and pressed down on his boner. "That's the way I want it to feel three days from now...in Paris."

Alfons watched her leave, never taking his eyes off her swaying ass. The first thing he had to do when he got to his office suite was take a cold shower.

***

Across town, and oblivious of the sisterhood's trials, Maggie finally got in to see Doctor Jackson, primarily to get a refill for her HIV pills, she only had half a bottle left, and hopefully to get an optimistic update on her condition.

Robert waited in his dad's Mercedes. He sat there unconcerned about Maggie's office visit since she had told him that the doctor's appointment had to do with her blood pressure meds and nothing else.

Maggie sat on the examining table, picking at her fingernails, hoping beyond hope that the disease hadn't progressed to the next level. Doctor Jackson's assistant had already taken a blood sample, and she was waiting with fear in her heart for the results.

Jackson was one of the leading experts in HIV treatments. He came into the room, sat on a stool in front of a computer, and looked through her medical records. "Maggie, your antigen/antibody blood tests have been steadily improving. It's perfectly normal today. Could be the NRTI drugs you've been taking, which interrupt the HIV virus from reproducing in the early stages, have improved your immune system, or your antibodies were fired up for some other reason, creating false positive results. Borderline as your tests were, I think either possibility holds true, but the good news is you aren't HIV positive, probably never were."

Maggie jumped off the table and hugged Doctor Jackson. "Thank you, thank you, thank you."

"I see no reason to continue your medication."

Feeling on top of the world, Maggie got in the car and climbed all over Robert, smothering him with kisses. "Be careful," he managed to say. "Your blood pressure—"

She covered his mouth with hers until she had to come up for a breath. "We're going to do it twice a day, every day."

"The doctor's news must have been great."

"My heart is healthy enough for sex."

"He actually said that?"

Maggie continued to shower Robert's face with kisses. "You

wanna go ask him?"

"I'll take your word for it."

"And no more condoms. Let's get pregnant."

"Hell, let's have twins."

She hugged Robert and put on her most sexy voice. "How fast can you get us back to your quarters?"

***

One thousand five hundred fifteen miles to the southeast on Haiti, in the Ultimate Fitness Gym, Aurora had just finished up with a call from Brenda and returned to curling weights to bulk up her biceps as she gave Reinhard and Albert the good news. "The three of us are to leave Sunday night and fly to Paris to join up with Monica on Monday."

Albert set the 300-pound weighted bar on the stand and asked the same question that was going through Reinhard's mind as he ran on the treadmill. "Is this a setup so Brenda can have us killed?"

"No. She swore an oath to Loa, her Goddess, that no harm would come to us."

Reinhard didn't look convinced.

Aurora explained further. "Swearing an oath to Loa and then breaking the oath would result in Brenda being cursed for all time. She needs the three of us to assist Monica. I assume that means somebody is going to die, but I don't know who. I only know it won't be the three of us."

Back in Brooklyn, while Monica was still trying to console a very despondent Debbie, a cell phone rang and everyone checked to see if it was theirs. Brenda did not check hers. She waited until all the sisters put their cells down, and then answered the call.

It was Jackie. "I want you to come over."

"I'm kinda busy right now. What's the problem?"

"I want to paint a portrait of you...in the nude."

Brenda didn't know what to say but thought it might be pleasurable getting naked with the new Jackie. "I'll get there as soon as I can."

"I've sent the limo. Jorge should be there any minute."

"Brilliant." Brenda hung up. *She's a little presumptuous, but then again, that's Jackie.* "Monica, stay with Debbie and let her pour her heart out."

Chloe said, "In light of all that's happened, I'll go alone to the church on Sunday. Let Debbie grieve while I keep Leroy interested."

A horn honked out on Montford Lane. "I have to go." Brenda was glad to get into the limo and go to Jackie's. She sounded pleasant enough on the phone. *Perhaps she's not angry with me for turning her into a Lesbian Zombie...*which reminded her of Cassandra. She decided to call, but the phone went straight to voicemail. So she called Jenny, but it was Cassandra who answered. "Hello?"

"Why do you have Jenny's cell?"

"Brenda. It is a great honor to hear from you, my Queen."

"The phone, Cassandra. What's going on?"

"I lost my cell but Jenny's belongs to both of us now."

"You and Jenny? Why is that?"

"We fell in love, my Queen, and we were married last week in a Catholic church by a priest from the United States. I hope you will bless our union."

"Sure, why not." Brenda rolled her eyeballs. "I want you to set up the LZ Foundation. I'll be sending a lawyer from the U.S. in the next few days. You do what he tells you. Your bride is not to have any financial dealings with the foundation. Your second in command is Aurora. She, Reinhard and Albert are going to Paris on assignment, so Carlos and Jason are to provide muscle there if you need it. I'm putting a lot of faith and trust in you. Don't disappoint me."

"I will never disappoint you, my Queen."

"Give my congratulations to Jenny."

After hanging up, Brenda stretched out on the seat to get some well-deserved rest, only to be awakened by her ringing cell.

A little groggy, she managed to answer it.

Jackie was all in a tizzy. "Brenda, goddamnit, I cut my finger in the kitchen and it didn't hurt. It didn't even bleed, but my heart is beating. What the fuck? Am I dead? What good is being beautiful again if I'm dead? My skin restoration cream didn't make me look younger. I *am* younger. I'm a fucking Lesbian Zombie."

"Jackie, now settle down—"

"You did this to me. That rubdown, the kissing, the orgasm...it was all in your plan—"

"I gave you what you asked for."

"I didn't ask for this."

"What's the matter, Jackie? Don't you like your new body, your firm and perky tits, your smooth skin and supple lips?"

"Of course I love the new me, but what's it going to cost? This sisterhood of yours demands everything."

"Yes, you're one of us now. It's only money. We'll put it to good use."

"You robbed me without firing a shot. Didn't you?"

"If we're going to take the control away from men, it's going to take the both of us to succeed. I have the moxie, you have the cash. We're partners, like I'm the CEO and you're the CFO, right?"

"Bullshit. You're a thief."

"As CFO, it's still your money. As CEO, I'll tell you where to spend it. The sisterhood is a team, not Ocean's Eleven. When you're sitting on top of the corporate world and men are groveling at your feet, you'll thank me."

Jackie laughed. "When you put it that way, this might not be so bad."

"We're almost there."

"Yes, I see the limo coming up the drive. My front door is open. Come on through to the pool in back. There's an exquisite bottle of red wine on the poolside table. I've been saving it for a special occasion."

George S. Naas

"Nothing could be more special than this."

"Pour yourself a drink and don't forget to take off your clothes. I want a good look at your tits for comparison."

"Sounds like fun." She hung up.

The limo stopped under the pillared portico. She didn't wait for Jorge to open the door for her. Rushing through the house, she was surprised by all the excitement coursing through her body. Poolside, she found Jackie skinny-dipping. Brenda rid herself of her light blue pantsuit and yellow blouse and took off her bra and rubbed her tits. The sunshine felt sublime on her naked body.

She took a drink of wine from the bottle, and careful not to spill it, stepped into the pool and swished through the water to a smiling Jackie. She looked ravishingly beautiful, the glow of her skin and flow of her hair, and the way her full breasts bobbed in the rippling water made Brenda want to see more of her body. She handed the bottle to Jackie, whose taste for alcohol hadn't changed.

"A toast." She held up the bottle to the sun god, if there was one. "On this spot and on this day, two women will go down in history as surpassing all the great leaders of the world, men such as Alexander the Great, Genghis Khan, Julius Caesar, Napoleon Bonaparte, and a dozen lesser known men from the present era. It's women's destiny. When we come to power, we'll erect a marker on this property, engraved with the words: *Where women changed the world forever.*" She chugged from the bottle and passed it to Brenda, who took a much less exuberant swallow.

Now sitting on the edge of the pool, drinking wine and splashing the water with their legs, Brenda and Jackie laid out their plans for the future of the planet. Jackie contemplated the nearly empty bottle in her hands. "I think we should use the same plan the male gender has used on us females since the beginning of time...only reverse it. Women have always had to defer to their husbands, boyfriends and dads when it came to their own destiny. This is because women were considered to have sinned the original sin."

Brenda kicked water high in the air. "Convenient how that came about. Wouldn't have been that way if women had written the Bible."

"Men think we're stupid when it comes to handling money. I run into this all the time. Some fucking prick tells me where to invest my money while he can't afford a pot to piss in." She handed Brenda the bottle.

Taking another drink Brenda said, "I want the LZ Foundation to destroy the myth that women are not as strong as men. I propose that we have cage matches between men and Lesbian Zombies. We both know how those fights will turn out."

"Spoken like a true man-hater." Jackie grabbed the bottle away from Brenda and downed the remaining contents.

***

Back at headquarters on Montford Lane, Debbie, with red, swollen eyes, took a piece of paper and started making up the death plan. She wrote down in great detail exactly how the killers would die. Impalement, cage drowning, fire, disembowelment...nothing seemed fitting, terrifying, or torturous enough. Because Pedro watched her family die, maybe he should watch his family die too. Brenda and the sisterhood would never agree to the killing of women and children. Then putting more thought into it, she decided the sisterhood could help with the executions, but the manner of those deaths were solely hers, not Brenda's, not Monica's, nor the devil's himself, and she would relish the vengeance.

Still, what manner of death would befit those snakes?

Not all the sisters thought of murder and mayhem that night. At Fort Dix, New Jersey, a contented Maggie slept in Robert's arms. He, on the other hand, lay awake in silent prayer to his mother and father. *Thank you, Dad. I know you and Mom are together now, and because of you, Dad, I have found the love of my life.* He kissed Maggie and closed his eyes to sleep.

On Long Island, all around her art studio, Jackie had hung,

stacked, and boxed her canvas creations. Colorful sheets of paint-dappled plastic protected the floor, and there were rows of shelves that housed an enormous supply of paints and brushes and canvases yet to be used.

Jackie had Brenda right where she wanted her: naked in a director's chair, legs crossed at the knees, her back straight, and her long red hair a-flow over her shoulders. Those gorgeous round breasts looked perfectly scrumptious poised between her extended arms, her fingers interlinked at her knee. A tall potted plant with yellow flowers served as the backdrop for the painting, a watercolor canvas on which Jackie dabbed a few additional highlights.

The beauty of Brenda's body is unmatched in nature, anywhere.

During the process of painting this exquisite specimen, Jackie's libido stirred with desire. De Vinci, Van Gogh, Rembrandt, and Picasso, how they missed the turn-on of painting Brenda Ayler, Queen of the Lesbian Zombies.

With a final dab of gray-brown shade under her perfect chin, Jackie set her brush across one of the many cans of watercolors strategically positioned around her. "Now you can relax and come see."

Brenda flowed from the chair like pure honey and rushed to see what Jackie had created. She was surprised to see herself as Vincent Van Gogh might have seen her, with blotchy brush strokes of vivid color and exaggerated shading that highlighted her every curve. Almost speechless, she managed to express her wonder. "Jackie, you're a master."

"I was highly motivated by my model." She gleamed, all young and beautiful and sexy. "I think my impasto style suits you quite nicely."

When Brenda looked down and smiled, she noticed a blob of cream colored paint on Jackie's left breast, near enough to her nipple to awaken any Lesbian Zombie's craving for the pink flesh. "Let me get that off for you." She used her finger to wipe off the paint, but instead, only managed to smear the splotch across her tantalizing nub. "Oh, dear."

Jackie gasped, not so much on account of the mess, but more-so because Brenda had touched a very sensitive place. "You did that on purpose," she teased then grabbed the brush and swiped a gray-brown stripe across Brenda's right breast.

"Ahhuugh...why you..." Brenda's eyes shifted back and forth then landed on the can of red watercolor used to paint her hair. She grabbed it up and splashed it on Jackie's chest, as a woman would toss a bar drink on a disrespectful man.

Jackie screamed, bent down, and retaliated with the yellow of the background flowers.

Greens and blues and every shade of skin-tone flew in every direction, turning two naked women into a living, breathing kaleidoscope. Dripping paint from every body part, Brenda tackled Jackie to the plastic on the floor, and as Jackie tried to wriggle free, their slippery bodies became entwined in positions that would put the Kama Sutra to shame.

In the midst of all the squealing and giggling, red lips found yellow lips, and breast colors mixed to a vibrant orange with swirls of green and blue as they twisted and clung to each other and fought for domination. Nipples rubbed nipples and labia rubbed labia, and as the girl-play got serious, their breathing became more intense, more desperate, and the giggling turned to moans of pleasure until they both used God's name in vain and came like screaming banshees in each other's arms.

Then the laughing began as each assessed the damages. Besides the body-painting extravaganza and their hairdos a gooey mess, Brenda's image on the canvas had become imprisoned behind colorful bars of paint streaks.

"It's ruined," Brenda cried.

"On the contrary. It's the best painting the art world will ever see."

Instead of cleaning up, they lay embraced on the paint-splattered plastic and soon fell fast asleep.

***

Chloe went up to Debbie's bedroom with a can of beer and two Valium pills. After handing them to Debbie, she watched her put the pills in her mouth and take a drink. Debbie didn't swallow the pills and beer right away. It was as if she considered spitting it all out so she could stay miserable and full of hate. But she didn't. They too were soon asleep with Girlie Dog lying at the bottom of the bed, her body keeping both girls' feet warm.

Only Monica was still awake. She sat in the back porch swing, swinging to and fro, and thought of how she would pleasure Alfons and kill Baby Doc and his family, all within forty-eight hours of reaching Paris. Her cell phone rang. The display read *International* and she knew it was Jacque calling from Paris, right on time. She answered: "Is everything set?"

"Oui, Madame."

"And the house in the country?"

"Vos invités seront à l'heure, Oui."

"Our guests had better be there on time."

"Ne vous inquiétez pas."

"I worry about everything. Merci." She hung up. Her France connection had come through for her, opening the door for her final act of revenge. Of course, *house in the country* and *guests* were code words to make their conversation seem benign when, in fact, the meanings were quite deadly.

Under the porch light, she studied a group-picture of Baby Doc and his two grandkids. He was dressed in a white t-shirt, green Bermuda shorts, and flat walking shoes without socks. He was skinny for a rich man, five—foot—seven with graying hair. She couldn't see his entire face because of his sunglasses. Francois, Baby Doc the Third, the great grandson of Papa Doc, was a frail little boy wearing a Mickey Mouse t-shirt and shorts like his grandfather. He was no more than six years old.

His sister looked about nine but must not have had the same mother because of her strawberry blond hair, and at five feet tall, she looked too small for her Minnie Mouse shirt and Haitian style Bermuda shorts adorned with embroidered flowers.

Monica referred to the Lesbian Zombie creed that said they would not kill women and children. *Fuck that. My daughter wasn't spared.* There had been no mercy for her, so there would be none for Papa Doc's descendants.

With that final thought, she put the picture back in her side pocket and went to bed, thinking about how she would outwit Alfons.

***

Thursday, Maggie and Robert were on their way to New London and Galaxy International Incorporated. Both were bleary-eyed after another night of lovemaking. The October morning was unseasonably warm, so Maggie ran down her window and enjoyed the wind blowing in her face. Her auburn curls flew back and away from her shoulders.

At the same time, she tried to ignore the pain between her legs from all those love sessions. Robert had the looks of a Mercedes and the stamina of a Mack truck. She glanced at him and smiled. "You really love me, don't you."

"Can't get enough, Maggie. Just wish my father could see how happy you've made me."

"I'm really going to miss your father. He was such a good man and a good friend when I really needed one."

That earned her a questionable glance. "What do you mean? When did you really need him?"

Realizing that she had made a mistake, she punted. "I was going through a rough patch with my patient Isabel."

"You knew that she was not long for this world."

"That's true, but it didn't make losing her any easier." She changed the subject. "What all do you have to do when we get to your company?"

"Mainly, I need to go through dad's personal papers and find things I want to keep. All of the company's financials, powers of attorney, and legal transfers of all the properties are being handled by our legal team. He had a small house built close to the plant. There's where we'll find personal property that may mean something to me."

"I thought he commuted from New York."

"When mom died there were times he couldn't stand to stay in the home they had shared for thirty years. Too many memories."

"So he built the small house."

"He also had an apartment in Brooklyn, close to Sam's Donut Shop."

"I'm so lucky that I met him." Remembering Brenda's advice to the sisterhood, *"You won't get into trouble saying too little but you can get in a lot of trouble saying too much."* Maggie acted out a pretend yawn and put her head back. "I'm going to take a little nap. Don't get much sleep lately, thanks to you, dear."

"Rest up. I'll wake you when we get there."

***

Monica got up to leave for work but got another call from Alfons. She sat in the porch swing and answered it. "This is Monica."

"Change of plans. We're going to leave at one a.m. Saturday morning."

"But I have our itinerary set to start on Friday."

"We're still in good shape. Just tweak it."

"Then I will need the rest of the day off to do it."

"That's fine."

"Then I will need tomorrow off to make arrangements for our trip to Mexico City."

"What do I get in exchange?"

"I will be eternally grateful."

"Not good enough. Try again."

"How about an unbelievable experience in the mile high club on the way to Paris."

"I have had that many times before."

"Not Haitian style, you haven't."

"Okay." He cleared his throat as if the prospect of a Haitian blowjob at thirty-five thousand feet had choked him up. "See you Saturday morning at one. LaGuardia. Don't be late." He hung up.

Before Monica could put her phone away she heard the incoming call tone. The display said it was from Brenda. She answered. "Where the hell have you been?"

"Busy with our new Lesbian Zombie sister."

Jackie grabbed the cell. "I'm sending my limo to pick up the sisterhood, of which I'm now a member. I look forward to meeting you. By the way, Brenda is on fire in bed, but I guess you already know that."

Monica groaned in annoyance.

Brenda took back the cell. "The sisterhood is going to love Jackie. I want to have a strategy session and for you to meet the woman who will play a huge role in helping us achieve our ultimate goal of taking what has always rightfully belonged to us females."

"We can all be there, except Maggie." Monica huffed. "She is off somewhere with Robert, God only knows."

"The limo will be there in an hour and a half."

"I better go then, get Debbie and Chloe up and feed Girlie Dog. What should I wear? Never mind. See you soon."

Brenda hung up and finished telling Jackie the short history of the sisterhood, right down to what was going to happen in Paris and Mexico City. "Once everyone's personal problems are solved we can get down to business."

"Do you need me to help?"

"It's not your fight. Remember though, we only kill evil men who have it coming, never the innocent."

Melinda, dressed in a short maid's skirt, brought out a huge breakfast of raw Rocky Mountain Oysters, egg yolks on toast, and more wine.

Jackie waved her off. "That will be all, Melinda."

"Wait," Brenda said. "Rule number one, Jackie. Melinda is now part of the sisterhood so you can't order her around like she's your servant anymore."

"She is my servant."

"We're all equal." She turned to Melinda. "Where's your breakfast?"

"In the kitchen where I always eat."

"Get it. You eat with us from now on."

Melinda shot Jackie a questioning glare. "Really?"

Jackie answered by kissing Brenda on the lips, then: "You heard our Queen."

***

Back on the road to the palatial estate, Jorge had been telling the sisterhood about Jackie's rags-to-riches story. The sisters enjoyed his entertaining narrative and polite manner.

When the limo glided up the drive, the sisters saw the place for the first time. The mansion walls made of redstone blocks rose three levels in stages, the roof gables and windows trimmed in white, as were the arched garage doors and the rising tower of windows, much like a castle's keep.

Chloe got out of the limo and asked Jorge about what she couldn't see. "What's around that way? A tennis court?"

"No, Miss Chloe. On the south side there's a short breezeway that leads into a greenhouse in dire need of a gardener's caring hands."

"And the beach?" Debbie asked.

"A very nice path on the east side, just off the swimming pool."

"There's a pool?"

"Out back, Miss Chloe."

"We should all move in here. I got nothing against Maggie's house, but this place is amazing."

Melinda appeared at the front door and escorted them to the pool where they found Brenda and Jackie naked and lying on lounge chairs, drinking wine.

Debbie looked at three kitchen plates under the umbrella of a poolside table that cradled a few leftover Rocky Mountain Oysters. "Are those balls?"

Jackie pulled her sunglasses down her nose and looked at Debbie over the rim. "Not human balls but bovine balls."

Chloe picked one up and took a bite, chewed and swallowed. "Not bad."

Monica chimed in, "Human balls are better. Trust me."

Chloe, still enraged at men in general, made a suggestion. "Let's sample Jorge's balls."

Jackie scoffed. "We can't do that. If you develop a liking for them I'd have to run an ad for a new limo driver every week."

Chloe chomped on another bull's ball. "Just kidding."

"Girls." Brenda called everyone to gather round. "The first thing on the agenda is for all of you to get naked. Jackie and I aren't the only eye candy around here, so chop, chop. Hurry up."

Now, with the entire sisterhood naked and floating on individual air mattresses, Brenda made an announcement. "I want you all to meet Jackie O'Neal, our LZ Foundation's new Chief Financial Officer. As CFO, she's in charge of all finances. Monica is VP in charge of day-to-day operations. Debbie, Chloe, and Melinda are assistant VPs in charge of recruitment."

Monica questioned, "What about Aurora, Reinhard, Albert, and the two clowns, Carlos and Jason, we de-balled on the beach in Port au Prince?"

"Aurora's in charge of the lady-boys. Reinhard and Albert are just grunts who do our bidding. You know, like kicking the shit out of someone we need to teach a lesson for causing us problems."

Monica said, "You left out two people, Jenny and Maggie. What about them?"

"Jenny's in charge of security on Port au Prince. I've instructed her to keep a watchful eye on what's taking place on the island. Anything she deems out of the ordinary she'll report to me or our lawyer."

"We have a lawyer?" Chloe asked.

"She's a damn good one," Jackie assured the girls.

"As far as Maggie goes, she'll help us by getting donations from Robert's company, even after they get married. Outside of that, she won't be around much, but she'll always be a member of the sisterhood, whether she's a Lesbian Zombie or not. We'll always love her as a sister, and no harm will ever come to Robert."

"What if they have a daughter? Will we convert her to a Lesbian Zombie?"

"That'll be up to Maggie's daughter."

"But I want a little Lesbian Zombie niece." She pouted.

The girls laughed and splashed water on each other.

"Girls. We come to things that need our attention for the following weeks. Monica will be leaving for Paris Saturday morning with Alfons, and I assume when she comes back she'll have delightful tales of her sexual adventures with Alfons..." she paused when Monica booed, "...and how she'd sent Baby Doc to the next world."

Monica cheered.

"If you feel up to it, Debbie, you can go with Chloe to the church and begin the process of seducing the preacher and his wife."

"Chloe's going to eat his balls for lunch," Debbie said.

Chloe covered her mouth as if she would urp.

"Debbie, you decide how and when you indoctrinate Janice into the sisterhood. When she's one of us, she's sure to surrender a large amount of cash to the LZ Foundation."

"Yeah, our motto," Debbie reminded them. "Before we can fuck 'em over, we gotta fuck 'em or suck 'em." She sighed. "Fuck is such a wonderful word."

"Lastly, Jackie had the idea to put the Lesbian Zombie virus in her skin cream, which sells worldwide."

"Oh, wow," Monica said. "You sure that's a good idea?"

Chloe responded with, "Fuckin' A."

"Once we've perfected the idea, we can use the women in The Church of the Risen Jesus as guinea pigs to see if it's effective. Now we all know it takes the virus and an orgasm to make the conversion. Imagine the husband's surprise when, after a night of uninhibited sex, he wakes up to a brand new woman who hates him."

That got a laugh from all the sisters.

"Tomorrow, Jackie and I will meet with her lawyer to get the LZ Foundation set up in Haiti. She'll be working with our COO, Chief Operating Officer, Cassandra, in Port au Prince. We already have a sizable deposit for our overseas account."

"How much?"

"Five million three hundred thousand so far, thanks to Jackie and Monica."

"More is on the way." Jackie smiled.

"Next, some of us will be going with Debbie to Mexico City to help her slaughter the killers of her family. She'll be solely in charge of how the assholes are to die."

"We'll get them good," Chloe assured her.

"And that concludes business for today."

"Yea," the girls cheered.

"So this afternoon, Jackie is going to paint our Lesbian Zombie sisterhood, in the nude, of course. You'll have to stand still for a while, so no playin' grab ass and titty twisters. Got it?"

Jackie laughed and added, "And you better love my work. I don't take criticism well. The husband of the last person who criticized my painting blew his fucking brains out. Well, he shot himself in the head. I don't know if that qualifies as blowing his brains out or not."

Brenda chuckled. "So cross Jackie at your own peril, girls."

After she and Jackie high-fived each other, the girls rolled off their air mattresses and frolicked in the water like kids at summer camp.

"We need more wine," Jackie shouted over all the chatter.

Brenda got out of the pool and headed for the kitchen where

she selected a nice Chardonnay from the wine rack. When she turned around she saw Melinda standing there with her arms folded. Brenda gasped in surprise. Something about a naked woman in the kitchen really turned her on. "Melinda? What's wrong?"

"You left me out, Brenda. What am I supposed to do on Friday, play with my dildo all day?"

Brenda tucked the wine bottle in the crook of her arm, like a football but way more fun. "Melinda, I did that on purpose because I have something very special in mind for you."

"Special?" She relaxed her arms to her side.

Oh, those beautiful curves.

"I want you to shadow a woman for the sisterhood. She could be of service to us if we can get her to convert. Her name is Donna. Chloe was getting close to her until her butch girlfriend decided to shoot it out with the cops and lost."

"Donna? Is she pretty?"

"A knockout and she's already gay...or at least bisexual. She has a congressman for a sugar daddy. I want you to befriend her."

"What about Chloe?"

"That's why I didn't say anything in the pool. I don't want her to know. Chloe thinks Donna hates her, blames her for Joanne's death, because she inserted herself in their relationship. Joanne felt threatened, decided to kill them both. Cops got to her first."

"Oh dear."

"Donna won't have anything to do with Chloe, but a new face might be welcomed. I'll give you all the information tomorrow."

"Tomorrow?"

"I'll be staying here with Jackie. Now go have fun with your sisters in the art studio."

***

Friday morning, at Robert's dad's little house in New

London, Maggie and Robert had just finished another vigorous round of lovemaking. She fixed a breakfast of corned beef hash and scrambled eggs and toast and orange juice.

Robert's knees were a little weak when he came to the table. "You just fixed my dad's favorite breakfast." He dumped hot sauce on the hash. "How did you know?"

"When you have donuts and coffee with someone as much as we did, you learn a lot." *Another lie to add to the list.*

He dug in. "This is delicious. Thanks."

She brought a plate of her own and sat with him. "What's on the agenda for today?"

"I'll save all the photo albums and my dad's diary. All the other stuff can go to Goodwill."

After breakfast, Robert loaded up the Mercedes with the memories of his mom and dad. Then they stopped by the funeral home where Robert stood at attention beside his father's casket and saluted.

Maggie sat in a chair behind him. "Why did you do that?"

"Because my dad was Fifth Army, put in twenty years. I owe him that respect."

"What will we do for a headstone after the burial service?"

"One is on order. We'll come back in a couple weeks when you are my wife and place it. Then we can put flowers on both graves and say our prayers." He stepped back and performed a military about-face to face Maggie. "By then I'll have sorted through all the albums and read his diary."

In the car heading back to Brooklyn, Maggie feared what might be in the diary. Her angst put a damper on this beautiful October day.

Things were great from Robert's perspective but Maggie kept picking at her fingernails. This brought an immediate response from Robert. "I've noticed that you only pick at your nails if you have something on your mind...the way you did on the way to your doctor's appointment. So what's up?"

"Nothing, dear. I'll just be glad when we're married and

pregnant."

"Something is bothering you. I know it."

"The only thing wrong is that I have a headache because you kept me awake last night."

"If you want to get pregnant, you have to do the work." He laughed at his philosophy.

"I'm going to put the seat back and rest and think about Las Vegas and our wedding. Wake me when we get to your base."

"I'm sorry you don't feel well."

Maggie turned away from Robert and lay there with her eyes closed, but her mind was running at maximum speed. She kept churning through her memories of the times she'd spent with Robert's dad. And she remembered the money he'd given her, not knowing it was to keep BBBD happy. As a father figure to her, he didn't hold her home care occupation against her just because it didn't pay squat. One day she'd invited him to Isabel's house for breakfast. He was thrilled with the meal and went on and on about how his late wife had fixed it the very same way, even down to the hot sauce on the corned beef hash. It dawned on her that he'd taken a selfie of her and him and the breakfast plate. That photo could be in with all the stuff that Robert had in the car. Innocent enough, she could explain it away.

She then thought of the time she was holding hands in a father-daughter sort of way with Robert's dad at Coney Island where they ran into General Lawrence Taylor. He'd recognized her as his on-again off-again concubine but lied to Robert's dad when he said he'd met her at a VFW dinner with her boyfriend, BBBD. She'd dodged a bullet there, for sure, but there could be a picture of them in all that stuff. Robert could find out she'd known the general long before the party in the hanger on base.

That'll be tough to explain.

In his diary he might have written his impressions of her, but surely they'd be positive. After all, he wanted his son to meet her and possibly fall in love. He wanted her to be a part of the family. No way would he write that she was a prostitute.

Thinking her past was probably safe, she managed to put it out of her mind enough to drift off to sleep. Much to her dismay, she woke up too soon. Thinking they were back at the Army base, she sat up and looked around. They weren't. They were at a rental storage facility. Robert had the trunk open. She got out and rushed to ask him, "Why did you stop here?"

"I have a storage locker here." He pulled a bag out by its straps and set it on the ground. "I'm going to put dad's stuff in it, along with my junk I don't want to get rid of."

Thinking fast Maggie said, "I have plenty of space in my house." *That way I can go through it...* She took hold of the straps on one of the bags and tried to put it back in the trunk, but Robert took it from her. "Don't be silly."

"What if someone steals it?"

"Maggie. Nobody's going to steal this stuff. It only has value for you and me. We'll go through it all when we're back from Vegas. Maybe we'll buy our own house to put it in."

"At least let me take the diary home."

"That should be interesting. He'd write about everything. I'll bet you're mentioned in there somewhere. We'll find out together. Later. What do you think of that?"

Maggie forced a smile. "Whatever you say, dear."

I'll get the storage locker combination, and when he's at work, I'll come here and go through everything.

But a complication set in. As he drove up to the closed storage facility gate to leave, he punched a pass-code into a drive-up keypad. The gate opened. On the highway back to his base, she asked, "What's the code for the gate?"

He looked straight ahead, driving. "I could tell you but then I would have to...well...you know the drill."

"Funny, ha ha."

Now she'd have to come up with a new plan to get her hands on those pictures and that diary, because if her lies were exposed, her life would be ruined.

***

Life was more upbeat for the sisterhood. Since they had partied most of Thursday night, the girls had gotten up late for brunch. Afterwards, Jorge took them back to Maggie's house in the limo. When they opened the front door they were attacked by a tail-wagging Girlie Dog.

This brought a roar of laughter from the sisters, some still splotched with paint from yesterday afternoon's festivities in Jackie's art studio.

Monica had already cleaned up. She had a lot to do, making last minute arrangements for the Paris trip. However, when she got online, she found out Alfons' mother had already done everything for her, and worse, she'd decided to go along with them, and even worse, she'd reserved separate hotel rooms for them.

Alfons is going to be really pissed but at least not at me.

Now that she didn't have to work on the itinerary, she could go shopping. He'd told her to get some European style outfits to make herself look like a million dollars, so she was just following orders.

***

At the Church of the Risen Jesus, Tim Dawson had arrived, feeling for certain that someone must have seen Chloe. As he climbed the stairs to enter the church, a fat woman in her late forties came waddling out. He took out a picture of Chloe and stopped the woman. "Pardon me, ma'am. I'm looking for my ex-wife. Here's her picture. Have you seen her?"

The woman put on her glasses and studied the picture. "Yes. She was at last week's Bible study...with a friend. They left right after it was over."

Excitement ratcheted up his voice. "Do you know where she went?"

"I didn't talk to her directly. You could ask Reverend Leroy.

He might know more about her."

"Leroy?"

"He's in his office. Just up those stairs to the right."

"Thanks." He started up the steps again, but she grabbed his arm and stopped him.

"I hope that you find her, and I'm sorry she's your ex-wife. She sure is lovely. I'm sure the blessed Jesus wants you back together."

Tim said, "Okay," but before he could continue on his way, the lady squeezed his arm. "Pray with me, young man." She closed her eyes but didn't let him go. "Lord, let this true believer find his wife who has gone astray."

"Amen." He pulled his arm free and ran up the steps and into the church. Hell, it looked more like a theater or auditorium than a place of worship. He spotted an old guy who looked like he might die before the day was out. "Reverend Leroy's office?" he shouted. "Do you know where it is?"

"I'm old," the man said. "Not deaf." He pointed a trembling finger at Leroy's office.

Tim turned around and saw a closed door with OFFICE painted on it as clearly as the wart on the old man's face.

He knocked.

A panicked voice responded, "Just a minute."

"Reverend Leroy, is that you?"

Inside the office, a young intern hurriedly pulled up her pants and made a quick exit through a side door. Reverend Leroy combed his mussed hair back and checked his zipper to be sure it was up and secured. Then smiling like the network star he was, he opened the door, thankful he wasn't in the middle of a fantastic orgasm when this clown showed up. "Can I help you?"

Tim took out the picture. "Have you seen this woman?"

Leroy instantly recognized Chloe and remembered how much he wanted to fuck her. He scowled at the visitor. "Who wants to know?"

"I'm Tim Dawson, her ex-husband."

Not welcoming the competition, Leroy grumped. "What do you need her for? She owe you money or somethin'?"

"I love her and hope to get her back."

"What part of ex don't you understand, boy?"

"Do you know her or not?"

Leroy sighed. "She was here last Friday for Bible study. I expect she'll be back tonight. Her soul needs savin', son."

"Thank you, Reverend. I'll be back."

***

Unaware of what was going on with Tim, Chloe was playing with Girlie Dog in the backyard. She threw a stick and the dog brought it back, all full of slobber.

Debbie came out and sat down in a lawn chair.

"How are you feeling?" Chloe threw the stick again. "Are you up to going with me tonight?"

"As much as I hate to go back to that asshole's church, I know it would make Brenda happy if we were at least trying to seduce those two born-again TV Christians."

"I don't see why we need to con that church out of their money." She threw the stick again. "Jackie has plenty."

"We need to get it over with. I'll go with you. Besides, I don't have anything to do until Mexico City."

Girlie Dog brought the slobbery stick and Chloe threw it again. "I hope I don't puke."

Chasing the stick again and again made this Friday a good day for Girlie Dog.

***

Monica was having a good day too. She came in with two new suitcases full of expensive clothes for her Paris trip.

The doorbell rang. Moments later, Debbie strolled in and threw Monica a package that had just been delivered.

She shook the box and something rattled inside.

"It was sent to the Waldorf Astoria and forwarded to this address. Let's hope it is not a bomb from Donna."

Monica set it aside and returned to removing price tags from her new clothing.

"Are you going to open it?"

"What is the rush?"

Debbie yelled, "Open the damn box."

"Jeeze." Monica used her fingernails to carefully cut through the tape then opened the flaps. She stood there looking at the contents, her mouth agape.

Chloe huffed. "Well, what is in it?"

"I'll be damned. Cherry lollipops."

"Really? From who?"

"And two notes...one from Caroline's mother and another from Caroline herself."

Monica read the mother's note first:

Dear Monica, I have wonderful news. Caroline is completely free of the disease that ravaged her body. The doctors say there is no explanation. I say it's a miracle from God. You must believe in miracles. I remember how you spoke with such conviction when you said that Caroline would be okay. Jesus said faith can move mountains. Maybe your faith had something to do with this miracle. I will always be eternally grateful.

Sincerely,

June Crandall.

Monica felt warm inside. "You are welcome, June."

Caroline's note:

Dear Lollipop Lady. I am all well now and doing good in school. I think I got well because there was something magic in the lollipop you gave me. I can now play on the girls' soccer team. Last time I scored twelve goals. I always eat a cherry lollipop before the game. I think it makes me run fast. Billy the school bully always made fun of me because I had to be in a wheelchair and he would laugh really loud and make me cry. Yesterday on the playground, he hit me and I hit him back so hard I heard a crack. He ran away crying and that made me feel good. Don't eat all these lollipops at once. Mommy said it will make you sick. I ate a whole bunch of them and I threw up.

I love you.

Caroline

Monica carefully put the notes back in the box. "This almost made me cry."

"You should send them your phone number so you can talk sometime."

"I will." She looked at the clock. "Now what are we going to do until it is time for me to go to the airport?"

Chloe suggested, "You could go to Bible study with us."

"You know what? I will go with you two. It beats staying here talking baby talk to Girlie Dog."

***

On Long Island, Brenda and Jackie were also discussing the Church of the Risen Jesus. "If Chloe and Debbie succeed in seducing Reverend Leroy and his wife, we'll have leverage over him to promote your skin cream laced with the virus."

"Brenda, you need to think this thing through."

"What's the problem?"

"Let's say it works. What are we going to do with all of those new sisters? They won't know what's happening to them. Someone might link the changes to my skin cream. We'll be found out for sure."

"Jackie, now I know why you're so successful. You're right. We need a chain of command to keep everyone under control."

"Brenda, we're going to need an army."

"That's the whole idea, an army of Lesbian Zombies to rid the world of men."

"What do we do if some sisters band together and strike out on their own? They might not want to kill men. And you should reconsider the consequences: we cannot, and should not want to kill off the entire male gender."

Brenda chuckled. "Then let's turn them all into lady-boys."

"You don't get it. Three point nine billion men in a long line, waiting to get their balls bitten off. Three point six billion Lesbian Zombies that can't get pregnant. The entire world will die within four generations."

"Leaving just us zombie girls to have fun." She cupped her breasts and shook them about.

"That man you killed really fucked you up, Brenda."

"Men got it coming."

"So what's the rush? Have you heard the story about the frog?"

"Frog?"

"If you put a frog in a pot of boiling water, it'll immediately jump out. But if you put the frog in a pot of cold water and slowly raise the temperature, the frog won't jump out and it'll eventually boil to death."

"Are frogs really that stupid?"

"The point is, if we go about changing the world slowly, we'll eventually succeed."

"What do you suggest?"

"We need just enough Lesbian Zombies to infiltrate the governments of every country on earth. Campaigns and elections take time. Convert a candidate or two, a senator here and there, governors and school board members. Replace religious leaders with lady-boys and Lesbian Zombies. All the captains of commerce started somewhere low on the ladder. Have Lesbian Zombies apply for the mail room. Convert a secretary or two. Slowly, they'll replace all the CEOs in retail, manufacturing, energy, television, Hollywood, every news network, and of course the internet dot coms and social media moguls. Then we can change the curriculum in kindergarten through the twelfth grade to emphasize the importance of women and de-emphasize the importance of men. Change the corporate pay structure. Give women opportunities in the world they'd otherwise never have."

Brenda frowned. "And we won't get rid of men along the way? Why not?"

"Just the men who harm women. Besides, what good is a victory over men if there are no men left to defeat? Women don't want advantages given to them. They want the opportunity to earn those advantages...on a level playing field."

"Are you saying what happened to me isn't divine intervention by the Lesbian Goddess Loa?" Brenda wouldn't hear of it. "I'm not just some victim of a virus that invaded my body from the Tree of Life. I didn't just pass the virus on to the sisterhood who'll pass it on to others. It's not a domino effect no better than Ebola. We matter."

"We do, yes, but the future of the human race is depending on us. We have to keep the sisterhood in check, can't indiscriminately go spreading the virus around or there won't be enough fertile women left to reproduce. And we need men with balls for that."

Brenda sighed. "Guess we'll have to stick with Rocky Mountain Oysters."

With that wise crack, they both broke out laughing. The virus-laced skin cream idea was tanked.

***

Monica, Debbie, and Chloe went to a Mexican restaurant right down the street from Maggie's house, unaware that Brenda and Jackie were making plans without them. While stuffing down a smothered burrito, Chloe pointed her fork at the two of them. "If that fucking Leroy makes a pass at me while saying one of his praise-Jesus lines, I'm going to slit his throat and watch him choke to death on his own blood."

A couple sitting in the next booth left twenty-five dollars for their food and made a quick exit.

"Cool it, Chloe," Monica whispered. "Everybody in this place just heard you."

"You're not the one who lost the coin toss."

"Twice," Debbie sang. "I get to seduce Janice."

"I'm sick of men thinkin' we're only good for fucking, and

when they don't get their way, they beat, rape, and murder us."

"Stop it. Your husband beat you. You divorced him. Get over it."

"I swear I'll throw up when Leroy touches me. Fuck 'em to fuck 'em over...fuck all that. I want some pussy."

Monica had enough, "Let's get out of here. I have got to check all my paperwork and passport and my suitcases. I don't want to be running around tonight at 12:00 with Joseph waiting for me in the limo. The Bible study will be over at 7:00. So time-wise we are good."

***

At Fort Dix, Robert and Maggie were having dinner at one of the Post Exchange restaurants. Robert felt like confessing. "If I hadn't met you, and the circumstances were the same with my dad dying and all, I would've agreed to extend my active duty and serve out my six-year commitment."

"Six years?"

"Four active and two inactive, but I did meet you, so the army is gonna have to go on without me."

"I'm glad we met...so you didn't stay in."

"The Army couldn't drag me back in."

Maggie was sitting next to him in a booth. She leaned over and kissed his cheek. "If they try, I'll drag you back out. I'll tell them you're going to be a father so they better get someone else."

"Yeah, you tell 'em, girl." He pushed his cleaned plate away. "I'm full. It's almost seventeen-hundred hours. Let's head back to my quarters."

"What are we gonna do there, big boy?" she cooed.

"Watch planes take off and land, and if that gets boring, we can go online and make reservations for Vegas. Have you ever been to Las Vegas?"

"Have you ever been popped in the nose?"

"Huh?"

"You didn't mention we could have sex, silly."

"You're going to love it in Vegas."

"Sex?"

"That too."

"I'll really love it when I can say that I'm the wife of Captain Robert Mark Johnson Jr."

***

During the limo ride to the church, Debbie was the most sedate. Chloe was still on a rant about how she hated the whole goddamned church assignment and especially Leroy the Lecher.

Jorge laughed. "Leroy the Lecher. I like that."

Arriving five minutes late, they found the usual women with their Bibles open to some verse that the girls had never heard of before that night. The sisterhood was happy to see Janice leading the group.

After fifteen minutes of sheer boredom with the sisters checking their watches every other minute, Reverend Leroy came into the room followed by Tim Dawson.

Chloe gasped at the sight of the man who'd beaten her for not wanting to let him fuck her when he was drunk, obnoxious, and mean. Her stomach knotted. Leroy would have been a welcome lay right now.

Tim walked over to her and got down on one knee in front of her. "Please forgive me, honey. Let's renew our love now and let Reverend Leroy remarry us tonight."

Chloe and her sisters stood up and walked toward the door.

Tim grabbed Chloe's arm. "How dare you walk away from me, bitch."

She spun around and caught him with a right closed fist to his teeth. In that split second she felt her fist break his jaw.

Tim hit the floor without muttering a word, now flat on his back with his tongue hanging out the side of his bloody mouth. All the church women screamed, and Reverends Leroy and Janice just stood there in a state of shock.

The sisterhood beat a hasty retreat to the limo and got away without being stopped. To be sure they weren't followed, they had Jorge pull into a Subway sandwich shop and drive around back by the dumpster.

Three cop cars with lights on and sirens blaring flew past them, heading for the church. A New York EMT fire truck was in close pursuit.

The joyous sisterhood high-fived each other.

***

On Long Island, a nude Brenda was posed on some rocks along the shore. Floodlights were arranged in a manner that highlighted her voluptuous breasts from a side angle.

The pose wasn't exactly what Jackie wanted, so she moved Brenda's left foot off one rock and put it in the soft sand, thus exposing a tease of red pubic hair.

Jackie ran back to her easel. "Now don't move."

She didn't. In fact, she stayed mostly motionless for the better part of an hour. Zombies could do that. When Jackie set aside her brushes and palette, Brenda stood and stretched. "Let me see what you painted so far?"

"Oh, no. Just like last time, you'll get to see it when it's finished."

"This one better not get ruined."

"Then don't start something you have to finish with an orgasm."

Draping a towel around her bare shoulders to ward off the cool sea breeze that also brought in the tide, Brenda followed a very cocky Jackie up to the house.

***

Back at 127 Montford Lane, Monica, excited about her upcoming trip to Paris, gave a hug to Debbie and Chloe. "You better stay away from the church for a while." Then she bent to Girlie Dog, took her by the ears, and turned her head side to side.

George S. Naas

"You be a good little doggie while I am gone."

Girlie Dog tried to follow Monica out the door but Chloe pulled her back.

Walking to the limo door Joseph held open for her, she turned and waved goodbye to the sisters.

Chloe looked at Debbie and in unison they said, "Time for a hot tub hoedown." They stripped and headed for the bubbly water on the back deck.

Arriving at LaGuardia, Monica was struck by the size of Alfons' private jet. "It's a 787 Dreamliner," he shouted down from the top of the aircraft passenger stairs parked at the front entrance door. She started the healthy climb. As soon as she got in range he pulled her up to his body and hugged her. "I've been counting the minutes, waiting for this moment."

"Big deal. Your mother is going to be on the plane."

"Don't worry about her. She'll be asleep soon after takeoff. Then you can suck my cock completely dry."

"No kissing and no blowjobs." Monica didn't want to infect him with the virus, not yet anyway.

No blowjobs? No mile-high club? She heard this pinball through his brain.

She stepped into the cabin. The plane was not like any plane she had ever seen. The exquisite arch of the ceiling was highlighted in different shades of blue backlights, and the first class seats were plusher than any ritzy hotel recliner, set two abreast and each sporting a pillow and blanket. The seats farther back were enclosed in their own compartments, each with its own television, wifi, dining table, and privacy door.

Alfons mother, Maria, came out of one compartment to greet her. "Welcome aboard, Monica." She hugged Monica who had her head turned to look right at Alfons' angry expression.

No blowjobs? His thoughts were so loud he could have been screaming in her ear.

Maria said to Beverley, a cute little African American attendant, "Would you bring us a bottle of white wine?"

"I'll get it right now, Missus Duda."

Monica sat down next to Maria in the first first-class row and heard luggage compartments being closed. Alfons was still mad as she watched him stop Beverley and slip something in her hand.

A roofie, she heard in his mind. *Mom's gonna sleep like a stone.*

A few minutes later, Beverley brought the wine. *Left hand for the pretty black lady, right for Alfons' mother.* She offered Maria a glass first. Reading Beverley's mind also brought her to the conclusion that Alfons had humped her on this plane many times before.

To pass the time, Maria quizzed Monica about Poland, the war and Polish history. After a dinner of red beet soup and pork tripe stew with sauerkraut and rice, followed by more wine, Maria yawned. "I'm suddenly so tired." She decided to go to bed.

"Me too." Monica knew Alfons would be around to see her.

Beverley showed her to her compartment. The Dreamliner compartments made up into real beds. Monica closed the door but didn't lock it then stripped to the buff and slipped her dark slim body under crisp white sheets. It didn't take long before a knock came on the door. "Yes," she called out in her breathiest voice.

"Monica..."

Crap, it was Beverley's voice.

"Mister Duda would like you to join him for a drink."

Annoyed, "Tell him to bring the bottle here," Monica demanded.

"He won't take no for an answer, this I will assure you."

"Okay, tell him I am coming."

"I'm sure you will be very soon."

"Huh?" *Oh. The other coming. This cat and mouse game Beverley is very familiar with.*

Monica got up and redressed, this time in a French-lace dress, lace bra, and no lace thong. *It's a private jet, right?*

Barefoot, Monica made her way to the front of the plane, which suddenly hit turbulence over the Atlantic. Her stomach fell out from under her, and she got banged back and forth. The seatbelt light came on with a chime. Clinging to the overhead bins, she turned around to go back to her compartment. She didn't make it. Alfons came up behind her and put both hands on her shoulders. "You're not afraid of a little turbulence, are you?"

"I can't walk a straight line. The seatbelt light came on so I thought I had better buckle up."

"And so you shall...but in my compartment." Alfons led the way, escorted Monica inside, and locked the door.

His compartment was four times the size of hers, and it had a permanent bed that didn't pull out. The small dining table was set with fine linen, which was in stark contrast to the built-in bar-fridge under the tabletop. The floor threw her off balance so she grabbed a wardrobe closet set in the front wall and noticed a shower stall next to it. Finding her footing, she ran her hand along the polished walnut armrest of a glider rocker. "Nice."

Alfons leaned back on the tipsy bed. "How do you like it?"

"Where's the garage to park your car?"

"Actually, Joseph's limo is in the forward cargo hold. He sleeps in it and flies for free."

"I fly for free. Where do I sleep?"

He patted the mattress. "You don't have to stand. Come on over and sit down."

Monica strode two steps to the bed but, in spite of the turbulence, didn't sit down. "I am not going to be your whore, Alfons."

"But why not? You would be so good at it. Now let's see what your high-dollar salary and my AmEx card has bought me."

The floor bucked as she pulled her dress over her head and let her hair settle back on her ebony shoulders.

Alfons didn't take his eyes off her. "My my."

Monica stood in front of him no more than two feet away. *Brenda, I should kill you for this humiliation.*

Alfons leaned forward and slid his hands up her torso, following those luscious chocolate curves to the perky mounds of her breasts. He explored beneath her C cups and discovered nipples the size of quarters. "I like the feel of your tits. Now take off your bra so I can see all of them."

Slowly, she reached back, unfastened the clasp, and let the straps hang loose as she held the cups in place with both hands and turned her back to him. She jerked her head around to look at him, her hair a fan of black silk, then winked at him.

"Why you fuckin' tease." He adjusted the growing lump in his pants.

She let the bra fall to the unstable floor then turned to face him, hands on her hips, legs spread like Wonder Woman. "Well?"

"Your tits are beautiful. I knew they would be."

The constant tipping and shaking of the plane made her boobs bob all on their own.

He ran his hands up her charcoal thighs, grabbed her perfectly round butt, and pulled the V of her scented thong to his face. "Ah, the smell of a woman so fine." He kissed the soft skin under her bellybutton then licked a trail down to the top hem of her thong where he stopped to savor the flavor of this woman, *a little salt, a little spice, and everything so nice.*

Monica closed her eyes, thought of Brenda, and shuddered.

He took the shudder as a sign of approval, hooked a finger on the hem of her thong, and whispered, "Now for the pièce de résistance." He gently pulled down her thong far enough to allow his tongue access to her most private place, which he licked with slow long strokes.

Even though Alfons wasn't Brenda, or Chloe, or Debbie, not even some hunk of a man, quite the opposite actually, Monica began to feel the heat rise inside. The turbulence added a thrill-ride effect to her growing want, and she had to steady herself with her hands on his head for support.

He took that as a plea for more, tore off her thong, and let his tongue wander down her meaty folds and dip into her honey pot.

She gasped and moaned, and the plane threw her forward so hard she lost her footing and fell over, pushing Alfons to his back on the bed where she landed in a sitting position on his face.

He never complained; his tongue never missed a stroke.

Her heat became a fire only one hose could put out. She keeled over on her back, which gave Alfons the opportunity to worm out of his cloths as if they too were on fire.

Monica smiled up at him...and one of the biggest boners she'd ever seen. No wonder this guy was in high demand. Sure, she wasn't that excited about his big gut, but the fine hairs on his stomach were soft and inviting. At least he wasn't a hairy beast, if she didn't count his beard, but it was still nicely trimmed. "Come on, big boy. Give it to me."

By now, the turbulence was knocking them around pretty good, which made it difficult for Alfons to line up for his plunge. On his knees between her spread legs he did something he very seldom did: asked for help. "Take hold of my cock and put it in."

"Thought you'd never ask." She grabbed a handful of wagging meat, pulled it to her valley, rubbed the head around to get it good and wet then, when she felt it was in the right place, she gave the order. "Go ahead, shove it in."

He did and then laid his gut on top of her, not bothering to use his arms to keep from crushing her. But man oh man did he ever fill her up. That was the reason she couldn't breathe, with all that cock inside her. He grunted then started thrusting, deeper and deeper, she didn't think it would ever hit bottom.

The things I do for the sisterhood.

"Oh, yes, Alfons. That's it. Harder. Fuck me harder. Oh please don't stop."

The bucking plane added to the effect of a Brahma bull ride. One pocket of dead air knocked his dick right out of her just as he was ready to come.

"Put it in, put it in." She grabbed for his cock but missed.

Too late.

"Oh, oh, oh..." He shot white ribbons of cum all over her tummy.

She gasped. "Oh my god, no." Actually, his cream felt rather warm as it pooled in her belly button.

On the other hand, Alfons was as frustrated as a World War II bombardier who'd just dropped his bombs on the wrong target. The plane knocked him over on his side as he held himself and squeezed out every last drop. "Fuck."

Monica thought the whole episode was funny and covered her mouth so she wouldn't laugh out loud in his face.

"I'm gonna kill that fuckin' pilot," Alfons quipped.

"Please wait until after we land."

Alfons lay on the bed, still holding his dick, and looking defeated.

She got up and kissed his forehead. "While you play with yourself, I am going to try out your private shower."

The plane hit a bump of air.

While hanging on and soaping down, she directed the handheld sprayer to her vagina and let the water finish what Alfons had started.

Now cleaned up and dressed, she slapped Alfons' ass as he lay on the bed, facedown and snoring. "Wait until we get to Paris. You won't believe the sex I have in store for you."

He snorted.

She knew the value of her second lease on life, having been old and crippled and now young and vibrant. Sure, she was a lesbian, but she wasn't about to let her youth and vitality go to waste just because the sisterhood wasn't around.

I will love the one I am with, and he will be the first of many.

Staggering back to her compartment on a floor that wouldn't stay still, she was amused at one of Alfons' vice presidents and his wife staring at her. Snickering, they knew what she and Alfons had been doing in his compartment. She leaned to them and whispered, "You two should hope you can get it on that good sometime."

Passing by Beverley, Monica said, "I just love this plane."

Beverley responded in a curt manner, "You're not his first fuck on this jet, you know."

"I know you want to fuck him again," Monica retaliated.

"But he is not interested in you anymore."

***

Meanwhile back on Montford Lane, Debbie and Chloe had been rehashing the fiasco at the church. Chloe got each of them another beer, and they moved to the back deck and sat in the swing. Debby swigged beer like a sailor on shore leave. "You know you cannot go back there. If they see you again, they will call the cops."

"I didn't think I could hit him that hard."

"You're a Lesbian Zombie. You could have killed him."

"I should tell Brenda what happened." Even though it was getting late, Chloe called Brenda.

She was in bed with Jackie. Jackie handed her the phone. "Something is wrong. I can tell by the tone of Chloe's voice."

"Fuck." Brenda put the phone to her ear. "How did things go at the church, Chloe?"

"My ex showed up and I broke his jaw in front of the whole Bible class."

"What the hell was he doing there?"

"He wanted me to marry him again."

Jackie spoke up. "What's the matter?"

Brenda put her hand over the phone. "Chloe turned down a marriage proposal."

"I'm sorry," Chloe cried. "What should we do now?"

"Don't worry about it. You two get some sleep. I'll send Jorge to get you both in the morning. Goodnight." She hung up and handed the phone back to Jackie. "Goddamned personal problems keep getting in the way of progress."

"I guess that means the church's money is history."

Brenda put her finger on her lower lip. "Hmmm...not necessarily. Chloe can't go back. The cops probably want her for simple assault and battery, but Melinda has never been there."

"But she's going to recruit Donna."

"We may have to wait until Monica gets back."

***

At the Aeroport International Toussaint Louverture in Port au Prince, Aurora, Albert, and Reinhard boarded a wide-body jet to Paris, with one stop at Pointe-à-Pitre in Guadalupe. Now sitting in the three middle seats C-D-E of row 34, they quietly discussed what they could do for entertainment once their work was finished.

But business first.

Aurora, dressed in a flowery flowing gown and sandals, passed around pictures of Baby Doc and his grandchildren.

"The kids too?" Reinhard asked in disbelief.

Aurora nodded. "Monica's orders."

Albert whispered to Reinhard, "I don't know what this guy did to get under Monica's skin, but he sure made her mad as hell."

"I guess we'll find out when we get there." Then Reinhard leaned to Aurora. "As you know, Albert and I are just two Brooklyn guys who like to have a good time fucking and breaking bones. I've heard that the French women like American men." He elbowed Aurora's arm. "I don't know how they'll feel about the likes of you."

Aurora flicked her curly hair. "I go both ways, prick, so be careful...unless you want my dick in your ass."

Albert jumped in. "Don't worry. Maybe we can hook you up with some French whore or gigolo. You'll have to tell us what you're in the mood for, beauty or brawn." He laughed.

Aurora wasn't amused. "Maybe I should have killed you both in BBBD's basement."

"Ah, we're just funnin' with you."

"Ha, ha." If looks could kill, those Nazis would have been dead men.

***

At Fort Dix, a wide-awake Maggie lay in bed next to a very

sound asleep Robert. For some unknown reason, she missed her sisters and wondered what they were up to. A phone call seemed in order.

As she sat up, the sheet slipped down off her chest and gathered at her waist. She was still naked from last night's sexual adventures with Robert, and a little sore considering the crazy positions they'd tried out on each other.

Carefully reaching over Robert's nude body, *why don't men care if they're covered or not,* she retrieved her cell from the nightstand and called Debbie.

As the phone rang, Maggie got out of bed and shuffled bowlegged to the tiny dinette in Robert's tiny kitchen.

Debbie answered in a voice full of slumber. "Hello."

"It's me, Maggie." She could've bet money on what would come next.

"How many times did he fuck you today?" she asked sleepily.

"Three and a half."

"Huh? What is a half a fuck?"

"My pussy was getting sore so we finished up with me giving him a nice blowjob."

"Are you pregnant yet?"

"No."

"Then why waste his juice on a blowjob?"

"We just thought it would be a nice change of pace. I can hardly walk as it is. Besides, we'll start over again in the morning. So what's new with my sisters?"

"Let's see. What is new? Chloe about killed her ex-husband in the church. He wanted to marry her again. She broke his jaw and separated the wife-beating bastard from a few of his teeth."

Maggie laughed. "Served him right, I'm sure."

"Monica is on a plane to Paris to kill Baby Doc, and Brenda is fucking Jackie O'Neal."

"The rich painter?"

"Yeah, that is another story...oh, I almost forgot. We got a box of cherry lollipops from that little girl in the wheelchair, ah, Caroline. She survived her disease, and now she is some kind of child-wonder soccer star. So things are good."

"What about you?"

Silence then a sniffle.

"Debbie?"

"My family...a cartel kingpin in Mexico City killed them all."

"Oh, no."

"We are going back on the Day of the Dead to make things right."

"The sisterhood hit squad?"

"When do we get to meet the world's greatest stud?"

"In Las Vegas next Sunday. You're all invited to the wedding, and bring the lollipops."

"Where? When?"

"I'll send you the details by Monday. I gotta go. Robert is up. Oh...he's just going to take a leak. I want to get back in bed before he gets out of the bathroom, surprise him with an offer he can't refuse."

"You go, girl. Call me."

"Bye."

***

At 28,000 feet over the English Channel, Alfons' plane began its descent to land at Charles de Gaulle International Airport in Paris. Eighteen hundred miles behind them at their four o'clock position, the wide-body flight from Pointe-à-Petri and Port au Prince was approaching with the three killers onboard, destined to meet with another killer, the sexy one smiling at Alfons and drinking his wine and whispering in his ear, "You have no idea what I am going to do to you in Paris."

Alfons whispered back, "I get to find out in about three hours. We should be checked into the hotel by then."

"Too bad your mom booked us separate rooms."

"Since when has she stopped us?" He produced a whole

bottle of *roofies* from his pocket.

Monica and Alfons ticked glasses and toasted Maria, still fast asleep in her compartment.

***

In a very rich suburb of Paris, Baby Doc, a contented and loving grandfather told his grandchildren that he would take them to the zoo. They jumped up and down in excitement and hugged their grandfather. He had no idea that his life span and that of his grandchildren were now down to twenty-two hours.

Back in the states, Brenda got out of bed and left a sleeping Jackie to go for a walk on the beach. The sun would be coming up shortly, and she loved the ocean view of the rising sun's rays on the water, like the scattering of diamonds. Bending over to pick up a handful of cool sand she felt her cell vibrate. *Who can be calling me at 5:35 a.m.?*

She answered it to hear Jenny bawling on the other end.

"What's so urgent that you have to call me this early?"

"I'm stuck down here in Port au Prince while everybody else is off having a good time, and that's not fair." After that outburst she wailed into her cell.

Big baby. Brenda let her sob for few seconds and then broke in. "Stop it right there."

"What?" she muttered.

"You're a thief...not only stole my money, you stole my fiancé. Why should I give a shit what's fair to you? I spared your life and gave you a job. Shut the fuck up, already."

"This place is the pits." She sniffed. "Doctor Gomez's old medical clinic, I live here with the rats and no air conditioning."

"I know the Bellagio is more your style."

"All right. I fucked up. I'm sorry. How long are you going to punish me?" The crying began again.

Brenda rolled her eyes. "Okay, maybe you deserve better." She thought about how to appease her Head of Security and stop the waterworks. "Our lawyer, Lisa Swartz, will be down there this coming week to meet with Cassandra and set up home operations for our LZ Foundation. While she's there, I'll have her get you a bungalow right off the beach. Furnish it however you want, on me. How's that?"

"I'm a Lesbian Zombie, for Chrissake, and I'm sick of fucking Aurora. She only looks like a woman. Her dick isn't getting it for me anymore. Why can't I be a part of the sisterhood?"

"You are, dear, but in absentia. Look, I'll arrange for you to come back to the states for a visit? Who knows, you might find the woman of your dreams and stop bellyaching about everything."

"That's so nice of you...*sniff*...I'm sorry. I love you and the sisterhood."

"One last thing, Jenny. What has Cassandra been doing to keep herself busy these days?"

"I don't know. Back in the woods doing her voodoo thing, I guess."

"Has she made any more Lesbian Zombies?"

"Not that I know of."

"All right. Back to work. Eyes open. Let me know if you see anything out of the ordinary."

"I miss you, Brenda."

"Bye, sweetie."

After putting her cell back in her pocket, Brenda walked along the shore, her feet cool on the sand as the waves rushed in and raced up the beach to tickle her toes. *All we have going for us is Jackie, and to a lesser degree so far, Monica with Alfons Duda. We have to expand our cash donors and our influence with the rich and famous and the kingmakers.*

Running one bad idea through her mind after another, bank robbery included, Brenda came up with something that might work. *A charity ball.* She turned around and started back to the house.

"Brenda," Jackie called out.

Brenda met her halfway up the path to her house. "What is it?"

"I woke up and you were gone." Jackie hugged her. "What have you been doing out here in the dark?"

"I have an idea."

Jackie put her hands on her hips. "How much is this going to cost me?"

"Let's throw a big fundraising party to announce the launch of the LZ Foundation."

"Here?"

"Where else? We'll invite the rich and famous and tell them to bring their checkbooks. We'll supply the food, booze, and the pens. What do you think?"

The sun cracked its morning glow on the horizon, as if it too were happy about the idea.

"It's a great idea." With an arm around her back, Jackie turned Brenda toward the house. "I'll make up a list of people to invite. I know them all. Throw in a few movie stars and pro football and baseball players to sweeten the pot. And it's an election year. How about the mayor and a senator or two? They love to be seen at high-profile events."

"I'll get the sisters to use their feminine charms to butter up the bastards then squeeze them for hush money."

"Business as usual for those guys. But there's a problem."

"I should have known."

"We need LZ to stand for something other than Lesbian Zombies. You know everyone is going to ask."

"LZ? Little...Zebra? Fuck, I don't know."

They got back to the house, then: "Race you to the pool." Jackie peeled off her nightgown and took off running.

Brenda lit out right behind her, shedding her nightie, and both women dove into the pool and surfaced, gasping and laughing.

Each commandeered an air mattress and climbed on. While floating on their backs to watch the sky brighten, Jackie made a disturbing comment. "We may have to change the foundation's name."

Brenda replied, "I don't want to do that. I really like the name. We gotta think of something for LZ."

Melinda, naked as the day was young, strode to the edge of the pool. "Lily Zaharias."

"Who?" both women asked.

"She was an obscure feminist way back in the 1680s."

Jackie huffed. "Never heard of her."

"She was hanged as a witch."

"How do you know this?" Brenda asked.

"I walked with a limp and couldn't get a date if I put whipped topping between my legs. So I read books, remembered her name from one of them."

Jackie laughed. "I didn't know you were so smart."

Melinda walked down the steps into the pool, more glamorously than any perfume commercial. "You only knew me as an ugly old lady housemaid." She did the breaststroke to a floating air mattress and slipped onto it, smooth as vanilla ice cream. "I was afraid you'd fire me if I showed I had a brain so I remained mute, played dumb, even though I knew I could win on Jeopardy."

"Melinda, you're a life saver."

"At least now I don't have to worry about being fired."

Jackie paddled her air mattress over to Melinda's, and eating a little crow in the process said, "You sure don't, honey, you sure don't."

"The Lily Zaharias Foundation," Brenda said. "If she were here today, we could use her as a spokeswoman to tell everyone how women have been shit on over the centuries."

Melinda dabbed her hands in the water. "I overheard you talking about a fundraiser. Jackie, you left out one very important category."

"I did?"

"The military."

"That should draw a big crowd."

"You should include General Lawrence Taylor. He's slated to

become the next Chairman of the Joint Chiefs of Staff. You know he's divorced and has a hard-on for you. Remember the Christmas party two years ago? He was fawning all over you."

"What would he think of me now?"

Brenda jumped on that one. "The question is how much would he pay to fuck you now?"

"I hear he likes to pay a woman for sex. That way he doesn't have to buy her a house."

Melinda laughed. "Jackie, would you like a drink?"

"I think we could all use a drink."

"Okay." She pushed down on the edge of Jackie's mattress and dumped her in the water. "Then you better go get our drinks."

All three had a good laugh.

***

Worlds apart, none of Monica's team of killers was laughing while going through customs in Paris. They were there to lower the population of France by three.

Monica had arrived in Paris four hours earlier. She was busy putting her new clothes away in the most expensive suite in the five-star Shangri-La Hotel. The magnificent Eifel Tower rose majestically just outside her window. She reflected on how she'd come from the slums of Port au Prince to the pinnacle of society, thanks to Brenda. *God how I love that woman.*

Alfons was having a drink in the hotel restaurant with some of his equally rich business associates. They discussed the upcoming North Sea Oil Association Dinner for the following night, but his mind was on Monica. *God how I love that woman.*

Monica carried one of her suitcases into the bedroom and slid it under the bed. Having everything in place in the suite, she called her Paris connection, Jacque.

"Madam Monica," he answered with a heavy French accent.

"Are we still on for our guests to be at the country house?"

"Oui. Et l'argent, mademoiselle?"

"The money will be wired to your bank on delivery, Jacque, as agreed."

"Merci." He hung up.

She smiled. The kidnapping plans and the abandoned farmhouse that would be used for the executions were still on track. Now she had to get the money to pay Jacque.

For now, she had nothing to do but wait until Aurora arrived with Albert and Reinhard, the assassins. It would be up to Jacque's people to get the victims to the killing place.

***

Back in Brooklyn, Debbie and Chloe were now on their way to Jackie's, and at the same time, Robert and Maggie were looking at houses in New London. All their thoughts were light-years apart. Maggie was worried about the photos and diary in storage; Debbie counted the days until the Day of the Dead celebrations in Mexico City, Monica was wondering how to get ten Gs from Alfons to pay Jacque in Paris, Chloe contemplated how many years she'd spend in prison for each of Tim's teeth she'd knocked out, not to mention how she might have to kill him sometime in the future. Then there was Jenny who had been mad enough at Brenda to tell the cops about Vegas and what happened to John. Now, as she stood on Kat-Kalen beach, forty miles north of the squalor in Port au Prince, and looked at the perfect bungalow for sale, she was grateful she'd kept her mouth shut, for now.

However, as usual, there was trouble brewing on Long Island. Brenda, Jackie, and Melinda were compiling a list of people they'd invite to the Lily Zaharias Foundation Charity Ball when the phone rang. *International.* Brenda answered, "Salut, Jacque."

"Ils veulent que je kidnappe le garçon et la fille."

"You're going to kidnap the boy and girl?"

"Oui."

"I said no kids."

"J'ai pensé que vous devriez savoir."

"Thanks for letting me know, Jacque." She hung up. "Fuck."

At 3:34 p.m. Paris time, Monica got a call from Brenda. As she answered, she didn't even have time to say hello.

"We don't break our creed. So don't do it."

Monica was speechless. *How did she know—?*

"I can tell by your silence that you disagree. Well, I don't give a goddamn. It's chickenshit to involve the kids You got it?"

"Brenda, I wasn't going to unless—"

"We all agree he has it coming. Need some ideas? Shove a pissed off king cobra up his ass. Give him a sulfuric acid enema. Actually, I like that idea best—"

"Good god, Brenda, you are really upset. I have it all mapped out and I will think about our creed. All right?"

"Do more than just think about it. Not a hair on those kids' heads gets even so much as bent. When will it be done?"

"Tomorrow about this time. I have been waiting forty-seven years for the day to come. Right now I am waiting for Alfons to come up to our suite. I have something special for him that I hope is worth ten grand."

"I have no idea what you're talking about, but I'm sure you'll tell me tomorrow." She hung up.

Monica threw the phone on the bed. "I do not need this shit right now."

***

In Waterford, Connecticut, Maggie fell in love with a country chalet that had been recently remodeled and was on the water's edge. "Robert, this place is perfect."

He exhaled. "I don't know...one million, six hundred thousand dollars is a lot of dollars. Five bedrooms? Do we really need a house this big?"

"We will if you do your duty, dear. We'll need all five bedrooms for all our kids, and it's easy driving distance to your company. Please, please...can we get it?"

Robert looked into her sweet, adorable face. "Sure, honey."

"Thank you, thank you, Robert." She hugged his neck, felt the bristle of his two-day beard on her cheek. "I'll do my part. I can't wait to fill those rooms with babies."

What could he do...other than smile?

***

Back in Paris, Alfons opened the door to their suite and found Monica wearing a see-through nightgown that was only long enough to reach the tops of her thighs. "Whoa, hello there young—"

She held up one finger to shush a very hot Alfons right as he was speaking. "Do not say a fucking word." Taking him by the hand, she led him into her bedroom. "I will tell you when you can speak. I will tell you when you can fuck me. I will tell you when you can come. Got it?"

"Monica, what the—"

"It's Mistress to you from now on."

A fast learner, Alfons bowed. "Yes, Mistress."

Wait 'til I sink my teeth into her bare butt, she'll be calling me Master.

"Just stand here by the bed."

"Yes, Mistress."

She pulled out the suitcase from under the bed and opened it up. "Get your clothes off."

He immediately obeyed, kicked off his shoes, tore off his suit coat, his tie, and destroyed the buttons on his shirt getting out of it. He liked the way she watched his enthusiasm at following her commands. Belt off, zipper down, he had to feel for both under his belly, shucked off his slacks, his shorts, and stood there in only his socks. When he looked down, he couldn't see his socks, but he could see the head of his hard-on reaching out beyond his belly. Wondering what was coming next, he watched Monica sort through the suitcase and slowly remove a riding crop. Her wicked smile gave him a shiver. "What are we gonna do with that?"

Brow creased, she marched up to him and smacked him in

the leg. "No talking."

Fuck. He bowed. "Yes, Mistress."

She stood there hitting her left palm with the crop over and over. "I know you are a mama's boy, and she is really the one in charge at the office, but in the bedroom, I am in charge."

"Yes, Mistress."

"Now lie down on the bed on your back."

Easy enough.

"You have been a bad boy and you have to be punished."

He thought to ask what for but quickly decided to stay quiet.

She picked out a blindfold from the suitcase and put it on him. "And no peeking." She looked at his gorgeous erection and actually felt a pull inside. However, knowing Alfons, he wouldn't play submissive for long, so she fished out a pair of Velcro wrist straps. When she attempted to wrap one around his wrist, he pulled back. "What the fuck?"

That earned him another *smack* with the crop, this time very close to his nuts. "Keep it up, Alfons, you'll be peeing through a tube."

Tube? What's she going to do to me, whip my junk?

"Trust me. This will be fun."

He relaxed his arms so she could tether him to the bedposts. *What the fuck is next?* He quickly found out as Monica straddled his hips and went down on his completely erect cock. Tight, warm, and wet, he was beginning to like this, well, until she said, "Giddy up." She smacked his leg again.

Owe!

"Now we are going to play horse race. I am the jockey and you are the horse. I am in the saddle, very nicely I might add, but if you don't obey me I will whip you." She started riding his cock like a pogo stick. "Faster." She struck his leg. "Go, go, go."

Alfons was in the race of his life, ramming his hips up as her ass came down, finding a rhythm and speed that promised he wouldn't get smacked.

"I want to ride faster," she cried. "Move that big butt of

yours up and down, faster and faster, or I'll have to use the crop."

He couldn't see a damn thing but figured she must be a sight jumping up and down on him, her tits bouncing, and her crop poised to strike. The vision in his mind brought him to the edge of a wildfire in his loins. "Oh, oh..."

"Shut up." *Smack*

"I'm gonna come."

"Don't you dare." *Smack.* "Faster."

The bed frame sounded like it would turn into scrap iron any second.

"Monica, please. I can't hold it."

"Hold it." *Smack.* "I'm not there yet."

"I can't."

Smack

"Yes you can."

"I can't."

Smack "Yes you can. Oh, oh god, yes, yes, yes...you did. You did. Ahhhh... Ahhhh, okay, okay," she screamed. "Now you can come. Come, you bastard, come." *Smack. Smack. Smack.*

Alfons stopped pumping and exploded inside her. He couldn't breathe. His heart was racing one hundred fifty times a minute as every muscle between his legs delivered the goods. "Oh fuck."

Smack.

The crop felt like heaven striking him with lightning bolts. Every nerve in his body rejoiced. *This woman is going to change my life.*

Monica reached up and peeled off his blindfold. She swore his eyeballs were crossed.

He saw two black beauties atop his mighty stud. "What happened?"

Monica leaned over and kissed his neck and his face and his sweaty brow. "You did well for your first race, The Kentucky Derby. The next one will be the Preakness. It is a longer race so you will have to hold out longer or I will not hesitate to use the

George S. Naas

crop. The Belmont will be last. You will need a lot more endurance for that."

His whole body shuddered as he came down from his equestrian high. "I've never met a woman like you before."

She tossed the crop toward her open suitcase. It hit dead center. "Okay, you've had your pleasure, now for the business."

"Business?"

"I need ten thousand dollars in cash."

"I thought you weren't going to be my whore."

She smiled. "I lied."

"Now, Monica, I don't think—"

"Do you want to run the Preakness or not?" She pressed her pussy down hard on his cock, still happily buried inside her, then rose up as if to let it pop out.

"Okay, all right. The Preakness, sure. Chump change. I have that much in the hotel safe, but I got a feeling ten grand's not the end of it."

She patted his cheek and settled deeper into her saddle. "I also need a check for six million dollars made out to the LZ Foundation."

"You're shaking me down for a donation?"

"It is an organization to help battered women worldwide."

"No, no, no. Monica that's too much."

"It will be worth it. A big tax write-off for you plus you will get it back ten times over when you bust your brother."

"Karol?"

"He has been skimming from your company for the last five years."

"No way."

"He told your mother it went to Polish Nazi hunters."

"How could you know that?"

"You gave me the passwords, remember? If I found all those discrepancies in one night working at home, how long would it take the IRS to find the errors in *your* tax returns? They will not blame Karol. Hell no. They will blame you."

"I am so fuckin' screwed."

"Alfons, you have been getting screwed all your life in more ways than one." She climbed out of the saddle, and legs spread above him, gave him one last look at her jockey. "Write the check for the best secretary you've ever had."

"And we're still on for the Preakness?"

She sat on the side of the bed with her butt up against his right calf. "In the bedroom I will always be the dominant and you will always be the submissive. I am a lesbian at heart. No kissing on the lips. No blowjobs, but I will always make you get your rocks off. This pledge will be good until your last horse race. Then we will see. If this does not appeal to you, then you can fire me and hire back that bimbo, Adrienne."

"Oh no, anything but Adrienne."

She removed his wrist straps. "Then you won't mind me taking off tomorrow while you are in meetings. I must take care of a small problem here in Paris."

He sat up. "What's in it for me?"

Good old Alfons. Always got an angle.

"Your main competitor, Scottish North Sea Drilling Corporation will announce that OPEC has accepted their bid, which was higher than what you offered for the drilling rights. Karol told them your bid. They paid him ten million Euros. Is that worth a day off?"

"Yes, and if it all checks out, about my brother, I'll hand you the check for six million myself."

"And the cash."

"Of course. If it doesn't check out, you find your own way home. I can fuck Beverley on the way back."

"Sorry." Monica grinned with confidence. "Beverley is shit out of luck again."

"I don't know what to do about my mother."

"I am sure she means well and I feel sorry your own brother would stab you in the back. If you ever want him to permanently disappear, I know a guy who knows a guy who can handle that for you."

"How much?"

"Six million seems like a good number." She stood and patted his bruised leg. "Just something to think about."

His eyes teared up. "I've been such a fool." He keeled over and sobbed into a pillow. Monica looked at her watch. *Baby Doc's life is now down to twelve hours.*

She called Brenda with the good news of her six million dollar score. Brenda didn't answer. She was busy holding still while Jackie finished her new portrait with Debbie, Chloe, and Melinda looking on.

Jackie applied the last dabs of color. "Done."

Brenda stood, relieved she didn't have to pose anymore, and strode over to the easel. The rocks looked like wilted mushrooms and the incoming surf looked like spilled champagne. "I liked the other one better."

Without responding to Brenda's criticism, Jackie tapped on her wine glass and made a big announcement. "Listen up, ladies. I think it would be a good idea if the entire sisterhood moves in with me. This is a ten bedroom house. Plenty of room for everyone. We could make my mansion our new headquarters. Do we need to vote?"

Brenda spoke up. "That is actually a very good idea. Our place on Montford Lane really belongs to Maggie."

Jackie asked, "When do I get to meet Maggie and her fiancé?"

"Oddly," Chloe stepped in. "She's not a Lesbian Zombie. For some reason the virus didn't take, however, we still consider her a member of the sisterhood. She's working on a big donation for the foundation from her incredibly rich husband's company. Isn't that right, Brenda?"

"Yes, Chloe. That's the plan."

Jackie sipped wine, then: "What company?"

"Galaxy International."

Surprised, Jackie raised her voice. "Hell, I got a lot of stock in

Galaxy International. Maybe Maggie can get us some inside information on any upcoming stock splits or government contracts before it goes public."

Brenda cupped one of her breasts just because it felt good. "We'll invite them to our launch party. Mister and Mrs. Robert Mark Johnson."

Jackie made her second announcement of the night. "Let's all pile into the limo and go eat at Hernandes. It has great Spanish fare."

The sisterhood did not have to be told twice. Brenda and Jackie got dressed in casual wear, jeans and t-shirts while Jorge brought the limo around. As he drove them to the restaurant, the sisterhood, to a woman, was excited about the new living quarters.

Brenda watched the sea shore rush by at sixty miles an hour. Monica and the hit-squad in Paris were on her mind. Baby Doc definitely deserved to get whacked, and the cartel boss in Mexico City shouldn't have killed Debbie's family, but Brenda was sick to death of all the killing. She was living the dream with her sisters, Jackie, the mansion, the limo, and the nightlife. Why bother changing the world for the betterment of women? *Who cares if men are in charge?*

Then that black hunk of coal she called her heart lit fire. The humiliation, degradation, and violation John inflicted on her for the sake of a blowjob and fifty grand, she couldn't let that go. Sure, he paid the ultimate price for his treachery, but he wasn't the only man to fuck over a woman, to steal her money, to run off and fuck another woman.

Those assholes have it coming.

She heard Chloe tell Jackie, "I hope you like dogs," which broke Brenda out of her morbid thoughts of death and revenge. "Ours name is Girlie Dog. She'll bite the balls off any intruder."

***

At precisely 10:00 a.m., a silver limo in the Saint-Germaindes-Pres neighborhood of Paris drove up to the curb. Waiting there was Baby Doc and his two grandchildren, Francois and Anya. Each child was holding one of their papa's hands. Since their father died, Baby Doc was the only papa they'd ever known.

After the driver, Sophia, got them seated in the limo, she headed off in the wrong direction to get to the zoo. The kids were excited to color in their new coloring books of animals at the zoo. It wasn't until Baby Doc glanced out the window and saw a road sign that read Boulogne-Billancourt that he realized they were on the wrong road.

"Pilote." He worked the switch to lower the privacy window separating the back seats from the driver's compartment, but it wouldn't go down. Confusion dumped a load of hot adrenaline into his bloodstream. "Driver," he screamed into the limo's intercom, but Sophie didn't respond, maybe because she wore the ear buds to her iPod.

The traffic light ahead turned red. As the limo stopped, Baby Doc pulled on the handle to open the door. Locked. The window switch did nothing. He tried the handle several times, more frantic at each pull.

The grandkids noticed his panic. "What's the matter, Papa?"

He got a grip on his emotions for their sake. "Nothing, kids. The door is stuck. Probably just the child-lock system. The driver may have hit the switch by accident. We'll relax. Then she will open it when we get to the zoo."

While his grandkids colored their elephants and giraffes, Baby Doc tore a page from a book they weren't using, found a black crayon, and over a fat hippo wrote the following in French: *We are kidnapped! Call the Police! NO Joke!"*

He held up the sign to the window, but no one in the cars they passed paid any attention. What's wrong with you people? You are looking at the magnificent limo. Why don't you see...?" Then he realized it was due to the dark tinted windows. *Fuck.*

The limo turned off onto a rutted dirt road.

A terrible foreboding sank in his chest. Several bumpy

minutes later, the limo stopped in front of a deserted farmhouse. He gathered his grandchildren into his arms, not knowing if he could protect them from the two men and two women who approached the car.

"Papa?" Anya cried.

Francois put his arm around her protectively.

Sophia got out, and as dust swirled up around her, she pulled a basket off the front seat.

A fucking picnic basket? What the hell?

Sophia opened the back door. "Hey, kids," she sang. "Let's have a picnic down by the pond."

"We want to stay with Papa," Francois said.

"Your papa has to talk to these nice people. Not for children to hear."

They looked up at Baby Doc, their little eyes wide with fear.

Sophia added, "There are fish in the pond you can feed."

Baby Doc knew he had no choice but to cooperate. "Go, kids. Feed the fish. Have a nice lunch with the nice lady. We will go to the zoo later."

Reluctantly, they broke from his embrace and scooted out to stand with Sophia.

"Are they going to be all right?" Baby Doc implored.

Sophie forced a smile. "Of course."

When they disappeared into the woods, the door on his side opened, and two tattooed motherfuckers dragged him out. "Easy s'il vous plait."

"Yeah," the black woman said. "Go easy on him."

The muscular pale woman stood behind the two Nazi-looking bad-asses.

"Who are you people?"

"Your worst nightmare," the black beauty spat, "but you can call me Monica."

"Monica. Mademoiselle, what do you want with me?"

"Get him inside."

The bruisers wrestled him into the farmhouse, a boarded up

dusty place, and shoved him to his knees.

Monica stood in front of him, looked down, and spat. "I am going to take your fucking life, you worthless piece of shit, and maybe the lives of those sweet little grandkids of yours."

"W-why? I don't know you. Are you terrorists? Robbers? I can give you lots of money."

Monica smirked. "Fuck you and your money. Think of your execution as death by proxy."

"Exécution?"

"I can't kill the one I would like to kill...that would be your father, Papa Doc. His Tomtons Machetes raped me, murdered my parents then raped and murdered my daughter. She was just a child."

With a look of disbelief he said, "That's impossible. My father died in 1974. You are too young, not even thirty, born long after he was gone. You are making some twisted terrible mistake."

"I knew the monster, the tyrant, and you were no better. You did nothing when my daughter was killed."

"How? It's not possible. You are too young—"

Monica snapped her fingers to one of the Nazis. He handed her a knife, big enough to gut a deer.

"Watch this." She stabbed her left arm with the knife and then pulled it out.

No blood. He saw with his own eyes the wound heal up.

Is this whole thing a bad dream? Maybe he would soon wake up. But the terrors kept coming.

She grabbed him by the hair. "You know what I am?"

"Pas de ce monde."

The muscular woman stepped in and slapped him. "Speak English."

"Not of this world, Madame."

"Wrong. I am a zombie. You don't think we really exist but I am living proof. I am over eighty years old." She turned to her henchmen. "Prepare him to die."

The thugs took hold of his arms and dragged him into the

next room. He looked in terror at the method of his execution. Less than ten feet away stood a guillotine, maybe the last one in the world. Its frame barely fit in the room, and the angled steel blade was raised to the ceiling. Terror lit fires in his bloodstream. "You would cut off my head for something my father did fifty years ago?"

Monica shot him a vicious look. "What better way for a Frenchman to die than by his own invention, the National Razor."

"When I get to heaven, who shall I say sent me?"

"Monica Abelard, your angel of death."

"Abelard?"

"Put him in position," Monica ordered her men.

"I know that name."

The Nazis manhandled him to the death machine, forced him to his knees, and shoved his head in the stock and locked him in.

"I remember you now."

"Aurora," Monica said. "Do the honors."

The muscle-bound woman grabbed the release lever, looked down at the condemned man...then backed away. "I cannot do this."

"What? Are you fuckin' kidding me?"

"I am...er...I was a doctor. I took an oath to do no harm. For the same reason I could not kill Albert and Reinhard, I cannot kill this man."

"Fuck you then. I'll do it." Monica grabbed the lever. "Any last words, Baby Doc?"

"Your father came to my father and told him the Tomtons Machetes had raped you. He was devastated but could never admit, not to the world or to his country that his soldiers had done such a horrible thing to a citizen of Haiti. Five years later, you came back and told me those same soldiers had killed your parents four years earlier and had just raped and killed your five-year old daughter. I too could not make that public knowledge, so in secret I had my men round up the nine Tomtons Machetes. In the dead of night, they were executed by firing squad."

"You are lying."

"I swear on my grandchildren's lives."

Monica had come too far and hated him too long for his lies to stop her now. She pulled the lever. The blade came down at lightning speed, but her second thoughts came faster. In the blink of an eye she grabbed the cable attached to the blade, instantly stopping it with her bare hand, only inches from his neck.

A man who has only his grandchildren left would never swear a lie on their lives.

Monica pulled the blade back up and locked it into position. "Get him up."

The Nazis unlocked the stock and pulled him to his feet. His entire body was shaking and sweat oozed from every pore. "Merci, Mademoiselle."

She poked her finger in his face. "If I ever find out you lied about executing those soldiers, I'll come back and kill your grandkids no matter how old they are."

"Yes, I understand. They will live long and happy lives. Merci. Merci."

Knowing the rapists and murderers had been dead for decades lifted a great weight off Monica's shoulders. She reached up and touched the blade's sharp edge. "That little fucker can really cut. Remember those TV commercials where they chop up tomatoes and cabbages and aluminum cans to show how sharp their knives are? Well, Baby Doc, they would have to take a fucking back seat to this big son of a bitch. Wouldn't you say?"

He cranked his neck and touched his throat. "Yes, I would say so. What happens to me now?"

"Go back to your life and enjoy your grandkids. Oh, I forgot one thing. You will donate the two hundred forty million Euros you stole from Haiti and stashed in banks all over Europe to the LZ Foundation in Port au Prince."

"The LZ Foundation? Is this something new?"

"One day it will save your granddaughter a lot of grief."

They followed the lady-boy and her Nazi musclemen outside where the kids had returned to the car with Sophia. "Who is ready to go to the zoo?" Monica asked them.

The kids ran over and hugged a much relieved Baby Doc. Then Sophia loaded her passengers and sped off in a cloud of dust.

Monica waved then called Brenda.

"Is it done?" she asked when she answered.

"I almost made a terrible mistake. He's alive and well."

"What did you learn?"

"Revenge is a soup best served cold."

Brenda agreed. "Going off hot-headed can bite you in the ass, girl. See you back here soon."

***

Back in the USA, the sisterhood had to do some brainstorming. Chloe led off. "I think I should be the one to seduce Donna, not Melinda. Donna knows we didn't kill her lover. Joanne shot the cop and he shot back. We're not to blame. Donna didn't have many friends, thanks to miss possessive, so she might be receptive to a little cheering up the Lesbian Zombie way."

Debbie was next. "I don't care who I have to seduce as long as I kill those fucking cocksuckers in Mexico City."

An annoyed Brenda countered Debbie's rant. "Okay, already. We all know you want revenge, and we'll be there to help you kill the cartel pricks. Getting back to the subject, there are certain people we need to bring to our side, and a U.S. Senator would definitely be one of them. Chloe holds that key along with Donna. Since Chloe can't go back to the church, Melinda, you can go after the preacher and his wife. Chloe, you get Donna and the senator."

Melinda grumped. "But I want to recruit Donna."

"Plans change. Lesbian Zombies have to be flexible."

"What are you and Jackie gonna be doing?"

"We'll make sure everybody is doing their jobs and that the foundation is up and running. There's no need to think you all have to spread your legs while we don't have to. We'll be doing our share of fucking for the sisterhood. Thanks to your suggestion, Melinda, Jackie has agreed to target Four Star General Lawrence Taylor."

Jackie stuck out her tongue and flicked it real fast, simulating the act of cunnilingus.

The sisterhood stood up and clapped.

"What about Brenda, our Queen of the Zombies?" Putting her arm around Brenda's waist, Jackie kissed her cheek. "Who do you have in mind to fuck so you can fuck over?"

"I don't know yet. I'll let it be a surprise at our launch party. When you see me groping someone, you'll know I've made my decision. Until then I'll just keep sleeping with you, Jackie." With that said, Brenda bent Jackie over backwards and gave her one very passionate kiss.

The sisterhood all yelled, "Ooh la-la."

The sisters then came together and made a circle with arms interlaced and swayed back and forth.

Brenda spoke up again. "We can't change the world with just words. There're only three things needed to reach our goal. Money, influence, and sex. We'll make the world a much better place that'll never go back to what it's been in the past. This I promise you. We will win."

***

In Paris, Monica was getting all dolled up for the big oil drilling in the North Sea association dinner. She was happy when the BBC had reported that Baby Doc had made a historic donation to a foundation in Port au Prince. Alfons stalked up to her as she looked in the mirror, fixing her hair, and kissed the side of her neck. Before he could say anything she had already read his mind. "So, Alfons, I assume you have confronted your brother and he has confessed. Am I right?"

"Yes. I banished him from the family."

"And your mother?"

"Well, you know. She's my mom and I'm a mama's boy..."

"Do you need a pen to write out my check?"

"I've written it out already. Monica you are amazing, saved my company. You're a godsend."

"Well, you are right about that. Loa is my goddess. Have no regrets, because whatever Loa wants, Loa gets, and little man, Loa wants you."

"Right here? Right now?"

She got on her knees and, making sure her gown would not get wrinkled, unzipped his pants.

"A blowjob, fuckin' okay."

"No. A hand job." She went to work stroking him, didn't take long for him to finish. The evening got off to a great start for Alfons and provided Monica with shot of heady hand lotion.

Later, in their suite in Paris, Monica woke up to her vibrating cell phone. She looked at the clock. *5:20 a.m.* It was Saturday. She glanced at Alfons, sleeping like a bear. She covered his white butt with the sheet, reached over him, and picked up her cell. Though she didn't recognize the number, she answered it anyway. "Hello?"

The connection sucked. "Hello?" *Static.* "I can't hear you."

"This is Mrs. Robert Mark Johnson."

Monica, still in a sleepy fog said, "I don't know anyone by that name." She hung up only to hear her cell vibrate again. This time she answered irately. "I said I don't know anybody by that name. Bother someone else." She was about to hang up when she heard: "Monica."

What? She put the phone back to her ear. "I am Monica."

"This is Maggie. I'm in Las Vegas. We were married an hour ago."

"Oh, Maggie. I am sorry for being so rude. Congratulations honey, but...I thought you were getting married next weekend. We all wanted to be there."

"We decided to speed it up and that's not all. I took the pregnancy test and it came back positive. I'm also pregnant. Isn't that wonderful?"

"I am so happy for you both."

"Robert wants to say hello."

"Monica." His voice came on the line like a freight train compared to Maggie's meek little voice. "I'm glad to meet you even if it's over the phone."

"Hello, Robert. I am so glad you two are married and expecting. You are getting a wonderful girl, and from what Maggie tells me, you are the catch of the century."

"I don't know about that. I'm feeling pretty lucky."

"I know that I can speak for the sisterhood when I say we are looking forward to meeting you."

"The sisterhood? What's that?"

Realizing her blunder she explained herself, well, loosely. "Just a nickname for us girls. We are going to have a party in a couple weeks. You two are invited. Brenda will send the details to Maggie."

"Okay, here she is."

"Monica, have Brenda call me to set up Skype here in our room at Circus Circus. I want to talk to everyone."

"Sure, honey. You are sweeter than any of us. Love you, sugar, and we are so happy for you."

"Bye, Monica."

***

Once more Monica and Alfons were at 35,000 feet, heading back to Manhattan, and doing the same thing they did going to Paris. She had a big fat six million dollar check in her purse for Brenda.

Also at 35,000 feet but going another direction, Aurora, Reinhard, and Albert were headed back to Port au Prince with a big fat two hundred forty million Euro check from Baby Doc. Cassandra would soon deposit it into the LZ Foundation coffers.

As the sun caught up with Long Island, the sisterhood had no plans for the day. They were drinking wine by the pool, topless, giving each other massages, and discussing their Lesbian Zombie virus.

Jackie was already plowed. "I wonder if it...works on men."

Brenda stared into her glass. "Monica isn't taking any chances with Alfons. She has two rules. No kissing on the mouth and no blowjobs."

"Hell." Debbie stopped rubbing skin cream on Chloe's back, spread eagle on the massage table. "That can't be any fun."

Chloe murmured, "What if it gives men boobs?"

Brenda threw in her two cents. "Do we really want transgendered Lesbian Zombies in the sisterhood?"

"Creepy." Debbie shuddered.

Brenda explained, "We just want men to become zombie-like and carry out our orders."

"Lady-boys *with* balls?" This came from Chloe, who sat up and took a drink of her wine.

Jackie laughed. "We won't know how...*hic*...the virus works on a man until we...try it. But I don't think any guy...man is going to volunteer, do you, Brenda?"

"I wouldn't."

"Hey." Jackie's eyes lit up. "I know a test subject to try it out on...right now."

"Who?"

"Jorge."

"Your driver? He'll never volunteer."

"But he might be up for a massage...with a happy ending."

Chloe almost spit out her wine. "I won't do it."

Melinda jumped in. "He won't do it."

"Don't tell him he's...a guinea pig."

"What if he turns gay?"

"I don't...picture Jorge sucking cock."

Melinda groaned. "It seems kind of rotten to do him that way."

"I might do him." Debbie sat next to Chloe on the massage table and rubbed herself through her bikini bottom. "He is tall, dark, and handsome, well-proportioned, got one hell of a schlong too, I bet."

"Let's all do him...might be fun." Picking up her cell, Jackie called Jorge.

"Yes, ma'am," he answered.

She cast an evil glance at her sisters. "Jorge, I have a new skin cream formula for men I want to try out. Would you be a dear—?"

"I don't use skin cream."

"Us girls will give you a massage...with it."

"I don't know—"

"Come on, be a sport. We're all topless."

"I was on my way to fuel the limo."

"Forget that. We're out by the pool."

"Okay."

"You're a dear."

"Yes, ma'am."

Closing her cell, Jackie looked around at the dismay on her sisters' faces. "What's the matter...with all of you?"

"You should tell him," Brenda said.

"Maybe the virus doesn't...work on men."

Debbie scowled. "And what if his dick falls off?"

"Quiet. Here he comes now."

Jorge stepped out onto the pool deck, took in each of the topless sisters and all that bare skin aglow in the sunshine. He hadn't seen this many nipples at Dandy Dandy's strip club. *This might be my lucky day.* He could only hope they'd all jump his bones. *Wow.* "I'm here for my massage."

Brenda strode up to him, and in her usual commanding voice said, "Take off your shirt."

He was glad to oblige her since he was proud of his physique, which was the product of countless hours of working out.

"The pants." She snapped her fingers.

He was quickly down to only his boxers.

She led him to the massage table. Debbie and Chloe scooted off. "Get up here and lay face-down."

He found himself surrounded by the sisterhood, all dipping their fingers in familiar jars of *Jackie's Soft Skin Restoration Cream.* Even the label read: *This cream can change your life by making your skin soft and smooth.* "Hey, you said this was something new for men."

Jackie smacked his behind. "Shut up and enjoy the massage."

Melinda dipped her fingers into the wide-mouthed jar and dug out a large glob then began applying the cream to his broad shoulders.

At the same time, Jackie was at work on his back, Debbie on his legs, Brenda on his neck and arms, and Chloe on his feet, as far as she could get from his man parts.

The warm sun, the greasy cream, and all those kneading hands coaxed Jorge's cock into full bloom. He closed his eyes but couldn't relax with his erection crushed beneath him, and throbbing. Finally, relief when Brenda told him, "Roll over."

The girls gasped when they saw his tented boxers.

He smiled.

Gentle hands caressed his chest, his abs, his arms and legs, my god, their nipples were touching his skin, so close, so hot, so hard. He opened his eyes to a blinding sun and smiling faces all surrounded by heavenly coronas. One face came toward his face. Long red hair blotted out the brightness, and hot lips touched his lips, and he welcomed in a wet and probing tongue.

And something else was happening down below. The tent pole had been freed from its confines. Slippery hands glided up and down his shaft and cupped his balls, more hands than two, maybe four, maybe six, and as he stole quick breaths between her lips, the redhead kissed him harder and deeper while those eager and energetic hands massaged his nipples and his erection, and strangely his feet, in ways he'd never dreamed possible.

A fire lit in his loins, a spark turned to flame, a ladder to heaven, each rung afire as he climbed higher and higher. He was a sex slave to a tribe of feral women on a planet in another galaxy. No. Make them women cannibals. One of the sisters had put him in her mouth, all the way in. His engorge tip slammed against the back of her mouth, then the tight grip of her throat strangled the rim, deeper and deeper as he raised his hips to invite her all the way down. Whichever sister it was, she was a deep-throat pro, took his breath away, and set every nerve in his body on fire.

The redhead withdrew long enough for him to suck in some air, and a familiar face took her place. Melinda, her beauty restored to her youth, kissed him with as much passion as the redhead. He couldn't explain her transformation, didn't want it explained to him, he just loved the feel of her wet and warm tongue in his mouth while the fire inside him churned to a raging inferno. At the top of the ladder, everything let loose, and the sisters backed away, leaving his suddenly abandoned cock to jerk and throb unrestrained.

Melinda released him from the kiss and whispered in his ear. "I'm so sorry, Jorge."

Sorry? His breaths came in short spurts as he lifted his head and opened his eyes to see the mess being made on his stomach. "Holy fuck," he managed between gasps.

Debbie wiped skin cream from her lips. "Do you feel any different?"

"My whole body is on fire." His dick kept pumping out cum. "I can't stop coming." It was actually very painful now. "What did you do to me?"

"Do not worry about it." Debbie didn't know what else to say.

"Make it stop." His heart beat so hard he thought it would explode, and the fire inside was so hot he thought he would melt into a puddle on the ground. Dick squirting, he sat up, saw the pool...*water, I've got to cool off*...leaped from the table, and dove into the cold water.

When he didn't surface right away, the sisterhood rushed to

the shallow end where they stood by the steps in a semicircle, all expecting his body to bob to the surface, face-down.

"He drowned," Melinda screamed.

A rush of bubbles boiled to the surface. His head rose slowly from the water, eyes glazed and focused on Brenda as his chest appeared then his abs, tightly muscled and newly bronzed.

The girls stepped back, all but Brenda.

He glided toward her and walked up the steps to the deck where he promptly dropped to one knee at Brenda's feet and looked up into her haloed face. "I serve only thee, my Queen."

***

Later that day, across town, Chloe didn't know what to expect as she knocked on the Barclay suite door of the U.S. Senator from New York, James Hoffman. She knocked and knocked again. Finally she heard a deadbolt lock click, and the door slowly opened.

Donna stood there dressed in a pink nightgown and holding a glass of scotch and a cigarette in the same hand. She looked at Chloe with a *what-the-fuck* expression then turned around and walked back inside.

Chloe followed her, mesmerized by her statuesque frame and runway-model gait.

Donna sat on a black leather couch and propped her feet up on a coffee table, kicking a half-empty beer bottle to the floor. "What are you doing here, Chloe?"

Chloe sat next to her, close enough to savor the scent of her perfume, but far enough not to invade her space. "I've been worried about you, just came here to see how you're holding up."

"What does it look like? I don't have a goddamn care in the world. The love of my life is dead and I have to suck and fuck James every other weekend to keep from being homeless. Outside of that, things couldn't be any peachier."

"You have every right to be pissed off at life but not at me and the sisterhood."

She flipped the cigarette into the fireplace. "How are things with you and your girlfriends? Has the redhead beat the shit out of anyone in a restroom lately?"

Chloe countered, "Anybody beat the hell out of you lately?"

She sighed, contemplated then: "Do you want a drink?"

"I want you to join us."

"Great. I want another drink." Donna strode to the bar, poured another glass of scotch, and returned with a rant. "Every time I look at the sliding glass door, I remember James swearing up and down that miss redhead threw a bottle all the way across the street. Is that crazy?"

"He wasn't lying."

"Do you realize that's over a hundred yards?"

"And she almost hit him."

Donna sucked down some more scotch. "Is she from Mars?"

"Donna, come and meet Brenda and my friends. Join us. You won't be dependent on James anymore. You'll be your own woman with the sisterhood."

"Sounds like a cult."

"We're something so unusual that you can't imagine how your life will change. Beats drinking yourself under the table. Come with me to Long Island."

"Are you all fuckin' rich bitches?"

"What have you got to lose?"

"I'll think it over. Now scram. I got some serious drinking to do."

"Okay. Let me give you a hug before I go."

"Suit yourself."

Chloe hugged a stiff body that smelled like ten packs of cigarettes and the bottom of a scotch bottle. "I'm not going to give up on you, Donna...not ever. I left a wife-beater husband in Ohio. He would've eventually killed me. You and I have suffered the same pain. We need to stick together."

Donna started to sob. "Just go, please."

Chloe stood and dropped her card on the coffee table. "Call

me."

***

Later, as Maggie and Robert landed at JFK, back from Vegas, two limos arrived at Jackie's place within forty-five seconds of each other. Monica was in Alfons' limo, and Chloe was in Jackie's with Jorge behind the wheel. He didn't say anything when he picked her up in front of the Barclay Building, acted like an oversexed zombie, playing with himself at stoplights. At least his dick hadn't fallen off.

Walking up the driveway with Monica, Chloe filled her in on her progress, or lack thereof, with Donna, her rebuff still a fresh sting in Chloe's heart. Monica all but bragged about what happened in Paris and the Kentucky Derby race with Alfons.

"I don't know how you can stand touching his dick."

"Spoken like a true lesbian. I go with what makes me feel good, and having Alfons wrapped around my little black finger feels great."

They walked through the house to the pool and saw everyone lounging around, taking a nudist-camp-style siesta. Monica strode to Brenda's chair and shook her awake. "What's going on here?"

Brenda stretched and, arching her back, inadvertently displayed the finest breasts in the universe. "Oh, you're back from Paris," she said sleepily then noticed Chloe. "Did you bring Donna back with you?"

"She has a drinking problem."

Jackie snorted from two chairs away.

"Not another one." Brenda sat up. "Take off your clothes and join us."

Monica pursed her lips, then: "New dress code around here?"

"Not a bad idea." Brenda yawned. "We wanted to see what effect the Lesbian Zombie virus had on men, so we made Jorge an offer he couldn't refuse, not from five topless sisters, anyway."

Topless now, Chloe chimed in. "They gave him the best massage of his life. I just did his feet." She shuddered. "Ick."

Monica frowned. "Are you telling me Jorge is now a Lesbian Zombie?"

"No. And he's not gay. He's not transgendered, he's, in fact, all male and only loyal to me."

"And he plays with his dick at stoplights," Chloe added then dropped her panties.

Monica shot her a you-gotta-be-kidding look. "What progress have you made with Leroy and his wife?"

"Don't look at me." Chloe snuggled up to still snoozing Debbie on a cushioned lounger, shaded by potted ferns.

Brenda folded her arms under her superb chest. "You're supposed to get Donna onboard so we can snag Senator Hoffman. My concern is that you're more interested in getting Donna's panties off than you are in seducing the senator."

"He wasn't there...and yes, I'd do Donna in a heartbeat. She's hurting now. Give her time to come around."

"I need him at the launch party."

"You'll get him when Donna's damn good and ready."

Debbie stirred, found Chloe snuggled up in the lounger with her, and kissed her neck. "What is all the yelling about?"

"Lesbian Zombie interrogation," Chloe grumbled.

Monica spoke up. "Debbie, we will have the use of Alfons' jet and limo...departing LaGuardia on the twenty-ninth. What is the news in Mexico City?"

Still nuzzling Chloe's neck: "My friend Polo has a taco bar restaurant and many connections. He will get one casket, a cheap one, and the costumes we need. I am depending on you to get Jacque and Sophie there on time."

"Jacque is flying in from Paris a day before the Day of the Dead celebrations."

"How is he going to deliver Pedro and El Paco to the rendezvous place?"

"Don't ask. Don't tell. Have you decided on the manner of

their deaths?"

Debbie sat up, her perky nipples excited by Chloe so near. "Oh, you will not believe the surprise I have planned for those pricks. Best of all, none of us will have to get blood on our hands."

***

Later that night, the sisterhood, all bundled up now, sat around a bonfire fire and roasted marshmallows while waves from the Atlantic Ocean washed up on the shore. The sand was warm and felt good on their bare feet but the October ocean breeze was cold on Long Island.

Jackie lay on her back, resting her head on Brenda's stomach. "For the first time in my life I feel at peace. Here with my sisters I'm content. Sure, I know hundreds of people and I've been to countless parties, but I always felt alone compared to now."

Monica watched her marshmallow turn black and catch fire. "Only a few months ago," she blew and blew and blew out the flames, "I went from decrepit and old to overwhelmingly beautiful and filled with joy...the night that I met Brenda."

Melinda's marshmallow turned out beautifully brown. "I'll throw in my two cents worth. If not for Brenda, I'd be dead and Jackie would have hired another maid to terrorize."

"Melinda, you're such a drama queen."

"See what I mean? She still doesn't respect me."

"I love you," Jackie told her.

Chloe took her turn. "If Tim hadn't been a first-class prick, I'd still be in Ohio sucking his cock. Thanks to Brenda taking me in and Debbie taking me on, I found out why I didn't enjoy men so much. I'm a lesbian and proud of it."

Debbie had to laugh. "I didn't know about sex until I got waylaid in Haiti and shacked up with Dr. Gomez. Now I like sex, man sex, women sex, self sex, I am good with it all. But you should thank me for botching Brenda's anesthesia for surgery. If I had not goofed up the dosage, none of us would be here today.

"Thank you, Debbie."

"Yeah, thank you."

Jackie stabbed another marshmallow on the end of her stick. "Brenda, you haven't said a word."

The fire warmed her face but didn't melt the ice in her heart. "My journey here was hard and cruel. Hundreds of people went out of their way to make fun of me, laugh at my fat body, and say terrible things about my pimply face. I'd pretend I didn't hear them though each insult was like a knife making small cuts in my flesh. Then, in the solitude of death, thank you, Debbie, the Lesbian Goddess Loa came to me on that night in Haiti and told me her story as we dined, how she was oppressed and ridiculed by the male gods, how she killed them all and took over as sole ruler of the universe."

Jackie inhaled, then: "You mean God is dead?"

"God has been dead in the hearts of men for a long time. Loa thrives in the hearts of many, many women who long for equality and respect. She had seen enough of our struggle and sent me to right the wrongs of men. She is with us now, and our actions will be her actions."

Melinda had to ask, "How is it that we're young again and can never grow old?"

Brenda munched on a marshmallow straight out of the bag. "It's complicated," she managed while chewing the goo. "In all of our cells there are chromosomes capped at each end with Telomere proteins that protect the genes during cell division. They get shorter each time the cells divide, and as a result, the body ages and dies. Our Telomere proteins get longer, thanks to the virus and the incredible surge of energy during orgasm. We get stronger, smarter and more beautiful."

"How did you come to know this?"

"The Goddess Loa told me as we dined the night I died."

The sisterhood sat silent. Then Debbie asked, "How did she kill the male gods?"

"The Lesbian Goddess Loa got naked, seduced the gods to have sex with her in a celestial orgy, and got all of them drunk.

While they slept off their stupors, she cut their Telomeres. When they woke up they looked at their bodies and saw they were turning to dust. They cried, 'We are sorry,' but their cries fell on deaf ears."

"So we are the embodiment of Loa?" Jackie asked.

"And that's the truth, sisters."

***

Sitting on a mattress on the floor in their new million dollar home, Robert and Maggie were discussing what kind of furniture they wanted. Just then Robert's cell vibrated. It was an email from General Taylor. Robert read it and responded.

[I'm sorry, General, but I now have a pregnant wife and my late father's business to run. I cannot stay in the Army for another four months and go on another mission in Afghanistan. Sincerely, Captain Robert Mark Johnson O17595313.]

Maggie's brow bent with worry. "What was that all about?"

"Nothing." Robert took her in his arms and kissed her. "I love you."

***

Back on Long Island, the sisterhood was walking in the cold surf of the Atlantic Ocean. Brenda felt a pull in her heart and an idea blossomed in her brain, one planted by Loa herself. The idea was the most spectacular feat of engineering ever to be envisioned on earth.

"Sisters, we must erect a shrine to the Lesbian Goddess Loa for the kindness she has poured out on all of us. Jackie, we need to use the old greenhouse attached to the south side of the house."

"But I was going to make that a sunroom and giant terrarium."

"It will be the perfect place for us to pay homage to the Goddesses Loa when the moon is full."

"All right." Jackie sighed. "You design it and I'll have it built in time for the party. While you're all gone to Mexico City."

"But there's something special we need."

"Special?"

"Seeds from the Tree of Life, to grow a sister tree in the shrine. Loa has commanded it."

"We certainly can't get those seeds from Home Depot."

"I know exactly where they are."

Back at the house, Brenda called Cassandra.

"Hello, my Queen."

"Is the LZ Foundation in business?"

"It is. Your lawyer, Lisa Swartz, a nice gal and very smart, has left the island. We have already over five million on deposit."

"And what about Jenny's house on the beach?"

"We are enjoying the new digs very much."

"Don't let Jenny anywhere near our money or she'll break the bank."

"She has been acting very strange. Something is on her mind."

"Keep an eye on her."

"Yes, my Queen."

"Now for the reason I called. I need at least three seeds from the Tree of Life."

Cassandra huffed. "They are very rare, Brenda. And very costly."

"How much?"

"The blood of a Lesbian Zombie."

Brenda's chest felt like a truck had parked on it. "A little blood?"

"A life."

"I can't sacrifice one of my sisters."

"Loa demands it. I will go down into the Pit of the Ages and look for the seeds. They come in pods of three for wind, water, and fire. If I am successful, and find only one pod, I will FedEx it to you, on credit. You will have thirty days to make payment." The Voodoo High Priestess hung up.

"Cassandra?"

"Bad news?" Jackie asked.

Brenda swallowed hard. "Loa is a very demanding Goddess who must not be denied." She put her head in her hands and cried.

Who will I choose for the sacrifice?

***

Chloe answered her cell phone and heard a very subdued voice. "Chloe, this is Donna. Would you please come over? I keep thinking about what you said and I need some company right now."

"Just relax. I'm on my way." She hung up, her heart all aflutter. "Jackie. Can Jorge drive me to Donna's?"

"I don't know. Brenda is keeping him pretty busy. I'll call and see."

"Jorge," she said into her phone. "Are you available to drive?"

"Yes, ma'am. Fifteen minutes."

Waiting in the driveway, Chloe practically got run over by the limo as Jorge pulled up. She didn't wait for him to get out and open the door, just jumped in and told him, "Take me to the Barclay."

As they drove down the interstate, Chloe asked him, "How have you been?"

He stared straight forward.

She sensed that something was different about him. "Jorge, are you all right?"

Silence.

"I hope Donna doesn't kill herself. She's been really depressed since the cops killed her girlfriend."

That earned her a glance in the rearview mirror from Jorge. "I feel so bad for her," he muttered and sniffled.

Chloe saw a tear slip down his cheek. "Don't worry, Jorge. I'm going to take care of her."

"Please, miss Chloe. I don't want to talk about it." He went back to staring straight forward.

He doesn't sound like the old Jorge that I knew.

Arriving at the Barclay, she saw Donna waiting for her outside.

Jorge said, "Is that her?"

"Yes."

"She looks so upset." His voice was all sobby. "I feel sorry for her."

"Are you for real? Guys don't give a shit about a woman's personal problems. You all just act like you're listening just to get in our pants."

He threw his head on the steering wheel and broke out in tears.

"Jeeze." Chloe got out and noticed Jorge had his cock out of his pants, holding it in a death grip. "Oh, yuk. Wait for me here, even if it takes all night, and play with your new toy."

Donna rushed up to her, "Chloe," and threw her arms around her neck. "I've been such a fool."

"Let's go in and talk about it."

The last Jorge saw of them, they were arm in arm as they disappeared through the entrance doors.

Once in the senator's suite, Donna led her into the bedroom. "Wait here." She went into the bathroom, and when she came out, she was completely naked, standing there, hands clasped in front of the V between her legs. She heard Donna's pleading thoughts. *Please, Chloe, tell me I'm beautiful. Tell me you want me. If you don't, I'll throw myself off the balcony.*

"Donna, you are absolutely gorgeous." Chloe started to unbutton her blouse, but Donna stepped in.

"Let me help you."

Chloe just stood there like a sex goddess being attended to by her slave. The blouse came off, the bra, and then Donna worked her way down to the skirt. Everything ended up in a pile on the floor. Now wearing only a black thong and white high heels, she stood before Donna and listened to her thoughts.

God I want this woman so bad.

"Chloe, you're the hottest blonde I've ever known." Donna dropped to her knees and slid the thong down Chloe's magnificent thighs, revealing her shaved mons and delectable lips.

Donna's mouth watered in anticipation. She pressed her face into Chloe's woman-flesh, inhaled the most wonderful woman-scent, and began kissing circles around her perked up clit.

"Oh, Donna, please...you're teasing me."

With that, Donna let her tongue loose on the most wonderful place on a woman's body.

Chloe shuddered. Her vagina clenched. Bolts of electrified nerves raced up her back. *This is what I've been waiting for. I'm not going to tell her how this night will change her life forever.*

As Donna left a trail of butterfly kisses up Chloe's body, she paused at her bellybutton for a swirling lick then moved up to her breasts to lavish her nipples.

Chloe stepped out of her shoes. Her nipples were hard and ready to take all that Donna's lips had to offer.

"You taste so good," Donna breathed. With a light shove, they tumbled onto the bed where Donna delivered herself to her destiny. Her mouth met Chloe's with hungry abandon. Their legs intertwined and Donna slipped her hands around Chloe to her smooth and soft ass. One hand explored no-man's land from behind where her finger pressed into her pink and moist valley.

Chloe gasped in surprise at Donna's slick maneuver. It quickly became apparent that Donna was a pro at lesbian sex, whereas Chloe was just a beginner. All the while Donna's finger dipped and slid about, the juicy kissing continued. The virus had been administered. Now all that was left were the fireworks.

***

Sitting in the limo in a loading zone, Jorge's obsession for his new sex drive had him stroking himself off for the third time. As the tip ejected more cum on his trousers, he leaned his head back and opened his bleary eyes in time to see U.S. Senator James Hoffman enter the building. Jorge recognized him from all his campaign ads and posters, and his trademark pinstriped suit, courtesy of U.S. taxpayers. His imagination went to Chloe and Donna fucking each other's brains out upstairs when the senator catches them in action. *Oh my god, those girls must be a sight to see.*

Another surge of pearly cream erupted onto his trousers.

***

In suite 1524, Donna and Chloe never heard the door unlock. Wrapped in their own noisy affair, they'd wriggled themselves into the 69 position, each pleasuring the other until:

"A-hum."

Tongues stopped licking. Throats stopped moaning. Both craned their necks toward the open door to see Senator James Hoffman leaning against the doorframe.

"What do we have here?" he said with a smirk.

Chloe rolled off Donna and promptly fell off the bed.

Donna just lay there, legs spread and glowering at James.

"Who's your attractive and very sexy girlfriend?"

Donna brushed a lock of ebony hair from her face. "What are you doing home, James?"

Chloe was near panic, naked in front of this man whose expression just flipped from amused to angry.

"I should ask you the same thing."

"Isn't it obvious? We're having sex, you know, when two people love each other, not like you and me, two caged animals fighting for survival."

Chloe was suddenly struck with a dilemma. Donna hadn't come yet, and her mood was quickly deteriorating. The tension in the room could've turned the air to mud. And her main goal, the senator, was suddenly within reach. *Brenda won't be happy if I let him get away now.* She steeled herself against the grossness of his hairy balls and slimy cum for the sisterhood.

Forcing a smile, she got up off the floor and strode to him as if she were fully clothed. "Well, hello there. My name is Chloe."

His smile returned and he stood up straight. "Chloe."

"You must be the great and awesome senator I've heard so much about."

"Not from me," Donna spat.

"Lighten up, girl," Chloe cooed. "We've got a live one here."

"Yes. I'm Senator James Hoffman."

"I knew it." She clicked her fingers. "How did I get so lucky?"

He unzipped his pants. "Meet Lucky."

"Really? You'll let me give you a blowjob?" She sounded as coy as a high school girl on prom night.

Donna sat up. "James, don't be a bore."

Chloe dropped to her knees and reached in through the zipper hole. "Donna, please don't ruin this for me." She pulled out his cock, not quite hard but obviously interested, forced a hungry stare, then kissed the tip. "I've always wanted to suck off a senator."

"Oh yeah," he breathed.

She looked up to see his wicked smile. *He has no idea what I'm going to do to him.* She shifted a sly glance to Donna. "I could use a little help here."

Donna groaned, got off the bed, and joined Chloe on her knees before man's best friend, his cock.

Chloe angled the growing shaft, offering the head to Donna in a tease. "Wanna taste?"

"You go first."

"I want to see how you do it."

"Guests always go first."

"Goddamnit," James blurted out. "Somebody suck the damn thing."

Chloe shrugged, swallowed like she was about to eat spinach, and plunged the cock into her mouth. And she sucked him with reckless abandon, not for the love of sucking cock, but to

George S. Naas

get it over with as quickly as possible.

Donna undid his pants and pulled them down around his ankles, then went to work cupping his ball sack and kissing around the base.

"Oh fuck," he moaned breathlessly.

Funny how a man's knees go weak at a time like this.

Chloe made sure she got him good and slobbered up. She slipped her hand around behind Donna's ass and slid her fingers into her wet opening, now pleasuring both at the same time.

Donna moaned in delight.

James groaned in delight.

She worked them both in Lesbian Zombie style, occasionally giving way to Donna's lips to kiss her then letting her suck the cock a little before taking it back into her own mouth to suck it again in earnest. With Donna so close, and her fingers inside Chloe, this cock sucking didn't seem so bad after all. The three of them got on a magic carpet ride that took them to the moon and ended in a crazy three-way orgasm. He pulled out of Chloe's mouth and offered the reward to Donna, who'd been there and done that before. She swallowed him down while enjoying her own orgasm.

Chloe backed away and let them finish each other. *Brenda's going to be so proud of me. Two at the same time. Slam bam thank you ma'am.*

Then something went horribly wrong. James had both hands on Donna's head, making it impossible for her to retreat. He kept pumping cum in her faster than she could swallow or spit.

"Suck it, suck it, suck it," he shouted. "Fuck. I can't stop coming."

Donna started choking and gagging and turning blue.

Chloe screamed, "No," and bulled into them, dislodging Donna from James' grasp. They both landed on the floor, Donna gasping for air and James holding his cock like it was some kind of vicious cobra spitting venom.

"Make it stop. Make it stop."

Chloe scrambled to Donna, turned her head to the side, and made sure she hadn't swallowed her tongue. "You're going to be okay."

Donna coughed and wheezed and finally caught her breath. "What happened?"

"I should have known he'd go whacky."

They turned to look at James. To their surprise and shock, James was on his feet, completely naked, his hard-on drained and bouncing with muscular spasms. He was looking at Chloe. "Take me to your Queen."

Donna scooted away from him. "What's he talking about?"

"Get dressed. You're coming with me."

As they scrambled into their clothes, James stepped forward. "Take me to your Queen."

Chloe slipped into her shoes. "You'll get an invitation to the LZ Foundation charity ball. You will meet her then, I promise."

"Queen?" Donna muttered.

"Donna, let's go, unless you want to get laid for the next twenty-four hours straight."

Hand in hand, they fled the suite and rushed down to the curb where Jorge was holding open the back door to the limo. It was impossible to miss the wet stain on his pants. "Ladies."

They tumbled inside.

Jorge got behind the wheel. "Did you have an enjoyable evening?"

"Take us home. We'll explain later."

"Yes, ma'am."

Chloe was surprised to find that Jorge was back to talking like his old self. She was even more surprised when Donna dragged her down on the seat and started smothering her with kisses.

***

The morning found a very excited Maggie sitting in front of her computer with a headset on, talking to some high-priced furniture store in Manhattan. The excitement in her voice woke up Robert. As he shuffled into the room, massaging his back from sleeping on the floor all night, he heard Maggie say, "Yes, I want the mahogany dining room set and the walnut bedroom set too. Can you deliver them tomorrow? Oh, today is even better. I'll put it on my husband's credit card."

He stepped up behind her and kissed her neck. "Did you buy out the entire furniture store?"

"I'm working on it."

"Let's go get some breakfast. Bacon, eggs, and grits."

"Good idea. Baby Johnson and I are starving to...to..."

"Sugar?"

"Oh, no."

"What's wrong? You're looking a little pale—"

She threw her hand over her mouth and ran into the bathroom where she promptly vomited in the toilet. "Agghhr."

Robert didn't know what to say.

She coughed and spit. "I hate this shit." Another wave of nausea gripped her. Just the thought of eating eggs spawned another round of rank spew. "Morning sickness sucks."

***

Back on Kat-Kalen Beach, Jenny and Cassandra were lying in bed cuddled up just yards from the breaking surf. "I don't want to do security anymore," Jenny complained.

Cassandra rubbed her wife's shoulder. "But you are doing such a great job. Aurora and his goons just sit around drinking rum all day."

"I want to be in charge of discretionary spending."

This brought a laugh from Cassandra and a firm comment. "Honey, that ain't never gonna happen...not in a million years. You have a lot of good qualities but safekeeping someone else's money isn't one of them."

"Says who?"

"Brenda, our Queen."

"Fuck her."

"Don't be so pissed off. It don't look good on you."

"It's time for Brenda to bow to me."

Cassandra rose up on one elbow. "What have you been smokin', girl?"

"I can make her promote me to CFO."

"You know Jackie is CFO."

She turned to face Cassandra. "I have a secret weapon I can hold over Brenda's head. She'll do whatever I want. Fire Jackie and put me in charge of the finances, if she knows what's good for her."

"What would that weapon be?"

"She killed my ex-husband. I was there. Crushed his skull with a big rock, she did. I could threaten to rat her out to the cops. She'll fold like a bad poker hand or she'll go to prison for a long time. You and I could spend that money on ourselves and get out of this stink hole."

"This stink hole is my home."

Jenny caressed Cassandra's cheek. "Think of it, Las Vegas, Hollywood, Monte Carlo, the Riviera. The world will be our oyster."

"Oysters are very slimy."

"We can eventually get out of this Lesbian Zombie rat race."

"You forget somethin'."

"What?"

"I am not a Lesbian Zombie, just an intermediary, a Voodoo High Priestess."

"You'll always be my princess. Please. You do love me, don't you?"

"More than anything, girl, but Brenda is very smart. We have to be careful, plan very well. You threaten her, she will kill you, me too if she knew what we are planning."

"That would be against her creed to never kill women and children."

"I don't know. She might make an exception for us."

Chapter 9: THEY DON'T CALL IT THE DAY OF THE DEAD FOR NOTHING

After arriving in Mexico City on Alfons' jet and clearing customs, the sisterhood: Brenda, Monica, Chloe, and Debbie, walked out into the unseasonably warm afternoon of seventy degrees on this late October day. Jackie, Melinda, and Donna stayed in New York to facilitate the construction of Loa's shrine. The seeds for the Sister Tree of Life had arrived by FedEx just before they all left for LaGuardia.

A long black hearse pulled up to passenger pick up and stopped. The Mexican driver popped out, dressed like a mariachi guitarist, sombrero and all. "Miss Lopez, it is you?"

"Polo, my friend."

"My how you have grown since your mariachi days." He hugged her.

"The hearse is a nice touch."

"A rental for Day of the Dead."

She rushed to look through the tinted window, her hand cupped on the glass to block the sun. "Is it in there?"

"Si, and a bag of surprises, very big surprises."

She could barely make out the shape of a casket inside.

Just then, a long black limo careened around the corner with Joseph behind the wheel and Alfons riding shotgun. The car glided to a stop next to the hearse.

"Get in, sisters," Debbie instructed.

"Where are we going?"

"To the place of my father's betrayal." Debbie got in the hearse with Polo. The others piled into the limo then the procession sped out of the airport and soon looked out of place among the shanties and broken-down vehicles in the slums of Mexico City.

Debbie turned to look behind her, saw the black painted casket befitting a Day of the Dead parade. There were two cardboard boxes set beside it. "What's in the boxes?"

"The costumes you requested."

"And the surprises?"

"They are safely riding in the spare tire well."

"Smart."

The hearse took a turn down a dirt road and into a familiar neighborhood. Pedro's house stood in disrepair, windows boarded, the lawn overgrown with weeds and cacti. Even in the daylight, the terror of that night and her fateful escape threatened to choke off her air.

The procession drove around back to the shack. It looked so much smaller and frailer than she remembered.

Polo stopped. The limo stopped. Everyone got out. Alfons and Joseph inspected the shack, found a way to open the patched-up garage door. Birds flew out in every direction.

"Come on, girls. Let's get the hearse unloaded."

The casket was heavy for a Halloween prop. They set it on the dirt floor of the shack where the old pickup was once parked. The boxes came in, and finally, a burlap bag Polo set apart from everything and everyone. It made a rattling sound when it hit the floor.

Debbie turned a full circle and wondered how many other women had been successfully raped in this disgusting place. She saw the same busted up toilet and even spotted shards of glass from the Tequila bottle she'd busted over Pedro's head. That brought a smile to her face.

She unhooked the two sturdy latches and opened the casket lid. With a hiss and the twang of springs, a skeleton sat up, its eyes flashing red, its head twisting about, its jaw flapping as if to say, *Get me out of here.*

The sisters jumped back in surprise.

Polo laughed. "It is the best I could find for cheap."

Monica huffed. "Very funny."

Joseph and Alfons removed the automaton and set it on the broken toilet as if it were taking a dump then stripped out the cheap casket liner, leaving only the rough boards inside. Polo closed the lid.

Debbie bent over a five-inch hole he'd cut in the lid and looked in, half expecting to see a dick jump out. "Perfect." She backed away.

"Okay, let's try it out." Polo opened the lid. "You and you." He pointed to Joseph and Alfons. "Get in."

"Not on your life." Alfons shook his head.

Monica applied the pressure. "We have to be sure two full-grown men can fit with the lid closed, dear. Be a sport."

"What's in it for me?"

"Shut the fuck up and get in."

Joseph got in first, on his back, then Alfons climbed in on top of him, on his back. Polo closed the lid just fine.

Monica reached in the hole and grabbed Alfons' cock through his pants. "Perfect."

"Are you done fuckin' around?" Alfons spat.

Polo opened the lid and both men bailed out.

Alfons scratched his beard. I don't get it. You're gonna bury the cartel guys alive, so why put an air hole in the casket?"

"It is not an air hole," Debbie assured him.

"What? A glory hole?"

"They will only wish." Debbie laughed at her cunningness. "Let's get our costumes on. Jacque will be here soon with our special guests."

The sisters got into skeleton costumes with white skull masks, drank some Tequila, and got in the mood for the real Day of the Dead celebrations.

Joseph and Polo and Alfons left for the hotel where they would meet later to celebrate. Monica closed the garage door and they waited in the dark and dusty air.

As dusk settled over Mexico City and the streets came alive with the haunting screams of partygoers and loud fiesta music, tires crunched dirt outside the shack. The garage door rolled open to reveal the grim reaper. "Aidez-moi avec ces Bozos."

"Jacque needs help with those bozos," Monica translated.

Brenda and Chloe rushed out in skeletal haste to a silver limo. Monica nodded hello to the driver: Sophia, dressed as Wonder Woman.

Inside, they found Pedro and El Paco trussed up like pigs at a pig roast, well...minus the apples, but plus the Armani suits. They protested under their duct-tape gags, just sounded like a bunch of frantic mumbling.

The costumed girls wrestled their captives into the shack. Monica gave Jacque an envelope fat with cash. "Thanks, again, my friend." The silver limo sped away in a cloud of dust. She closed the garage door.

The killers were forced to sit in the dirt, back to back, and Debbie roped them together. She walked up to Pedro, leaned down and ripped off his gag.

"You fuckin' cocksuckers," were the first words out of his mouth.

El Paco squirmed against his bindings.

Debbie knelt to Pedro's eye level and glared at him from under her mask. "Bet you really want to fuck me now."

"Fuck you? I want to kill you, you...ah...your voice is familiar. Do I know you?"

She lifted her mask to show him her white-painted face.

He laughed. "Debbie, of course. Now I see you are into bondage. What a pleasant surprise."

"You will soon be screaming for mercy, fool."

"Why you little fuckin' cun—"

She slapped the duct tape back over his filthy mouth. His

eyes glared at her, wide and round and filled with defiance.

Standing, she moved around to the man who had murdered her father and brothers, raped and murdered her mother, all because her father wouldn't let him get his greasy paws on her. She knelt down and ripped off the duct tape from El Paco's mouth. "You killed my family."

He said nothing.

"You too will be begging for mercy." She left the tape off his mouth and backed away. "Get them up."

Brenda lifted both of them off the ground, easy peasy, while Chloe and Monica stripped them of their shoes, slacks, and boxers, then tossed the garments in the corner with the skeleton on the toilet. The killers' little pee-pees were shriveled up so tight they couldn't rape anyone if they tried.

Debbie opened the casket lid. The hinges squeaked. "Put them in." This was Debbie's show and the sisters moved to obey.

Now El Paco spoke up while bracing his stocking foot against the coffin rim. "You will bury us alive?"

Debbie scowled. "You should be so lucky."

Pedro's duct tape dammed up a slew of expletives. Debbie ripped off the gag and let him roar.

Brenda singlehandedly slammed both condemned killers into the casket, Pedro on the bottom, El Paco on top.

"My people will find you and kill you."

Brenda looked down at their sorry asses. "Your people will die too, motherfuckers."

Debbie shut the lid and secured the two latches. The men jostled about like two cats in shoebox.

"Now for the coup de grâce." Debbie retrieved the burlap bag. The disturbance set it to rattling. She untied the string that secured the top opening, reached in and pulled out one pissed off Diamond Back rattlesnake. It twisted in her grip, turned and bit her hand, so she grabbed it behind the head and pried the fangs from her flesh. Looking at the snake eye to eye she ticked her tongue. "No wasting your poison on me. Save it for these clowns."

She stuffed the snake in the hole, rattling tail first then let go.

"What the fuck?" El Paco screamed. "Something bit me." He screamed. "It bit my dick."

"Hold still...you're crushing me," Pedro yelled. "I can't breathe." He screamed. "Something bit my balls."

Debbie dispatched a second snake through the hole. All the rattling and screaming blended so well with the Day of the Dead festivities outside.

By dawn, all was quiet in Mexico City.

***

Back in Waterford, a very happy Maggie was telling the furniture delivery men where she wanted everything put. First in one place and then, to the chagrin of the men, she would have them rearrange everything again. Robert saw what was going on and asked Maggie to come downstairs. She followed him. Standing by the staircase he put his hands up to her cheeks. "Honey, you are driving those delivery guys crazy."

"Robert, are you mad?"

"No. But I can't speak for those guys. They might be. So go up there and tell them that everything is perfect now."

"But what if I want something moved a little bit?"

"Sugar, I'll move it. Now go tell them what I told you to say."

"Maybe you should."

"I'm on my way out to Fort Dix to sign some mustering out papers, and then I'll get Dad's things from the storage locker."

Maggie almost fainted. Those papers could be the end of her and Robert. "I'll go with you."

"It could take several hours and you have more deliveries coming today." He gave Maggie one more kiss. "Now go on upstairs."

After watching Robert drive away, she didn't go upstairs. She went into the bathroom and got down on her knees and clasped her hands together and rested her arms on the side of the bathtub. She closed her eyes and prayed, "Dear God, don't let Robert find out the truth about me. I'm not all that bad."

**

At LaGuardia, Alfons' jet landed on runway 31 and taxied to area H where private aircraft were serviced. An aircraft passenger stairs truck pulled up to the front door, even as the engines whined down.

A long black limo pulled up with Jorge behind the wheel. He was sweating profusely as he rushed around to open the rear door for the sisterhood, now deplaning and chattering up a storm.

Alfons stopped at the aircraft door to watch them pile into the limo. Debbie and Chloe were giddy in their Mexican Day of the Dead makeup. Brenda looked irritated at them. Monica brought up the rear. Sure, the women were stunning, but his eyes kept going to Monica's black sleek form, and he wondered how she'd look when they got old together. Gray hair. Wrinkled skin. Then he wondered if, by then, they'd ever kiss like lovers kissed. *And a blowjob once in a while would sure be nice.*

Joseph stepped up behind him. "You really like Monica, don't you, boss."

"Yeah, she's special all right. Sometimes I'd like to make her the next Mrs. Duda. Other times I'd like to..."

"To what, boss?"

"Ah, hell. Who am I trying to buffalo? I'd like to make her Mrs. Duda those times too."

By now, the girls were inside and seated. Jorge closed the door, and as he walked around to the driver's side, he kept monkeying with his trousers as if he had a burr in his boxers. Or was he playing with himself?

Alfons' limo rolled out of the plane's belly doors. It was covered in Mexican dust. "Let's go," he told Joseph. "On the way home, stop at a car wash."

"Yes sir, boss."

***

Meanwhile, Captain Robert Mark Johnson, still wearing the uniform of his country, picked up his father's stuff from the storage unit. He threw everything in the trunk except his dad's diary. That he put on the front seat.

At the new house in Waterford, now with all the furniture in place and the furniture people gone, a very anxious Maggie sat in a two thousand dollar glider rocking chair, waiting for her fate to come through the front door. Her chest felt heavy, as if an elephant had pulled up her heart to use as a chair. She was sure that if Robert read anything bad in his dad's diary, he would tell her to get out. Sticking her hand under her blouse she rubbed her pregnant belly and consoled herself. *I will always have our baby even if Robert kicks me out. I have Isabel's house to live in and nobody will bother me because of my rose tattoo, so I can get a job as a waitress, even on a nightshift if I have to.*

She heard a car door slam, and the elephant on her chest knew her fate was only seconds away. She stood and adjusted her clothing to look presentable for when Robert handed down his sentence. He opened the door. Her wait was now over. "How much trouble am I in?"

"What?"

"Did you read your dad's diary?"

"This?" He showed her the dog-eared book. "I read this the week after he died."

"What did he say about me?"

"He loved you like a daughter."

"The elephant became a dove and flew away."

Robert frowned. "Do you have some deep dark secret that I should know about? What did you do...take a donut without paying for it?"

"Let's go to Sam's Donut Shop and celebrate your father. I'm starving for a rainbow-sprinkle." Then it hit her like a brick to the forehead. "Why are you still in uniform?"

"Sit down." He guided her to the new five-thousand dollar dinner table. "There's something I have to tell you."

As she sat in the plush dinner chair, the elephant returned with his buddies...in a stampede. "You're supposed to be mustered out of the Army."

"Something happened. There's been a change of plans."

"What the hell does that mean?"

"Three U.S. Army soldiers have been captured by the Taliban and they're going to be executed."

"Did you know those men?"

"They are my friends from Charlie 2-5."

"What's that got to do with you?" Tears stung her eyes.

"I've been ordered to go on an S-A-D mission?"

"What's that?"

"Search and Destroy. We're going back to Afghanistan to rescue our men."

"What about the plane full of men who flew out of here? Why can't they rescue their own men?"

"The Taliban has them pinned down in a valley. They can't reach them."

"But you have a wife and a baby on the way. You can't just go back to war."

"We're going to get our troops out alive and kill anyone who tries to stop us."

"I don't want you to go."

"I have no choice. If I refuse, I'll never be able to look at myself in the mirror again, not to mention the time I'd have to serve in Leavenworth. That's a prison."

"They'd send you to prison for staying with me and your baby? For being a husband and father?"

"For not obeying a direct order. For not being an honorable soldier. Kinda like you not being an honorable wife." He dropped a picture on the table.

Choking back tears, Maggie looked at a picture of her in bra and panties, sitting on General Taylor's lap. She remembered the party. BBBD supplied the girls, for a price, of course. Her secret had been released from its dark cave.

"Where did you get this?"

"The General gave it to me in answer to my plea that I stay here with my wife...as a civilian. Needless to say, he doesn't think a whore makes for good wife material. I was in shock. You knew him all along. You lied to me about that. What else have you lied to me about? What else haven't you told me?"

"Okay," she shouted and stood to face him. "I was a whore. I was afraid to tell you for fear of losing you. Now I'm your wife. I'm never going back to that life. We have a baby coming. Please give me a chance to show you I'm better than that now."

"I don't care about the whore part. It's the lies. How can I ever trust you?"

She slumped back down on the chair in defeat. "You don't have to worry." She stared across the room at nothing. "I'll move back to my house on Montford Lane. I won't contest a divorce, but I won't give up our baby. I will raise him by myself but I'll always let him know who his father was. I'll be gone when you get back, and you won't have to see Maggie the lying whore again." She threw her face down on the table and burst out in tears.

He glared at her for a long moment then exhaled. "I can't leave you like this. Don't go. Promise me you'll be here when I get back."

"Do you really mean it? You want me to stay?"

"Of course I do. You're my wife. I love you. Just because you lied doesn't change that. You can make it up to me when I come home."

"You *are* coming home, right?"

"I promise."

Robert left a crying Maggie with tears in his own eyes, got in his car, and drove back to base to leave on an impossible mission.

***

On Interstate 55 just outside Springfield, Illinois, a Class-A diesel-powered motorhome took a wrong turn. The eighty-year-old driver missed the *No Left Turn, DO NOT ENTER,* and *WRONG WAY* signs. His seventy-six-year-old wife in the passenger seat didn't notice either, as she was knitting a pair of booties for their new great-granddaughter whom they were on their way to meet. Now northbound in the southbound lanes, he had to honk at cars coming at him in what he perceived to be the wrong lane. "What's the matter with these fools?"

Up ahead, a semi was passing another semi and suddenly veered into the median just in time. However, the compact car behind him became an immediate problem. Following the semi too closely, the driver had nowhere to go. The motorhome instantly turned the car to scrap metal, and the elderly great grandparents met the panoramic windshield with such force that both would never meet their new great granddaughter.

The highway patrol was the first to get to the accident scene. Smoke pumped from the diesel engine, and the officer could smell a mix of oil and fuel and death. An ambulance screamed down the highway to join him, but a quick survey told him the MEs would not be needed. Within the debris-field he found the elderly couple mangled on the highway, having been thrown from the vehicle, and inside the crushed compact car, the obliterated bodies of the driver and passenger were still buckled in. He called dispatch. "I've got four deceased—"

"Hey, mister."

The hair on his neck stood up as a little girl's voice pleaded from somewhere inside the unrecognizable car.

"Can you please help me get out of here?"

"I've got a survivor," he shouted into the radio. "Send fire rescue."

Using the Jaws of Life, firemen soon freed Harold and June Crandall's ten-year-old daughter Caroline, unscathed.

***

Jorge dispatched his passengers, freshly back from Mexico City, under the portico of Jackie O'Neal's spacious mansion. His goddamned cock was hard again and he couldn't wait to get to his room and take care of this persistent and painful problem.

Jackie, Melinda, and Donna stepped out the front door to greet the returning sisters and offer them fresh margaritas.

Brenda wasn't in the mood to party. She noticed construction workers with white hard hats were loading up their vans and pickups. She pointed them out to Jackie. "Are they finished?"

Jackie downed the margarita Brenda had waved off. "Come and see the shrine." She led a procession of sisters, all giggling and laughing, around the mansion to the south-side greenhouse. When it came into view, silence fell over the sisterhood.

Brenda stood in awe of the majestic shrine before her.

The roof glass panels had been replaced with crystalline sheets that reflected the sunlight in a rainbow of colors, and the side-wall glass panels were now rich amethyst and quartz in interlacing bands.

"Come see inside." Jackie led them through the breezeway to the double doors that led into the heart of Loa's master design. Gold tiles made a path through red floor tiles that ended at a solid gold railing around a six-foot-square pit from which grew the Sister Tree of Life. Its reaching branches and broad leaves drew in the crystallized sunshine and shaded a variety of flora native to Haiti.

Brenda, her breath stolen by the splendor, stepped to the pit railing, leaned over it, and looked in. Six feet below, roots and vines intertwined and wriggled about. A few of them sensed her presence and wormed their way up the side to wrap around her legs and slither up her body until the tips wavered before her eyes.

The girls shouted out in alarm. "Brenda, fight back."

"Don't be silly." She petted a smooth root as if it were Girly Dog. "They missed me, is all." She looked up at the Sister Tree of Life and saw that it had grown around a blood-red pedestal on which sat a golden throne. Her heart swelled with pride and the regal honor of serving the Lesbian Goddess Loa. With a final loving stroke, she said to the roots and vines that had come to welcome her, "Go back to our sister tree, make her grow and keep her healthy."

The welcoming committee sank back into the pit and joined with the others wriggling about.

Brenda stepped back. The beauty of this shrine almost made her forget the cost, the life of one of her sisters. Who would die to appease the sole goddess of the universe?

***

Later that chilly November afternoon, while lounging in the hot tub, Monica got a call on her cell phone. She didn't recognize the Illinois number but answered it anyway, braced for a telemarketer. "What are you sellin'?"

"This is the Illinois Department of Children's Service calling," the male voice said in an official tone. "May I speak to Monica Abelard?"

"Speaking." Her heart rate ticked up a notch. *What does DCS want with me?*

"I'm Investigator Webb. Do you know Caroline Crandall?"

She sat straight up in the bubbling water. "Yes."

"There's been a terrible accident, four fatalities, but little Caroline escaped without a scratch. She says you're the only family she has left. Is that right?"

"I don't know." One thing she did know. Being a zombie just saved her life again. "Is she there with you now?"

"We have her in protective custody."

Monica's brain was running a mile a minute. *I have to get her out of there before she's lost in the foster care system forever.* "I am in New York. I will fly out tonight and pick her up in the morning."

"You'll have to petition the court for custody."

"I will get my lawyer on it right away. Meanwhile, can I have temporary custody?"

"That can be arranged."

"Can I speak with her now?"

"Hold on a minute. I'll go get her."

A minute seemed like an hour. "Monica?" Caroline's sweet voice came on the line. "My parents are dead. You're all I have now."

"Everything will be okay. I will protect you and take care of you. Have you ever been on a plane before?"

"I always wanted to."

"Honey, I am on my way. You will never be alone. You now have a lot of sisters, and they will love you like I do. I know your Mommy and Daddy are in heaven and they are very happy that you will be living with us. See you in the morning."

She hung up and flew out of the hot tub like it was suddenly full of electric eels. "Jackie."

She awoke from a margarita-induced nap. "Not so loud." Squinting, she saw naked Monica standing above her.

"Get Lisa Swartz on a custody case for me. I will text you the details. Meanwhile, I have to catch a flight to Springfield, Illinois to pick up Caroline."

"Caroline?"

"The sisters will explain. Can Jorge drive me to the airport?"

"I'll call him."

"I will be out front." She dialed Alfons as she ran to get dressed.

***

Surrounded by crumpled tissues, Jorge lay on his bed, hard-on in hand, yanking it for all it was worth. His entire life he'd loved his cock, listened to its whims, and kept it safe from harm, but now it had become his burden, like the ploughshare to the oxen, the leash to the dog, or the pack to the pack-mule. It wouldn't leave him alone. It wouldn't let him rest, and no matter how much it hurt, he had to satisfy it, over and over again.

His cell phone buzzed. He had to stop pounding his pud long enough to answer. It was Jackie. "Yes, ma'am."

"I need you to take Monica to the airport."

"Now?"

"You got something more important to do?"

He looked down at the throbbing, beet-red blister between his legs. "As a matter a fact, yes."

"She'll be waiting out front." Jackie hung up.

"Fuck." Jorge got up, managed to stuff his boner in his trousers and get dressed. "What the hell did those girls do to me?"

***

At 10:27 p.m. the next night, Caroline awoke to the screeching sound of the plane's wheels touching the ground at LaGuardia. "Are we there yet, Monica?"

"Yes, honey."

Monica, having all the perks that money could buy, had already called the sisterhood to tell them to throw a big welcome party for Caroline. Alfons had sent his limo to pick them up.

Caroline took in all the sights as Joseph drove her and Monica to Jackie's palace. Just as the limo stopped in the driveway, Brenda yanked the door open. "Hello, sweetie." She took the child by the hand and led her to the waiting sisterhood, six steps up to the porch.

The outpouring of love and affection from her new sisters overwhelmed Caroline until Girlie Dog ran up to her, tail wagging a hundred times a minute. Then she liked Girlie Dog best.

That night, Monica put Caroline to bed in her own room. She was soon fast asleep with Girlie Dog curled up at the end of the bed.

***

Wednesday night brought Debbie and Donna to the Church of the Risen Jesus. Melinda had stayed behind to help take care of Caroline. Donna, having no clue what she was getting into, volunteered to take on the unholy task of desecrating the church.

As they walked in they were met by Reverend Leroy himself. His belly was so fat his tie looked three feet too short. Debbie had visions of giving him a blowjob and biting off his balls. However, she took a breath and remembered what she and Donna were there to do, recruit Janice for the sisterhood, and destroy the hypocrite Reverend Leroy Parker.

"We really need a private session with you and your wife, Reverend," she told Leroy in her sweetest, most innocent voice. "This is Donna. She lost her lover, Joanne, and is hurting really bad."

Leroy leered at her. "Welcome to my church. We specialize in treating the homosexually afflicted. Shall we get started?"

Donna nodded meekly.

Being ushered into Leroy's private office, Debbie and Donna were shocked to see the missus sprawled spread-eagle on the polar bear rug. "I saw her walk in." Janice pointed to Debbie. "You're not getting a second crack at her without me."

Leroy swallowed hard. "Honey, this is Donna. She's new."

"Go get her," Debbie whispered in Donna's ear.

Donna did her runway model walk to the bear rug. "And you must be Janice."

She patted the white fur. "Come join me and confess your sins."

Donna dropped her dress around her ankles and stepped out of her shoes. "Don't we have to sin first?"

"My my, you are a pretty one." Janice extended her arms and wiggled her fingers in a come-hither way. "I can't wait to chomp on that bush."

Donna dropped down on Janice and delivered her first Lesbian Zombie kiss.

Debbie turned to Leroy the Lecher.

He'd already shed his pants and his little pecker was sticking out like the nose on Pinocchio. "Praise Jesus," he hollered.

Debbie slipped the straps off her shoulders, let her dress fall to the floor, and then joined Donna and Janice on the back of the bear. Donna was a pro the way she humped her pussy against the clit of the soon-to-be newest member of the sisterhood. Debbie laid her nakedness down next to the writhing women and spread her legs for the Reverend.

He stood there, mouth agape, and ogled the most beautiful pussy he'd ever seen. His fingers trembled with excited nerves so badly that he fumbled with the condom until he finally tossed it aside. "Ah fuckit." He jumped on top of Debbie and put the meat to her while she delivered her form of venom with a juicy French kiss.

Donna slid down between Janice's legs and licked her into a frenzy. Debbie reached over and caressed Janice's pert nipples to help her libido build while Leroy humped her like a horny rabbit on steroids.

As the two Reverends reached their crescendos, they both cried out, "Hallelujah Lord."

Leroy pumped Debbie full of cream, but she wasn't concerned about STDs or getting pregnant. She just laughed when he couldn't stop humping her. He couldn't stop coming.

Donna rolled off the newest Lesbian Zombie to let Leroy see her wet and wanton vagina. He immediately stopped fucking Debbie, and still spurting jizzum, he climbed on top and put it to his wife. Problem was, his body now disgusted her and she fought him off. "Get away from me, you pervert."

This left Leroy a desperate, oversexed zombie with a hard-on that was about to pop. He looked around for somewhere to put his prick and spotted the more-than-willing look on the polar bear's face. He dropped to his knees and just before he rammed his rod into the bear's open mouth, he froze and glared at the girls. "Take me to your Queen."

The girls and Janice got the hell out of there as fast as they could. They ran right into Tim, Chloe's ex. He recognized Debbie right away. "Hey, you're Chloe's friend."

"I do not know anyone by that name." She kept walking in a hurry to get out of the church before Leroy turned his sex-crazed cock on them.

Tim blocked her progress. "You know where she lives."

"Get out of my way." She ducked around him.

He blocked her again. "Tell her I'm sorry. I want her back."

"She's not interested in getting beat up again."

"Look, bitch—"

Janice stepped in front of him. "You can't call my sister a bitch."

"What are you gonna do about it, bitch, bitch bitch?"

She poked him in the chest and forced him to walk backwards. "You'll never change. You're disrespectful to women, to your ex-wife, a disgrace to every decent man on this planet."

He kept walking backwards, into the sanctuary and slammed into the back row of pews. "You want some of this?" He showed her his fist.

Janice, unaware of her new Lesbian Zombie speed and strength, threw him a left roundhouse that sent him flying over the pew. His head hit the back of the next pew and his neck bent with a sharp crack. He hit the floor, jerking around like a chicken with its head cut off.

Janice backed up and looked at her fist. "What did I do?"

"We will explain later," Debbie said. "Until then, do not hit anybody else."

By now, Tim lay still. His life was over in less than a minute. He wouldn't be terrorizing Chloe anymore.

The sisters carried his body outside to the limo where Jorge wasn't on duty at the rear door. A quick peek inside found him in the back seat area playing with himself...or something of that nature. Without distracting him, Debbie reached in through the open window and pulled the trunk release. They threw the corpse in the trunk, slammed the lid, and broke Jorge out of the sexual assault on himself.

"Home, James," Donna quipped.

Before Debbie got in she had a last word with Janice. "You're one of us now, the sisterhood of Lesbian Zombies. Your job is to funnel church money into the LZ Foundation account in Port au Prince, Haiti."

"That's easy enough, but who's going to tame the wild beast in Leroy?"

"Sorry. He's still your problem." She got in the limo and Jorge accelerated away from the Church of the Risen Jesus, never to return.

***~

Now back at Jackie's, the limo parked in the driveway. Chloe wanted to take a look at her now late ex-husband. Donna opened the trunk and Chloe peered in. His eyes were wide open and glazed over, and his mouth hung open. Problem was his jaw. It was behind his right shoulder. "I can honestly say Tim has never looked better."

All the sisterhood came to look then high-fived each other. Chloe slammed the trunk lid closed, a symbolic way to close forever that horrible chapter of abuse in her life.

Caroline ran out of the house and tried to join in the high-fives by jumping up, but she was too short. Melinda picked her up and walked over to each sister so that she could slap their hands.

Jackie said in a low voice, "Get rid of the body."

"How?"

"Chop him up in pieces and run the pieces through the meat grinder in the basement, then put the scourge into fruit canning jars."

"What do we do with the jars?"

"Put them in the pantry. They'll be a tasty meal substitute for Girlie Dog, and we'll save a bundle on dog food."

Chapter 10: THE DAYS DWINDLED DOWN TO A PRECIOUS FEW

Captain Robert Johnson and his men of Second Platoon parachuted into the Sistan Basin and soon found themselves wading through a marsh on the outskirts of Zaranj, a trade route hub in Southwestern Afghanistan near the Iranian border, population 160,902 plus a contingent of thirty-seven Taliban and three American soldiers. The U.S. had no permanent presence in the region, just an occasional patrol to make nice with city officials. Charlie 2-5 had drawn the short straw for the fateful mission and drove into town with nine soldiers and one reporter in three armored trucks. A suicide bomber had struck the middle truck with a pushcart full of explosives and ball bearings. The ripped apart truck landed in the median then Taliban insurgents opened fire on the patrol. The three survivors of the ambush would be beheaded in the morning, 15 November.

The sun came up at 6:27 a.m. on that fateful day. A crowd had gathered in front of a platform where the three American soldiers were to die. Each wore an orange jumpsuit and stern faces. Three masked executioners stood behind them on the platform, knives at the throats of their captives, waiting for the signal to cut off their heads while being filmed for Aljazeera and various sites on the dark web.

Three shots rang out, and the three would-be killers lay dead. Each had been hit with a single shot to the forehead. Second

Platoon raced in, killing everyone with a weapon. Bullets and grenade shrapnel filled the air as the Taliban fought back. Seventeen minutes later, the firefight was over. Thirty-seven Taliban insurgents lay dead. Second Platoon suffered only one wounded. Captain Robert Johnson was hit by shrapnel and suffered a severed spinal cord below the neck.

The Captain was flown back to the states and admitted to Walter Reed Army Medical Center. Though the mission was a success, the men of Second Platoon returned home in a somber mood.

***

In Waterford, Maggie ran to answer the doorbell. When she saw General Taylor standing there, her first thought was to kill him for ratting her out to Robert. However, the serious look on his weathered face told her not to act so irrationally.

"Maggie." He took off his cap. "I'm sorry to tell you—"

"Is he dead?"

"Well...good as dead, maybe. He suffered a very serious injury to his spinal cord."

"That's not right. He's coming home." Tears flooded her eyes. "He promised."

"He's paralyzed from the neck down."

"Will he ever walk again? Play ball with his kid?"

"The VA will outfit him with a special wheelchair that has a built-in ventilator."

"I want to see him right now."

"I knew you would. I can take you to Washington on a military transport. I have one waiting at Fort Dix."

Maggie stared him down. "Why should I trust you? He looked up to you, respected you, and you turn around and crush his respect for me."

"He wanted to refuse the assignment and run home to you. The best man I had chose you over his country. I simply put his priorities back on track."

"I'm not a whore now."

"You should have told him the truth."

She agreed. She'd known it all along, feared it all along. Now, for all she knew his injury was her fault because he went into battle with her lie on his mind. One second of lapse in concentration could mean the difference between life and death. She needed to see him, tell him she was sorry, even if meant catching a ride with the devil himself.

***

At Walter Reed Army Medical Center, Maggie rode the elevator up to ICU, intensive care. The air smelled like medicine and distant voices and footsteps echoed down long tiled halls. She found Robert's room and peeked inside. The greatest, bravest, strongest man in the world lay on his back, his body suspended in a huge contraption that resembled a black hamster wheel. The multitude of wires and tubes running in and out of him would rival any submarine. There were no words to describe the helpless feeling that dug holes in her heart.

Forcing a smile, she walked in to face an unimaginable sorrow. "Hello, Robert."

His eyes shifted to her. He couldn't turn his head, so she leaned in closer. "You're going to be all right."

He couldn't speak due to the ventilator tube in his throat. He just stared through her, and the heart monitor beeped a little faster.

"You know who I am, right? Blink once for yes."

He blinked twice.

"I'm Maggie, your wife."

He blinked twice.

"I'm not your wife?"

He blinked once.

"Don't talk like that. Of course I'm your wife."

He blinked twice.

"You want a divorce?"

He blinked twice.

"Robert? You want me to forget about you?"

He blinked once, shifted his eyes forward, and stared at the wall.

"Never. There's something that can be done to heal you."

He blinked twice.

"I'll be right back."

Maggie stepped out of the room and made a call on her cell. "Brenda, this is Maggie."

"We heard the news. We're all in shock. How is he?"

"You've got to help me."

Silence.

"Brenda, please."

"Are you sure he would want that?"

"He'd rather die than live like this."

"You don't know what you're asking. We experimented on Jorge. Now he's a sex maniac zombie."

"Hmmm. That side effect doesn't sound too bad."

"Very well. I'll fly down tonight."

At precisely 11:21 p.m., Maggie greeted Brenda in the hospital lobby. This time of night, the place could have been a morgue. Security checked Maggie's floor pass and admitted Brenda as her guest.

In the elevator up, Brenda implored Maggie once again. "The virus will heal him, but when you two tie it on in the bedroom, his bliss will turn into a nightmare."

The elevator opened to ICU. Maggie took Brenda aside. "I know why I'm not a Lesbian Zombie."

"You're immune somehow."

"These pills." Maggie removed a half-full prescription bottle of HIV medication from her purse.

Brenda recognized it right away, the bottle she'd found in the bathroom after she'd relieved BBBD of his heart.

"The pills kill the HIV virus in its early stages by not allowing it to reproduce. We know the LZ virus restores the body to its youthful state. So kiss my husband with everything you've got. When he's better and healed, I'll give him these pills to kill the LZ virus. He should go back to his old self in no time."

Brenda huffed. "In the meantime, you better stock up on KY Jelly and buy yourself a pair of crutches. You're gonna need them."

Now in Robert's room, Brenda approached the wretched man in the spinal injury contraption. He had so much potential, so much hope for the future before serving his country, now reduced to a glob of immobile protoplasm. When she bent to his face, his eyes popped open wide at the sight of a beautiful redhead.

"Hello, Robert."

Who are you? she heard him think.

"I'm Brenda. Maggie's friend."

One of her sisters?

"Yes. I've come to help you."

There's no help for me. Tell Maggie to go home. Start a new life with our baby.

"I'll tell her no such thing. You're going to walk out of here tomorrow."

That's impossible. Look at me. I can't move. They put a tube up my dick so I won't piss on myself."

She patted his arm. "Pretty soon that'll be the least of your problems." She puckered her lips and moved in to kiss him.

What are you doing? The heart monitor beeped furiously.

"It's okay, Robert," Maggie said from behind Brenda. "She's going to kiss you."

At 11:52 p.m. the LZ virus was administered by the sweetest lips on the planet, well, Maggie would argue that point, but nonetheless, Brenda gave him her tongue and ravaged his mouth.

His mind erupted in a whirlwind of thoughts: *What's going on? Why is Maggie allowing this gorgeous woman to kiss me? Her wet tongue tastes like sugar candy. What's happening to me? I'm tingling all over.*

Brenda released him from her Lesbian Zombie kiss. "Take

two aspirin and call me in the morning." She turned to Maggie standing behind her. "My work is done here."

"Thank you."

"I have to get ready for a charity ball on Long Island. Good luck with him." She strode out like what she had done was nothing.

At 12:17 a.m., Maggie noticed Robert's fingers twitch. The heart monitor went crazy with excitement. He started flexing his arms and legs against the restraints that held him in the hamster wheel bed. A passing nurse rushed in and dropped the tray she was carrying. Jell-O cups bounced in every direction. Disbelief clouded her face. "Doctor." She ran out of the room.

A team of doctors and specialists converged on the scene, all flabbergasted at the writhing man. One doctor removed the ventilator tube from his throat. Others sewed him up. Others stopped the beeping machines and disconnected tubes and wires. The place had exploded in chaos.

At 1:01 a.m., Maggie and Robert walked out of Walter Reed and got into a staff car driven by General Taylor, who was just as confused as Robert over what had just happened.

"Don't ask." Maggie pressed a finger to Robert's lips then pulled him to her and kissed him with all the love she had in her body. The HIV medication in her system would fend off any backflow virus from Robert. They were going home to have a baby and live happily ever after.

Chapter 11: THIS INVITATION IS EXTENDED TO YOU ALONE

THE LZ FOUNDATION CHARITY BALL
TIME: 7:00 FRIDAY, 23 / NOVEMBER
PLACE: HOME OF JACKIE O' NEAL
LONG ISLAND

T he first to open his invitation had been General Lawrence Taylor. He was the new Chairman of the Joint Chiefs of Staff, riding a wave of popularity after the rescue of Charlie 2-5's soldiers. His military position was vital to Brenda's plan to conquer a man's world. She also knew he had the hots for Jackie O'Neal. *Wait 'til he sees her now.*

The second invite went to Larry Evans the Attorney General of the United States. He had been divorced five times and was now looking for ex-wife number six. His position in the justice system would be crucial to Brenda's influence over the courts.

The third invitation went to Senator James Hoffman, Chairman of the Health and Human Services Commission; however, he wouldn't make it to the party. He was currently sitting in jail and under investigation by the ethics committee for taking pictures of his dick and posting them online. The Feds had to put him in a private cell because he wouldn't stop masturbating all over the other inmates.

The fourth invitation went to Stuart Jackson, an internet

mogul with inroads to all forms of social media, the content of which Brenda wanted to control. His stance that women should be pregnant and barefoot in the kitchen would no longer fly in the Lesbian Zombie's new world order.

The fifth invitation went to Charlie Mantella, CEO of the World News Network. His three hundred television stations and nine news outlets would be a gold mine for Brenda's message to reach women around the world. His crime: he only hired blue-eyed blondes who could pass for the Stepford Wives in their devotion to the sexist bastard.

Number six on the list went to Matt Simmons of big banking and Wall Street fame. If he sneezed, the stock market dropped five points. Brenda needed his clout in the financial sectors, for obvious reasons, even though he advocated for women to have unlimited credit card use to boost his bottom line, regardless of the consequences of overbearing debt.

There was to be an invitation sent to Reverends Leroy and Janice Parker, but Janice was already a sister with her hands in the Christian cookie jar, and nobody wanted a preacher around who couldn't keep his dick in his pants.

That left Alfons Duda for the seventh slot, a business tycoon with his hands on the wheels of commerce and big oil around the world. Even though the womanizer and sex fiend deserved to be brought to his knees, Monica fought hard to keep him out of Brenda's clutches. The night of the party would be a turning point in their relationship.

Cassandra and Jenny didn't need invitations. The Voodoo High Priestess and Lesbian Zombie Head of Haiti Security would attend as a couple. Aurora, her lady-boys, and the Nazis would stay behind to hold down the fort in Port au Prince.

Chapter 12: BLACK FRIDAY

It was misty and cold on the day of The LZ Foundation Charity Ball. Jackie knew that everyone invited would show up because no one wanted to have her wrath poured out on them, and besides, she always threw one hell of an X-rated party.

They all showed up right on schedule, except Senator Hoffman. General Taylor made a play for Jackie right away. He walked up behind her and covered her eyes with his hands. "Who do you think this is?"

"Let me guess. The General who is in charge of saving us from the assholes of the earth."

"Close enough." Smiling at her, his gaze kept dropping to her red low-cut dress that showed off her cleavage and made him wonder if this would be the night to see her all in the flesh. "You look terrific. How do you keep such a youthful glow?"

"Skin cream." Jackie had to look up to see the tall man's face. He'd been an Army Ranger in years past, and he still had a good build. He stayed in the same shape that he required of his men. She slipped her hand into the crook of his arm, and they strolled to the path that led down to the shore. They stopped and looked back at the crowd laughing and drinking within the lighted windows.

He decided to go for the downs, put one arm around her, and slowly pulled up her dress in the front.

She wasn't wearing any panties.

"Maybe you had this in mind all along?"

George S. Naas

"You got away last time, big boy." She kissed him on the lips and gave him some tongue.

His fingers found a playground within the soft folds between her legs.

Just when he had things going for him, she broke away and got down on her knees. "My turn." Pulling his erection out of his pants was like pulling a tent pole out of a gunny sack, but she managed and quickly set to suck him off.

Yeah, I'm a lesbian, but a girl's gotta do what a girl's gotta do.

For the sisterhood, she would do anything.

Monica had to do something too. Reluctantly, she led Alfons to a secluded corner of the pool deck, and among the potted ferns, she sat him down on a lounger, and gave him the best and longest kiss ever. His beard was a little itchy, but she gave him her all. One thing led to another, and before long she had his cock in her mouth, sucking it for the glory of the sisterhood.

Alfons was on cloud nine, a cloud that had no silver lining.

Chloe found Charlie Mantella sitting on the porch rail, drinking a beer. *If the other sisters can do this, I can too.* After taking a deep breath, she sat beside him and offered a wan smile. "Some party." She sighed. "Nobody is paying any attention to me."

This blue-eyed blonde bombshell had his attention. "Where have you been all my life?"

"Are you single, or just another married man who wants to get in my panties?"

He chugged beer and chuckled. "I'm single and still want to get in your panties, but what woman would want to be with an overweight man in his mid fifties and going bald? I forgot to mention I'm also boring as hell."

Chloe felt a little sorry for the guy. *No wonder he's out here drinking alone.* She was suddenly presented with a challenge that trumped her general disgust for a man's body. "If you're horny we can go fuck. Bet you wouldn't be boring then."

"Where?"

She held out her hand. "I'll show you."

They climbed the stairs and met Donna and Larry Evans descending. He had a hand shoved down the front of his pants and a desperate look of embarrassment on his face. "Take me to my Queen."

She high-fived Donna. "Score."

They found a vacant room where Chloe kissed Charlie on the lips and slipped him some tongue.

Boring Charlie turned into a maniac, knocked an assortment of figurines off the dresser, bent Chloe over it, and fucked her from behind.

Well, at least I don't have to look at him.

She yawned.

He got off with a growl, and a growl, and a growl. "What the fuck?" He pulled out, and still squirting, made a mad dash for the bathroom down the hall.

Some men just can't control themselves.

Chloe put herself back together and stepped out of the room, proud she'd done her share for the sisters.

Just then, Caroline came stomping up the steps and went into the bedroom Chloe had just left. All of a sudden the kid screamed bloody murder. She stormed out, fists clenched at her side. "Who was in my room? You assholes broke my figurines. I'm going to tell Brenda."

Chloe shrugged. "Don't look at me," then escaped down the stairs.

Jenny had a hot one in Stuart Jackson, the Internet mogul who would beat women back to the 1960s, barefoot and pregnant in the kitchen. She figured him for a missionary-style kind of guy in the dark, but he dropped his pants, rolled her over, and shoved it in her tush. And he wasn't gentle about it, either. She made a note to herself. *When Brenda is out and I'm in charge, I'll order Aurora to give Stuart a taste of his own medicine.* Meanwhile he took his disgust for independent women out on her ass. Trying to appease him, she cooed, "That feels great."

"Shut the fuck up."

Yeah, I'll tell Reinhard and Albert to take sloppy seconds when Aurora is through with him. Maybe I'll even invite Carlos and Jason. They'll ream him all night.

Meanwhile, Brenda had coaxed Matt Simmons to join her in the hot tub. The clock was ticking. In a half an hour it would be time to start the ceremony to pay homage to Loa.

She'd have to speed things up. As she kicked out of her high heels and peeled off her long white dress, Matt got out of his clothes in a hurry. She saw that he was hard and ready, mostly because he'd been thinking about fondling her tits for the past hour.

As they settled into the bubbling water, his hands were all over her breasts.

"How about a nice blowjob?"

"I thought you'd never ask."

He propped his elbows on the side of the hot tub while she slipped between his spread legs and lifted his ass up until his bobber broke the surface.

"You're never going to forget this one." She went down on him like gangbusters. Reminded her of when she would go down on John Marshall, when she did it for love. Those days were long gone. Now her lips and tongue, and a little teeth, did it as a means to an end.

His breathing accelerated to desperate gasps and his legs clamped around her shoulders. She had the world's banking system right where she wanted it.

"Ah...ah...ah..." When he let loose, she backed away and watched 'ol faithful' explode and explode and explode. He grabbed his throbber and shoved it under the water, screaming, "Motherfucker," the whole time.

Damn. Now I gotta clean the hot tub.

As she got out and stood there naked, wishing for a towel to dry off, a dark figure stepped out of the shadows between the potted ferns. "Casssandra?"

"It is I, my Queen."

"What are you doing here?"

Matt kept hollering, "I can't make it stop."

"My Queen, there is something important that I must tell you."

"I'm listening."

"Jenny has betrayal and mutiny on her mind."

"Against me?"

"She thought she was confiding in me when she told me she had a weapon to hold over your head to get whatever she wants from you."

"What kind of weapon?"

"She will threaten to go to the police and tell them you murdered her ex-husband in Las Vegas unless you make her CFO in charge of all the money."

Brenda saw red. "The little thief. I gave her a second chance..."

"She thinks I am a partner in her plot against you, but you are my Queen and I will die first before I would ever betray you."

"Thanks for the heads up, Cassandra."

"Will you kill my wife now?"

"I don't kill women and children. There must be another way to get rid of her."

"Good luck, my Queen." Cassandra melted back into the shadows.

Seeing the moon was now high in the sky, soaking-wet Brenda hurried into her long white dress and high heels and ran across the lawn toward the breezeway. She got one shoe stuck in the grass and left it there, much like a Lesbian Zombie Cinderella.

The partygoers had assembled inside the breezeway. Her sisters escorted their captains of the world, the men fearful and sweaty, Monica with Alfons, finally all smiles, Jenny standing bowlegged with Stuart, her ass on fire, Jackie with a stooped and defeated Lawrence Taylor, Donna and the Attorney General, Larry Evans, still muttering "my queen, my queen." Chloe had to hold Charlie up to keep him from falling over, and Debbie and

Melinda flanked Matt, still naked and dripping hot tub water.

Cassandra walked in. "It is midnight, my Queen."

As Brenda moved toward the double doors, now barefoot and her long white gown a bit soggy, the crowd parted to let her pass.

Jackie and Monica opened the doors and Brenda led them all inside the shrine to Loa. Rays of light radiated spokes of colorful beams that rotated all around. The air smelled of rich soil and lush vegetation.

Brenda stepped to the golden railing where the roots and vines of the Sister Tree of Life rose up and gathered her in their loving arms. The onlookers gasped, and even the sisterhood stood in awe of this otherworldly spectacle. Up Brenda rose until the tree set her down on the golden throne atop the red pedestal within its bosom.

Alfons muttered, "What the hell is going on?"

General Taylor turned to Jackie. "Is this for real?"

"You'll see."

Brenda looked up and saw that the moon was directly overhead, and the rays from the moon shined down on her through the crystalline roof panels, giving her body a heavenly glow.

Cassandra stood on the left-hand side of the pit and proclaimed, "Now all bow down to Queen Brenda as ordained by the Goddess Loa, Lord of All that exists now, or will ever exist."

"My Queen, my Queen," the captains of industry chanted and took a knee.

Everyone bowed except Jenny. She remained standing and put her plan into action. "I will not bow to her," she cried. "If Brenda doesn't bow to me, I'll go to the police and expose her for what she is. A murderer. Your so-called queen will be in prison and I will reign in her place."

Brenda hardened her heart for Jenny. "I've been told of your plot against me, Jenny, but I'm not sorry to say you have failed."

Jenny glared at Cassandra. "You. You betrayed me, your

wife. How could you?"

Cassandra pointed an accusing finger at her. "Better to betray you than Brenda, our Queen."

Vines and roots wormed their way out of the pit and along the floor while Jenny concentrated her hate on Cassandra.

"I'll kill you." She charged toward Cassandra.

The roots and vines grabbed Jenny's legs, pulled her off her feet, and dragged her toward the pit.

Brenda shouted down from her throne. "You have sealed your own fate."

"Please forgive, please forgive."

The arms of Loa dragged her under the golden railing.

Screaming, she clawed at the red-tiled floor but found no purchase and disappeared into the abyss, never to be heard from again.

"Payment accepted," Cassandra said.

Caroline ran in through the double doors and jumped up into Queen Brenda's lap. "What's all the excitement?"

Cassandra spoke. "From this day forward until the end of time it will be women who are superior to men. Our original sin in the Garden of Eden has been forgiven by the one ruler of the universe, our beloved Lesbian Goddess Loa. Come now and kiss the hand and swear allegiance to Loa's consort on the earth, Queen Brenda."

Everyone lined up to kiss her hand.

The General swore the allegiance of his armies, the Attorney General, his courts. The bankers, the networks, the world wide web all followed suit. Donna kissed Brenda's hand and spoke for U.S. Senator, James Hoffman, that he would sponsor bills to protect women's rights and recruit his cohorts in Congress to do the same. At the end of the line was Alfons. Kissing her hand he said with a smile, "I knew there was something special about all of you. I will be forever at your service."

"Go in peace, Alfons." Brenda stood. "Everyone go back to your chosen professions and initiate changes on behalf of all women."

The men bowed and filed out. Her sisters stood at the door, proud as could be.

Caroline climbed off Brenda's lap. "I didn't get a turn."

A smiling Brenda held out her hand. "Here."

Caroline kissed it then jumped off the pedestal and ran to her sisters.

Brenda joined them, took hold of Caroline's hand, and they walked out together, with Caroline skipping all the way back to the house the sisterhood now called home.

Postscript:

Maggie gave birth to a beautiful baby girl, Zoey, and the men rebelled, as usual, thus, to make a better world for Zoey and all women, the War of the Lesbian Zombies started in earnest. Stay tuned.

About the Author

George S. Naas is a long-time Colorado resident who owns Golden Publishing Company and writes in a variety of genres. He's an ancient history buff, a military strategist, and a romantic at heart. When he's not writing or working, he enjoys bowling and cross-fit. He lives in Lakewood with his wife Dana.

Look for Other Works by George S. Naas

God's Assassin

Finding True Love at 35,000 Feet

Anything Goes

Charlie the Cherry